Best of
Wondercon!

Kath
NAC

Living
Lies

Kate Mathis

POWWOW PUBLISHING

PowWow Publishing
P.O. 31855
Tucson, AZ 85751-1855 U.S.A.
info@powwowpublishing.com
http://www.powwowpublishing.com

Printed in the United States of America
First Printing July 2009

Library of Congress Control Number: 2009902937
Mathis, Kate.

Living Lies/Kate Mathis - 1st ed.

1. Female Spy – Fiction. 2. Mystery – Fiction. 3. San Diego State University – Fiction. 4. La Jolla – Fiction. 5. Dating – Fiction. 6. Suspense – Fiction.

ISBN-13: 978-0-9819789-0-1
ISBN-10:   0-9819789-0-8

Book design and composition by PowWow Inc.

for Brent

CHAPTER 1

Melanie Ward was running on pure fear as she raced down the marble corridor. In 30 minutes the sleeping pill would wear off and he'd come hunting for her. There would be no hesitation or remorse in his dark, cold eyes. He'd give the nod, and one of his thugs would cut her life short. But … there was no turning back.

Melanie stopped at the door that, according to blueprints, was his office. She took in a deep breath, looked in either direction and, with a sweaty palm, twisted the gold handle.

Moonlight streaked through two slits in the heavy drapes, throwing her just enough light to navigate around the ornate furniture to an imposing desk that presided over the room. Melanie lowered herself into the leather wingback chair and pulled the chain of the small desktop lamp. Without a sound, she felt behind the drawers for false backs, hidden compartments or locks that would reveal the cache. Tracing her frozen fingertips along the underside of the pencil drawer Melanie gasped and sprang out of her seat. Sending the chair skidding across the tile and crashing loudly into the credenza. Her heart leapt with the thunderous noise and she dropped cowardly to the floor, waiting for the outcome of her recklessness.

After a handful of seconds with no sign of Malik's brutes, her confidence resurged. Melanie examined the hidden lock she had found and rummaged through the obvious places searching for the key. Without success, Melanie contemplated where an arrogant, self-absorbed primate like Malik would hide the key. She checked her watch not having the luxury of time, hastily she began righting the damage she had caused on the credenza. A thick gold frame that had been knocked over, a photo of a young Malik with a woman caught her eye. They were both smiling, he at the camera and she at him. The woman was pretty, with flowing dark hair and features like Malik. As Melanie righted the frame, something shifted inside.

Broken glass, she thought, giving it a stern shake to dislodge the fragments.

Instead of glass, a small gold key dropped to the Italian tile floor, bouncing and clanking to its final destination, an inch from Melanie's left foot. Using one hand to steady the other, Melanie slid the tiny key into the lock and the latch released with a soft pop. Among the guns and stacks of cash was the thin folder she was looking for. She delicately laid out its contents on the desk and photographed it all, page by page. A continuous prayer of thanks looped in her mind as she meticulously replaced all as it had been and tucked the camera into her waistband.

Taking a deep breath, Melanie poked her head into the hallway - empty. Filling her lungs beyond capacity and with her stomach in knots, she prowled through the corridor and back to the parlor where she'd left a drugged Malik. His face was buried in an overstuffed pillow on his spacious red couch. The fire, though less intense than it had been, was still blazing, sending the beads of sweat that had collected on her brow rolling down her face. She wiped her temples and dumped the remainder of Malik's Cabernet Sauvignon into a nearby potted palm. Taking her seat next to him, Melanie smoothed her hair back, steadied her trembling hands and prepared to deceive. Never having been a skillful liar, she now felt the pressure to perform.

"Hey, wake up." Melanie lightly shook his shoulder.

His eyes fluttered as he struggled to gain consciousness, licking his lips and clearing his throat.

"I fell asleep?" he asked, wrestling with the pillow to sit up.

"Yeah, while I was talking to you," she said, her voice ringing with impatience.

She'd been out with Malik every Friday and Saturday night for three weeks and, fortunately, tonight she was going to break up with him. It had been increasingly difficult to avoid his advances, and although his kisses were surprisingly pleasant she was not eager to go further.

This was her longest relationship since high school and Melanie was nervous, unsure of how to end things without offending him or raising suspicions.

"I should take you home," Malik said, obviously still groggy.

In the car, Melanie tried to recall how Hollywood handled break-ups. She was drawing a blank, distracted by the Beach Boys CD. All she could think of was "Ah, ba ba ba ba Barbara Ann."

Malik's black Mercedes rolled to a stop outside her building. With the camera pressing into her hip, Melanie began to speak, her voice cracking and tripping over a list of incoherent words. It was Malik who finally stopped her in mid-incomplete-sentence.

"You know, baby, you're too much work and you don't give Malik the love he needs," he said, his piercing dark eyes devoid of emotion.

Her momentary speechlessness gave way to an absurd pang of rejection and, finally, the joy of relief as she realized she was off the hook. He was breaking up with her. Melanie almost laughed.

"I'm sorry, baby, but this was our last night together," Malik leaned across her chest, his spicy aftershave searing the inside of her nose.

Preparing for a last kiss she closed her eyes and paused, suspended for a moment ... until a gust of chilly wind swept in from her opened car door. Malik wasn't pursuing a farewell kiss, he was kicking her out. Embarrassed, Melanie stumbled out onto the broken curb and stared dumbfounded as his cackle drilled into her ears, sending prickles down her spine.

"All you American women hate rejection," he said, leaning over the passenger seat to get a good look at her.

"Whatever," Melanie spat back, slamming the door.

He sped down the narrow residential street, his laugh still ringing in her ears.

Heated and offended, she stomped to the top of her stairway and sat, pulling her jacket tight around her trembling body as a cold wind whipped through the stairwell. Her assignment for the United States Government was over, successfully completed, the spy camera tucked safely away. Freezing, Melanie ducked into her apartment as a group of giggling girls spilled into the hallway.

Filling the tub with the hottest water possible, she twisted her long auburn hair into a messy heap and rubber banded it in place.

Her nerves were raw and her mind raced as she lowered her 5'6" frame into the steaming water.

In May she'd graduate with honors. She worked hard and was proud of her scholastic accomplishments, but tonight she proved that she was capable of more than just good grades. A senior at San Diego State, Melanie had earned and maintained a full academic scholarship. But classes were over for the semester. Her three roommates had left for winter break. For weeks she'd wanted to share her experiences and gossip about Malik, but the Covert Defense Division – the CDD – had prohibited her from divulging any information, so Melanie had censored every dialogue. The stress of such a huge secret had weighed heavily. She was relieved there would be no more lies.

The next morning, her daily six-mile run followed the well-pressed path that weaved deep inside the 1,200 acres that made up Balboa Park. She pushed herself harder than normal, her lungs stinging and her nose pink from the brisk morning air. The familiar path was lined with evergreens, but today Melanie's mind was on the destination, not the journey. She'd cut five minutes off her best time and her legs burned from the extra strain as she reached the 200-foot California Tower of the Museum of Man.

Sitting on a bench, a man buried his nose in the daily paper and waited. Melanie couldn't believe it had been just five weeks since he'd appeared at her library study cubicle, back when her life was as predictable as this trail - every curve known, every tree familiar and safe. Her well-planned steps had been charted out well past graduation.

"Melanie Ward, I'm Agent Gary Collins with the CDD," he said quietly, flashing his badge. "I was hoping to speak with you for a few minutes."

The minutes turned into an hour as Agent Collins explained his situation. A man who had approached Melanie on Friday night at the local hot spot, the Jungle Jim, was Malik Razul, the suspected leader of an information theft ring. The CDD had been unable to penetrate his tight inner circle but now they hoped Melanie would gain access to his home office. Female agents had attempted to lure Razul, none had succeeded and it was time for a new tactic. Melanie.

"He's not a nice man and if you're caught … well, he has people for that. But we have people, too and we'll keep you safe." Agent Collins had promised.

Collins awakened her sense of adventure and there was no masking the thrill. She felt alive and passing on the opportunity was not an option.

"I have confidence in you, Ms. Ward," Agent Collins said, his expression taut and stern.

⟨∞⟩

The following Friday night, Melanie changed her outfit three times and only nibbled at the sandwich she'd made for dinner. The poorly ventilated nightclub was packed, as usual. Lights from the dance floor illuminated the cigarette smoke that permeated the air. Melanie sat on her usual stool at their usual table.

"This is my last year of college and I am going to meet someone tonight," she told her best friend and roommate, Carla Wagner.

Scanning the faces she recognized from school, Melanie kept an eye out for Malik Razul.

"It's about time. You're missing out on the college experience by studying so much," Carla said, her Southern accent almost undetectable.

For a year, Melanie and her friends upheld their weekly ritual of gathering at the Jungle Jim. Only a mile from campus, it was a popular school hangout, and although the name denoted a sense of the tropics, there were neither plants nor animals to be found. There was, however, a large dance floor, a loud DJ, pool tables and, of course, alcohol.

"What about him?"

Melanie's gaze followed Carla's discreetly pointed finger toward Danny Ashe. There was no need to look. She already knew his face, his eyes, his smile. He had been in at least one of her classes every semester since freshman year, but she had long ago given up hope that there could be anything between them. Danny was a jock, on the university's rugby team, popular and handsome, and Melanie was an academic. She wore little makeup, kept her hair imprisoned in a tight ponytail and wore a uniform of jeans, freebie T-shirts and tennis shoes. Hardly the type of woman Danny Ashe dated. But her crush lingered.

"Yeah, he's cute, but he's got a girlfriend."

Melanie took one last, long glance at him as he ran his fingers through his blond hair. Perpetually bruised and broken from his battles on the rugby field, tonight he sported a fresh black eye. Her gaze shifted momentarily to Carolyn, Danny's girlfriend, who laughed with her friends and pointed at people who were not as popular or beautiful as they were.

You wouldn't have fit in with them anyway, Melanie told herself with a heavy sigh.

At a nearby table, her other roommates, Jenny and Trish, shamelessly flirted with two boys who were relishing the attention. Melanie watched as Jenny lit up a cigarette and Trish leaned forward, pulling down the waistband of her skirt. She'd recently added a butterfly tattoo to the small of her back, its bright blue wings stretching out several inches. Trish was 5'10" without her stiletto heels and was as beautiful as any cover model. At the start of the semester she'd dyed her hair a brilliant red and cropped it military style. She was playful and carefree and it seemed to Melanie that, whatever the circumstance, Trish always got her way. The flashing strobe from the dance floor reflected off Trish's short haircut, deepening the color to a rich violet.

Jenny, though not as skilled as Trish in the art of the come-on, kept up with Trish, boy for boy. She was the classic girl next door, baiting the male species with her bouncy golden hair, which she forever tossed back and forth, her large baby blues giving the false impression of innocence. A long cigarette had become her signature over the past few months as she tried to lose the extra 15 pounds she'd put on since her high school cheerleading days.

"Hello again, foxy lady."

Completely absorbed in the activities of her friends, Melanie hadn't noticed Malik standing beside her.

He had a strong Middle-Eastern accent with eyes that looked right through her. He wore shiny shirts with wide collars, unbuttoned down to an uncomfortable level. Melanie had dated sporadically, mostly study dates, but her usual type was of the geek variety. Her friends were surprised when she agreed to go out with Malik and, because of his gruff behavior, confused that she kept dating him. Here was a man who regularly struck the "gotcha" pose, interrupted any conversation and honked from the car instead of ringing the bell. But to Melanie's surprise, Malik was funny and at least polite, if not gentlemanly when they were alone. Guarded about his life, Malik pressed for each of their dates to end back at her apartment. Finally, after three weeks of charm and diligence, Malik invited her to his house, where he cooked her dinner and she slipped him the sleeping pill the CDD had provided. That evening had been the most intense of her life and she loved every scary, sweaty second of it.

"How did it go?" Agent Gary Collins asked, not looking up from the paper as she sat down next to him and tied her shoe.

"Task completed," she muttered, masking her delight.

From the pocket of her red hoodie Melanie took out a small brown bag that held the tiny camera and an energy bar. She ate the bar and left the crumpled bag on the bench between them.

CHAPTER 2

The window from the second story room gave a perfect line of sight. It was spring and the sleepy town in the Italian Alps was about to awaken. This was only the second time his target had been a woman. He took one last look at her photo – an elegant blonde with bright blue eyes and red lips – before stashing it inside his large backpack along with the rest of his gear. The hotel room had been wiped clean of fingerprints and any other signs of his existence.

He waited patiently, keeping vigil through the night and watching for her to emerge, ready to fire the fatal shot.

Every task, even murder, became routine if done often enough, and eight years was a long time. He no longer felt the fear or the horror of his work, no longer cared who or why a hit had been hired. Payment – it was all about the payment.

His blood was icy and his heartbeat slow and steady as the woman, in a sable coat, appeared in his scope. Her scarlet lips were now a pale pink but the blue eyes were unmistakable. The barrel of his gun rested on the wooden flower box as his gloved finger caressed the trigger.

An uncharacteristic uncertainty flashed through his mind as he gently squeezed. The victim dropped heavily to her knees, dead before her head cracked on the wet cobblestone street. Blood sprayed the vibrant flowers outside the chic inn and ran down the street like water. Her small entourage screamed in unison and crowded around the collapsed, lifeless body.

Indifferently, he collected his few possessions and walked past the fallen target, noticing her eyes, still open, staring up at him accusingly.

Quickly, he left the scene, ignoring his reflection in the blood-spattered window. Three blocks later he ducked into a dusty tavern as police cars and an ambulance screeched through the quaint streets. The weapon, tucked into his backpack, leaned against the sturdy wooden chair as he ordered breakfast.

A stout blonde woman, sitting alone, flashed him a yellow smile.

CHAPTER 3

Melanie's holiday plans were always the same: Christmas at her parents' house in La Jolla, sleeping in her old bedroom before being drained of tolerance by her parents' idiosyncrasies, and leaving for the peace and freedom of an empty apartment. By the end of her winter seclusion, she'd be eager to ditch the hermitage and impatient for the return of her roommates.

Traveling beneath the canopy of tree branches that blocked the clear blue sky, Melanie drove Carla's run-down Toyota and dreamed of snow and blizzards. Instead, green front lawns showcased their holiday spirit with festive lights winding their way up the tall palm trees and garnished gates with wreaths of holly and pomegranate.

The steep roads descending from downtown La Jolla to the cliffs at the shore were lined with multi-million-dollar homes, granting them an unobstructed view of the Pacific Ocean. Moderate family homes were nestled among the ostentatious, all of them painted in an array of pastels and adorned with neat lawns and flowering shrubs. Often tourists in search of sea lion coves found themselves pointing from the windows of their family vans, admiring the quaint and grand neighborhoods.

The Ward home did not overlook the ocean.

Melanie climbed the porch steps to the pale yellow two-story home with the white shutters, careful not to drop the bundle of presents for her mom, dad and little brother, Brucey. Bruce Ward was only two years younger than Melanie but as the baby of the family, he was still treated as if he were 10.

"Merry Christmas, dear," her mom said with her expected big, warm hug and kiss.

Rita Ward's hair was cut stylishly short at the nape, newly colored a strawberry blonde, and she wore her trademark knit vest over a colored turtleneck with a long, heavy gold chain. Roger Ward's thick brown hair had grayed at the temples and the hours working in his garden were evident from his tan skin.

"Annie!" Her father called, using her pet name when seeing her in the hall. His eyes sparkled and Melanie returned the same smile.

Without fail, Melanie knew that Christmas Eve morning the family would go out to breakfast before hunting down the largest tree left on the lot. A struggle would ensue between the family members, the tree and the top of the car. In the end the family would emerge victorious, only to repeat the struggle with the front door and then again with the hallway to the living room, where the tree would stand for the next week.

"Honey, when are we going to meet your boyfriend?" Rita interrogated innocently as she opened a box of ornaments.

"Right after I meet him," Melanie said, gritting her teeth and bracing for the aftershock.

It was such a small sound, her mother's tsk, but it held the force to rattle her foundation and raise her blood pressure.

Ignore it, she repeated silently – her mantra.

"Why don't you ask Trish for help, she's very popular."

Melanie counted to 10, still hooking silver orbs onto the evergreen branches.

"That's a good idea, Mom."

"Your Aunt Paulie will be here in the morning with her kids. You don't mind giving up your room for a night, do you?"

"No." Melanie sighed.

The next morning, Melanie sat on a hard pew wedged between her mother and a fidgety Bruce. Rita and Roger were weekly members of their congregation but had long ago surrendered in forcing their children to attend, saving Christmas Day.

❧

"I've got a date," Bruce announced four days after Christmas. He'd been on the phone all week and the ominous cloud that had been hanging over her head broke. "I won't be here for New Year's." He grinned and struck his fist against Melanie's shoulder.

She glared.

"Well, I've got a date, too." She was a miserable liar.

"Now that's just pathetic," Bruce said, taking a bite out of an apple.

"Hush," Rita reprimanded but with her eyes filled with suspicion. "You know you're welcome to come to the lodge with your father and me."

Melanie tried her best to look offended. "Really, I have a date with a guy in my econ class."

"Hah, what's his name?" Bruce probed.

"Felix. And shut up." Melanie turned back to her mom. "Really. I didn't want to tell you because I didn't want to get your hopes up. It's just a date."

"Dear, that's wonderful."

Rita followed her children. "Are you certain you're going to be all right?" She asked when they reached the curb.

"I'm fine, how about you, Brucey?"

"I told you not to call me that."

"At least take some of the leftovers," Rita begged.

"I've got some," Melanie tapped the box she carried in one arm. With her other hand she yanked her jeans up. She always lost weight when she came home. Her mother was a horrendous cook whose feelings could be hurt with even the slightest remark. Bruce's waistline had the opposite effect. He snuck in Hostess powdered doughnuts gobbling them with Doritos and washed both down with Mountain Dew.

"Call when you get to your apartment," Rita waved as Melanie drove away.

Melanie was grateful to have her family so near – and even more grateful to be on her own.

∞

New Year's Eve, wearing old, bleach-stained jeans and a threadbare T-shirt, Melanie got to work. She spent the afternoon scrubbing the kitchen floor on her hands and knees, cleaning out the refrigerator and reorganizing the cupboards. She was exhausted by nine.

With a bowl of milk and a can of tuna, Melanie whistled outside her building.

"Happy New Year, Felix," she said, scratching the tabby on the head.

Plodding up the stairs, her date over, she settled in front of the television, a book in one hand and a fork in the other. Steam rose from the microwaved macaroni and cheese she balanced on her lap. A glass of milk rested on a coaster.

Her phone never rung, there were no knocks on the door and she left the apartment only to retrieve food and a slew of epic movies from Blockbuster. In her flannel polar bear pajamas she stretched out across the couch. The soft cushions contoured to the curves of her body, and she sank in deep and comfortable charmed by Cary Grant in *The Bishop's Wife*. The disruption of the phone ringing startled her awake.

"Hello?" She yawned.

"Hi, is Melanie home?" a deep voice asked.

"This is Melanie," she reached for the remote to turn down the volume.

"Hi, Melanie, this is Dan Ashe."

Melanie bolted upright and turned off the television.

"Hi," she said, more like a question.

"Is this a bad time?"

"No, it's fine." Melanie's heart and stomach both synchronized a leap to her throat. "Are you, um, still in Denver?"

"No. I just got back. Hey, I was wondering if you were busy tonight?"

"Well, um," microseconds ticked off loudly in her head. "No, I'm not busy at all."

"Great. How about I pick you up at 7?"

"Okay." A tentative smile stretched across Melanie's face.

"I'll see you then. Bye, Mel."

"But," she said, limply, into the dead receiver, "I have questions."

Her melancholy, fluffy sock day was replaced by panic and fear.

What could he possibly want? Cary Grant was forgotten, the laundry that waited for her downstairs was forgotten, all that she had left were questions. Questions flowed in an endless torrent, and hours of mulling caused her brain to ache. Melanie swallowed three aspirins with a single gulp of water and laced her running shoes.

The fresh air helped. It didn't stop the burning, nagging, uncertainty mixed with insecurity, but it did make her tired enough to stop thinking.

After a long shower, Melanie dressed in a skirt and blouse she found in Jenny's closet. Taking great care, she primped and prepared for a heart-stopping, mind-blowing date with Danny Ashe. The excess energy flitted up from her belly and traveled as a soundless scream out her mouth. She added curls to her hair and applied makeup. It was the stranger with her eyes that brought her back to reality as she scrutinized her reflection. *What had been his exact words?*

She was fuzzy on the specifics and now she worried that she might have mistaken his intent. She strained to recall the precise words he had used when he called.

"Maybe he's returning some notes or a book he had borrowed," she pondered out loud.

What if, she thought, filling with horror and humiliation, *he shows up at the door with Carolyn on his arm?*

"You'd look like a complete idiot," she said, looking down at her legs, bare to mid-thigh.

Melanie reconsidered her outfit and purposely put a damper on her excitement. Pulling on a pair of dark jeans and a red sweater that was warm though less fashionable than Jen's outfit. Tying the laces of her black work boots that had never seen a day's work, she grumbled at her lack of confidence and slipped back into student mode.

Combing out the curls and clipping back her auburn hair, she scaled down the makeup and looked more like the girl he saw daily in class. She glanced at her watch. It was 6:58.

He'll be late, she thought just as the doorbell rang.

"Oh, shit," she said, dragging all the cosmetics off the counter and back into their basket. "I'll be right there."

The thick rubber soles of Melanie's boots barely hit the tiled hallway as she bounded to the door. Sucking in a deep breath with every intention of letting it out slowly, an unsubstantiated remedy to cure erratic nerves, she forced it out in one sharp gust and opened the door. Danny Ashe. Her heart swelled as she stole a quick glance over his shoulder, verifying that Carolyn was nowhere in sight.

"Hi," he said, looking around. "Are you expecting someone else?"

"No, come inside," she giggled. Her cheeks flushed with embarrassment, excitement and nervousness.

"These are for you." He smiled, the light catching golden streaks in his brown eyes, she embraced the flowers she hadn't even noticed he was holding.

"Thank you, I'll put them in water." She tucked her face into the petals and breathed in the fragrance. Trish had half a dozen vases in the kitchen cupboard and Melanie knew exactly which one she would use.

He trailed her into the kitchen where she contemplated hopping onto the counter to reach the top shelf before he asked, "Can I get that for you?"

"Please, the blue one."

As he brought down the vase they were just inches apart and Melanie could feel her blush rising from beneath her sweater.

"You look really beautiful."

"Thanks," she felt awkward accepting the compliment distracting herself by unsystematically arranging the flowers. "I need a second."

"Take your time," he said, his hands shoved deep inside the pockets of his heavy canvas jacket.

Oh My God, she cautiously glanced at him before gliding back to the bathroom. She held her breath, unplugged the curling iron, took one last look in the mirror and smiled.

It is a date with Danny. Her heart sputtered as she unclipped her hair and grabbed her lipstick.

Danny had draped his coat on the back of a chair, his back toward her when she returned. Melanie took a moment to admire the Levi's that lightly hugged his muscular contours.

"You have a nice place," he said, turning when he realized she was behind him. Assessing a photo that had been taken at Sea World in September. Trish had dated a guy who fed the dolphins and had arranged a private showing for the girls. In the picture they were all making faces and Trish had tried to give rabbit ears to the dolphin. "You seem to have good friends. I've seen you together at the club." He smiled, and looked embarrassed as he placed the frame back on the crooked TV unit she'd got from a second-hand store. "So, are we ready to go?"

He ran his hands through that perfect blond hair. How many times had she dreamed of this moment?

"I'm ready."

The warmth of her happiness spread from the pit of her stomach to her cheeks and despite the cool evening air she felt toasty. He opened the door and Melanie climbed into his faded, old red Jeep. The CJ-7 had seen better days – it smelled of motor oil, the top was ripped and the plastic windows were cloudy.

She sank comfortably into the warm sheepskin seat covers.

"Where are we going?"

"Pizza and a concert in the park?"

"Really?" She hadn't heard about a concert, but then she'd been holed up for the past few days.

"Too cold?" He glanced at her sideways.

"No, it sounds great."

"I'm sorry the heater doesn't work too well," he said, fiddling with the switches.

"It's okay, really." Melanie placed her hand on his wrist.

"Mel, your hands are so cold." He cupped both of her hands inside one of his as he drove, letting go only to shift gears. His rough hand was warm and strong. Though the ride was noisy, wind whipping in and around the tattered top, she hardly noticed.

The pizza place was a nicer than the usual college hangout, with muted lighting enhanced by candles in red jars on red-and-white-checked tablecloths. Hand in hand, Danny led them to a private table in the back. Melanie bit her lip. This wasn't a dream, she was holding Danny's hand and they were on a date.

He ordered two beers and turned to her, looking puzzled.

"What do you like on your pizza? It's funny, all this time we've known each other and I don't know anything about you."

"You know things about me." She was beginning to feel very hot beneath his curious stare.

"Tell me," he said, his eyes narrowing to slits.

Melanie was suddenly afraid he might be expecting too much. She was just a student and she wasn't allowed to talk about the only thing interesting that had ever happened to her.

Danny smiled and leaned forward, "I know you're beautiful and a genius with numbers, but otherwise I'm here with a stranger." His gaze was intense. "Like, why are you studying finance? You're so smart, you could do anything." He touched a lock of hair resting on her shoulder.

Melanie flushed, even a bit dazed as she answered, "A PBS documentary on the stock exchange. I wanted Wall Street, millions of dollars, balanced in my hands. It's exciting without being dangerous." She took a sip of beer. "Why did *you* choose finance?"

"I wanted to be able to invest the money I make as a professional athlete."

She liked the sound of his laugh, the slight overlapping of his front teeth and even the cocky glint in his eyes. The bump on the bridge of his nose was endearing, giving character to his otherwise perfect face.

She found herself staring and grasped at the first strand of conversation she could come up with.

"So, you were in Denver over break?"

Ugh, she only knew this because she'd overheard him talking in class.

"Yeah, I grew up in Denver and my mom still lives there," he answered, without noticing her slip.

Melanie took a swallow of the strong beer, a taste she didn't particularly like.

"Why'd you come back early?"

"You," he said without hesitation, staring directly into her eyes.

"Smooth, very nice." She rolled her eyes but her skin tingled at his wonderfully sweet lie.

"When do your roommates come back?"

"A week from tomorrow. I'll be glad to see them. It's getting lonely in that apartment."

"Well, now I'm here to keep you company." His eyes sparkled, making her heart skip.

"I don't think Carolyn will be very happy about that."

It was a question, posed as a statement that she'd been dying to ask.

His battered fingers ran a single course through his sandy hair. "We broke up right before I left for Denver." Then guzzled the last of his beer.

"Oh," she said, delighted. "I'm sorry to hear that."

He laughed. "No, you're not!"

"Okay, I'm not," she shrugged.

"Didn't like Carolyn?"

"It's not that, but if you were still with her then you wouldn't be sitting here with me." The beer was clearly having its intended effect. She felt giddy and light-headed, warming to the idea that Danny was seriously flirting with her. Or was she flirting with him?

"Smooth, very nice," he said.

Melanie was extremely self-conscious; Throughout dinner his stares never left her face, hair or neck. Her first plan of trying *not* to make eye contact failed miserably and made her even more self-aware. Quickly, she checked her reflection in the window and ran her tongue over her teeth and closed her eyes.

Opening them slowly, he was looking directly at her and this time she couldn't look away. He was handsome. She met his gaze, and the look in his eyes took her breath away. She'd never had the courage before, and was surprised by what she saw. His chocolate brown eyes were soft and warm. This wasn't the tough rugby player she pilfered glances at in class.

"You know, you ate three pieces of pizza," he observed, not adjusting his eyes.

"You're counting?" she asked, her eyebrow arched high in mock offense.

"Yeah," he grinned, offering her the last slice.

Melanie declined, mildly embarrassed.

"Most girls I go out with order a salad and then only pretend to eat," he laughed. "What's that about?"

"I don't know. I get irritable when I'm hungry."

"Maybe *that's* what's wrong with most women."

"You do realize you've just insulted half the population?"

"No, I said *most* women."

"Technicality," she said, glancing sideways at him. "Maybe it's indicative, simply, of the women you've been choosing."

As the words were still forming on her loose lips she knew she'd said too much. The higher his eyebrows lifted, pushing his forehead into his hairline, the worse she felt.

"I'm sorry." She shook her head, "I should never drink." It was a lame excuse but it was all she had.

"No, it's okay, you're probably right." His warm fingers pressed on her icy hands as her face reddened. Gently he lifted her chin and drew her face up to meet his eyes. "You're sweet, and gorgeous and honest," he whispered as if the past three minutes never occurred.

Melanie sat frozen until the waitress broke the spell.

Danny looked at his watch. "Wow, it's late. We should get going. The concert starts in half an hour." He reached for the check and Melanie reached for her purse.

"Can I pay half?" she offered, unsure of the current policy.

"No way," he said, ordering two coffees to go.

The Jeep roared to life and she wouldn't have guessed that speeds over 80 miles per hour were a possibility, but now car lights and street lights all blurred into a long stream. Melanie did what she could to mask her white knuckles as she gripped the edge of her seat cushion.

"It's Elvis' birth week," he explained, his eyes not kept nearly enough outside the windshield. "It's a concert to honor him and his music. You're okay with Elvis, right?"

"Yeah, but I don't think we're dressed appropriately. Shouldn't you be wearing a white jumper and tunic?"

"He wore a cape, not a tunic, and it was my first choice, but since this is our first date I decided to go with the jeans."

She let go of her grasp on her seat. Dating Danny was going to be a wild ride, Melanie decided, biting her lip in excitement.

The outdoor arena was draped in gold lamé, and behind the band hung a huge sign lit by hundreds of colored bulbs that spelled out "ELVIS". Melanie was impressed.

The lead singer wore head to toe black leather, a guitar strapped across his shoulders. The crowd was wild, most in costume with muttonchops and TCB sunglasses to pay tribute to the King of Rock 'n Roll. Melanie couldn't resist joining in the dancing. The party turned to karaoke when the band took a break, and Melanie and Danny found a spot away from the pack, far from the speakers.

It was a brisk, clear January night. The big-city lights obscured the stars but the almost-full moon shone dramatically overhead.

They huddled together for warmth, arm against arm, thigh against thigh. He wound his arm around her shoulder and Melanie shivered at his touch.

"Take my jacket." He slipped his arm out of the sleeve.

"I can't take your jacket, you'll freeze."

"Really, Mel," he said with a chuckle. "I'm from Denver, remember? This is like spring for me."

The inside of his jacket was lined with flannel and still warm from his body heat. His cologne permeated the fabric, making her swoon.

Danny scooted in tight and practically pulled her onto his lap, his muscular arms encircling her shoulders.

"Better?"

She nodded. *You have no idea*, she thought.

Braving the winter night, they stayed through the last song.

"I had an incredible time tonight," Danny said at her doorstep.

"Me, too."

Melanie hung onto the doorknob for support. She'd been waiting for a kiss all evening.

"I'll call you tomorrow," he said, in a husky low voice. "Melanie, I, um, I don't usually ask this but..." He chuckled nervously. "Could I kiss you?"

Before Melanie could answer he was there, ever so slightly brushing his lips across hers. She felt his breath and hers sped up to mirror his. It was almost torture to have him so close, and just when she thought she couldn't bear it any longer he pulled her in, his arms holding her tight and kissed her.

Melanie was overtaken and ran her hands up his neck and through his hair, pulling him lower.

His hair, she thought from some sane region of her brain, *its so thick and soft, no wonder he's always messing with it.*

For a moment after the kiss they held each other, hearts racing and blood rushing. She was grateful to be in his arms, unsure if her legs would support her.

Danny let out a sigh. "Melanie." He caressed her cheek then gently kissed her forehead. "I'd better go," he said with a laugh.

A laugh? What was the laugh? She wondered if she was missing something as her key became difficult. Clumsily, she wrestled with the door, he waited.

Alone inside, she melted to the floor. It was 20 minutes before she felt solid enough to make it to bed.

She wished Carla were home, they would rehash every detail of the evening. Melanie lay on her back, her head cradled in her pillow, and let the otherworldly sensation take over her body while her mind wandered. The concert had been romantic, and the kiss goodnight incredible. His cologne lingered on her skin as she drifted off to sleep. She was shaken out of a dream by the phone ringing.

"Hello?" It was late and she couldn't imagine who'd be calling.

"Hi, you weren't asleep yet, were you?"

It was Danny. Blissfully she pulled the blankets up to her chin and snuggled into her pillow.

"No," she whispered, though she was alone in the apartment.

"I was thinking about you and I wanted to hear your voice." He, too, was talking low, and Melanie wondered if he had a roommate or was this just how people spoke in the middle of the night.

"I'm really glad you called. I'm not sure I thanked you for the great time."

"You did. Hey, look, I've got a couple of things to do in the morning but I'll come by your place in the afternoon."

Melanie nodded in silent darkness, her heart pounding. *Another date with Danny!*

"Goodnight, Melanie Ward."

"Goodnight, Danny Ashe."

All the attention and tender words were more than enough to make the little hairs on the back of her neck to stand on end. She wanted to believe, oh, she wanted to believe, but how? It was unbelievable that Danny would be attracted to her. It was unnatural, unsettling. Her instincts told her to beware: the whole "too good to be true" thing.

Life's equilibrium was being set off balance.

How could she accept his compliments or express her crush on him when she doubted his sincerity? Being on the lookout for an ambush was not an idyllic condition for romance.

She was going to have to be brave and confront him with her concerns.

Melanie woke early, too early but too restless to linger in bed. Lacing up her running shoes she went out to meet the cloudy gray morning. It was an hour before sunrise, her favorite time of the day. The air was crisp, clean and quiet, with just the hint of morning promise. Most of the city slept and the aroma of coffee brewing and donuts baking wafted from nearby bakeries, arousing her senses.

The track was deserted, and the dew from the grass clung to her shoes as she cut through the field.

Danny, she thought, her body airless in mid-stride.

She was scared of saying the wrong things or pushing him away and wrecking the possibilities. But she couldn't just sit and wait for the proverbial "other shoe" to drop.

Melanie sighed. The red track was hypnotizing and she was at the top of the turn again, having lost count of the number of laps. She started back at zero and kept running.

It was tempting simply to go along with it, to surrender to his attention. It was exactly what she wanted. Kissing Danny – Danny Ashe! – in her apartment, being in his Jeep was amazing, but the fear that she was the butt of a practical joke was overwhelming.

Through the misty morning, Melanie ran while mentally rehearsing possible scenarios, complete with reaction and commentary. She edited questions and responses until they were perfect; subtle yet definitive.

At the sound of knocking she was ready, with preparation as her line of defense. Never mind that the sight of him constricted the passage of oxygen through her airways or that her heart trembled just knowing he was behind the door – she was strong.

"Hi, come in," she smiled, wondering how he could be *more* gorgeous than any image she'd conjured all day.

"Hi," he greeted her without a kiss, but walked right into the apartment.

She locked the door and when she turned back around he was watching her, a crooked grin cut across his face.

"You look beautiful." His hands were on her waist.

"Danny, I'm in jeans," she said, trying to squirm out of his trance-like gaze.

He shrugged. "Doesn't matter what you wear, you're still beautiful."

Oh, my God, who cares why he's here, she thought nestling against his chest.

"You say the nicest things." She looked up into his eyes, unmarred at the moment, making her chuckle.

"What's funny?" he asked, squinting.

"I was just thinking how handsome you are even without a black eye or tape on your nose." Before she realized what she was doing she reached up and caressed his face. Danny turned his head slightly and kissed the palm of her hand. It was too much. Her body stiffened as she backed away, planting her butt on the couch.

"Everything okay?" He sat next to her.

None of her scenarios had begun this way, and Melanie was left to improvise. Unconsciously, she chewed on her bottom lip.

"I don't know," she said, looking him straight in the eye.

He said nothing, waiting for her to continue, his eyebrows low and knitted tightly together. Melanie wasn't sure but she thought she saw a look of anxiety beneath his confusion.

Maybe that's your own reflection, she considered.

"Why are you here?" It blurted out so fast that she hadn't time to stop or think. "I mean, don't get me wrong, I like that you're here. I really, really like that you're here, I just don't understand why." *So much for tactfulness, finesse and grace,* she thought, nervously squeezing tight fists and then drying her palms on her jeans.

Danny ran his fingers through his hair. "I'm not sure I know what you mean. I thought it would be nice to spend time with you, that's all."

Melanie bit hard into her lip and felt sick.

"Danny?" she breathed, disappointed by his response.

Their eyes locked, and he sighed.

The lump in her throat had swollen, choking her breath as her worse-case scenario played out. Looking away, she blinked to clear her watery eyes.

When she spoke, her voice was small, "I've had this huge crush on you forever and now you're here and it doesn't make any sense. There's something you're not telling me, and if this is just a big joke, well, I don't think it's funny." She stood with her arms folded and her jaw set.

"Melanie, this isn't a joke. I want to be here with you." He stood to face her, "Wait," a slight smile emerged, the sadness faded and his eyes danced. "Did you say you had a crush on me?" A bit of his usual cockiness returned.

"Danny."

"No, Mel, this is good, it makes it so much easier." His calloused hands on her arms gently pushed her back onto the couch. He crouched in front, resting his weight on the edge of the rickety coffee table.

She tried to read his eyes but they were filled with emotion and hers were blurry.

"It's crazy, Mel." He dropped his eyes and his voice quivered slightly, releasing a deep, pent-up breath. He began slowly. "Before finals week, do you remember?" He looked up only for an instant. "At the coffee shop, you were sitting at the back table with some old guy. I didn't think anything of it at first but you were looking at him with such intensity, hanging on his every word. I'd never seen you like that before. Then you smiled at him, so beautiful, so easy, that I wanted you to look at me that way. I waved to you but you didn't notice me." He twisted his twined fingers, nervously.

Melanie knew what he was talking about. She'd met with Agent Collins a few times prior to her assignment; at the library, in an empty classroom and once at the Java Hut. She'd been engrossed, not with Collins but with the mission. The café had been merely background noise that day. She couldn't recall having seen Danny at all.

The corners of his mouth pulled down. He looked embarrassed.

"I told you it sounded crazy. Then, the following Friday, I wanted to talk to you at the club but you were never alone. When I finally worked up the courage to approach you, I couldn't find you. I know it's irrational." He shook his sandy hair then smoothed the rough edges with the pass of a hand. "I can't explain it, you and I barely know each other outside of class, but that day I saw you differently. I left for Denver thinking that I could just shake it off but instead you followed me. I thought about you constantly, picturing you with him and you with me." His unsure brown eyes on hers. "You know what I mean? I couldn't stop torturing myself, so I decided to find out why you'd suddenly become so intriguing, changed my flight and came home."

Danny Ashe couldn't stop thinking about ME?

"Mel, you're making me a little nervous." His smile was crooked, different somehow. "I was afraid to call you yesterday," his smile widened, "I had no idea you liked me. I thought you'd say no – why would you waste your time with a dumb jock? Melanie, say something." He shook her knees.

"How could you *not* know I had a crush on you?"

Danny laughed, "You never speak to me outside of class. If we collide somewhere, the club or the coffee shop, you barely acknowledge my existence. How could I have known?"

She had never considered his angle. Could this be right?

"I'm shy," she said, narrowing her eyes.

"Four years of shy?" His laugh was light, relieved. "What do you think about what I just told you?"

She shook her head, numb.

"Okay, then how are you feeling this instant?"

"Like I swallowed a pit bull and he's chomping and clawing to get out."

"A pit bull? I was hoping for butterflies."

Melanie laughed.

Then an unsettling thought weaseled its way into her mind. *What if I can't compete with his imagination?*

She was constantly worried about living up to her scholarship and to everyone's expectations. It was exhausting, mentally and physically. Was there room to add Danny to the mix?

"I hope I don't disappoint you," she said, wearily.

"Mel, I don't have any expectations. I just want to hang out with you and we'll take it day by day. Besides, you said you've had a crush on me for 'forever'" he lifted his left eyebrow, grinning, "What if I'm not who you think I am?" He knelt in front of her. "What do you say, can we give this a try?"

What could she say? She'd been in love with him for years, or at the very least infatuated, and here he was on his knees. She chuckled at how easily it had twisted.

"Yes. I guess it's you and me." It was an effort to pull away from his soft lips. "Danny, you're more than I thought."

"You are, too."

"So, you're here, like, for real?"

Danny's eyes widened, devilishly, his grin mischievous.

"I'm here," he smiled, his eyes were focused and sure, "until you kick me out."

Melanie nodded. "Get comfortable."

His skilled lips firmly pressed against hers as she toiled with her own lack of experience. He'd kissed too many girls.

"What'd you have planned today?"

Melanie shook her head, "I've done it." She felt awkward not having any pressing engagements. "I ate breakfast and I ran, almost ended things with you. Actually it's been a busy day."

He shook his head, his golden hair swaying perfectly with the movement. "You run?"

Melanie laughed, "You don't know anything about me. It's really my only hobby."

"Tomorrow I'm running with you." Danny stood and pulled her up with him. "Let's go somewhere."

They drove to the roller coaster at Mission Beach.

Danny's zest for life was contagious. Trotting toward the carnival booths, he held firmly to her hand, slowed his gait and kept her alongside.

"I'm going to win you a bear," he declared.

"Maybe I'll win *you* a bear." She offered, laughing at his exhilaration over a stuffed toy.

They headed toward the only game she knew she had a chance, throwing a Nerf ball through a basketball hoop. Even as a child she had a unique dexterity for the game. She'd passed the pretzel vendor and the ticket booth before realizing she'd lost Danny.

He stood 10 paces back with an euphoric grin.

"What's wrong?" she asked, closing the distance.

He wound his arms around her waist and forced her until her back was against a wall.

"I could have sex with you right now." His lips had already found a ticklish spot on her neck.

"Danny!" she gasped, nudging his shoulders.

"I know, I know." He came up from behind her veil of hair with a groan. "Everyone says I move too fast and you're not *that* girl, so I *am* going to be a perfect gentleman." He smiled, stepped away from her and winked. "At least for a day or two."

Melanie froze, still pressed to the wall.

"Well, come on woman, win me a prize."

A bear, monkey and dolphin later they stopped to eat a burger.

Riding on Danny's shoulder the large blue dolphin mocked Melanie in a high-pitched voice.

"Seriously, I can't believe how you ruled that game."

With Danny's egging, Melanie had upgraded three smaller dolphins for the one that was mocking her. She shrugged, squeezing the silent monkey.

"Ring toss is no easy challenge."

She bit into her tasteless, waxy burger as the roller coaster whooshed overhead.

"Let's do that," he challenged.

Melanie looked at the shaky wooden structure and scrunched her face.

"Chicken?" asked the "dolphin".

"No," she thought of the two lonely dollars in her wallet. The dolphin clucked and she smiled. "It's too expensive."

"Who's asking you to pay?" Danny was back.

"You're a college student, you have no money."

"I'm on scholarship, the school gives me a stipend and I get cash from my dad."

I'm on a scholarship, she thought, a bit ruffled. "Save your money, Danny."

"My dad pays me to be happy," he said, seriously. "It's the least he can do, and right now you and me on that roller coaster would make me happy."

Melanie's heart sputtered.

"You're not really scared, are you?"

"No," she wasn't. She was wistfully absorbing the moment.

"Come on, chicken," the dolphin said, rubbing its nose in Melanie's face.

"You do know that I'm going to toss that fish off the side."

Danny laughed, "Don't get mad at him, he likes you. Besides he's going on my bed." Melanie thought their laugher was harmonious. "These burgers suck. Let's grab something else on the way home."

That evening Melanie and Danny kicked back on her couch. She turned on the TV but Danny watched her.

"You're comfortable," he said, scooting closer and draping his arm over her shoulders.

She pulled her feet under her and leaned into his chest. This was remarkably easy, she thought as images blinked across the screen.

By eleven Danny was kissing her goodnight.

"You have to leave?" she asked, no longer drowsy.

"Yeah, but I'll be back in the morning," he said, his fingers threaded through her hair.

She nodded, her mouth was busy.

Lonesome once he'd gone, she took a shower. Clean, dry and bored, she lay on her stomach and willed him to call. *Please ring.*

It did.

"Hi," she said, knowing it was him.

"Hi," Danny said.

"I was hoping you'd call."

"Are you in bed?"

"Yeah, where are you?"

"In bed," he chuckled, "where'd you think I was?"

She honestly didn't know. "It's early and I thought, maybe you had someplace else to go?"

"You're crazy. I'm in my apartment, in my bed *alone*, thinking about you." There was a pause, "So, what are you wearing?"

The truth was impossibly boring. "I'm getting undressed," she said, blushing.

"You're wearing your pink bra?"

"Danny!"

"What? I took a peek when you weren't looking," he growled, "Melanie, I'm trying to behave here. Tell me you're wearing a long flannel granny nightgown and save me."

"A T-shirt and a pair of boxer shorts."

"I bet you look cute."

Each morning at about five to seven, Melanie's pulse began to race. A response triggered by a knock on the door. Danny had claimed a spot for himself on her daily run, moving it to the more difficult terrain of the beach.

"Hi," she said, her enthusiasm at his presence still discomforting.

"Ready, Gorgeous?"

She blushed. "What's up for today? Bowling? More racquet ball?" She tiptoed to receive his kiss.

"It's a surprise," he beamed. "But you'd better put on an old sweatshirt."

In four days of dating Danny, Melanie had learned enough to take him at his word. She changed.

An hour drive, (that should have taken two) later, Melanie was strapping on a helmet.

"Are you sure this doesn't hurt?"

"That jersey should help but … you'll still feel a sting. My advice is, don't get shot."

"Excellent." She looked down at the camouflage.

He smiled apologetically, "I won't let anyone tag you." He kissed the side of her head and handed her a paintball gun.

Divided into teams, she reluctantly followed a group of very tall, very enthusiastic warriors out to a desert-like field. Instructions were condensed into a few sentences – no overzealous shooting, no swearing, smoking or illegal drug use and stay off the bunkers.

Danny had paid for three hours of terrifying paintball battle. Neon green paint grazed her pant leg within the first three minutes. Pissed, she sat out, observing, until her team's flag had been snatched.

"I don't like that team," she whispered to Danny. "They cheat."

"You can't cheat in this game. All's fair."

"All's fair," she repeated softly with a vague sense of what she was about to do.

She wanted to kick Mr. Neon Green's ass. Settling in behind a sand bunker she motioned for Danny to go ahead when the start buzzer sounded. He rolled his eyes and she waved him on. What she had to do, she had to do alone. Fly below the radar, picking off the other team one by one until she had the one she wanted in her cross hairs.

Melanie almost made it to the end using this strategy. Salty sweat stung her eyes and she turned to wipe away the beads when the paintball smacked her square between the shoulders just below her neck. It was a force strong enough to heave her to the ground.

Dust coated her goggles but she saw enough to send goose bumps up her spine.

Danny.

Jumping out from behind a pile of branches yelling, "You shot her in the back you Mother…" that's when the rapid fire of orange paintballs were released, tagging Mr. Neon Green across the chest.

"Sorry I got us kicked out," he said, cranking over the engine.

"It was worth it." She laughed. "He looked like a radio-active orange giant when you got through."

"He's an ass. I'm barred from that place forever." Danny shook his head. "Not like there aren't a dozen more fields."

"Well, I think you were brave."

"It was paintball, Mel." He laughed before turning serious and reaching over to tenderly place his fingertips at the base of her neck. "How are you?"

"There's going to be a mark." Understatement. *Maybe it was worth a gigantic bruise.*

"Keep the ice pack on." His glance fell to the baggie of ice dropped between the seats.

"Are you sure it's necessary? It's really cold."

The orange sun slipped below the horizon while Melanie and Danny huddled beneath a blanket.

Even from his profile she could tell he was deep in thought.

"What are you thinking?" she asked, shadows from the bonfire dancing on the sandy shore.

"That it's getting cold out here. How about we move back to your apartment?"

She couldn't argue, but wasn't convinced that he was engrossed only by the weather.

Melanie had never felt more comfortable in her apartment. She lowered the stereo and the pair sank into her couch.

Distracted since the beach, out of the blue Danny answered her earlier question. "I was thinking about the other day when you said I'd never noticed you before. That's not true. I always looked for you on the first day of class. Borrowing notes and partnering up for projects, that was no accident." He rested his hand on her stomach.

"No, it was because you knew we'd get an A," she said, stating what she'd believed.

"Not totally true," Danny continued, "It never occurred to me that you'd be interested."

"Seriously Danny?" she asked rolling her eyes. "You had to know I had a crush on you."

"I didn't." He propped himself up on his elbow. "I can tell when someone likes me." His arrogant lips shaped in a high curve. "But, you," he shook his blonde head, "no idea."

"I was embarrassed," she said, believing him. "I always thought you knew," she said, more to herself as he settled back down and she rested her head on his shoulder. "I'm glad we're together now."

"Me, too." A kiss on the top of her head sent warm shivers down to her toes. "How about we take it easy tomorrow."

"What, no flying trapeze?"

"Cute, no. But I know a guy who works on a whale-watching boat. I thought we'd check it out." He was scooting off the couch. He was leaving.

"Sounds great," she said, trying to push away the disappointment. It was stupid, how could she miss him? He wasn't even gone and they'd spent the day together with the promise of another.

"Goodnight, Melanie Ward."

"Goodnight, Danny Ashe."

The other nights had ended with the same playful formality and heart-stopping kiss.

◈

"You're going to need another jacket," he stated. "It looks like it might rain again."

"Welcome to sunny California," Melanie smiled. She added a

third sweater and donned a windbreaker before they set out in his drafty Jeep, where a large, steaming black coffee waited for her.

The low, heavy clouds let little light pass but as the 30-foot excursion boat motored out of the marina the fog drifted quickly. Once out on the open sea, patches of blue sky gave way to shafts of golden sunlight.

The cruise was not luxurious but perfect for the dozens of school children that ran amuck.

Melanie and Danny picked their way to the top deck. The wind blew and they leaned close to each other. He was strong and warm and she felt safe though the sea was rough. An hour into the rocky trip a pod of humpbacks were spotted off the starboard side. For 15 minutes they followed the mystical creatures rising out of the dark ocean, their enormous gray backs glistening above the water's surface. Hundreds of seagulls greedily hovered around the feeding whales, gobbling up any fish that escaped the giant jaws.

She was in awe as the final fluke descended into the icy sea.

"That was incredible," she said.

Over the loudspeaker a crackly voice instructed children to meet on the bow for activities. Kids ran around pretending not to hear their weary teachers. Melanie smiled as an especially rambunctious 10-year-old boy raspberried an adult and darted down the stairwell.

"I bet you were just like that kid," Melanie teased, smiling at the thought of a young Danny.

"He pales in comparison."

"Is that why you got into rugby, to beat up on people?" The salty breeze pushed away the clouds and the winter sun warmed her back. "I bet your mom freaked when little Danny Ashe came home from school wanting to join a rugby team." Melanie could only imagine.

Her parents freaked when she joined the track team in high school.

"Actually, it was my mom's idea."

"Really? Wow, I worried about you getting hurt, and I was just a girl with a crush. I can't imagine your mom."

Danny's eyes were thoughtful, his voice was deep and he brushed back the loose hair that had escaped her ponytail. "I was 10 when my parents split up. My dad left us for his secretary, Connie." The resentment rang in his words.

"I'm sorry," Melanie didn't know what to say.

"We sold our house and my mom and I moved into an apartment. I hated it, hated being traded every weekend, hated Connie. She and my dad were together for almost two years before she kicked his sorry ass to the curb. He came crawling back to my mom but it was no good. Too much time had passed, she said she had moved on with her life. Though she had no husband or boyfriend, I didn't understand and God, I was pissed."

Melanie could feel his anger. He shifted and leaned forward, his elbows resting on his knees.

"Then I blamed my mom for not taking him back, for him leaving in the first place, for all the mess we were in. I thought it was her fault. I missed him and all I wanted was for us to be a family. I thought everything could be like it had been. We'd move back to our house, get a dog." He leaned back and wrapped his arm around her shoulders. "I was 13 when I started smoking, ditching school and using drugs." His voice held the tone of contrition. "My revenge. I treated her like shit, calling her names, slamming doors. She felt guilty about how unhappy I was so she took my abuse, but the day she found my cigarettes her head nearly exploded. She pulled me out of school and found a place to live across town. I raised hell, but she wouldn't let me out of the apartment. She made me box all our stuff. I hauled every box from the old apartment to a truck she'd borrowed and then into the new apartment. By the end of each day I was too exhausted to fight anymore. She enrolled me in a new school and signed me up for football and boxing. Every day for three years I was in two sports with only a couple of hours to do homework and no TV. She threatened military camp if my grades fell below a B average. I believed her." His voice was calm, his eyes sparkled and his face flush from be whipped by the wind.

"She put me in tough sports, letting my aggression out in a monitored environment. Basically, she saved my life." He rubbed Melanie's thigh. "More than you wanted to know?"

"No, I want to know everything."

He put his lips on her mouth and kissed her more completely than he had before. "I haven't told many people about my past." The creases in the corners of his eyes deepened as he smiled.

"Thank you." Melanie looked at the people around her, all carrying their own stories – secrets that they hid, masking private moments that created the essence of who they are. Even she had one.

Starving when the boat finally pulled into port, Melanie and Danny headed for the nearest hamburger joint.

"I don't know what it is about you, but it feels like I've known you all my life," Danny said.

"So I don't make you nervous?"

"It's not nerves, it's excitement. I'm excited walking up to your apartment or thinking about you or even now sitting here talking. I think we're more than dating, I think we're friends, don't you?"

It sounded innocent, but Melanie hesitated, "Yeah, I'd say we're friends."

"Are you all right? You look kind of funny." Danny reached for her arm.

Melanie nodded, but she could feel the tendons in her neck tightening.

After a pause Danny grinned just slightly. "Do you think I just pulled the, 'Let's just be friends' line?"

"Did you?"

The amusement on his face was unmistakable. "I'm psycho about you, okay? Don't you know that?" He grabbed her by her shoulders and gave her a soft shake.

She did know. The electricity in their touch was too intense for them both not to have felt it.

God, I hate being insecure.

Kissing goodbye inside her apartment, Melanie was startled by the sound of a key in the door.

CHAPTER 4

"Melanie, I'm home."

It was Trish. She hadn't seen Melanie and Danny as she wheeled her luggage down the short hallway and into her room. Melanie's sad expression reflected Danny's as he placed a soft kiss on her forehead. She cleared her throat, fixed her sweater, and went to greet a now-blonde Trish.

"Hi, how was your trip?" Melanie asked, giving her friend a hug.

"Not too bad." She paused and narrowed her eyes. "Okay, where's the guy? I smell male." Trish walked into the living room to find Danny.

Melanie held her breath throughout the introduction. This was proof, her relationship with Danny was real.

"I'm going to let you two catch up," Danny said, jacket in hand.

"Aren't we going to the club later?" Trish asked.

Melanie hadn't thought about the club, but it could be fun. "Club?"

"I'll pick you up at 9:30." Danny leaned in for a quick kiss before walking out the door.

"My little Melanie did good. What a hottie," Trish said making a purring sound in the back of her throat. "How long have you been seeing him?"

"This past week," Melanie gushed.

"You look awfully comfortable with each other for only a week," she said with a note of skepticism.

"We have been together every day. It's been wonderful."

It was the first time she'd been able to share her heavenly secret and Melanie swooned.

"Slow down girl, or a certain boy is going to think you're in love. Trust me, that's not what you want," Trish said, from the kitchen, ready to fix a sandwich.

"Trish, when was the last time you dated the same guy for over a week?" The bitterness in her voice filled the room.

Trish set the plate on the table before responding to Melanie's snide remark. "I'm trying to protect you, Mel. You've never been heartbroken and a guy like that breaks hearts. I'm speaking from experience. It takes a long time for a heart to heal. The next time passion comes along you won't be so eager to respond. Love and pain go hand in hand and it can change a person forever. So don't be naïve."

The words of her friend cut deep, Melanie didn't want to admit that Trish could be right and was about to pout alone in her room when Trish broke the awkward moment.

"I'm sorry, I didn't mean to be such a bitch. I'm sure he's a great guy and you know exactly what you're doing."

"I do," she said, while the back of her mind shouted *No, you don't!* "Why are you back early?" Melanie squirmed, easing into a neutral conversation.

"Oh, a huge storm was expected so I decided to get out while I could. Lots of people had the same idea. O'Hare was packed by the time I arrived. So I took the initiative with a very powerful ticket agent," she giggled. "He even bumped me up to first class, so to speak."

They talked until it was time to get ready for their evening. Melanie hadn't been back to the club since she was dating Malik and her stomach twisted at the thought of seeing him there.

"Oh, Mel, I brought a blouse that's perfect for you," Trish said excitedly as she opened her luggage and dumped its contents all over her bed and onto the floor. "I loved it but it's so not me. Let me see." She rummaged around and finally pulled out a tiny black shirt.

"Trish, that's too small." It looked like it belonged to a sixth grader. But it was cute, black with blue rhinestones around the collar and along the sleeves.

"It stretches. Not over my ample bosom but definitely over your tiny boobs." Trish was very proud of her newly purchased breasts and took every opportunity to share them with the public.

Melanie gave Trish the evil eye for her rude comment before trying on the shirt. It did stretch but clung to her body.

"I have the perfect skirt, too." Digging once more through her clothes.

"It's too cold for a skirt," Melanie protested.

"Please! No one's ever said beauty was easy." Trish strapped on a pair of four-inch heels, a micro-mini skirt and a tank top.

Unbelievable, Melanie thought.

"Wow," Danny said when Melanie opened the door.

"I told you that shirt was great. It even makes you look like you have boobs," Trish said when she saw Danny staring at Melanie's chest.

Melanie shook her head. "We don't pay attention to her," she said.

"Come on, I didn't get all dressed up for you to ogle her in our doorway." Trish pushed Melanie out the door.

The club was more crowded than usual. The line to get in wrapped around the building but Trish, Melanie and Danny walked right in.

"Hey, Trish, you are looking especially hot tonight," said the huge bouncer guarding the entrance.

"Hi, Bubba, aren't you sweet." Trish kissed his cheek and then wiped away the lipstick mark.

"Mel-A-Nee," he said, bobbing his big round head, smiling until he saw Danny. "Friend, you need to wait over there." He pointed to a smaller crowd waiting in the corner.

"No, Bubba, he's with me." Melanie patted Bubba's enormous arm.

"This guy?" He asked looking Danny up and down.

Melanie smiled. Bubba was totally messing with Danny.

"You watch yourself, pretty boy. This here is my girl." Bubba gently elbowed Melanie in the arm and gave her a wink.

"Thanks, Bubba."

"Where's my kiss?" he asked leaning down so she could place a peck on his cheek.

But Melanie patted the big mans arm. "Sorry, Bubba."

"Understood," he said, narrowing his beady eyes to glare at Danny.

Once inside, Danny asked, "You guys never wait or pay a cover?"

Melanie shook her head and pointed at Trish. "She comes with perks."

Trish took the "reserved" sign off their table and headed for the bar, returning a few minutes later with three beers.

"I'm going to do the walk," Trish said and left to scout out the territory.

"She is something," Danny replied.

Melanie sipped her beer, thinking about how their relationship was changing. Whether she wanted it to or not, they were back on familiar ground and Melanie had seen his friends gathering across the room.

During their week there had been an adjustment to Danny's behavior. His cocky, peacock strut had all but faded, his reckless flirting and urging comments of sex had vanished as well. And whenever they were together somewhere they were touching, hands, arms, legs – somewhere.

She wondered if he'd change back once he was again among his cohorts.

"Dance?" He stood, holding out his hand.

The dance floor was crowded and people were everywhere, on the tables, speakers and on the platform above the D.J. Melanie and Danny found a small space where they danced close.

The music slowed and his tender gaze led to a soft, passionate kiss as they held each other on the dance floor. A rainbow of lights reflected off the huge disco ball spinning above. Melanie closed her eyes and pressed her cheek against his chest, breathing in the scent of his cologne.

"Are those your hands?" she asked, looking up into his eyes.

With a small chuckle he said, "These are my hands."

He gave her butt a squeeze. "And these are my hands and these are my hands." He was running his hands slowly up to her waist, along her sides from her hips to her breasts, caressing her shoulders and into her hair.

"Okay, I was just checking."

Her desire was engulfing her senses, drowning out every other emotion, more intensely than she'd even thought possible, and now she wanted Danny to be her first.

"Danny, can we talk?"

"Hey Dan!" His friends yelled, beckoning him from off the dance floor.

Melanie felt each pair of scrutinizing eyes on her as she and Danny approached. Wanting to shrivel and hide, she tried to convey confidence, standing straight and returning the stares. Danny coiled his arm around her waist, pulled her close until their hips met and he introduced her to the group. Danny was cool and if he noticed the six people get suddenly quiet and exchange glances and smirks he didn't let on.

"I didn't know you were in town," said one of the guys, moving over so Melanie and Danny could sit down. "When did you get in?"

"Last week."

Watching him with his friends was like being invited into your favorite TV sitcom. You knew the characters, their places, their faces and yet they were always just beyond reach. Tonight she was sitting in with Danny, Joe, Barbie, Kaitlyn, Sara, Angelo and Chaz. The only one missing was Carolyn. Was she the new Carolyn? The thought almost made her laugh out loud. She could never be Carolyn.

But Danny did look happy, his grin was wide and with ease he moved from their seclusion to his regular seat at his regular table – she was the only thing *irregular* in this picture. His laugh was genuine, carefree, his voice loud enough for the entire table but directed to the boys. Even his perfect hair had its natural buoyancy. Beneath the table his hand had snaked its way over her thigh and his fingers wiggled beneath her leg. It was a clasp of reassurance and protection. He turned toward her and gave a heart-melting crooked smile.

"So, how did you meet Dan?" one of the girls asked for what must have been the second time.

"What?"

The girl, Sara, rolled her eyes, shook her head and tried again. "Where did you two meet?" her words were slow and precisely annunciated. She even had the gall to use hand gestures. The three girls laughed heartily.

Right, Melanie nodded, *I'm the idiot here*.

"We have classes together," Melanie said, guarded but not wanting to make eternal enemies.

"Well, Dan goes through a lot of girls," another girl snickered. "Don't get too comfortable."

"Dan usually goes for blondes. I guess he's testing out the old adage, if blondes really are more fun."

"If blondes *do* have more fun."

"Same difference."

Okay, it's official – I hate these girls.

"How are things going over here?" His deep voice was rough and she cherished its raspiness.

"We're just discussing your usual appetite for blondes," Melanie said, defiantly.

"Okay, then." His chuckle was casual but sent ripples of excitement through her that were only intensified when Danny cocked his head and whispered in her ear. "I want you to consider letting me spend the night tonight."

His warm breath was soft and tickled her ear.

"Don't decide right now. Just think about it."

Then as a bonus he kissed her, not a regular peck, but lustful, tongue laden, full-mouth kiss.

"Think about it," he said, looking squarely in her eyes. Then he squeezed her hand and returned to his conversation.

Melanie clung to his hand, her heart pounding. Blood coursed through her, first draining to her toes before riding a roller coaster right back up to her woozy head.

The girls were talking yet she heard nothing – her blood was pumping, his words, his breath filling her. In her panic it seemed she'd forgotten to breathe. She was no longer Melanie, a whole person, she was a billion molecules frantically colliding into each other.

"Mel, I need you." Trish was leaning over the chair behind Melanie.

Melanie saw the boys gape, each hoping her tank top would give away and reveal what little was hidden.

"What's up?" Melanie asked, shaking, panting and dizzy.

"I met someone. Are you okay if I leave?"

Melanie took a quick look at Trish's "someone" as Trish motioned for him to approach.

"Mel this is, um, what's your name again?"

"Leo Miller."

Leo was a completely average college student, brown shaggy hair, a few too many pounds around his midsection, wearing baggy jeans and an old faded gray T-shirt.

"You go to the U?' Melanie quizzed.

"Yeah."

"What's your major?"

"Haven't exactly decided. Liberal Arts, I guess."

Trish handed her a slip of paper with Leo's phone number.

"Okay, be safe, Trish."

"Thanks, Mel." Trish gave her a kiss on the forehead.

Trish and Leo hadn't reached the front doors when Melanie was faced with a burst of her own reckless freedom. Danny's hand, resting warmly on her leg, sent her pulse rising.

"Are we getting out of here?" She breathed softly in his ear.

"Yeah?" he asked sounding surprised and delighted.

"Yeah," she answered with certainty.

Danny immediately stood. "We'll catch you guys later."

He grabbed her hand, ignoring the questions from his confused friends, and whisked her toward the swinging front doors. The crisp night air came in puffs as replacements for exiting patrons were let in. Melanie could barely feel the chill on her burning cheeks.

"Dan the Man! Dan the Man!" The cheers echoed across the noisy, smoky nightclub.

A group of bulky guys blocked the exit. Danny lowered his head and gave a faint groan.

"Hey guys."

The primal male greeting was that of low grunts, expanded chests, body slamming, all combined with a bit of wrestling. These guys were more "in your face" than Danny's other friends and Melanie liked them better for it.

"Melanie, these are my rugby mates, Kyle, Reed, Tony, Roy, Fletch, Wally and Hank. Guys, this is Melanie. We were just leaving."

"What happened to Carolyn?" As the words were escaping Roy's – or was it Tony's? – lips one of the other mates slapped him across the head.

"You don't ask that with *her* standing there." The teammates started arguing among themselves and Danny and Melanie slipped away, but not before hearing the rest of the conversation.

"I heard he called out another girl's name when he was banging Carolyn."

The howling drunken laughter abruptly died when Danny spun around and grabbed Tony or Kyle – they all looked alike to Melanie – by the shirt and shoved him hard against the wall.

Melanie stepped back as the rest of the team rushed in, yelling at Danny to get off Tony. They pulled at his shoulders while Danny shook them off, undeterred, getting right into Tony's panicked face. "Watch your fucking mouth!"

Danny pushed Tony into the rest of the group and grabbed Melanie's hand, swinging her around and out the open doors into the chilly night air.

Melanie jogged to keep up. *What had she just heard?*

"Danny, slow down."

She pulled at his hand and dug her heels into the asphalt. He let out a deep breath. They walked, slowly, to the Jeep where he leaned on the passenger door, his hands stuffed deep into his pockets.

"What just happened?"

Danny gave her a quick glance then studied something across the parking lot. Melanie glanced behind her to see what he was looking at – the line waiting to get into Jungle Jim's. She turned back to him.

"Danny?"

A wary smile lifted the corners of his mouth.

"Is there any chance of avoiding this conversation?"

"Not likely."

He tugged at his ear lobe. "I might have had a couple of fantasies about you."

Melanie blushed, his words and his eyes that had a way of undressing her. X-ray vision drilling beneath her 50 percent rayon blouse, Melanie chewed on her bottom lip.

Danny pulled his eyes up to meet hers, shrugging with a cagey grin.

"I was packing for Denver when Carolyn dropped by my place. We were messing around and at the very wrong moment I said 'Melanie.'" Melanie knew this was awkward for him despite his cool demeanor.

"Carolyn was justifiably pissed and I was embarrassed. It just slipped … I never meant to hurt her. Tony's my roommate, and he heard everything. I'm sorry, Mel."

She stretched on tiptoes to put her lips on his. His warm breath filled her mouth followed eagerly by his tongue.

Danny drove to her apartment in record time and was undressing her before she got the door open, shedding a trail of clothing.

"Danny," she tried to speak but all she kept saying was his name. His mouth on her neck, distracting, along her collarbone, distracting … she couldn't form her thoughts.

"Danny, I need to tell you something."

They were on her small bed, he was undressed to his unbuttoned jeans, when she tried again.

"Hmm?" He continued kissing her, his warm, strong body pressing her into the mattress.

"I've never done this before," she whispered.

It took almost a full minute before he stopped. He lifted himself up enough to look into her eyes.

"*We've* never done this or *you've* never?"

"Both."

He stared, processing her confession, the lust clearing from his eyes.

"Jesus, Mel!"

The words burned like she'd been slapped in the face. She bit the inside of her lip to keep from crying.

"You're a virgin and you thought *this* would be the best time to tell me?"

Melanie knew it was a comment made out of frustration, but it stung. She crawled out from under him and quickly covered up with his T-shirt, which he had tossed over the footboard.

"I'm sorry, I didn't know how to tell you. I tried."

Danny sat back against the wall.

"God, Mel. Just give me a second," he said, clearly irritated.

He blew out a long breath and closed his eyes.

Melanie stood next to her bed, waiting nervously for Danny's response. She had no idea where the rest of her clothes had been thrown but she knew this night was over and moved to get dressed. The rejection flooded through her and it was all she could do to keep her chin from trembling.

"Mel?" His voice gentle now.

"I'm sorry I didn't say something sooner."

"No, no." He rose from the bed to wrap his arms around her. "You surprised me, that's all." He kissed the top of her head. "It's me, I'm sorry." He pressed her harder into his chest. "So, you're a virgin?"

He said it like he'd never met one and Melanie pulled away to look into his moonlit face. He bent and kissed her tenderly.

"How about we hold off on this and I'll plan something special, romantic. We'll get a room and champagne." His smile was back, reaching his eyes. She felt the laugh in his chest but kindly he brushed the hair from her eyes.

Instantly, he was forgiven and she knew she was making the right decision. "I don't want to hold off. I haven't been waiting for the right place, I've been waiting for you."

Cupping her face in his hands he put his lips to hers, kissing her slowly, less frantic and more passionately than before. His breath was uneven and his mouth trembled slightly. Every touch was deliberate, gentle, and Melanie had no choice but to let go.

They didn't fall asleep until after dawn.

Waking first, Melanie looked over at Danny, sleeping with his head on her pillow.

Danny Ashe, she admired, and wondered how this had happened. *If I wasn't in love with him before,* Melanie thought, *I am now.*

She had always found it irresponsible for girls to be so gullible to think they've found love between the sheets. But now being her turn, she understood.

She loved the way his sun-kissed hair lined his face. His breathing was slow and soothing. Melanie put her face on his chest and drifted back to sleep.

It was almost noon when they stood at her door, kissing goodbye. Today was the first day of rugby practice and he had 15 minutes to be on the field.

"I hate to leave," he said, squeezing both her hands at her door.

"I'll see you later though, right?"

"Try keeping me away." He kissed her again his crooked smile beamed knowingly.

"Go," she urged, blushing and pushing his shoulder.

Melanie was floating back to her room when the front door opened. She was about to reprimand him when Carla's voice rang out.

CHAPTER 5

"Melly, we're home."

Melanie shrieked, running and jumping into the arms of her best friend.

There was so much to tell Carla. But she had arrived with Jenny.

"Hey, how was your trip?" She asked, dying from the restraint it took to bottle up her emotions.

"Oh my," Carla sighed. "I have so much to tell you."

Melanie followed as Carla dragged her oversized luggage to the corner of their bedroom.

"First, you'll never guess who was racing down the stairs when Jen and I were coming up."

Melanie turned to make her bed. She didn't want Carla to read her expression.

"Who?"

"That rugby guy you've had a crush on, what's his name?"

"Danny." Melanie grinned, she loved saying his name.

"That's right, he must have a girlfriend in this building. He looked disheveled, if you know what I mean."

Melanie knew exactly what Carla meant.

"But let me tell you about my vacation." Carla plopped down on her bed and pulled Melanie with her. Carla radiated a glow as she spoke. "Ted came down to Louisiana a couple of days after Christmas and we spent a glorious three days with my family. Can you believe I'm saying that? Mother behaved like an angel. I was so proud of her." Carla was excited and her Southern drawl was more pronounced.

It was a typical Carla trick used to complement her tale.

"Then we flew to Boston. I was so nervous, but Ted held my hand the entire flight. Isn't that sweet?" It was rhetorical. Carla continued, "Mel, you should see his home, it's so grand and his parents were fabulous. They accepted me right from the start. At dinner one evening, Mrs. Bradley asked me to call her Helen," Carla raised her eyebrows, impressed. "Anyway, Helen tells me how she's always been fascinated by the 'proper ladies of the South.' So, I kicked up the accent a bit and explained how Mother is engulfed in high society. Helen loved it." Carla detailed every moment of her stay with the Bradleys.

"Then the other night Ted and I were cuddling by the fire while the snow piled up outside and Ted started telling me how much his parents like me and how much he loves me."

Melanie waited for Carla to explode.

"He says that he can't imagine a more perfect woman for him and then, Mel, – I was entirely shocked – he knelt down with ring in hand and asked me to marry him!" Carla screamed, waving her left hand.

Melanie screamed, grabbing her friend's hand to get a look at the diamonds. She didn't know much about diamonds or carats but the square one in the center looked huge.

"Carla!"

"I know!" Hugging and jumping around the room they celebrated. "I couldn't wait to tell you."

Her drawl turned dreamlike as she admired her finger. "Oh, it was so romantic, his grandmother's ring, even. A perfect fairy tale proposal."

"What the hell's going on in here?" Trish asked, smiling with a bored looking Jen by her side.

"I'm getting married!" Carla screeched, and the high-pitched screaming began again. She fluttered her hands in a gesture meant to calm her nerves. Carla was big on presentation and her engagement was going to make an impact.

"Three nights ago the Bradleys held a huge ball with the who's who of Boston, easily 100 guests," Carla said, one eyebrow arched. "Ted stood on the steps of the grand staircase and began by clinking his champagne flute. Right there in front of God and everyone, he starts speaking about how he and I met and how he's grown to love me, and then..." she looked around, her brown eyes moist, "Ted announced our engagement. I was overwhelmed, I cried right there and then the toasts started and Helen gave me a peck on the cheek welcoming me into the Bradley family. It was magical." As Carla relived her proposal Trish's stomach gurgled.

"You said toast and I'm hungry."

Carla collapsed on a nearby chair. "Oh, my Lord, I'm famished, too. How about I tell the rest over a bagel sandwich?"

"You're back home now, you can cut the act, Scarlett," Trish snorted, while Melanie pulled Carla up by one arm.

It was a cool, sweater-perfect afternoon as Carla talked nonstop the half block to a frozen yogurt and bagel shop. The place was charged with the energy from the resurgence of students. The girls elbowed their way to a booth that was about to be deserted.

"Carla, don't you think you're way too young to be considering marriage? I mean, really, you're only 21," Trish said from across the table.

Melanie's glaring eyes locked with Trish's wide "what'd I say" stare.

"I was just asking," Trish said, twisting her porcelain face to grimace at Melanie.

"I love him, Trish. He's my prince."

Yikes, do I sound like that?

"There's no such thing," Trish mumbled but then dropped the subject.

Jenny, who'd remained mostly silent, spoke up. "Ryan and I have decided it's time to reinstate our commitment. We're backpacking across Europe this summer."

Melanie gritted her teeth. Ryan was Jenny's high school sweetheart and a complete jerk. He was a senior at Texas Tech, and their freshman year he dumped her to date other people. They lived in a dorm room at the time and Jenny's begging over the phone had curdled Melanie's stomach. It took months for Jenny to wrangle a compromise with Ryan – they'd each date other people with the assumption they'd reconnect after graduation. Melanie had to control her gag reflex each time Jenny uttered Ryan's name.

In a concerted effort not to be outdone by him, Jen's promiscuity was unleashed. She accepted his decision, defiantly, on her back.

Through the four years, Melanie didn't like it but stayed quiet as Trish and Jenny traipsed strange men in and out of their rooms.

"What, no more boys?" Trish asked.

"Nope, I'm done." Jenny lit up a cigarette.

"You can't smoke here, Jen, they serve *yogurt*." Carla drilled incredulously, as if the combination of nicotine and bacteria could incite chemical warfare.

Jenny crushed out her smoke. "Ryan loved my new body and I am not about to gain an ounce."

"You look beautiful, but smoking is so nasty," Mother Carla preached.

Jenny shrugged. "It's not like I'm addicted. I could quit if I wanted."

Passing over Melanie, Carla and Jenny wanted to know about

Trish's escapades in Chicago. It was always something with Trish, unabashed and brave as she was.

Speaking rapidly and skipping over the nonessentials, Trish highlighted her vacation, giving the CliffsNotes version.

Trish's mom had scolded, sobbed and reprimanded her regarding her breast implants as well as her short red hairdo.

"Fortunately, she didn't see the tattoo," Trish chuckled. "I'll save that for summer. But she forced me to dye my hair and swear never to cut it again. Does it look all right?"

"Better," Carla said, too quickly, and Trish shot a nasty look her way.

"Anyway, it's your turn, Mel." Trish grinned slyly.

"Did you do something this year?" Jenny snipped. "I did notice you moved the cereal boxes to the other cupboard."

When Melanie faltered Trish took the initiative, with a song to her words, her high-pitched voice sang, "substantial enough to rival Carla's holiday."

"Really? I don't believe it."

"So give," Carla insisted.

Melanie was pink before the first word was spoken. Biting on her bottom lip she stared into Carla's doe eyes.

"You remember seeing Danny run out of the building this morning," Melanie said, blushing so fiercely she matched the red vinyl booth.

"Yeah."

"Who?"

"The dude Mel's been hot after for ages," Trish said, turning to Melanie, "See, I pay attention."

"Who?"

"Come on, Mel, spill." Carla was at the edge of her seat.

"He was with me." Her toes curling in her tennis shoes, she waited breathlessly anticipating the reaction.

Stunned, Carla could only manage one-word questions, "What?" "How?"

"He just showed up last week and..." she looked at Carla and shrugged her shoulders. "I don't know."

"Oh my. Did you sleep with him?" Carla's brown eyes opened wide, accusingly.

"Carla!" Melanie turned a deeper red.

"I think I can answer that," Trish said raising her left index finger. "I found clothes, everything from shoes to black underwear that I didn't even know Melanie owned, leading from the front door to her room last night. I folded them nice and neat and left them in a pile outside her door."

"Melanie!"

"So, how was it?" Trish asked.

Melanie wanted to shrink into her sweater. "Amazing."

"Did he tell you he loved you?" Trish asked, snidely.

"No."

"No proposals?" Trish sarcastically, letting her opinion known.

"Great, now who am I going to spend my weekends with?" Jenny complained.

"Nice, Jen, because it's all about you," Trish said. "Besides, who am I going to spend my weekends with now that you're ditching me for Ryan?"

"I was just kidding. Really, it's awesome for you. Ryan and I have been together for years and it's tough to maintain a relationship unless you are truly right for each other."

Carla rolled her eyes.

The little restaurant had emptied by the time the girls finished their two-hour lunch.

Walking the short distance to their apartment, Trish draped her long arm across Melanie's shoulder. "If you want to talk or need anything, you come and see me, OK?"

"Thanks." Melanie hugged Trish. "I love you."

"You love everyone today." They laughed because it was true.

"It's for me," Carla yelled when the doorbell rang.

"No way. It's for me,"

"Jesus, you two," Trish said, opening the door. It was Ted.

Ted was six feet tall with cropped dark brown hair. He smiled broadly as he entered the apartment and greeted Carla with a hug and a peck on the lips.

In flannel pajamas and slippers, Jenny collapsed on the couch with a pint of Ben and Jerry's. In case she wasn't obvious enough she added a heavy, pathetic sigh.

"Jen, stop eating that!" Trish said, grabbing the Cherry Garcia.

Melanie looked up to see Danny standing in the doorway. A faded jean jacket hung loosely across his broad shoulders and his blond hair was long and shaggy, just the way she liked it.

"Hi, gorgeous," Danny said. "These are for you."

He handed her a bouquet wrapped in brown paper.

Roses.

His brown eyes sparkled and he looked at her as if they were alone in the room. With barely a moment to smile, Danny's lips were pressed against hers. His kisses were intoxicating and the apartment around her was forgotten. The flowers being pulled from her grasp brought Melanie back into the room, where her friends stood gaping in silence.

Melanie introduced Danny to her roommates and to Ted.

Ted broke the tension, and walked over with outstretched hand. "Ted Bradley."

"Dan Ashe." The two men shook hands.

"Dan Ashe, the rugby player?"

Danny nodded.

"Ted is our student body president," Carla announced proudly, holding on to Ted's left arm.

"Yeah, I recognized the name. Nice to meet you."

"So, were you two going to dinner?" Ted asked, looking from Danny to Melanie. "We were going to the Fisherman's Market. Best seafood in town. How about you join us, my treat?" Ted offered.

Carla's small mouth scrunched tightly. Melanie knew the look.

"Thanks, but we kind of have other plans," Melanie lied.

Ted's broad smile vanished and instantly she swam in guilt.

"I'm sorry to hear that," his disappointment seemingly genuine. "Is it something you can cancel?"

Was it the look in his eyes, the tone in his voice? Melanie wasn't sure what quality Ted possessed, but she felt compelled to please him. She didn't want to intrude on Carla but how could she resist Ted's plea?

"What do you think, Danny?" Melanie asked, not wanting to be the one to make the decision.

"Let's go out with your friends," he said.

"Terrific!" Ted's smile returned in full force.

"I need to get these flowers in water," Melanie smiled, pulling the bundle out of Trish's hold.

Danny followed her into the kitchen.

"That was awkward," he said, lifting her onto the counter and situating himself between her legs.

"I missed you." Melanie ran her fingers through the back of his hair.

"I missed you."

Danny tugged away from her lips, resting his head on her chest.

"Mel, I'd love to stay here kissing you, but I'm starving. When did we eat last?"

"Didn't you have lunch?"

"Five doughnuts and two Gatorades."

Melanie laughed. "Five?" She finished filling the vase with water and dropped the roses in.

"Ready?" Carla asked, linking arms with Melanie as they walked out.

"I'm sorry, Car, it's impossible to say no to Ted."

"I know, thanks for trying. Besides, it gives me a chance to get to know this boyfriend of yours."

Outside the indigo was deepening to violet and the temperature had dropped a few degrees.

"We'll meet you there," Danny called out as he opened the door of the old Jeep for Melanie.

"How was your day?" he asked, leaning to give her a kiss even before starting the engine.

"Good. Practice?"

He nodded, "I got pummeled but I'm sure glad we've been exercising." His lips spread into a smile.

The warmth of pure happiness spread through her.

"Was everything okay with Tony?" Melanie asked as the aged engine coughed and hacked before settling into a purr.

"Why? What was wrong with Tony?" Danny asked, pulling out into traffic. "Oh, right, because of last night." Danny accelerated and darted across two lanes to get onto Highway 163.

"Tony's fine. We said what we had to last night."

Saturday night traffic into downtown was light and Danny had no problem keeping up with Ted. Melanie looked up into the starless sky and felt sorry for lonely moon.

"Didn't you tell your friends about us? They looked, um, surprised to see me."

Melanie flushed. "I think it was the kissing that startled them."

"Can I ask you something?" Melanie asked, as silk-screened flags flying from lampposts featuring famous cherubs sailed outside her window.

"Anything."

"Why do I call you Danny, when everyone else, including you, calls you Dan?"

He smiled. "I have no idea. You're the only one who calls me Danny."

Melanie blushed. "Why had I never noticed? It's embarrassing."

"No, I like it." His eyes twinkled. "I was thinking that maybe we could go to my place tonight."

"Is that what you were thinking?" she asked coyly to hide her apprehension.

"What's the matter?" Danny asked, pulling to a stop in front of the Fish Market.

"Nothing."

He turned to face her directly. "Is something wrong?"

"It's just that I don't think your friends liked me and ... um ..."

"Why would you think that?' His brows pull together in a tight furrow.

"Oh, I don't know." Melanie said sarcastically.

Danny shook his head. "I don't think they care who I date." He smiled. "You're cute."

"What about all the other girls you've had there?"

The image of Danny and Carolyn streaked across her mind.

He breathed out heavily and ignored Ted motioning them to the entrance. "I like you. You're beautiful and smart and I wonder why you'd waste your time on a guy like me. Mel, we all have our insecurities. I could tell you that I like you more than any one of those other girls. It would be true, but it wouldn't erase them." His rough hand tenderly caressed her cheek and he leaned forward to kiss her. "Are we okay?"

"Yeah, but I'm still not sure about your apartment."

"Fair enough. I hope Carla doesn't mind."

Melanie laughed, figuring he wasn't serious but she wasn't totally certain.

An old warehouse adjacent to the harbor served as both restaurant and market. Melanie crossed the clean, white linoleum to the refrigerated glass cases that displayed fresh seafood. Sport fishing propaganda hung on the exposed brick walls with the remnants of many coats of paint still clinging to the corners. Along the back wall above the cases was a chalkboard menu of sandwiches, pastas, salads and lobster dishes, all fresh and made to order. Melanie chose a tuna on whole wheat. She had never been much of a fish eater and that preference intensified as she looked over the rows of silver, pink and blue fish dead on ice, their big, bulging eyes staring out blankly and their mouths still open from the fatal intake of oxygen.

"Carla, did you know that Dan is the best rugby player our university has ever seen?" He didn't wait for a response. "Yeah, I've caught a few games throughout the years. Tough sport. Dangerous. You should see how the other teams go after Dan. Last season against UCLA, didn't you crack a rib?"

Melanie flinched.

"It's really not that bad," Danny said.

Melanie's eyebrows raised automatically. "Danny, I know how many classes you missed last season."

For almost two weeks straight Melanie Xeroxed her notes, leaving them with the professor so Danny wouldn't fall behind. She'd been extra diligent, troubling over her handwriting and abbreviations. She was ready to breathe fire when she discovered he'd shared her notes with others in the class. She confronted him the day he returned and demanded, with as much force as she could muster given his repentant, beautiful eyes, that he not do it again.

Tonight when she looked into those same regretful eyes she knew they were sharing the same memory. His hands enclosed hers and a grin danced across his serious expression.

"Did I ever thank you for all your help while I was laid up?"

"I'm not sure I gave you opportunity."

"That's no excuse. Melanie, I am sorry and thank you for seeing me through these past semesters. I appreciate how much you've helped me."

"You're welcome."

"Are we going to my place, tonight?" Danny asked, as Ted and Carla looked on.

Ted cleared his throat. "Well, I think I'll go pay the check."

"I'm staying with Ted, so you can have our room," Carla whispered before joining her fiancé.

⚜

Danny had left early for a full day of rugby practice, so Melanie lay in her bed dreaming up excuses to get out of her family's Sunday dinner. It was going to be tricky. She'd wrangled out of last week's and her mother never allowed two cancellations in a row.

"Hi, Mom."

"Hi, Honey, I expect you here at 4:30 for dinner. No excuses," Rita said before Melanie had a chance to plead her case.

"But..."

"Nope. 4:30. I don't want to hear another word." Then the unmistakable *click*, indicating there would be no further conversation.

"Mom, Mom?" She glared at her phone as if it were to blame.

Melanie slumped on her bed.

"What's up with you?" Carla asked, finally home.

"Sunday dinner."

"You know you can't invite him," Carla said, sitting with Melanie on her bed.

"He's coming over after practice. What am I supposed to do?"

Carla shrugged. "Come to the bookstore with me and we'll talk about it there."

Melanie went, but her heart and mind were on Danny. After two hours following Carla around as she bought school supplies Melanie couldn't take any more. It was 3:45 and she'd have to make a decision, soon.

"Carla, do you mind if I ditch you?" Melanie was ready to bolt.

"Why?'

"I've got to talk with Danny and I think his practice is over at 4."

"Yeah, go." Carla waved her away. "Good luck."

Melanie sprinted across campus to the open grassy field where the boys played rugby. She slowed to a jog as she approached the golden sea of dry grass. The team was embattled in a full-force scrimmage. She spotted Danny immediately, his blond hair matching that of the parched field. Melanie held her breath as he hugged the oval ball, tucking it tightly against his chest right before he was tackled.

As Melanie approached she noticed that the two rows of benches, which extended half the length of the field on both the north and south sides, were mostly taken. She squeezed into a small gap between the edge of the bench and a girl wearing a Greek sweatshirt. The girl scowled, scooted four inches closer to her friend and resumed her conversation.

"Thanks," Melanie said, grateful that the sorority girl warmed half her seat and not caring that she was unwelcome. Now she was able to rest both her cheeks on the aluminum bench.

The second girl leaned forward to take a glance at Melanie. Melanie smiled and gave a quick nod.

"I have no idea. Whatever."

"Ashe is looking hot."

Melanie tucked her hair behind her ear so she could hear their conversation without interference.

"I know. Did you hear he broke up with that Carolyn chick?"

"No way! When did that happen? Oh my God, is he available?"

Nobody saw the small smile cross Melanie's face.

"Rumor has it he's already hooked up with a new bimbo."

The comment erased Melanie's smile.

"Are you shitting me?"

"Sorry. Do you think she's here?"

The two girls assessed the people watching the game.

"Maybe one of those skanks."

Melanie's gaze crossed the field toward three co-eds, with their dark brown tresses spiraling down their backs.

They had been standing, cheering since Melanie arrived. Their identical perms, sweat pants with seemingly harmless statements embroidered on the butt and layered baby-doll tees left no doubt to which sorority they belonged.

The coach, a short muscular man, blew his whistle and yelled out to the players to gather their stuff and meet back in the locker room. The Australian accent was a surprise to Melanie and she paid closer attention to the man hollering out names. Coach was maybe 5'2" with solid muscle and a bone structure far too thick for his short frame, giving him a prehistoric quality and putting him farther to the left on the "evolution of man" chart.

As she lost interest in Coach's genealogy, Melanie's mind went back to Danny. The Kappas had him surrounded, giggling and flirting, and he didn't seem to mind. Melanie watched the group as she crossed the field.

"Hi," she said, standing just outside the little circle.

Danny looked up at her. Dust had caked into the creases of his sweaty skin.

"Hey." He looked and sounded happy to see her.

"Excuse me," he didn't take another look at the other girls. "This is a surprise. I'd kiss you but..." he opened his arms and looked down to his dusty cleats.

"I don't mind."

He tasted of earth and salt as he pressed his hot, sticky body against her. His scent was strong, but she didn't mind.

"Come on Ashe, Hartnett," the coach scolded.

"I gotta go, but I'll be over tonight," he said, stepping out of the embrace.

Melanie clung a little tighter to his arm and pulled him closer.

"Well, that's why I'm here. I won't be home tonight," Melanie said, nervously.

"Oh, okay." He waited half an instant. "What's up?"

Melanie clenched her bottom lip between two teeth. "My family has a weekly dinner and I wasn't able to get out of it." She felt her guilt rise.

"Okay, well, that's all right," he said, looking back at the coach. "Call me when you get home." He ran the back of his fingers gently across her cheek.

"Ashe!"

"I'll be right there." Danny looked back to Melanie. "I gotta go. Call me, I'll come over." After a smile and a quick kiss, Danny slung his sports bag across his shoulder.

Melanie nodded. *Don't do it*, she told herself. *You cannot invite him.*

"If you want," she took two steps, cutting their distance in half. "If you don't mind, I mean, would you like to come?"

"I thought you'd never ask."

His smile was almost worth the inevitable torture.

⥈⥈⥩

Her warnings had fallen on deaf ears.

She had been fair when she cautioned him about her mother's cooking and how none of her girlfriends had ever returned for a second Sunday dinner. Even as she described her mother's quirky ways and her inability, yet undying determination, to prepare a edible meal for her family, Danny was undeterred.

"You're sure?" Melanie asked Danny outside the front door of her parent's house. "We could still make a break for it."

"Baby, I'm sure," he said, cupping her face in his hands and pulling her gently toward him.

"Okay, but don't say I didn't warn you."

The front door was unlocked, as usual. Danny followed her from the entry hall and through the swinging door into the kitchen. Her mom was leaning against the Formica counter, pots and pans in disarray on the stove behind her. Melanie wondered if he could smell that something was amiss.

"Hi, Mom."

Rita looked up from her cookbook.

"Hi, Honey," her expression was puzzled as her eyes fixed on Danny.

Melanie had known when she called to let her mom know she was bringing a friend that Mrs. Ward assumed it was one of the girls.

"This is my friend Danny."

"Boyfriend," Danny corrected.

A smile stretched across Mrs. Ward's face as she placed her glasses on the counter.

"It's very nice to meet you, Danny. Do you go to school with Melanie?'

"Yeah, we're in a lot of the same classes."

"Well, welcome. Excuse me," she said softly before turning. "Bruce Alexander Ward, what in the world do you think you are doing?" She said, punctuating each syllable with a note of abhorrence.

"Wha?" Bruce pulled his head out of the refrigerator, a can of beer in each hand.

"What are you doing? Can't you see we have company?"

"Oh, sorry. Hey man, would you like a beer?"

Melanie chuckled.

"You know that is *not* what I meant." Rita's lips were drawn into a straight, hard line.

"Thanks, but…" Danny started.

"Oh, go ahead. But Bruce, this is your last, understand?" Mrs. Ward's words had an angry edge.

Bruce tossed a cold can to Danny and fetched another one. "For Dad!"

"Why don't you kids go and visit with your father?" Mrs. Ward went back to flipping through the pages of the picture cookbook. She looked concerned as her finger traced over a list of ingredients.

"Something smells great, Mrs. Ward."

Melanie looked from her mother to Danny and then back again. Rita's lips parted into a wide, pleased, smile.

"Thank you. And please, call me Rita."

Melanie and Danny exited the side door that opened to a short hall leading to the garage, laundry room and a short cut to the living room.

"That was very sweet what you did for my mom."

"Well, your brother seemed to tick her off."

The living room, in the back of the house, had floor-to-ceiling windows, giving the illusion that the room was an extension of the outdoors. The scent from Roger's rose garden seemed ever-present to Melanie, even in the heart of winter, when the blossoms had been cut back and the plants themselves were dormant. The room, with its comfortable, lived-in feel, was where she could usually find her dad, sitting in his Barca-lounger watching a sporting event. Today was no different.

Bruce was literally on the edge of his seat, his butt almost floating above the cushion of his chair, as ESPN blared. On the small end table between him and the recliner sat the opened cans of beer, a remote and the current TV Guide.

"Hi, Daddy," Melanie said, stepping between her father and the television and leaning in to give him a kiss on the cheek.

Her dad's smile was warm, but she knew better than to stand in front of the TV for too long.

"Hi, Annie, how's school?" Her father asked not looking up from the game.

"Hasn't started yet," Melanie laughed, "but I'd like you to meet Danny."

Melanie stepped aside so Danny could come forward.

"Hello, sir."

Danny extended his hand.

"Danny, eh?" Roger lifted himself only inches from his seat. "So, do you like sports?" Daring to take his eyes off the screen for only a few seconds to size up the boy his daughter had brought to dinner.

Melanie hadn't considered that Danny was nervous, until she felt his body relax.

"Love sports."

"Great, have a seat."

Bruce yelled, uselessly at the screen. And Melanie foresaw a new favorite team in her brother's near future. He never had the staying power, fluctuating his loyalties behind whichever team was winning.

"I'm partial to the Broncos." Danny admitted.

"Good, Colorado is a good state."

"My dad likes West Coast teams. He feels that there isn't enough representation west of the Mississippi."

Roger began listing off teams and going in depth as to his beliefs of corruption and political unevenness. Melanie, having heard this hypothesis many times, turned to Bruce.

"Where's your girlfriend?"

"The same place Danny will be next weekend – at home." They laughed.

"Well, she seems nice."

"Yeah? I'm breaking up with her."

"Figures."

"Hey, I can't be tied down. I'm in my prime."

For a moment the memory of Malik crossed her mind.

"You know, Bruce, a little humility wouldn't hurt you."

"When you're this good, Mel, it's tough to be humble."

"You mean 15 pounds overweight, out of shape and with a C average?"

"Shut up."

"You get winded going up a flight of stairs."

"Shut up."

"You shut up. Don't be an ass."

"Okay, dinner is ready." Mrs. Ward invited everyone into the dining room, where five places were set with the Ward wedding china, which was used every Sunday.

Once the family was seated and thanks were given, Mrs. Ward doled out heaping spoonfuls of what Melanie recognized to be lasagna.

"I know, Melanie said you two have already eaten. But I think Danny might be hungry," Rita was delighted to add an extra scoop and passed the plate to Danny.

"Thank you, Rita. I'm starving."

Melanie sat quietly, gazing across the beautifully decorated table. Everything was meticulously presented, even the bowl of mixed vegetables was displayed in fine china. But the façade was broken by the crystallized ice that was melting, separating the frozen peas from the frozen cubed carrots.

⬤

"Thank you for inviting me to dinner," Danny said.

He had flown across the near-vacant freeway, zooming around the red tail lights of slower traffic. She reached for Danny's hand to distract herself from the lasagna that sat heavily in her stomach. He didn't slow as the off ramp approached and darted through the residential streets toward her apartment building.

"I'm not sure how I'm going to get you out of next week." Her mind was already working on strategies.

But Danny had agreed when Rita suggested he return the following Sunday, making Melanie's job that much more difficult.

"Why would you have to?"

"You were serious about enjoying dinner?" Melanie looked at Danny with curiosity.

Danny had been incredible. He'd charmed Rita by complimenting her food and he'd been a hit with Roger.

"I had a good time with your family."

The Jeep parked with a jolt as Mr. Toad's Wild Ride came to an end outside of Melanie's apartment.

"But you didn't *like* the food, right?"

"Does it matter?" he asked, chuckling.

"Only if you want me to consider you sane."

"No, I didn't like the food, but it's a small price to spend another evening with you." He stroked the side of her jaw and followed down her neck. "Do you mind if I don't come up?"

"Tired?"

"Yeah, Coach kicked my ass."

"I don't mind," Melanie said, inching closer to him.

Caressing his face she began kissing him softly, slowly.

"Maybe I can come in for a few minutes."

Melanie smiled.

"No, you'd better go. I didn't mean to tease."

"Yes, you did. Come on, I'll walk you to your door."

The students had arrived. Loud, obnoxious and partially dressed teens swarmed the halls. She wouldn't miss any of them.

"I'll see you in class tomorrow," Melanie said at her door.

Danny grinned. "Goodnight, Sweetheart."

"'Night."

Melanie fell asleep easily with those words ringing in her ears, "Goodnight, Sweetheart." They were still there when she awoke in the morning. It was the first day of her last semester, and Melanie was floating on air.

Danny was in her second class of the day. She took a typical Melanie seat, second row center. The smallish classroom with dingy white walls, green chalkboard along the front, a desk for the teacher and an assembly of aluminum chairs fitted with lap tables set in crooked rows was completely standard.

Attempting to chat with the other finance majors, she waited … aware of her pounding heart, as she watched for Danny.

"Hello, class. I expect everyone had a restful break," Professor McMillion, said dropping her canvas saddlebag on her desk.

Professor Loretta McMillion was one of Melanie's favorites. She wore her brown hair in a short bob and always, always dressed in long, flowing gauze broomstick skirts. In the spring she would trade her clogs for leather sandals with toe cuffs and straps that wound up her legs.

Melanie felt her heart lurch as the door opened and Danny walked in, handsome and confident. His backpack casually slung over his shoulder, she noticed his eyes scanning the room. Today, he was actively looking for her.

"Dan, hey man."

"Hey, Kevin good to see you."

"Well, it's nice of you to join us Mr. Ashe. Maybe, you wouldn't mind taking a seat so we can get started."

"Sorry, Professor," Danny said, adjusting his backpack.

"I saved you a seat over here, Dan."

"Thanks, Patty, but I see my girl over there," Danny said, smiling at Melanie.

"Sorry I'm late," he whispered with a quick kiss. "You look beautiful."

Melanie ignored the murmurs.

"Okay, now that Mr. Ashe is settled, let's begin," she said coolly.

But the wrinkles between her eyebrows gave a hint of disapproval.

CHAPTER 6

One Sunday evening, as they left her parents' house, Danny draped his arm across her shoulders. "That was the worse meal yet. She said it was catfish, right?" Danny never complained about Rita's cooking. He'd politely, even kindly eaten the unpalatable.

It'd taken much longer than Melanie thought possible, he had an iron stomach – but finally it was the catfish.

"I don't want to say anything about your mom, Mel, but..." He shook his head. "When we're making enough money we're hiring a cook so we never have to eat like that again." Danny pulled her to him roughly and kissed the side of her face as he opened the Jeep door for her.

His right eye was ringed in deep purple and the corner of his bottom lip was mending from a split.

"I love you, Melanie." He said, casually as if he expressed it everyday.

"Danny," she exhaled and the tears that quickly rimmed her eyes overflowed. "I love you, too."

⟡

Waiting with Carla outside of Ted's office building, Melanie was surprised when Danny and Coach emerged from the double glass doors.

"Hey, what are you doing here?"

"Petitioning for new uniforms."

"Ashe, wipe that stupid grin off your face," Coach griped as he walked off. "Practice is at 3, don't be late."

"You got it, Coach," Danny laughed.

"Where are you off to?" Melanie asked.

"I was gonna get a bite. You guys wanna come?"

"I do," Melanie stood. Glancing at Carla, "Ted could be another hour."

"I'll take my chances."

Butterflies flitted around the vibrant flowers lining the cement walkway, parading, chasing each other around the bright marigolds. Love was in the air.

"No one's at the apartment right now," Melanie suggested. "Unless you're too hungry."

"Was I hungry?"

Melanie shrugged.

"I'll race you."

Melanie laughed, and offered her conditions. "You give me a 10-second head start and carry my backpack."

She tossed her bag into his arms and sprinted away. She loved the ease of their relationship. Danny made everything better.

∝∾

"Mel!"

"Danny?" He sounded strange.

"Mel, they called. They're making an offer. Holy Shit, they're making an offer!" His laugh cracked.

"Which team?" Her heart raced.

"The Knights. I'm going to New York."

"Oh my God, Danny. That's perfect," her post-college destination, Wall Street.

"I know. Let's celebrate. Marry me, we could make it to Vegas in by ten." He was speaking loud and fast, full of adrenaline.

Melanie froze, confused. "I was thinking dinner."

"Yeah, that's probably best," he said. Melanie wondered if he had seriously just proposed – and if he had, had she just turned him down? "You were my first call. I'll pick you up tonight ... pack for overnight."

Melanie stood speechless, clinging to a dead receiver. He was gone.

All she had was a gym bag and her hands shook with each oddity she dropped inside.

"Car?" she asked, scared. "Are you really going to marry Ted?" Melanie looked into Carla's wide expression.

"Of course! I mean I know I've been complaining about Helen and Ruth. They're trying to be helpful – it's just so much easier for them to make the wedding arrangements, they're in Boston. And so what if they want to choose the dress? It's really very sweet. Don't you think?" As their eyes locked, her face twisted. "You don't think Ted thinks I'm changing my mind ... did he say something to you?"

"NO!" Melanie practically shouted. "No, Car, I was just wondering out loud – I'm sorry." *Crap!*

It was too late. Carla was in a panic.

"I've got to call Ted." Her fingers were already dancing over the familiar digits.

"Mel, Dan is here," Jenny yelled from the living room.

Melanie eyed Carla, "You okay?"

"Go," Carla commanded.

Melanie jogged, jumping into Danny's arms.

"Can you believe it?" He squeezed her tight enough to bow her ribs.

"Of course I can, I've always believed in you."

He stopped, beamed a heartbreaking smile and pulled her out the door.

"Where are we going?" She laughed, being shoved into the passenger seat.

"You'll find out." He planted a kiss on the side of her face.

Today, he spoke as fast as he drove.

"Wait, Danny, I think you went to wrong way." He was turning off at her parents exit.

"I didn't." He reached over to take her hand. "I've been seeing this place every Sunday for months." He bumped the tires on the curb as he parked in front of the picturesque hotel overlooking the ocean. "Two night stay in the honeymoon suite."

"No ceremony?" she asked, feeling secure enough to joke about the proposal.

Danny laughed. "So I got a little carried away. But, Mel, I swear right then it was like I could have it all – everything was at my fingers."

"And you don't feel that anymore?"

"I do but ... I've regained my reality. We don't have to get married now. Later is fine, right?"

"You are seriously asking me to marry you?"

Danny took a long moment, staring, and Melanie could see his brain working behind his clear eyes. "Yeah, I think I am. Do you think you would marry me after graduation, after I get settled in New York?"

"I know I would."

Melanie and Danny ditched their Tuesday classes. On Wednesday,

Danny was still skipping – he called it celebrating.

"Hi, professor," Melanie said, hooking her backpack to the back of the chair.

"Oh, Melanie, tell me how your interviews went!"

Melanie gawked at Ms. McMillan as the professor's expression gradually drooped. "What are you talking about?" she asked, feeling a cold dread seep into her spine.

"The job fair. Didn't you meet with any headhunters? Weren't they here this week?"

"This is the first I've heard."

"That's strange, your grades automatically put you in the running. Maybe I'm off on my dates." Her puzzled look disagreed.

"Do you mind if I skip another class? I'd like to check the job center out for myself."

"I think that's a very good idea," she said, concerned.

Melanie cut through campus, her heart racing and sweat building up at her hairline. Breathlessly, she ran right up to the information kiosk.

"Hi," she said, catching her breath and wiping her forehead. Noticing for the first time the other students dressed in suits and heels sitting in the plastic chairs that lined the walls. "Um, I was wondering about the job fair." She sputtered, the words didn't want to come out.

"All the interviews have already been scheduled."

"But ... why wasn't I notified?"

"The top five percent were mailed invitations last week."

"But ... I'm in that group," she said, the back of her eyes burning. "Could you please check?"

The girl behind the counter clicked at her keyboard, bored. "Hmm. Melanie Ward, right?"

Melanie nodded.

"Well," she scratched her ear, "I don't know what to say. Somehow you were left off the list of invitees." She looked apologetic.

"It's okay, but where do I sign up for the interviews?"

"You don't understand. All the recruiting officers are booked," she pointed at the other graduates waiting.

"No," she panted. "There must be something."

"Well," the girl winced, "there will be another job fair in a couple of weeks."

"Weeks?" She calculated the end of the semester.

Melanie walked out of the office feeling dazed and confused.

She tried to mask her growing depression, but her mood darkened each passing day. Everyone around her was keyed up for graduation. Carla had made peace with her future mother- and sister-in-law, Jenny was organizing her trip with Ryan and Trish had landed a paid internship with the university phys ed department as an assistant physical therapist. Melanie was envious.

Sick of her constant presence, her career counselor rolled his eyes each day she knocked on his door.

"Nothing new," he groaned. "I got a memo this morning ... the last of the interviews are being scheduled."

"Really?"

"Melanie, the big companies have filled their positions."

How could this be happening?

"Fine. Sign me up for anything you've got."

Tears streaked down her face as she took the long way home.

A week before graduation, Melanie spent the day at three interviews: Bank of America, Enterprise Car Rental and H&R Block.

The possibility of taking any of these jobs scared her. Envisioning herself stuck behind the same desk for 10 years, growing old and miserable.

I want Wall Street, not San Diego, not anywhere but the heart of the NYSE. Maybe, she toyed with the nagging thought again, *I should get my master's degree and postpone life a little longer.*

"No," she grumbled aloud. "I've got to grow up, get a job and become unhappy. It's the American way."

"When did you get so pessimistic?" Trish walked in and plopped down, her long legs dangling off the arm of the overstuffed chair. Melanie was sprawled across the couch.

"After three interviews from hell."

"That bad?"

"Actually, no, the interviews went fine." Melanie sat up. "Except it was for a bank, a car rental place and an accounting thing." She was mentally drained.

Trish made a face. "Well, the bright side is there was no insurance company."

Melanie looked up. "That's Monday."

"Are you serious?"

She nodded sadly.

Trish's hysteria was infuriating at first, and then contagious.

"You need a drink, and I don't mean lemonade. We need to get Dan over here." Trish stood up. "Go get dressed."

"I could use a drink."

"You could use two, moping about for weeks. Well, I'm sick of it. You haven't gotten your dream job? Get over it."

Melanie was about to comment when she noticed an envelope. White, plain with no return address, only her name typed neatly in bold, black letters.

"When did this come?"

"Today. It's odd," Jenny said, peering over Melanie's shoulder at the letter, "No return address, maybe it's that disappearing boyfriend of yours." Jenny gave Melanie the gotcha signal.

She hadn't thought of Malik in months, since their last date. Melanie chose to believe he'd been deported.

Alone, she tore open the envelope.

```
Ms. Ward,
We are pleased to inform you that you have
been selected for an interview.
10 a.m. this Monday.
Downtown Marriott.
Confidentiality is mandatory.
We look forward to seeing you again.
```

An interview with the CDD. This could be something.

Melanie's thoughts were interrupted by a knock on the door. Quickly she quartered the letter and stuffed it in the back pocket of her jeans.

"Hi." It was Danny, standing ... no slouching outside her door. "Mel, can we talk?"

Danny led her out into the hall, closing the door behind them. Somewhere down the hall a stereo blared. Brian Stetzer jamming on his guitar in another apartment seemed dreamlike as Melanie looked into Danny's somber eyes.

"What's up?"

"Mel, I leave for New York on Monday morning." His eyes would only briefly make contact with hers. "I only have one final and I've already made arrangements. I want to be first to meet the team and get situated."

"What about graduation?" Melanie asked, struggling not to sound hurt.

He shrugged.

"Danny?"

"It's just that I've been preparing my whole life for this moment," he jumped right to the point, hands shoved into his pockets and shifting his weight from one foot to the other.

Melanie waited, too scared to move or breathe, but instinctively knowing what was to come. He was breaking up with her.

"Things are coming together better than I've ever dreamed. I've made it to exactly where I want to be and I can't screw it up."

"When did you decide all this?" She thought back to any clues she might have missed. The truth was she hadn't been paying attention.

"It's been coming for a long time."

"A long time?" she echoed his words softly, seeing if they made more sense in her own voice.

"Mel, I'm sorry. I know you had plans."

"No, Danny, *we* had plans." How much time passed? "You've known since the beginning that we weren't going to make it?" It sounded incredulous.

Danny ran his fingers through his hair. "No. I mean, yes and no. In the beginning it was the plan, but as I fell in love with you I wasn't sure what to do. You have to know this is hard for me, too. I know you've been going through stuff and I haven't been there for you. I'm close, Mel, I can taste it. This is the chance of a lifetime and it's within arm's reach and … I have to choose the game. I'm sorry."

His voice was monotone, so unlike Danny's, it sounded – and felt

– final.

He reached for her hands but Melanie thrust them into her pockets. Her first impulse was to plead, beg, cry and force him to change his mind. But the elevator opened and she held her tongue long enough for the chirpy girls to reach their apartment. Long enough to search his face.

She couldn't bear to add to his burden. Melanie reminded herself that she wanted the best for him even if that wasn't her.

As much as his words devastated her it was her decision that caused the searing pain. A wave of nausea rose to her throat and clouded her head, and she placed one hand over her mouth and steadied herself with her other hand against the wall.

"Are you all right? Say something, react, hit me, anything," Danny pleaded.

"I can't," she whispered, her eyes watery. "You're going to be great," she managed to choke out before her lips and chin started quivering so hard she couldn't continue and the tears started to flow.

Her mind was screaming, she couldn't breathe.

"Melanie?"

She stepped up close and held his face, his skin warm beneath her cold shaky hands. Tears streamed down her face as she kissed his stubbly cheek. She didn't close her eyes. She wanted to remember every moment she'd spent with Danny. She wanted to remember the feel of his skin.

"I love you, Danny."

"Melanie," he called as she turned away, brokenhearted, and entered her apartment.

She slumped against the door, her legs unable to support her, and crumpled to the floor.

"Mel, what's wrong?"

"Danny broke up with me." She couldn't believe the words even as she said them. "I think I'm going to be sick."

✍

Melanie spent the weekend in bed, the covers pulled up over her head, quietly weeping.

"OK, Missy, enough is enough. You have an interview today and you're not missing it." Carla pulled the blankets, sheets and all off the bed.

"What are you doing?" Melanie asked, walking into their bedroom from the bathroom.

"Mel! I about had a heart attack when you weren't..." She pointed to the empty bed.

Melanie almost grinned.

"I'm glad to see you up. When's your interview?" Carla asked, changing her tone and throwing the covers back onto the bed.

"In an hour." She coughed trying to dislodge the lump that had taken up residence in her throat.

Carla gave a disapproving look as Melanie laced her tennis shoes and pulled the hem of her T-shirt out from the waist of a pair of faded jeans.

"Do I look horrible?" Melanie asked, thinking her eyes may still be swollen from the weekend of crying.

"You look great."

The world seemed heavier and the air thicker than before, Melanie noticed as she drove Carla's wreck to the Marriott. Maybe it was the weight of her sadness, or maybe the earth's gravitational pull had increased during the past 72 hours. Either way, Melanie was not looking forward to an interview. In between sobbing fits of losing ... she couldn't bare to think his name ... she had wondered about the means the CDD would take to ensure she accepted their position. Could they have been the reason she hadn't received any employment offers? It all seemed very egotistical but it explained the "glitch in the system." Throughout the weekend she had convinced herself, but she was out of tears, out of sorts and out of options. And the small, hateful, voice kept repeating "bank, insurance, bank, insurance" was getting louder the closer she got to the hotel.

At the Marriott she knew there would be no sign for her to follow, no welcoming committee. She went directly to the front desk.

"Anything for Melanie Ward?" She asked the lanky teenager behind the counter.

"What's the name?"

"Melanie Ward. W-A-R-D."

The pimple-faced kid handed her an envelope. Inside was a note that simply read, "711." As the elevator rose to the seventh floor Melanie examined her reflection. Her sullen, puffy face had dark circles under dark, flat eyes.

"Carla lied."

She let her hair down, hoping to cover at least some of her grim face.

Facing three black numbers on a white door Melanie knocked twice, took a deep breath and walked in. The surprise was the 10 people who abruptly stopped talking to size up the new applicant.

"Ah, Ms. Ward, right on time, very good." It was one of the men she had met in December.

What was his name? She searched her memory.

"Hello, Agent Jackson," Melanie greeted him.

His smile grew wide when she acknowledged him by name. "I am very pleased you made it this morning." Melanie shook Agent Jackson's outstretched hand. "We'll be meeting in an adjoining suite."

The conversations that had hushed when she entered resumed as Agent Jackson led her through double doors.

"These are all agents?" Melanie asked, checking out their casual dress, khakis or jeans. She fit in perfectly.

"Mostly," Agent Jackson looked at her and added, "You seem to have the knack of a chameleon. Exactly what we're looking for," he chuckled.

Melanie grunted. That hadn't been the statement she'd hoped to make.

In the other suite two men and a woman sat at a table littered with cans of Diet Coke and a box of doughnuts.

"Nice to see you again, Ms. Ward."

Melanie knew his voice. "Nice to see you too, Agent Collins." She shook hands and smiled away the sharp pain that stabbed her fragile heart. Agent Collins was the one responsible for bringing Danny to her door that cold January evening.

She took a seat at the table across from Jackson and next to the woman.

"Let us start with congratulations on your upcoming graduation," Agent Collins said.

"Thank you."

"Top of your class – that's impressive."

Melanie shrugged. She was no longer sure what it meant.

"You did exceptionally well at our winter trials. Best I've seen in years."

"I don't understand. Winter trials?" Melanie looked from Collins to Jackson.

"Let me explain," Agent Collins began. "We're a clandestine branch of the National Security Agency and each year we recruit a few, select individuals we find worthy and capable."

Melanie was trying to wrap her brain around what Agent Collins was saying.

"So, Malik…?" She asked, unsure.

"Yes, Malik," Collins laughed, scrutinizing her before looking to Jackson, who nodded, slightly.

Collins opened a door and called out into the other room, "Thomas?"

Melanie leaned forward to get a better view of the door.

"Melanie, I would like you to meet Agent Thomas Mitchell."

A young man in his twenties, dark hair and glasses strode through the door, smiling. Her puffy eyes widened. It was Malik.

What the…?

In flawless English, devoid of accent, Malik – Thomas Mitchell - said with a grin, "Hi, Melanie. How've you been?"

She was stunned. "You?"

"Oh, so the lady like this better?" As easily as that, Malik Razul stood wearing jeans and a white polo shirt. "You miss your Malik, baby?"

Melanie let out the breath she had been unconsciously holding. "You do that very well." She stared at Thomas. "You had me fooled. Was everything a setup?" She looked at Collins with wide eyes.

"Not exactly a setup. An assignment, a test."

Her gaze returned to Thomas. She'd kissed him. Weird. "So, how many times were you Malik this winter?"

"Seven."

"Wow," she said, shaking her head.

"Baby, you know Malik only had eyes for you."

"Thanks, Thomas," Collins sighed, opening the door in an obvious gesture.

"Really, Melanie, it hardly seemed like work." He chuckled out the door and Melanie wondered if she'd been insulted. It could go either way.

"He meant that in a good way," Collins said. "He had only good things to say about you."

"I've been doing this for 33 years, got recruited just like you," Agent Jackson piped in, smiling at her. "Most of the people in this room were recruited out of college. Ms. Ward, today the world is a different place than it was 20 years ago or even two years ago. Our job here is even more important and even more dangerous. For this reason we want only the best of the best and that, Ms. Ward, is why we conduct Winter Trials. To seek out top people."

Birds chirping outside distracted her momentarily as Agent Jackson continued.

"Each year we select about 100 candidates to test. We set up one scenario and watch the outcome. Oh, we vary the situations to accommodate men and women but basically everyone is on a level playing field."

"How do you select your candidates? Why me?"

"Our profile, yes. Well, we look at the overall person, skills, background, GPA and lifestyle. The folks at other federal agencies snatch up the techies or the multi-linguists, but we're interested in problem solvers, clever people who can fit into any situation and find their way out of a crisis. We research each of our 100 participants extensively, then we conduct our trial. We expect about half to decline our request and another 40 to break confidentiality. Of the remaining 10, we expect only a third to complete the task with any competence."

Melanie was surprised. "Only three of us got the job done?"

"You've reason to be very proud. We're excited at the prospect of having you on our team. You've shown great qualities."

Collins piped in, excitedly, "We're inviting you to join our elite group, Ms. Ward."

Staring directly into Agent Jackson's barely blue eyes she lied, "I'm flattered, but I do have other offers to consider."

"Melanie the decision is yours, obviously, but do you really believe you could be happy working for a car rental agency, checking gas tanks and selling the extra insurance?" Collins said, with a enlightened smirk.

He knows, she gasped, *I was right! They are responsible!* It was then that she began to realize the scope of their power. *I should be angry – why aren't I angry?*

Collins' stare was unyielding. Was there anything to lose at this point?

"When do I start?"

She was scheduled to report July 1st to Washington D.C. receiving a cover story, an address and some cash to get her across the country.

"What do I tell people?" she asked, wondering if she'd be able to lie effectively.

"The trick..." Collins told her, "is to be just on the edge of confusing. Keep it simple and no one will admit that they just don't know what the hell you do."

She nodded, numbly.

"Welcome aboard, Ms. Ward. I'm glad you accepted."

"Was there ever a doubt?"

Collins laughed and shook her hand.

Spy Melanie, she thought, a nervous excitement filling up the empty spaces in her body.

From the hotel Melanie raced to Danny's apartment. She even rang the bell before she remembered that he wasn't there anymore.

Danny's roommate answered the door. "Melanie? Hi, but you missed Dan."

"I'm sorry," she turned, "force of habit." Melanie looked regretfully at the Jeep, parked in the driveway as usual.

"He sold it to me," Tony said. "Five hundred bucks. You think I was ripped off?"

Her stomach rose inside her and her eyes welled with tears as she backed away.

She cried in the car outside of her apartment, finally wiping her nose and putting on a happy, swollen, red face.

"I got a job," she said, sitting on the couch, her legs curled up beneath her.

They congratulated her and opened four bottles of beer to celebrate. Melanie wasn't much in the mood but felt obligated. She didn't mention her brief stop at Danny's apartment.

"Dan called," Trish said, cautiously.

"When?"

"I don't know, he left a message." Jenny pushed the play button.

"Hi, Mel. I was hoping to catch you before your interview. I'm at the airport. Um, I think I made a mistake. I miss you and, well, you're my best friend. Shit, there's my flight. I'll call you from New York tonight. I love you, Melanie. Bye."

"Can you save that for me?"

"Sure."

"I'm going for a run."

The next day Melanie phoned her parents explaining her new career. "I'm not really sure, yet. But the company develops communication networks for huge conglomerates overseas." She had been practicing and was impressed with how simple that first lie had been.

Spy Melanie can do anything.

Agent Collins had been right. Everyone thought they understood but weren't totally sure. After two days they stopped asking Melanie to explain.

CHAPTER 7
10 years later

The drizzle outside her office had been non-stop for two weeks. The gloom had penetrated the brick walls of the agency's historic building and had seeped under her skin. Melanie's heart was heavy as she turned from the gray sky and wet pavement to the barren walls of her office. The last thing she saw before closing her eyes and leaning back against her chair was a file placed benignly on the corner of her desk. Disturbing images of Diane March's broken body played through her mind.

March was a fresh, naïve 22-year-old college student who had gotten involved with the wrong people at the wrong time. Melanie had been in Ben's office yesterday when March had called looking for Agent Finn Parker.

"Excuse me, Mr. Jackson, but I'm routing a call." Judith's voice was crisp over the intercom.

Ben pushed the flashing red button. "Can I help you?"

"Hi, I'm looking for Agent Parker." The voice was sweet and unsure.

Ben shot Melanie an intense glance. His pale blue eyes had streaks of red and his lower lids sagged.

"Who may I ask is calling?"

"My name is Diane March. I'm ... I'm helping Finn on an assignment." Her voice was giddy and nervous with a hint of possibility that came from youth. "He was supposed to call me tomorrow and I know I wasn't supposed to call this number but I wanted him to know that Leslie was way easier than he'd expected. I finished ahead of schedule and the disc is ready."

Finn Parker's image flashed, unwillingly, in her mind. His handsome face hid the demons that lay beneath the surface. And she knew Diane March was a victim to those good looks.

Parker had been recruited into the Agency two years before Melanie, and she was assigned to his sector for the first six months. They'd started as friends, comrades. She snorted at the memory, it seemed like another lifetime ago.

Finn's father Hugh Parker, a U.S. Senator on the Agency's governing board, was a true politician – tough as hell and a hand in every pot. Parker Sr. expected great things for his boy and bestowed unwarranted merits at every opportunity. Finn's failures were brushed aside, leaving nothing but his highly polished shell.

Melanie despised Finn. She hated that he was rewarded for his incompetence while she fought for every promotion. They had risen up the ladder at the same rate but she'd sacrificed everything and he'd given up nothing. While she studied, he golfed. While she worked long hours and dined alone, he vacationed with the members of the Board. Early on she brought his blunders to the forefront, it added infinitessimal dilemma to his career and painted a target on her back. However, privately she knew, it caused friction between him and his father. It was not enough but it had to be.

"Agent Parker is on another assignment, very top secret, so I'll have another agent pick up the disc."

The disappointment in Diane's voice was obvious.

"Well, Finn promised no one would see the video, and I was kind of hoping to see him again."

"I promise that only a select few will see the tape," Ben said in his most grandfatherly voice.

The trace showed she was in Atlanta. "I'm sending Agent Patal.

He'll be at The Lexington Hotel in 10 minutes so stay put, Ms. March."

"Okay but how'd you know…?"

Ben cut her off and called Mike.

"Mike, I just received a call and…"

"I've got it here."

"Great, block her number. I don't want Agent Parker getting to her."

Mike uttered a quick, "Yeah, give me a sec."

Melanie could read Ben's angry look. "I'm already gone," she said.

Two hours later, Melanie touched down at Hartsfield airport in Atlanta. Diane was already dead.

Patal was waiting at the terminal with the news. He'd met her at the hotel and the trade had gone smoothly but an hour later she "fell" from the third-story window of a known crack hotel, five blocks from The Lexington. The high humidity was unbearable as Melanie and Patal climbed into the back of a waiting SUV.

"Who's this Leslie she referred to and what do we know about him?"

"Leslie White is the founder of the National Coalition of Morals and Ethics in America. He was in the footage attained from Ms. March." Patal looked over the top of his glasses. "Some pretty kinky stuff."

Eyebrows raised, Melanie watched as Diane and White broke at least two Georgia state laws.

She studied the information before being dropped off at the lobby of the National Coalition of Morals and Ethics in America's new 87-story tower for some face time with Mr. White.

Stepping out of the revolving doors and into the sweet, sweet air-conditioned lobby Melanie stood for 10 cool seconds.

"Mr. White's limo has arrived," the security guard said into his two-way radio before turning his beady eyes on her.

"I was just trying to get out of the ... storm," Melanie said as the thunder cracked mightily outside.

"I'm sorry but you'll have to wait outside if you don't have business here."

Begrudgingly, she pushed her way out as the sky opened up and dropped sheets of rain. While all eyes were looking up in disbelief Melanie slipped into the back of the limo.

The monogrammed towel from the limo bar was perfect to soak up her dripping hair. Melanie didn't feel guilty about drenching the soft calfskin leather, nor did she regret placing the disc into the DVD player and pausing the picture with Leslie in a very unflattering position. Rain pounded the roof of the limo as Melanie waited for Mr. White to emerge from the multi-million-dollar skyscraper.

Leslie White staggered into his limo, dry but for the cuffs of his trousers and his $1,000 shoes, without noticing Melanie or the muted TV. He grabbed at the whiskey and took a swig straight from the Baccarat crystal decanter.

"What the hell?" he said, spraying whiskey across the interior and onto Melanie.

She wiped her cheek with a fresh towel as the moans from the TV violently blended with the beating of the rain.

Then, with a hollow shriek and a jerk back, White scurried to stop the movie, scrambling across the limo's carpeted floor. On his knees, he began to weep before breaking into Bible verse.

"Save it," she said, pausing the DVD with Diane's image frozen on the screen.

White stiffened, petrified.

"Who are you? What do you want?" He asked, giving up his holy stance and sliding back onto his seat.

Melanie tossed him the black-and-white police photos of Diane's corpse.

"I want to know why."

"I didn't do it. I just saw it on the news," he said, closing his eyes and shaking his head. "I swear I didn't kill her. She was very much alive when I left her this morning."

The limo phone rang and Melanie hit the speaker button and pointed for him to speak.

"Hello?" White cleared his throat.

"Leslie, how are you doing, my friend?"

Melanie's heart skipped, she recognized the voice – Hugh Parker, Finn's father. She pulled her cell phone from her pocket and hit record.

"Hugh? Now isn't a good time. Why don't you call back tomorrow and we'll talk?" White said impatiently.

"I don't think you understand," Hugh Parker said coldly. "We need to talk about your decision not to back Joe Perry."

"We've already discussed the Coalition's position on this election," White said, annoyed and clearly tired of this conversation.

"Listen, you dumb shit, you are going to do as I say." Hugh Parker's voice was ice.

Melanie was shocked, sickened – and elated.

"Have you gone crazy? Who do you think you're speaking with?"

"Have you seen the news?" the Senator asked angrily, losing his patience.

White's expression turned ghost-like.

"You? You did this? Because of an election?"

"I own you, White. Next week you are going to proudly announce that the National Coalition for *Morality* and *Ethics* in America supports Joe Perry for Senate." The disdain in his voice was emphasized by the sarcasm placed on the words "morality" and "ethics."

White, stupefied, said nothing, but gurgles escaped his clenched throat. Melanie's heart was hammering as loudly as the storm outside.

"I hope you wore a condom," Parker's vile laugh echoed. "You really ought to be thanking me."

"Thanking you?"

"She was only your lover. I could have targeted your wife or son."

"Thank you," White's low voice cracked as it shook.

"That's better. We'll play golf soon."

"Golf?" White asked meekly.

Melanie was grateful when Parker's hearty laugh was abruptly silenced. White had cut him off with the touch of a finger.

Melanie was shocked at Hugh Parker's brazen demeanor.

"I knew he was powerful. I started the NCMEA in an old building next to a strip mall. It was Hugh that got the momentum going. He's the reason we are where we are today." White was drained of color and sat slumped in the corner of his limo.

As she stepped back into the torrential rain, Melanie took one last look at White crying like a baby.

"That's what you get when you deal with the devil."

One taxi and a plane ride later, she was being rained on back home in D.C.

"Agent Ward, Agent Jackson is available to see you now," Jane called softly from the doorway.

Melanie was startled awake.

"Thanks, Jane."

Melanie's assistant, a young girl with fair, freckly skin and short red hair, had been with the agency for just six months and still seemed unsure of her place. Her unease, Melanie believed, stemmed from Melanie's reputation for ruthlessness.

"Do you need anything else, Ma'am?"

"No, that'll be all."

Melanie smiled. She somewhat enjoyed her bitch status, preferring to think of herself as ambitious.

File in hand, she headed for Agent Ben Jackson's office.

"Melanie, come in and have a seat." Ben was pouring himself a drink and offered one to her. She refused as always, and as always Ben handed her a scotch.

"Thanks," she said, setting the drink on a coaster.

"You know, Melanie, you're a fine agent. To tell you the truth, you're one of my best."

"Just *one* of the best?"

"Is that the file?" Agent Jackson's face creased into a frown.

She placed it on the desk in front of him.

"Yeah, it's all in there, including the DVD of White and Diane and audio of Hugh Parker's threats and confession."

Ben shook his head and blew out a heavy sigh. "You do realize that this will never leave this office."

"We can't just let him get away with murder!" If she was surprised, she shouldn't have been. Melanie could no longer easily distinguish her own emotions, stifled for as long as they had been. It would take effort to decipher what she was feeling and she just didn't have the time or the inclination.

"Hugh is at the peak of his power, and he's part of our governing board. Realistically, we don't have a choice. Right now we wait, hold our cards and hope he somehow slips up."

Melanie's hatred for both of the Parker boys deepened. She had learned long ago how things worked in this town. The powerful could literally get away with murder but usually they hid behind heart attacks and suicides.

She would keep quiet for now, for Ben. He held a spot in Melanie's heart with his fatherly air, which she appreciated being so far from her family. Though admiration for him was not the general consensus in the Agency.

"Are you feeling okay, Ben?" Melanie asked, noticing the new crevasses carved into his face. "You seem tired."

He smiled but shook his head. "I'm fine."

He handed over a dossier stamped CONFIDENTIAL. Melanie had never understood how this might deter someone from looking. *If anything,* she thought, *it made the contents more appealing.*

"Take it, and we'll meet in the morning."

"What are you going to do with the March file?"

"Mull it over." He sighed.

"Just so you know, Ben, I've made copies."

Melanie took the elevator to the Agency's state-of-the-art basement gym, complete with lap pool, sauna and steam room. She needed to work out her aggressions and push back the thoughts of Diane's family getting the news of her death. For them there would always be unanswered questions. Dying with whores and junkies – could there be any more disrespectful death for a young woman? Melanie's heart ached.

She thought of her own mom and dad, whom she hadn't seen in over a year. She'd systematically deleted everyone important from her life. She'd sent an occasional card or e-mail, and gifts on all the required holidays, but her devotion to work had taken its toll. Melanie missed the horrible family dinners. She was friendless in D.C. and it had been years since she had been in an intimate relationship.

Her thoughts drifted from Bobby, the only man she'd been with since Danny, to Danny.

You've got to stop thinking. Her thoughts had come out of nowhere and startled her by the longing that still found its way inside.

The gym was mostly empty. She increased the volume on her iPod and began her 50-minute simulated mountain climb. Imagining she was climbing in the Pyrenees, Melanie practiced her French. Fluent in six languages, she imagined the various landscapes as she mentally flowed from one continent to another. Melanie liked keeping busy. Too much free time wasn't productive, and it gave her opportunity to think beyond the agency's brick walls.

This five-story renovated apartment building, divisional head-quarters, was bought in the 1930s and completely modernized it in the late '90s. At that time the top two floors were devoted to conference rooms, offices and the kitchen. The basement was transformed into the gym and the first, second and third floors became small offices and apartments for the agents while they were between assignments. Originally, the Board of Executives had wanted all the agents to live in the building. Each apartment could accommodate up to three agents, but right now it was single occupancy at "Spy Manor."

After a shower and change into a pair of well-worn sweats,

Melanie was back in her office, opening the file marked confidential. She worked into the early morning. The damp streets were dark, the lamps barely able to glimmer through the fog. Melanie rode her bike the two miles to her apartment, which she rented from the agency, for a three-hour nap.

Ben was gathering papers when she knocked on his office door early the next morning.

"Come in."

His mood was lighter than it had been the night before. He was grinning and there were only three creases in his forehead, not five.

"I was hoping," she said in a sweet voice while walking slowly to his desk, "you'd come up with one of your brilliant plans to nail Parker senior to the wall and crush little Finn just for the fun of it."

Ben chuckled. "That is the worst attempt at persuasion I've seen in years." He laughed harder as he herded them out of his office. "Thanks. You have no idea how much I needed a good laugh."

Melanie was disheartened, but she knew Ben well enough to know the discussion was over. The conference room was buzzing when they arrived.

"Hey, Mike, grab me one of those glazed and a…"

"I know, a large black coffee. I know, I know."

"Thanks."

"OK, everyone." Agent Jackson started the meeting. "We have a new development in the Yakimoto case. There was movement yesterday so we're now actively involved. Agent Ward, you will head this up and Agent Scott will be your second. I've got our jet ready to take you to Seattle, where you'll take on your new identities. You're booked on American, leaving tonight for Honolulu."

The preliminary agents quickly appraised Melanie and Jack Scott of the situation. Melanie had worked with Jack before. He was a good agent, capable and reliable.

She and Jack were to pose as married tourists to get close to a Japanese businessman who was passing government information. A mole had been discovered in another branch of national security. The agent, before he disappeared, had destroyed every trace of data except for the name Bernard Yakimoto. Now Melanie and Jack were stepping in to answer the rest of the questions: What information had been leaked and where was it going?

Melanie made her routine call to her parents and sent an e-mail to Carla, letting them know she'd be unavailable for some time. They knew the drill and asked no questions. Melanie made it a quick conversation and within hours Melanie and Jack had become Lisa and Todd Abernathy, riding in a cab through the streets of Honolulu, Hawaii.

They were staying at the Prince Towers, a huge condo complex overlooking the marina and a sliver of sand and surf.

"I love Hawaii," Melanie said from the balcony.

"You know, that's where SS Minnow from *Gilligan's Island* set sail from," Jack said, coming to join her.

"There's speculation it set sail from Newport Beach," Melanie said, drawing a deep breath of the heavy air, scented with a balance of florals and salt.

"Rumors."

She looked over at Jack. "Anyway, how'd we check out?"

"We're clean." It wasn't safe to talk on the balcony. Melanie took in another deep breath, looked toward the green hillside and closed the door.

"Have you seen the revised kit?" he asked, excitedly opening one of his bags.

"Amazing."

This was not just a bag it was technological wonderland, loaded with the latest internal gadgets. They'd been educated on each of the new optical devices and Jack had used the bug detector to verify there were no listening devices, cameras or alarms set up anywhere in the apartment. Satellite scramblers protected them from unwelcome listeners. Cameras were so small that could be placed, without detection, on a shirt or dress while the suspect was wearing it. GPS trackers were in every shape and size. Special underwater equipment was specifically added for this mission. Melanie couldn't help but be impressed. Her favorite was the vast array of drugs that caused symptoms from nausea to death.

Melanie picked an apple from the fruit basket. "Did you check the fruit?" she asked, taking a bite.

"Actually, I did."

After installing the alarm in their room she stood on the moonlit balcony, watching waves crash on the shore as Jack secured the equipment.

Very romantic, she thought, fighting off the current of emotion.

It had been years since she thought of Danny and now here she was thinking of him twice in as many days. The churning in the pit of her stomach had started a month back when her little brother Bruce called to say that he and his wife, Cheryl, were expecting their first child in October. It was during the weeks that followed when Melanie spoke with her zealous mother that an unfamiliar feeling grew inside of her. Fear, jealousy, maybe both. And now she couldn't shake the agitation she felt over Diane's death. Someday her own parents could receive a similar call and Melanie wondered how her own life would be represented. Would she be portrayed as a crack whore? They could never know the truth, she accepted that, but she wanted them to be proud of her, and it was completely out of her control.

Pangs of loneliness seeped under her skin and she ached for a touch of a hand, an embrace, something. All this she would never admit to another soul. She could barely admit it to herself.

What are you doing, Melanie?

She had no business thinking of home. She knew better than to be distracted on a case, but she couldn't help watching a couple holding hands, laughing as the waves lapped at their toes. Closing her eyes, she touched her fingertips to her lips and felt the moist, warm air on her face.

Inside she stretched out on the bed. It was as isolated as she'd ever felt.

"Can we talk?" she asked.

"Yeah, the scrambler's on," Jack said, without opening his eyes.

"You're engaged, right?" She looked over at him and waited. Melanie had long ago lost the nervous habit of biting at her lip, but she felt the urge when he turned on his side and looked at her. "I'm sorry. Never mind. I shouldn't be asking you this."

She couldn't remember the last time she'd broken cover.

"No, it's okay. It's just in the all time we've worked together you've never asked anything personal."

"I usually don't, but I was curious how you're able to maintain a relationship with this job?"

"Sara thinks I'm in the Navy, on a sub."

Melanie nodded. Jack lay back and closed his eyes again.

"Are you dating someone?"

"Nope."

"How are you able to do that?" he asked.

Melanie knew there were rumors about her. "I block it out. I just can't lie to anyone else."

This time Jack nodded.

⌘

The next morning Lisa and Todd walked down the dock looking for a boat to take them diving. They stopped at a 30-foot white fishing vessel with the name THE MOTO-MAN painted in light blue.

"Excuse me," she called out.

"Wha'?" snapped a man from inside the boat.

"Hi, we are looking to go diving."

"10 a.m." A Japanese man in his late 50s, with sun-toughened skin, came out and looked them over. "We're back by 3. You bring your own equipment and lunch, I only supply the trip." He turned and went back into the boat. "Show up by 9:30."

"Well, Honey," Melanie said as they walked away, "looks like we've got some shopping to do."

Three dive shops later and they were equipped.

The next morning with their scuba gear, surveillance equipment and lunch they arrived right on time.

"Hello, I'm Todd and this is my wife Lisa." Todd reached to shake the man's hand.

"Captain Yakimoto." He ignored Jack's outstretched hand.

The water was calm and the blue sky stretched across the horizon as the agents got acquainted with the only other people on the boat, a young couple from Texas.

Melanie was feeling the excitement of being on a job. Sitting on that boat, knowing she had placed six cameras along the deck without being detected, gave her a rush. This, right here, was why she loved her job. Working on instinct, she was a natural at manipulation. During a case Melanie never felt lonely or empty. There was none of that melodrama. She was alive and in control.

"Those are awesome goggles!" she said.

"Yup, they're top of the line," the man from Texas said as he handed them over for Lisa to admire.

Melanie handled them with care and, without skipping a beat, placed a camera on the bottom corner. It looked like a piece of clear tape that could go unnoticed forever. The reception wasn't great, but for what she needed it was perfect.

"Very cool, but a little too big for me." Lisa handed them back and he exchanged them for his wife's.

"Here, these are more your size," he said.

Melanie tried on the wife's goggles, fitting them with a camera as well. She praised the goggles and returned them to their owner. Mr. Yakimoto dropped anchor and came on deck to point out the best diving area. They lowered themselves into the strange world of silence. Hearing only her own breathing, Melanie signaled for Jack to dive deeper. Beneath the surface lay brilliant coral reefs, with bright tropical fish hovering and soaring around her. The magnificent colors glistened in the sun's reflection. Melanie stopped by a lava formation that was home to thousands of sea creatures. Each life form was unique and yet they were able to build a functioning society; in fact their mere survival depended on the other species. Melanie marveled at the beautiful complexity for a nano second before tapping a few keys on her diving watch. She checked each of the cameras they'd placed on the boat as well as on the goggles of the other two divers. Mr. Yakimoto was relaxing on the boat reading the paper and the Texans were swimming around some tall green kelp. Jack was accessing these same images.

While still keeping tabs on the other divers and the captain, Melanie and Jack dove to the Corsair that had been resting on the seabed for over 50 years. Swimming amid vibrant fish and aquatic plants, sea anemones attached to the rusted metal, mussels and embedded shell fossils. Melanie examined the cockpit.

At the top, the sun glimmered off the crystal blue water. She attached a satellite tracking system to the bottom of Mr. Yakimoto's boat.

This job is going to save me a bundle on therapy, she thought, exhilarated, as she climbed aboard.

The cantankerous captain scoffed off her compliments and waved her off when she asked about the sunken plane.

With everyone back on board the craft headed back to shore.

The Texans also had brought their lunch and enough beer to share. They made a toast to Captain Yakimoto and his trusty ship.

For two weeks Melanie and Jack monitored every passenger on THE MOTO-MAN. They went on 10 more dives. Yakimoto knew the best locations, opting for secluded spots over heavily trafficked, touristy ones. The Texans were regulars and had been on seven of the dives. Melanie tagged each of them with tracking devices.

By the third week, with still no success or hint of a break in the case, Melanie could feel Jack's restlessness.

"How about we take today off?"

"Really? Ward, that'd be great."

Melanie and Jack prepared their apartment to go out, alarming the room and securing the equipment and transferring the satellite feed to go directly to headquarters for monitoring.

"What do you want to do?" Melanie asked as they left the building.

"I want out of this room and away from this equipment. I *have* been spying that sandy beach, with the umbrellas and the tourists."

"And the bikinis?" Melanie laughed. She had thought they might go inner-island hiking but Jack was happy strolling along the narrow stretch of Waikiki beach.

What the beach, in front of the multitude of hotels, lacked in width it made up for in length. Everything beneath the cheerful tropical sun brightened except for the deeply tanned skin of the sunbathers who marked their territory with vivid towels. They trudged through calf-deep water to avoid the masses lounging on the grainy golden sand.

"You look like you want to learn to surf," said a man with deep creases in his face and leathered brown skin.

Standing in front of two sandwich-board price lists, he waved her closer. Twenty colorful surf boards, varying in height and width, leaned against a wood frame and two catamarans were tied up behind him.

"Hey, want to?"

"No, thanks," Jack said, taking a step back.

"I guarantee you will stand on the board and ride a wave," the man added certainly.

"Go. I'll stay here and watch," Jack said, unrolling his red-and-white striped beach towel and stretching it across the sand.

"Let's do it," Melanie said to the man.

She paid "Big Bob" his fee and the sun-weathered man whistled to a young kid.

"This is Hardy. He'll be your instructor."

After choosing the right board for Melanie, Hardy demonstrated 'the pop' as he called it – she practiced on the sand. The warm water was shallow for a great distance as they paddled out to the waves. It was more difficult than it looked and even the small waves knocked her to the sandy bottom floor.

But in one beautifully, perfectly balanced ride she was hooked. Electrified, she'd forgotten the scrapes and bruises that would undoubtedly arrive. She wanted more, ditching Hardy to paddle further out to surf with the big boys.

"Hey, you did pretty well," Jack commented.

"It was amazing." Melanie sank into her towel. "The water is clear and so warm. You really should try, or at least take a swim." Melanie let the beads of seawater evaporate off her body she closed her eyes and soaked in the hot, tropical sunshine.

"I already take enough risks," Jack closed his eyes. "You *are* aware there are sharks out there, and they don't know the difference between you and their next meal."

Melanie ignored him.

"You know what we need?" she asked after a half-hour of basking.

"I'm almost afraid to ask." Jack didn't even turn to look at her. He, too, was enjoying the balmy weather.

"Souvenirs."

"Souvenirs?"

Melanie stood and wiped the sand off her. "I know the perfect place. Things that are Hawaiian and things that are not so Hawaiian can be found at the International Market Place," Melanie said, sounding like a commercial. "Come on, it'll be fun."

"They've got food?"

"Yup." Melanie waved to Hardy as she left. He was taking out another hopeful surfer.

She and Jack strolled the short distance to the market place.

"Oh, look, we can pick pearls." She said, stopping at a cart displaying jewelry and a bucket filled with oysters.

Melanie had done this once before and for some reason felt compelled to do it again.

"Why?"

She didn't let him dampen her spirits, choosing an oyster with two small pearls and setting them in gold earrings. Crowded aisles of overstuffed carts were filled with everything from jewelry to T-shirts and hibiscus-print luggage. She loved shopping and bartering with the cart keepers.

"What do you think of this swimsuit?" She asked, holding up a bikini in a blue and white print.

He was shaking his head again. "How about that one with the tropical pink and yellow flowers?" He pointed.

It was the first time he'd shown any interest in her shopping so she bought the suit.

They got lunch at a Vietnamese take-out counter and sat outdoors under the giant banyan trees listening to the ukelele music piped into the food court.

Carrying three bags of purchases, they headed back to their hotel feeling relaxed and ready to get back to work.

"Yoo-hoo, Lisa, Todd?" They both turned to see who was calling them. It was the Texans.

Lisa sounded happy to see them. "Hi!"

"Looks like you've had a good day," said the wife.

Lisa smiled. "We did. How about you? Did you go diving?"

"Just got back. Hey, we were wondering if you wanted to join us for dinner tonight." the woman asked. "We have four tickets to a Hawaiian show and there's just the two of us."

"We'd love to."

That night they met the Texans in front of their building at 8 o'clock. Hula girls and fire dancers reenacted ancient ceremonies for clapping tourists. Live music played before and after dinner when the dance floor was opened to everyone. The four danced, changing partners and sipping on mai tais. Melanie tried to get information from both Texans, she in the restroom and he out on the parquet floor.

It was after midnight when Melanie and Jack opened the door to the empty hotel room. The balcony glowed in the moonlight and Melanie stepped out of the air-conditioned room to clear her head.

There was definitely something about the Texans, though she wasn't convinced they were involved with Yakimoto. Something nagging, a secret she couldn't quite put her finger on, something she thought should be obvious.

By 7 the next morning Melanie returned from her daily run on the beach with breakfast. He had already showered and was reading the paper on the balcony.

"Are we diving today?" he asked.

"Look at the beautiful weather. I don't know how we could pass up a day like this." She smiled, handing Jack a croissant.

They arrived at Yakimoto's boat at 9:30, as usual.

Mr. Yakimoto barked the instant he saw them, "No, I'm not taking divers today," and waved them off.

"What? Why not?" Melanie questioned, irritated.

"I've got other business today. You can find someone else to take you diving." Agitated, he untied the tethers and shoved off from the dock.

Melanie and Jack jumped back on the deck when the motor revved up and the smell of gasoline filled the air.

"Okay, now what?" Jack asked.

"We'll take his advice and find another boat," Melanie said with a smile. She was glad to finally get this thing going.

Melanie drove the rented speedboat while Jack pulled up the satellite tracking and gave her coordinates. Yakimoto's fishing vessel was no match for the modern speedster. They quickly closed in and stayed just out of visual range.

"I'm getting another boat on the radar," Jack said.

"Let's get a little closer and see if we recognize anyone."

"Wow, that's a nice yacht."

Melanie got as close as she dared and wished she had something as simple as a pair of binoculars. Instead she typed in their location and tried to get satellite footage. As she waited Melanie called Mike at the control center. She wanted him to receive the satellite feed so he could get started on identifying who was on the yacht.

For 20 minutes she and Jack rocked on the gentle waves and watched the yacht. There was no audio reception and no movement on the decks.

"Melanie, he's one of ours," Mike said as he uploaded the photo from the satellite and transferred it to her computer. "Bill Fallon, the agent who's been leaking the information."

Melanie studied the picture on her screen: a middle-aged man with graying hair and tired eyes. Melanie slid the photo to Jack.

"Okay, thanks Mike." Melanie hung up the phone. "I say we get closer." She reached for their diving gear.

Three people had been detected by satellite infrared on board: Fallon, Yakimoto and the yacht's captain at the helm. Silently they climbed the rail access ladder onto the deck just as two rapid shots rang out, echoing across the calm seas.

Melanie instinctively ducked, her weapon drawn. She looked at Jack as they advanced cautiously. Suddenly, Yakimoto turned the corner in a full-scale run, charging toward Jack with wide-eyed determination. Rushing them at full speed, Jack threw his shoulder into the small man, attempting to stop him. The two men stumbled, struggling. Jack was smacked down by the weight of the tanks Yakimoto had strapped to his back. Melanie aimed her weapon at Yakimoto as Jack's head hit the deck.

"Stop!"

Yakimoto gave Melanie a confused grimace and plunged into the deep blue water.

Melanie checked on Jack who was regaining consciousness, "You OK?"

"Did we get him?" Jack asked, rubbing the back of his head, sitting up.

"No, I'm going to find Fallon." Melanie said, seeing that Jack was basically unhurt.

"You go after Yakimoto. I'll take care of Fallon."

"Sure?"

"Go."

Melanie jumped onto Yakimoto's boat.

"Yes!"

He'd used tanks she'd fitted with a tracking device, allowing her to follow him to a small, desolate island off the North Shore of Oahu. She made contact with Jack.

"Fallon is hurt pretty bad. A helicopter should be here in a few minutes but it doesn't look good."

"Okay, I've got to go. I'll call you when I can."

She got as close to shore as possible before swimming the remaining distance then running half a mile down the beach to an abandoned shack on the side of a lush, overgrown hill.

She ducked beneath the stilted shanty, tucked in the earpiece, and listened to Yakimoto pacing the floorboards above her head and speaking on the phone.

She quickly called Mike to put a trace on the call.

Yakimoto was speaking rapidly in Japanese. "Yeah, yeah he's dead. I shot him twice but I've got to get out of here."

A pause.

"No, there were no complications but I'm catching a flight out of Honolulu today."

The tension in his voice was thick.

"I'll meet you by the fountain the day after tomorrow."

His movements above her head were becoming more frantic.

"Hyde Park. Yes, I know where that is."

The call ended.

"Mike did we get the trace?"

The call was too short and the encryption too advanced.

"Can you send a helicopter for me and Yakimoto?" Melanie was ready to go inside.

She climbed the steps and gingerly pushed open the old crooked door that turned out to be steel inforced.

It was a one-room building. Yakimoto had his back to her, filling a suitcase.

She was surprised to see the magnitude of technology that lined the walls. She wouldn't have guessed the small hut was watertight or secure enough for such a setup. The thatched roof and palm siding was a sham. A table with sophisticated gear, including weather tracking, laptops and satellite technology was piled high with discs in a disorganized mess.

"Going someplace?" Melanie asked, as she thumped Yakimoto on the head with the butt of her pistol.

She easily dragged his light body across the hut and, using computer cords, tied his hands and legs then went to the computer to rummage through the documents while she waited for the chopper. Working quickly, she tried to get a grasp on what Yakimoto was doing and who was in charge of the operation. She searched the hard drive, and the third file she opened brought up a 3-D image of the globe, a satellite image of the rotating Earth, turning day to night in Paris, then London. Melanie watched until she'd viewed the entire rotation. Light clusters set the big cities apart and yellow flags dotted the planet in what appeared to be a specific pattern.

"I've seen this before," Melanie said out loud, remembering the first time she'd seen the sparkling lights of the big cities around the globe. The image was captivating.

She sent the file to Mike.

"Mike, does this look familiar to you?"

"I can't say I've seen this before."

Melanie strained. "Ask Judith. I know this image was up in the control center just before I left for Hawaii."

Melanie continued searching through Yakimoto's files, trying to understand the connection with the agency.

Minutes later Mike called back.

"The flags represent the locations of our agents. She's notifying

Agent Jackson."

Almost simultaneously Melanie heard Yakimoto moving about and the helicopter landing on the beach. The little man still secure, she went to meet the flight team, directing two agents to load up Yakimoto. Melanie grabbed a laptop and dumped all the discs she could find into a bag. On her way out she ordered a two-man unit to immediately scour the tiny hut inch by inch.

She spent the entire flight back to Honolulu on the cell phone. Fallon was pronounced DOA and Jack was back at the hotel awaiting further instructions.

"Melanie, I want you and Jack to resume your cover," Ben called as the blades of the helicopter whirled noisily and lifted off the roof of the agency's Honolulu headquarters.

"Give me a second, Ben." Melanie said, handing Yakimoto over to the guard who would escort him to a holding room.

Ben picked up the conversation once both the chopper and Yakimoto were gone. "Ward, there's still the question about the couple from Texas. I'm having another agent take over with Yakimoto while you and Jack get a definitive answer as to their involvement."

Melanie's fuse was short and she took a breath to maintain control. Absently she glared at a flock of pigeons.

"Who's getting this case?" she asked, knowing the answer and not liking it – Parker. "Damn it, Ben, with all due respect, how can you consider giving this to *him*?"

"I know your frustration, but believe it or not, Agent Ward, I'm still in command here. But," he sighed, "the Board is making this decision."

Melanie's blood boiled. Her pride stung and there was nothing she could do but fume. Her mind flew over expletives and threats.

"You can't do anything?"

"I know my place and Agent you should know yours."

"OK, Ben," she said, kicking at the cooing pigeons as they pecked at the gravel roof.

I'll be there for you when the sniveling, backstabbing, incompetent snake screws up again. Damn it! Melanie thought as she wound her way around the white corridors toward the interrogation room. Through a thin rectangular window in the door, Melanie looked at Yakimoto, who was already seated, his aged face defiant.

"Hey, Agent Ward, thanks for doing all the grunt work. The big guns'll take it from here," Finn said with a wink.

The taste of blood leaked from her bitten tongue. Thoughts of lunging at his throat were followed by contemplation of unleashing her firearm and releasing shots into each of his evil blue eyes.

Steam rose from his coffee cup as he lifted it to his grinning face. An icy shiver of revulsion shot down her spine.

She felt betrayed by Ben, and though betrayal was part of her profession she didn't expected it within the confines of their friendship.

"They're giving it to Parker," Jack said, cautiously.

Even as a timid sentence the words sent ripples of fury through her.

Melanie nodded, not surprised at Jack's trepidation. The entire agency was aware of her rivalry with Finn Parker.

"I've had enough of this. Come on, we're going to *bump* into the Texans."

Determined, she led Jack off the sandy beach and into Duke's for an afternoon cocktail. The Texans were balanced on stools with their backs to the bar and spotted Lisa and Todd immediately.

"Hey, look who's here!"

"I'm glad we ran into you," Lisa said. Tired and yearning to get back into the action, Melanie made an impromptu decision. She could explain herself later. "Today's our last day on the island and we hoped we could interest you in a farewell dinner."

"We should have done this weeks ago." Melanie said, throwing her evening wear on the bed and grumbling to herself.

Though dinner went uneventful, Melanie felt the tension between the other couple. Careful not to press too hard, it wasn't until after the third round of drinks, during a spirited retro disco, that the Texans looked at each other uncomfortably.

"Go on, ask 'em," he said, nudging her with his elbow.

"What's up?" Todd asked.

"Well, since you've asked," Mrs. Texas said nervously, "we really like you both and thought that you might be interested in a swap." She said the last part so quickly that all the words blurred together.

"A swap?" Melanie tried to smooth her expression as she strared. "Wow." She stalled. "As, um, interesting as your offer is, we're going to have to decline."

"Are you sure, 'cause we could have another drink and you might warm up to the idea," said the woman, who looked at her husband disappointed.

He picked up where his wife left off. "We understand. The first time we were approached we declined. But when we got home we discussed the possibility and when the opportunity came up again we accepted. Maybe when you get back to your condo you'll change your minds." He smiled and passed a piece of paper to Lisa. It was the phone number to their hotel room.

She accepted the number and promised to think it over. The rest of the evening was awkward and she was relieved to finally say goodbye to the Texans.

Walking along the dark beach, the sliver of moon cast a shallow light that guided them back to the hotel.

"I should be pissed, I wanted to finish the case, I wanted to beat the information out of Yakimoto." Melanie said, irritated that a couple of swingers caused her to lose the case, she shook her head. "But I'm just too shocked to be angry. Can you believe we were so wrong about them?"

"We weren't wrong, they did have a secret," Jack said, chuckling. "Just not the one we expected."

"I guess it's sort of flattering," Melanie admitted. "They weren't a bad-looking couple."

"Are you considering using that phone number?" Jack teased.

Melanie lightly punched his shoulder.

"You know, I'm going to miss Hawaii."

"It is paradise." Melanie looked up to the silhouette of Diamond Head and stepping into a wave that rushed up on shore and then rolled back into the ocean.

But she was still raw from Ben's actions.

"So, are we leaving tomorrow?" Jack asked.

"Yeah, maybe we can get back in time…" She knew it was no use. She was off the case.

Packing her gear early the next morning, she went back to the beach for one last time and rented a short board. The surf was up and she played for over an hour catching waves that carried her to shore. She had improved, riding the whitecaps. And just before she was ready to give it up for the day and head off the island, Melanie scored *the* wave of her career.

CHAPTER 8

Melanie slept on the plane to Seattle, where she and Jack would part and make their way home individually. Neither knew the other's route. It was standard, used to protect an agent's identity.

At the airport Melanie gave Jack a handshake and vanished. From Seattle she flew to Chicago then to Miami, finally taking a train up to headquarters. It was definitely the long way home. She wasn't sure she wanted to know what had come of her troubles in Hawaii, but true to herself, she went directly to Ben's office upon reaching D.C. She needed answers directly from him.

"You want a drink?" he asked as if nothing were wrong.

"No, thanks." He handed her a scotch and motioned for her to sit on one of the leather chairs facing his desk.

"That was a mess. You know I had to pull eight agents off their assignments. If you can believe it, three other cases may also be entangled. So," he said sitting down, "how are you? I heard you took the scenic route home."

"It's protocol," Melanie said curtly.

She sniffed at the drink, considering, then set the glass on a coaster.

"I had Jack picked up in Seattle. We looked for you but you had disappeared." Ben laughed and sipped his drink. "Just for fun, I put two guys to track you."

"Fun?" Melanie repeated. "We're in the middle of a crisis."

He leaned back, shrugged.

"I felt the tail," she admitted, thinking back. "Have they gotten back from across the border?"

"Not until tomorrow."

"Sorry." She wasn't. "They didn't do too badly tracking me."

He pointed at her with drink in hand and winked. "The Board has decided to let you continue with the Yakimoto case."

Melanie knew it but was too tired from the trip to even ask how Parker had screwed up.

"I understand your frustration, Ward, but trust me on this one."

"I always have."

In the control center Mike had set up an entire room devoted to the information retrieved from the little hut. He and his assistant Ed were sitting amid stacks of computer discs.

"When did you get in?" he asked, taking off his headphones when he saw her.

"Twenty minutes ago. How are things going in here?" Melanie asked, eyeing the mess.

"Too much information and not enough help. Besides going through this, I've got a 100 agents still needing to send and receive information. Mike overload."

"Jane," she said, leaning over the intercom. "I need you to get the three first-year agents to the communications center ASAP. Thanks." Turning back to Mike, "Well, that's a little help. What else has been happening?"

Mike recapped the events of the past few days.

Parker had dropped the ball with the Hyde Park meeting, and got nothing out of the Yakimoto interrogation.

"Maybe I can get something out of him." Melanie said.

"That'll be tough, seeing as he's still in Honolulu."

"What the hell?"

Forty minutes later Yakimoto was on a flight to D.C.

"Well, I'm not doing anything until he gets here," she said, with a sigh. "So how can I help?"

"You mean it?" Mike was joyous at the suggestion. "Here, grab some headphones, a disc and label everything." He pulled out a chair for her in front of a computer.

He did the same for the three freshman agents when they arrived.

Melanie went through 12 discs, looking at each file. Most of what she found was old information. It was nearly dawn when she opened the last one in her stack.

Immediately she knew this one was different. It was protected by encryption. Mike and Ed had left hours ago so she began the decoding process. Melanie's screen was covered in green, with letters, numbers and symbols spinning at high speeds. She watched for a few minutes before exhaustion set in and Mike's uncomfortable commercial blue rectangular couch was calling her name.

"Just a quick nap," she promised to the empty room.

Almost three hours later Mike, sweetly but clumsily, covering her with a blanket woke her from her dreamless sleep. The computer was still whirling.

"It's been going for hours?" Mike asked, amazed.

He went to the keyboard and hit a few buttons.

"Did I do it wrong?"

"No, everything's working right, it's just advanced." Mike laughed, giving his best 'mad scientist' impression. "But we are more advanced. Only nine more digits to decipher and these will go fast. Why don't you go get something to eat?"

"Good idea."

She went to the restroom to wash her face, brush her teeth and put her hair in a fresh ponytail. She got a change of clothes from her office. Half an hour later she was back in the control center with a cup of coffee and a doughnut.

"Another two minutes and this baby is ours." Mike had routed the information to be up on the five-foot tele-monitor. Melanie sat down and waited, hoping this was the real deal. She took a deep breath as the files appeared on the screen.

"Which do you want opened first?"

"Great job, Mike. Okay, let's see, the one marked Fallon/General. Who's the general?" Melanie leaned forward in anticipation.

"I guess we'll find out." Mike said, and with two clicks of the mouse he had the file open.

"E-mails," Melanie said, reading the first one, dated five years ago. "Mike, scroll to the more recent ones." Melanie, too antsy to sit, stood behind Mike with her hand on the back of his chair.

"Here's some dated last month," he offered.

"No, keep going go to the very last two messages." She stepped back so she could get the full effect of the large monitor. Reading the correspondence she felt chills running up her spine. She exchanged looks with Mike.

"Holy shit," he said, summing it up.

Melanie went to see Ben. He was sitting on the couch looking through case files.

She pulled up a chair to face him and went step by step, explaining the situation.

The General was a Chinese-American with no military background who had surfaced a few years back to protest the Chinese government. His name had hit the FBI's list of wanted terrorists when he claimed responsibility for a bacterial outbreak that killed more than a 1,000 people in Hong Kong.

Communication between The General and Fallon had described a plan to release the same virus in six global areas of dense population to commemorate his birthday, May 12 – tomorrow.

Fallon had supplied the satellite codes to detonate bombs filled with the bacteria.

"The General has linked all six bombs to one activation device, using our satellite to relay the feed. We need to find the General. Yakimoto is our only link and he's just arrived," Melanie said, looking at her watch, "I'm leaving now."

"What about disabling the satellite?"

"I'm leaving it up for now. I don't want to spook the General. If I can't find him then I'll have the thing shut down."

"It looks like you can handle this on your own," Jackson said. "Run with it but keep me in the loop."

She drove to the underground prisoner holding center.

"Good afternoon, Captain."

He huffed and crossed his arms. Melanie took a seat across the metal table from Yakimoto, who grunted at her. His face scrunched up, making all the creases squeeze together and making his features disappear.

"Since we both know there isn't much time, why don't you tell me where I can find the General?"

"You're joking – I'm not telling you nothing." He turned, angling his shoulder toward her.

"You are aware that you're sitting in a holding cell in Washington D.C., today, May 11."

"Either way I'm a dead man," Yakimoto nodded, his face no longer smushed together but sagging instead. "Besides, I've already told you what I know. He's on a ship somewhere mid-Atlantic, that's all I know. I'm not saying anything else until my lawyer gets here."

Melanie continued to press but the stubborn man sat staring blankly.

"I know nothing else. I was supposed to meet someone in London." He glared at Melanie.

With the little information he had supplied, Melanie went back to Mike.

"What do we know about the General's ships?"

A few clicks later Mike listed all the information that'd been gathered and labeled with the word ship. Accessing Yakimoto's information, the General's fleet consisted of four fishing vessels and one luxury liner, outfitted with the latest technology.

Mike loved the "latest technology" – his wide smile expressed it more than words ever could.

"What people don't realize is that everything is connected. Nothing's private, I can tap into computers, e-mails, cell phone, I can find anyone, anywhere. The worldwide web has brought everyone to my fingertips."

Mike located photos, taken from space, of the yacht drifting in the middle of the Atlantic Ocean.

It was almost sunset when the two fighter jets dropped their torpedos.

May 12 passed without incident.

On Friday the 13 the sun peeked over the eastern horizon at precisely 5:58 a.m. Five of the six bombs the General distributed already had been located and dismantled. The sixth was still at large but the team had leads and was actively seeking it out.

Melanie had spent an unusually restless night at her apartment and, during her bike ride to work, thoughts of Parker never strayed from her consciousness. An unexplainable sense of grief had taken root in her soul.

Spring had already sprung and the cherry blossoms had reached their pinnacle weeks earlier, so the trees had already lost their floral icing. Melanie had missed the bright pink flowers that cloaked the branches of the trees lining the capital building, too wrapped up in the events across the world to pay attention to the beauty that surrounded her.

As usual, Ben sat behind his big desk in his dark office, which hadn't changed in the 10 years Melanie had worked for the agency.

He stood when he saw Melanie. "Have a seat."

She did as she was told. The chair facing Ben's desk had never felt as stiff before, and she shifted trying to find comfort.

"You know, Melanie, these past few days have been inspirational."

It was 8 a.m. – she set the drink on the coaster.

"It's not quite over."

"Ward, as you've so keenly noticed, I've been distracted lately. Lilly, my wife, has been ill, and though I've tried to manage both work and her sickness I've decided that her health is my greater concern. I have chosen you to head up the domestic division while I take some personal time."

Melanie held her breath, scooting to the edge of her seat as she watched Ben place a level E badge on his desk in front of her. She was at a loss for words.

It's what every agent works toward, just one step below executive level. She wanted to be the first woman executive, and it looked like she was going to make that happen. Smiling, she held tightly to the badge.

"You will be co-chairing my position with Parker. It is the Board's decision that Finn will oversee international activity."

Melanie's heart stopped. She had assumed because of all that had occurred the past few days that Parker would have been sent packing with a ticket to a federal prison, or at the very least hiding in some dark closet until the situation blew over.

The elusive yellow plastic badge with "Melanie Ward" printed boldly on front stared at her. In an impromptu decision, she placed her ambition back on Ben's desk and slid it toward the man she'd admired for over 10 years.

"I can't take this." Melanie rose from the uncomfortable chair.

"You've earned it, Melanie."

"Damn right, I earned it – Parker did not. It's a slap in the face, and I'll have my resignation on your desk within the hour," she said, storming out of the office like a spoiled child.

Melanie left a shocked Ben Jackson, his mouth agape, unmoving at his desk. Fuming, she sat at her computer and typed out the end of her career as a secret agent in a two-sentence letter. She had reacted in haste and now her pride had forced her hand.

She looked around her office. Outside her window the skies darkened as clouds blew in, blocking out the soft rays of the New England sun. Inside, there was nothing of a personal nature: a couple of photos and a change of clothes hung in the closet. She turned off the lights.

Ben lowered his face and shook his head. "This is regrettable but not unforeseen. Today the world is less safe but I do wish you well. Judith," Ben paged his assistant on the intercom, "make sure the jet is ready to take Agent Ward to her choice of destination."

"Thank you," Melanie hesitated. "Ben, I did really enjoy working for you. I can't pretend to understand these motives but I'm sure that if there were an alternative you'd be there for me."

For an instant Melanie saw grief set into his eyes. "You are the daughter Lilly and I always wanted, but my hands are tied, Melanie."

Melanie nodded and turned to leave for the last time.

CHAPTER 9

"Hello, Ms. Ward," the pilot said. "We have your flight schedule and should be taking off in the next 15 minutes."

"Thanks, James," she walked onto the plane. "Am I alone today?"

"Just you and the crew."

She buckled into one roomy leather seat and looked out the window as her phone rang.

"Hey, Mike."

"What the hell is going on?"

"Ben is taking time off and you're getting Parker as a replacement."

"No!" His astonishment was mixed with a dash of disbelief.

"Yup, they offered domestic to me but I declined."

"You declined? Melanie, Parker needs all the help he can get. Now you'll have to work under him."

"No, I won't. I resigned. Right now I'm on a flight headed, headed … I'm not sure what I'm doing but I can't stay and watch Parker get what I've worked for, I can't."

"What will you do? The espionage game is all you know."

Melanie groaned.

"Sorry."

"It's all right."

"Let me know if I can help with anything."

"Thanks Mike. Just keep your eyes and ears open."

"I'll keep your phone intact for as long as I can, complete with all the gadgets."

"Thanks, Mike. Hey, do me one more favor."

"Anything."

"Call me if we're going to lose San Diego."

"You've got it. I'm being paged for a meeting upstairs."

"Bye, Mike."

"Oh, and Melanie, thanks for the Hawaiian shirt."

"No problem."

The gifts she'd brought for Mike and Ben had still been packed when Melanie opened her luggage to leave the Agency for the last time. She had a first-year distribute them after she'd left.

The flight was smooth and quiet. Melanie sat thinking of nothing. She was numb, emotionless. The probability that she'd just walked away from her life didn't seem real. Yet she knew exactly what she'd done – she'd thrown out her entire existence. Mike was right, she didn't know anything but being a spy. Where or how could she begin? How would she face her friends and most importantly, her mom?

Melanie hid from more than the bright sun behind a pair of oversized sunglasses. She wasn't ready for a new life, nor did she want one.

The taxi pulled up to her parents' home and Melanie paid the driver. She stood at the curb, a duffle bag in each hand, carrying everything she owned. She faced her future and her past.

"Anyone home?" she called out from the front door and dropped her bags at the base of the stairs.

The old, green carpeting had been pulled up years ago, exposing the original hardwood flooring. Melanie let out a deep sigh and caught a whiff of her father's rose bushes, her first welcome home.

"Melanie?"

The swinging door into the kitchen was propped open and Melanie followed the sound of her mother's voice.

Rita's hair was now a soft blonde, but still cut in her favorite style, something she always called an Italian boy. She'd worn it like that since she was a teenager. Her bifocals hung from a beaded chain around her neck. It had been over a year since Melanie had walked through these doors.

The mother and the disconnected daughter embraced without sentiment.

"You should have called, Dear, I'd have made something to eat," Rita nervously flittered around the kitchen. "Let me look at you."

Melanie smiled and took a step back.

"You're so skinny and you look tired."

"Well, you look great."

Her mother shuffled her feet and struck a pose.

"I've been taking tap dancing lessons."

Melanie laughed. "Hey, where's Dad?"

"He's out back tending to his roses, they came out especially beautiful this year. He is going to be so thrilled to see you."

"Hi, Dad," Melanie said as she pushed open the heavy glass door that separated the living room from the backyard.

"Annie! Hey, I didn't know you were coming home."

"It was a last-minute thing."

He pushed himself off the ground where he'd been kneeling.

"How long are you staying?" he asked, embracing his daughter.

"I'm not really sure." She closed her eyes as her dad put his arms around her, and sadness washed over her. "I've missed you, Pops." She said, and for the first time realizing how much.

"I've missed you, too. Come on, let's talk. How've you been?"

Rita brought out three glasses of iced tea and they sat on the patio, chatting about the weather, the roses, the neighbor's new car.

"The flowers you sent were beautiful," her mother said out of the blue.

"Flowers?"

"Mother's Day. I had hoped for a call but I guess that was too much for your secretary."

Melanie stared blankly. What could she say? She had been on the case in Hawaii and hadn't even remembered it was Mother's Day. "I'm sorry."

"That's not good enough."

Melanie brushed a clump of hair off her forehead and out of her eyes. She tried to push it behind her ear but suddenly it was exactly too short and exactly too long and kept falling into her face. She was in dire need of a haircut but hadn't even noticed before. "It's all I've got."

Mrs. Ward was hurt and the pain in her eyes bored into Melanie. She stood, appearing larger than her 5'2" frame, and stomped into the house.

"God, it was a bad idea to come home," Melanie said, rubbing her brow.

"You're going to have to make amends with her sometime, why not now?"

Words of wisdom from a man who'd spent the last two decades refereeing his two women.

Melanie smiled. "I'm afraid of her."

Roger Ward laughed. "She loves you. Just make an effort and I guarantee that she'll come around."

"Okay, Dad," she faced him, "you know I really am sorry for … everything."

"You don't have to worry about me, Honey."

"Thanks, Dad. You have my back, don't you?"

"Always have. Now go see your mother."

All the drapes and windows were open, allowing the ocean breeze to sweep through the house and keeping the temperature always perfect.

"Bruce and Cheryl should be here soon. They can't wait for you to meet the baby," Rita Ward said from behind her open cookbook as she leaned against the new granite kitchen counter.

Meet the baby? Melanie thought, completely confused. *Had the baby been born?*

"So, when...?" Melanie wondered how she was going to ask without looking like a complete ass. "Olivia, right?"

"Yes, that's her name and, no, she hasn't been born. Honestly, Melanie could you be more out of the picture?" Disgust dripped from every hurtful syllable. "The baby can recognize voices from inside the womb."

"I didn't know." Melanie sat on a counter stool and rubbed her tired, red eyes.

Her mother continued. "I must say this new secretary of yours has great taste. She's already sent the cutest things, you should see them."

"I get it, Mom. I'm a terrible daughter, sister and now I guess I can add terrible aunt to that list."

"Don't get angry with me, this is all you. Believe me, it's always all you."

Melanie was cut by the words but had promised to make an effort, so after a pregnant pause she tried again.

"The remodel came out really nice," she said of the distressed white cabinets and moss green countertops.

"It was finished over a year ago."

"You're right. I'm going to take a shower if you don't mind." Melanie was broken. "I did bring you something." Melanie reached into her pocket and placed the small red satin purse with the Hawaiian pearl earrings on the open cookbook. "I hope you like them."

She didn't wait for a response.

Upstairs Melanie lay down on her old bed, crawled beneath her lavender print spread and fell fast asleep.

The light was different when she awoke, confused by the bright sunbeams streaming in her bedroom window. Timidly, she climbed down the stairs.

"Good morning, Sleeping Beauty." It was her dad, sitting in the living room watching TV.

"What happened?" She plopped down on the old couch next to her father's chair.

"Bruce and Cheryl came over to see you yesterday but you were out."

"Yesterday?" Now it made sense. "I screwed up again." Melanie leaned her head back. "I had no idea I was so tired. Where's Mom?"

"She has a group of girlfriends at the church she meets with a few times a week. They'll be updated on every move you made yesterday." Her father winked.

Melanie groaned.

"It's a good thing, I think." He wondered to himself for a moment.

"What are we watching?" Melanie asked, kicking her feet up on the coffee table.

The first few days Melanie paced and when she wasn't pacing she was checking for listening devices in the phones and cameras in the fire alarms. She memorized each license plate that parked within a block radius, checking for suspicious activity. Any sign of espionage would have satisfied her, but to her intense disappointment there was nothing out of the ordinary. Manually she did a second sweep of the house, stopping when her father said, "Annie, you're like a caged animal," during an afternoon of wearing out a pattern on the carpeting. Dispirited, she found her way to the old couch where she hunkered down to wait out her misery.

Curtains were drawn and the bright sunny days weren't allowed into her cave as the TV's constant flicker comforted her aching ego.

The news was frustrating, only tidbits of information were released and Melanie knew there was an iceberg beneath each headline. She'd sat with a notebook and attempted to unscramble the fiction from the truth. No easy task, though she did know what to look for.

By the end of the first week, she gave up, boycotting every channel.

No CNN, no MSNBC, no local news, no paper – nothing that would cause her to obsess on all she was missing.

She intended to ride out this hiatus on the couch, which was more comfortable than she had remembered. Surrounded by the familiar smells of childhood, when life had been easy and uncomplicated, she sulked. Melanie flipped through the channels, surviving mostly on TV Land because she hated the handy do-it-yourselfers on the home decorating and cooking networks.

The battles between her and her mother had ceased. Apparently her church friends advised her against conflict. Melanie, left to her own devices, chose to do nothing but root into the cushions of the big old couch, under Nana's hand-knitted afghan. Moving on from TV Land's old Westerns, she switched to sappy Lifetime movies.

During the second week of her dismal new existence, she claimed her spot on the couch and curled up with her pillow, blanket and remote control. She battled the big decision of the day: a *Twilight Zone* marathon or a movie about a woman whose husband had three wives?

"Melanie, Honey, we need to talk," her mom said entirely too sweetly, causing the hairs on the back of her neck to prickle.

Rita entered the living room with Melanie's father, her brother and Cheryl, Carla, Trish and Jenny trailing behind her.

Melanie sat upright.

"What's up?" Melanie asked as her family and friends took their seats around the room.

They each looked at her mother. Melanie knew who the culprit was – and what the topic would be.

Cheryl opened the curtains to let in sunlight and Melanie squinted at the brightness of the day. Her mother turned off the TV and sat with her hands on Melanie's knees.

"Melanie, you are such a beautiful girl. We think that maybe you should take a more active role in your life. We're worried about you, Dear."

Right, they're worried about me, I've spoken to Jenny once in a year and only a few times more with Carla or Trish. Melanie rolled her eyes and doubted very much that any of them were worried.

She let out a heavy sigh. Her friends couldn't even look at her; they sat with hands in laps and heads down. But not her mother, the instigator, who had arranged this in the name of love. Melanie sighed and again waited for the barrage.

"You know what we're talking about," Rita said.

"Yeah, me taking a more active role. Right, I got it," she repeated hotly.

"Mel, what *have* you got planned for your vacation, another *I Love Lucy* marathon?" Bruce asked.

She had not been able to say she'd quit her job. They believed she was taking time off like a normal person. Besides, she was waiting for the Board to figure out they couldn't run the place without her.

"Actually, it was the *Twilight Zone*."

"This is not a joke!" Rita's voice was stern. "I have been angry with you, Melanie. But I've realized that I can't expect you to take an interest in my life when you don't even have an interest in yours."

"I'm interested."

"Good. Because I ... *we* have a plan."

Melanie could feel the anger beginning to simmer in the pit of her stomach – it was the most emotion she'd felt in days. She didn't want to fight with these people, but they had no idea what her life was about.

"You haven't talked about a boyfriend in some time and your father and I were wondering, well, what we thought was..." She stammered.

My mom at a loss for words? This is big.

"Your mother and I have this idea that maybe it's not a man that you ... prefer. We know there are other options these days and we're open to whatever it is that makes you happy."

"Dad!" Melanie suddenly remembered why she'd moved across the country.

"We're hip," Rita said.

"Well, I'm not." Melanie rubbed her eyes. "I am not a lesbian. Just because a woman chooses a career over a man doesn't mean she's gay.

"You think I'm gay?" She turned to look at each person in the room. She had limits and knew her fuse was much shorter than normal. She looked directly at her mom. "Not having a man is, like, the least of my worries. Seriously, Mom, I don't need a man to fulfill my life. Can't you understand that?"

"No, I can't. Melanie you are 33 years old and you're going to wake up one day old and alone. You'll have missed everything and I don't want that to happen."

Melanie closed her eyes, remembering the promise she'd made to her dad.

For her father sake, she asked, "What do you want from me?"

"As it turns out each of us has the name and number of a single man we think you'd enjoy meeting."

"Great." Melanie sighed and accepted the seven business cards from her mother.

"We're done here?" Trish asked standing to leave. "Sorry about this, Mel, but I was trapped." Trish kissed the side of Melanie's head. "I've got people to see and things to do. Or is it people to do and things to see?" She giggled and waved, "Hope you like Jason." She was out the door.

"Your first date is tonight," Carla said, also standing. "I, too, have got to run. Bye-bye." She hugged Melanie and raced to the door.

Jenny was the next to bolt. "You're not mad, are you?"

Melanie shook her head, too upset to answer.

"Why are you all leaving? I made lunch." Mrs. Ward was following the girls to the front door.

Melanie and Cheryl exchanged small smiles.

"You know, Mom, I'm tired. I think I should go home and rest." Cheryl said with a exaggerated yawn.

"Really, 'cause I think *Mom* would be happy to whip up a high-protein meal for you."

"Don't start, Melanie," Rita's said, lightly tapping Melanie's forearm. Jovial, that was her demeanor as she fished through the business cards. "This is your first date tonight," the card read Dennis Gossett, Divorce Lawyer. "He's picking you up at 8 for dinner."

Melanie shuffled through the rest of the business cards.

"I'm curious," she said, looking up at her mom. "What if I had turned out to be gay?" Melanie gestured to the cards in her hand.

Rita raised her eyebrows. "We had a whole different set if that had been the case."

Melanie leaned back in her seat.

They really thought I was gay?

"Get up," Rita chirped. "You and I are going to the salon and then to the mall. Honestly, Melanie, don't you own anything other than jeans?"

This is worse than actual torture.

Seven dates had been crammed into six days: two lunches and five dinners. The explanation: "We didn't want you to miss an opportunity with any of the men, in case you had to *get back to work*." Translation: ditch us and escape for higher ground.

Rita introduced Melanie to her stylist who enlisted a team to "fix" Melanie's hair and nails. The facial, manicure and pedicure were pleasant enough. She tuned out her mom directing the experts. The pain began with the reshaping of her eyebrows and the hot wax that stripped her legs. She won the clash against the Brazilian wax. After hours of trimming, soaking and primping, she left the salon a different person.

Sitting in the car, she looked over at her mom, who was staring out the front windshield.

"Do you really think this looks better?"

Rita stifled a smile. "Well, maybe it is a trifle overdone, but it's something."

"Yeah, it's something all right," Melanie said, dropping the mirror from the sun visor and pulling out the two-dozen bobby pins.

She saw the disappointment on her mother's face.

"The nails, I like." Melanie said, admiring her hands. "Thanks, Mom."

Rita beamed.

The next stop was the mall. Even Melanie had to admit her wardrobe needed updating. She'd forgotten the pleasures of the mall and she'd forgotten the enormity.

"With all these stores, how can I not find anything?" she asked, shuffling through racks and racks of undesirable clothing.

"Because, you're too picky. Always have been," Rita answered, pulling out a black sleeveless dress. It had a ruffle along the bottom and along the neckline, which dipped a bit lower than Melanie would have liked.

But it was the best so far, and it was her ticket out.

Melanie decided that the dates had a two-fold benefit. First, they would make her mom happy, and second, they took the focus off making a decision about her life and what her next step would be. She wanted her job back but her confidence was a roller coaster, one minute knowing it was just a matter of time before the Board came groveling, and the next minute wondering, ... what if they didn't? But the good news was: By the end of the week she would have successfully completed seven dates, eased the tension between her and her mom and accepted the sincerest of apologies from the

Agency. By this time next week she'd be heading back to D.C.

"Melanie? Hi, I'm Dennis." Average in height and slight of build, his morose eyes were dark against his pale skin, even as he attempted a smile.

"Nice to meet you, Dennis."

Melanie turned to wave goodbye to Rita, who was watching merrily from the screen door, gesturing with her hands to shoo them away. Melanie wondered if a 33 year-old woman should still be rolling her eyes at her mother.

It was Saturday night and she was on a date – albeit not of her own volition, but nevertheless, a date. A sickening feeling gnawed at her. She had less than zero expectations for any of the seven men she'd been set up with, yet still, sitting in a stranger's car added a slight level of apprehension.

How long has it been, she wondered, *since the last time you felt anything remotely similar?* The silent drive left her time to ponder.

"This was our favorite restaurant," Dennis said, steering his Lexus into a parking space outside a Japanese restaurant.

Melanie nodded, pressing her lips together so as not to ask the question.

"Oh, Mr. Gossett, it's been a long time," the man in the suit said, shaking Dennis' hand and checking Melanie out from the corner of his eye.

"Yeah, Clare and I split up two months ago," Dennis said.

His jaw was taut and a throbbing vein on his neck exposed his quickened heartbeat. Melanie took off her sweater and put her sunglasses inside her new purse. She was completely uncomfortable with the questioning stares.

"I am so sorry to hear that, you were a lovely couple," He said, leading them to a table in the back of the little restaurant. "Your table is available."

"No, we can't sit there."

The host stopped abruptly, then shifted course to a table near the front.

Quietly, a little Asian girl placed a square plate with thin slices of raw fish on their table.

"Thank you, Peggy." Dennis picked up his chopsticks. "She's the owner's daughter. Isn't she beautiful?"

Melanie nodded.

"She was only a baby when Clare and I started coming to this place."

Melanie didn't want to ask, but here it was being pulled from her. She looked around at the other patrons washing down their California rolls with tiny cups of sake, then back to Dennis, who continued to fiddle with his chopsticks as if lost in a memory. Melanie closed her eyes for strength.

"So, Dennis?"

He looked up, his eyes reddening and welling with tears, as Melanie glanced down at the plate with slivers of squishy white and pink fish.

Just because something is consumable doesn't mean it should be, she thought, giving Dennis time to man up.

"Sashimi," he said, pointing a chopstick at the bait. He cleared his throat and used the napkin to dry the wet patches on his face. "I apologize about this evening. It's been difficult moving on. Clare was in college when we met, young and beautiful. I fell immediately."

Dennis' words were sad and his voice was hypnotic. It was going to be a tragic love story. She barely looked up when he ordered for both of them. Intrigued as he outlined their six years of peaks and valleys, family deaths, a miscarriage, her graduation, his promotion. It wasn't difficult to leave her dish untouched as she listened. Even glancing at the squishy food made her stomach roll.

By the end, Melanie was engrossed. "Why'd you break up?" She anticipated some ancient Greek misfortune.

He sniffled. "She wanted to get married and I, well, I'm a divorce attorney."

"That's it?" Melanie was at the edge of her seat, disappointed at the lackluster end to a fabulous romance.

"Listen, you have no idea what I see on a daily basis – shattered lives. I can't do that to Clare, I love her. Don't you think I want all the things these other people wanted when they said 'I do'? Look where it got them ... screaming over Tupperware."

Melanie studied Dennis, his lost, weepy eyes that looked as dead as any corpse she'd ever seen. "You're making a mistake."

"Excuse me?' he asked, clearly offended.

"If you're both in love then what do you have to lose? You're being an ass."

Melanie picked up the less ugly piece of fish. The cold slimy meat slid down her throat whole. She suppressed her gag reflex.

Dennis sat with his mouth agape for a moment. "You women are all romantics. I can't marry, I'm a realist."

"I'm not a romantic," Melanie clarified, insulted by the charge.

"Do you believe there is true, everlasting love, like in fairy tales?" he asked with sarcasm.

Instantly she knew her answer, without a doubt. She did, somewhere, at least she hoped. She stayed quiet.

"My point. Marriage is an unattainable dream that ultimately only leads to disappointment."

Melanie shrugged, "Okay, then, stay stubborn. But do everyone a favor and quit crying."

She wondered if she pushed him too far – they finished their dinner in silence. Melanie hadn't hated the pink stuff but she wasn't a sushi girl. She liked her dinner cooked.

"Listen, I'm sorry, I was out of line," Melanie said when the silence stretched into the car ride home. *Like I'm one to be giving relationship advice, anyway.*

"No, you got me thinking," Dennis rubbed his ear lobe. "Maybe you're right, maybe Clare's right. What if…"

He stopped and Melanie smiled.

"What if?"

"Good luck, Dennis."

Melanie grinned as she stepped out of his car and jogged up the walkway to her parents' front door.

"How was your date?" asked an eager Rita.

"It was good," Melanie said, dropping onto the comfortable couch.

Rita beamed. "Will you be seeing Dennis again?"

Melanie sighed. "No, he's going back to his girlfriend."

Rita froze.

"Don't worry, Mom, you have six more chances." Melanie hopped off the couch, patted her mom on the back and raced up the stairs.

Rita would simmer overnight and Melanie knew there'd be consequences in the morning. But for now she laughed at the irony, or was it karma? Either way, she was amused at how the world had a way of kicking you right in the ass.

But the next morning Rita Ward's determination had returned in full force. The woman wasn't going down without a fight.

"Of course it's a disappointment, Dear, but this is only Round One," she said, coffee cup in hand.

By 11:15 am Melanie found herself driving her dad's 1972 metallic green Chevy Nova up Interstate 5, heading toward her date with Phil Malone, a grocery store manager. Sunday traffic was light and Melanie easily made it to the mall by noon for her lunch date. Pacing back and forth by the north side entrance, Melanie looked expectantly at every single male.

"Hi, you must be Melanie since there isn't anyone else loitering."

"Hi. Phil, right?" she said, with a polite chuckle.

"Yeah, Phil Malone. Sorry I'm late, I stopped at the store on my way over." He pointed across the street to a huge supermarket buzzing with activity.

Melanie nodded. "It's a big place."

"I work there and I live over there." He shifted his index finger toward a complex of beige apartment buildings skirting the edge of the asphalt parking lot of his store.

"Convenient."

"My drinking problem got worse after the divorce and my license was suspended, oh, what, seven months ago. Let's go inside."

He held open the tinted glass door as she processed her first impression of Phil. He looked normal, a typical man in his mid-forties with an extra 20 pounds around his waist, and receding dark hair that barely shaded his scalp. An enormous key ring jingled from a belt loop of his black Dockers and his black leather Rockports were scuffed.

The bright yellow booths of the food court were hard plastic and didn't give when she sat with her six-inch submarine sandwich, chips and a drink.

"I'm trying to lose some weight," Phil said, patting his stomach. "I saw that commercial about the guy who lost, like, 200 pounds eating this stuff."

Melanie wiped the glob of mayo from the corner of her mouth.

"So, how do you know Jenny?"

"The ex-wife and I used to socialize with Jenny and Ryan. She's a nice girl." Phil shifted his weight and sat up straight. "Jenny tells me that you're from D.C."

"Well, I'm from San Diego but I've lived in D.C. for 10 years."

Phil pinched down the end of his bread so his stuffed turkey sandwich would fit into the oval opening of his mouth. Melanie made a mental note. *Eating is not an attractive activity.*

"What are you doing on a blind date? You obviously have no problem getting your own dates, and I'm certain that I'm not what you're looking for, so why all this?" he asked, opening his arms in a wide gesture.

"Honestly," she looked him straight in the eye, "I don't date. I work a lot and there's no time for..." she mimicked his "all this" motion.

"Okay, okay," he repeated softly as she tried to explain.

"So, I thought it was time to give it a go, get back into the game."

"Okay, I can relate to that. It's been 18 months since my divorce and this is the first date I've been on. But if I'd have known what you looked like I'd have said no when Jen asked me to go out with you."

Melanie felt her eye muscle twitch.

"What I mean to say is that I wanted to ease into dating with someone more on my level," Melanie winced, as he continued, "you know, someone who's not so attractive and has let herself go a bit, someone who might think I'm a catch. My shrink says that I have a self-esteem problem." He licked his thumb and pressed it onto the potato chip crumbs.

Melanie wondered how much his therapist charged for that piece of information. "I'm sure you'll be able to find what you're looking for."

"Well, I had thought that we could maybe, would you, I mean only if you want, but I thought we could see a movie? The one with Bruce Willis opened on Friday."

The movie theater was located within the mall, and therefore within walking distance of Phil's life.

"Yeah, I haven't been to a movie in a long time." She could already taste the hot buttered popcorn.

◤

"How was your date with Phil?" Rita asked.

"All right," Melanie said with a shrug.

She was a little more than satisfied knowing the dates were bombing through no fault of hers.

"Will you be seeing him again?"

Her mother's sticky-sweet voice tried to sound casual, but Melanie knew that Rita was dying to know about Phil Malone. Melanie eased gently into an explanation of why things didn't work out with the grocery store manager. Her mother's eyes narrowed with each sentence until the beam from her eyes burned into Melanie's throat.

"What?" Melanie asked incredulously.

"You're doing this to spite me."

Melanie gave a sarcastic laugh. "Yeah, Mom, that's what I'm doing."

"You are doing this on purpose." Her mom stomped into kitchen. Melanie followed.

"Don't get mad at me, this isn't my fault." She tried not to get angry. "You think I like being rejected by men I didn't even want to meet?"

"There!" Rita pointed her perfectly manicured index finger in Melanie's face. "See, you're giving off bad vibes to these men and they can feel it." She turned and left the kitchen.

She's crazy, Melanie thought and reluctantly prepared for her evening date.

Third on the list was Lee Monte, a mechanic, a son of dad's friend.

Wearing her black dress again, Melanie sat on the white upholstery of Lee's souped up '66 Mustang. He'd restored her bumper to bumper, painted her a bright red and named her Rose, after his mother. Rose, the car, was pristine. She was all he talked about on the way to the pizza parlor, where he ordered an extra-large meat lover's pie. Melanie would have understood if Lee was a big guy, but he wasn't. At 5'5" he couldn't have weighed more than 130 pounds. But after Melanie ate two slices and the crust off a third, Lee polished off the rest.

"Do you work out?" Melanie sipped her soda as she watched Lee finish the slice without the crust.

He looked her with a gleam in his eyes. "I do. Would you like to see how?"

Melanie was taken aback for an instant, disturbed but curious. She agreed.

Lee drove rapidly across town to a two-story building. Colored lights lined the building and she could hear the music coming from inside.

"You dance," she said, trying to picture Lee breaking loose on the dance floor.

"I *salsa!*" he said excitedly. "I was turned on to it about eight months ago and I can't seem to get enough." He had parked the car and was running to Melanie's side to open her door. A mock gentleman, she knew his motivation was to protect Rose's door from being slammed.

Inside the club, the cigar smoke was potent and the waves of laughter only caused the band to raise its volume in a competition of sorts, music verses conversation. Neither won.

The women wore colorful dresses that hugged tight from shoulders to thigh, where the fabric flared out dramatically. Melanie's conventional black dress was out of place. Passing by tables she could detect a variety of Spanish dialects.

Lee stopped at an already-crowded table and squeezed in an extra chair. The group adjusted and by the end two women were sitting on one man's lap. It was very cozy.

"Would you like to try to dance?" Lee asked her over the music.

Melanie nodded. Although her dress was the wrong color it had the makings of a fabulous salsa dress, a low neckline and the skirt that fluttered when she spun. They had stepped off to the side to practice a bit, Lee showing her the steps and counting, letting her get the feel of the rhythm.

"Pretty good, pretty good," he assured her. "Now, see that woman in yellow?" he asked, glancing towards the dance floor.

"Yes."

The woman wore a thick layer of makeup and her blood-red lips matched her talon-like nails. In her long, wavy brown hair, sprayed stiff, was a yellow flower.

"See her attitude?"

Bitch, Melanie thought. "Yes."

"You do that while we dance, OK?"

Melanie smiled. She could do that.

The band was starting a new set as she and Lee made their way to the dance floor. In her heels she towered over Lee but he didn't seem to notice. Starting off slow so that Melanie could gain her confidence and absorb the beat of the music, Melanie kept her poise as they danced. Even when she flubbed it she kept on with the attitude. They danced until closing.

"I haven't had so much fun in years," Melanie said, rolling down Rose's window to enjoy the cool breeze.

Coughing from the smoke in the dance hall, she refilled her lungs with fresh air.

"You know, if we practice every day I think we could be ready for the tournament in two weeks."

Melanie tosseled her hair out the window, trying to rid herself of the odor that had soaked into her pores. Lee, hyped up on caffeine, talked nonstop. He'd worked out a plan – they'd meet every afternoon at a dance studio where Marcus would train them.

"Look, Lee, I did have a wonderful time dancing, but training for a competition is not how I want to spend the rest of my vacation," Melanie told him when they parked in front of her house.

He tried feverishly to change her mind.

"We could win. I believe we have a shot." He seemed astounded that she would pass up an opportunity like this. "Winning a tournament is an honor."

"I'm sure it is, but I'm just not interested right now. Thank you very much. I had a great time." Leaving the car door open, she jogged hastily into the house.

It was past 2 a.m., and her throat and eyes burned from the dense cigar smoke of the dance hall. She showered and went to bed.

Another one down.

CHAPTER 10

The next morning marked the return of her daily jogs and her date with Bruce's friend, Ty, a musician. He played lead guitar in a local band. Melanie called for reinforcements – she needed new clothes and Carla was the expert.

Through the years she had kept contact with Carla, even though her prim and proper ways had exaggerated themselves when Ted was elected to Congress. Now, Carla didn't utter a word unless it was politically correct and well thought out.

"I'm really glad you called. I haven't seen you much since you've been back," Carla said as she drove to her favorite boutique.

"I've been on my blind date marathon. Tonight I'm meeting a musician at the club where he plays and I don't have any idea what to wear."

"Sweetie, you don't have to enlighten me on that one. I thought you'd never wear out those old jeans," Carla said, linking onto Melanie's arm and sounding too much like Rita. "Well, you're in good hands now."

A lunch and 42 shops later Melanie, had doubled her wardrobe and had been re-educated on the U.S. electoral process. Carla spoke of nothing but Ted's upcoming run for a second term. His years in office had taken its toll on Carla's personality.

Later that evening, after dinner at a 24-hour drive-through Mexican restaurant, Melanie met Ty at a bar near the naval base, wearing her new tight dark blue jeans, spiked heels and a sleeveless white cotton tank top. She circled the full parking lot twice before finding a spot between a big-ass truck and a hotrod. The club was filled with off duty military men in their twenties, all of whom seemed to be sporting crew cuts and holding a drink and a cigarette in one hand. Their muscular arms, covered with tattoos, wrapped possesively around the waist of their woman.

"Are you Melanie Ward?" shouted the woman from behind the bar.

Melanie stepped closer, nodding.

"Ty's waiting at that table for you." She pointed to a table up front by the stage. "What can I get you to drink?"

"A beer."

The cold bottle was still wet from the ice as she went to meet Ty. He was the brother of a friend of Bruce. That could mean anything.

"Hi, Melanie, I'm Ty."

He was very young with curly brown hair that reached his shoulders, full lips and a cleft chin. His loose satin shirt was unbuttoned, exposing a rock-solid set of abs above the belted jeans that sat low on his waist. A thorny tattoo armband wrapped around a well-developed bicep and Melanie sensed she was being undressed with his sexy, dark brown eyes.

They sat at a small table next to the stage before his set. He dragged a chair up too close to her and made himself comfortable.

"Busy place," Melanie said to the over-confident youth.

A boisterous group gathered, pulling tables and chairs together and ordering pitchers of beer.

"My band is pretty well known."

"So, Ty, are you even old enough to be in a bar?" Melanie asked, her eyes starting to burn from the smoke.

"I'm almost 24," his pearly whites glistened and his eyes danced down her blouse.

Melanie laughed uncomfortably. Ty was more than handsome and he knew it, he worked it. Sitting close so their legs pressed up against each other, he draped his arm around the back of her chair and leaned in to her ear to speak. The scent of his musk mixed with a hint of pot was, surprisingly, not completely unpleasant.

Melanie was enjoying the attention. She played along, flattered by the advances of the sexually driven Adonis.

During his sets Ty kept eye contact with Melanie. It wasn't sweet, it was erotic, and by midnight Melanie was, humorously, considering her options.

He joined her after his set and his sweaty closeness had lost its appeal. No longer was he musky, he just stunk. Melanie decided to make her break.

"You have a great band," Melanie said, ready to leave. "I had fun."

"But I thought we'd hook up after this gig, you know, go back to my place. Tumble around the sheets."

Melanie smiled. "Sounds romantic, but you need a shower and I'm old enough to be your, well your big sister." She stood and he blocked her path. "Ty," she said, her eyebrows raised. She could feel his horny determination.

He flashed a smile before he put his lips on hers, pulling her up against his hot, wet, bare chest. She pushed his chest without much force causing him to dig his fingers into her back. His lips were powerful, confident and they maneuvered the strength right out of her bones.

The crowd enjoyed the show as they hooted and clapped.

Wow, nice kiss, Melanie shivered, inhaling, stepping away.

"Sure you won't stay?" Ty asked, in a full pout with a damn arrogant look of satisfaction stretched across his smooth face.

"Sorry, kid."

Melanie felt flushed walking to the parking lot. Her body was on fire – lit up from Ty's lust, youth, zeal, and from his kiss. Her body stirred. A man's arms had embraced her hard and hungry, and she could still feel his lips and tongue.

༺

It was a tough night. Restlessly, she tried to force her desires back where they belonged, locked away and forgotten. But Ty's passion lingered through the next day when she was finally able to spend some time with her friends.

Excitedly she dressed in one of her new outfits, a sheer light-blue blouse, skirt, a pair of fine Italian shoes and her favorite item – a camel-colored fitted leather jacket. She was thrilled to feel like a college student getting ready for a night out with the girls.

Jenny and Carla were both married but in totally different situations. Jenny was a stay-at-home mom with three kids while Carla and Ted – *now Congressman Bradley* – had more of a business relationship than a marriage. Trish had not married and was always saying how lucky she was to be free. Still as outspoken as ever. Melanie's relationship with her friends had fragmented through the years, each owning their part but Melanie taking most of the brunt.

"What a relief to be going out with you guys again, I've missed you." Melanie hopped into the front passenger seat of Carla's large SUV.

Settling into the soft leather seat, Melanie let out a huge sigh.

"How've the dates been going?"

Melanie rolled her eyes. "About as well as could be expected.

Oh, and by the way, thanks, Jen, for setting me up with Phil."

"You didn't like him?" Jen grinned.

"Well, within the first two minutes he tells me his license has been suspended and he's divorced. But, gee he sounded like a winner."

"Yeah, he's gotten a little chatty since he started therapy."

"Let me just say that you will *not* have that problem with Jason," Trish said, leaning forward from the back seat.

"I did good, too," Carla added at the stoplight. "Nick's a pilot, although I think he's been divorced once or twice."

Melanie closed her eyes and leaned her head against the headrest, instantly tired of this conversation.

Carla's tone was defensive. "You aren't going to find a man your age who hasn't been married."

"Hey, she's not old," Trish countered. "Besides, why does he have to be her age? Look at her, she's hot. Mel, you could definitely catch a younger man. It's the *in* thing, anyway."

Melanie smiled, thinking about Ty.

"Speaking of young," Melanie started her tale ending with the kiss.

"Oh, my God, you should have slept with him," Trish laughed.

"No, you did the right thing."

"Jesus, Car, you're with us, not those judgmental prudes you have to schmooze for Ted's campaign," Trish said, giving Melanie a look of frustration.

"So, you think Melanie should just jump into bed with anyone?"

"I think you all need to lighten up and get laid. When was the last time you had sex? Mel? Car? Jen?"

The car dropped into a dead silence.

"I rest my case."

Sitting at a corner table of a Mexican restaurant that had just opened, the girls ordered a pitcher of Margaritas.

Carla lifted her glass of ginger ale, "I will try to be less puritanical."

"I will try to have more sex." Melanie raised her glass.

Trish lifted hers. "I will try to keep my mouth shut."

"And I will try and put up with the rest of you," Jenny said, clinking her glass to the other three.

"To friends." They all drank.

"I can't believe your mom tricked us all into this whole mega-blind-dating spree. She actually had me believing you were a lesbian," Jenny said. "She's good."

"I have to confess that I think it was a good idea and way past due," Trish added. "You needed to get off that old, ugly plaid couch."

Jenny laughed as she dipped a chip into the green salsa.

"Okay, I'll agree that I needed a kick in the butt. But what you don't understand is that I am happy with the way things are right now. Besides, don't you think an intervention was a tad melodramatic?"

Taking a sip from her drink Melanie licked the clumpy rock salt from her lips. She could hear Jenny talking but it was the man standing with the hostess who captured her attention. He was tall with dark, wavy hair and a strong jaw line, wearing black trousers and a white dress shirt with the first two buttons open.

She stared, taking in his every detail: the square shoulders, the full lips that stretched perfectly across his face into a broad smile. She imagined his kiss and didn't doubt that it could exceed expectations. Carried away in her daydream she looked up to his eyes – which were looking directly at her.

She sucked in an embarrassing gasp – he'd caught her openly gawking. Her heart skipped and she could feel the warmth of his smile from 10 feet away. She nodded sheepihsly at him, ashamed, before turning her attention back to her table, trying to act undisturbed by his presence.

Torturing Melanie further, the hostess seated him facing her at a nearby table.

Just a quick glance, she looked up cautiously, and again he was looking right at her. His mysterious eyes caused goose bumps to rise on her flesh.

Damn it, this is Ty's fault! Melanie scolded silently. *Mel get a grip, have you never seen a handsome man before?*

Ty's lips touching hers had begun a chain reaction beneath her skin and now she was foolishly being carried away by the marvelously green eyes of a stranger.

Angry at her own weakness, Melanie reengaged in the debate ensuing around her.

"Mel, do you think you'll see any of these guys again or not?" Jenny asked for a second time. "What's wrong with you?"

"Nothing," Melanie answered quickly, "These dates are purely to satisfy my mom, not me."

"I told you," Trish exclaimed.

"But," Melanie hesitated. "Maybe…" she hemmed.

"Really?" They said in unison, surprised.

"Wow, your mom's trick worked."

"Some of the dates have been kind of fun."

Melanie's eyes shot to the man sitting only feet away. Again he caught her glance, *damn!* He smiled and she tightened her mouth in a scowl, wishing he'd stop looking at her. Her desire was granted when the hostess escorted a modelesque woman with flowing blonde hair to the table where he was seated. He stood as she approached and Melanie, stealthily, kept track of the manner between the two. The woman on closer inspection was as beautiful as her first impression although her dress, a light-blue satin gown, seemed too fancy for the casual atmosphere – it was hardly a flaw.

The girls, excluding Carla, indulged in a second pitcher of strawberry margaritas.

The arrival of the woman acted as a repellent. Melanie was mostly able to keep her eyes and her mind at her own table. The alcohol had loosened the atmosphere and she enjoyed her friends while savoring her cheese enchiladas with a side of rice and beans topped with a layer of sliced lettuce and goat cheese. But even as she ignored the couple she was also painfully conscious of her every move.

When the bill was paid there was nothing left for her to do, she looked directly at him and memorized his face.

"Where to now?" Trish asked, as they headed out the door to the cool night breeze.

"Shoot, I forgot my jacket. I'll be right back," Melanie said, running back into the restaurant.

The excuse sounded fake even to her, but she hadn't left it intentionally, had she?

A little tipsy from the tequila, Melanie stopped short, almost passing by her jacket still slung over the high-backed chair. The move startled a waiter carrying a single glass of red wine on his tray.

Melanie gasped, the waiter gasped. The glass was airborne and heading directly for the handsome man she'd been fantasizing about all evening. Without thinking Melanie lurched forward, quickly catching the stem. The wine splash down the front of his shirt, and horridly, at the end it was she who held the empty culprit.

He'd tried to get out of the way, standing only few feet in front of her with the right side of his shirt, from shoulder to the rolled-up cuff, stained.

"Oh, my God, I am *so* sorry," She bit down tightly on the flesh inside her mouth and slowly raised her guilty eyes.

She looked up into the greenest eyes she'd ever seen. A short gasp escaped her lips and she held her breath.

"I usually have to go out with a woman before she's throwing her drink at me," he said, a small smile forming.

His voice was deep, *absolutely luxurious*, and his ease immediately comforted her.

"It was an accident," she felt compelled to explain as she stepped closer and reached for his arm.

Her heart jolted as her fingers closed around the tight muscle beneath his shirt.

"I know," he laughed a low bass note.

Melanie was absorbed by every feature: dark hair framing tan skin, brilliant emerald eyes, salmon lips against white teeth.

"Club soda, I need club soda, now!" yelled the woman in blue, startling Melanie out of her revelry.

"Yes ma'am." The waiter scurried off.

"There is wine on my dress," she glared at Melanie, punctuating every syllable.

"I'm so sorry." Melanie tried to locate any stain on the fancy dress.

"Someone is going to pay for this," screeched the beautiful woman.

"Daria, calm down," said the man.

"Hello, I'm Mr. Gomez, the manager. I'm sorry…"

"Look at this," she interrupted, hotly pointing out a discoloration on the fabric.

"Daria, it's all right."

His tone was not as patient as it had been. Daria seemed to have noticed it, too, because she quieted down and gritted her teeth as Mr. Gomez rubbed a spot on her dress and apologized.

"I'm sorry," Melanie said, quietly to the man in merlot, writing her number on the back of a coaster.

"It shouldn't be a big deal," he said calmly, his smile crinkling the edges of his eyes.

He was handsome and behind the wood scent of the wine he smelled vaguely of rosemary.

"Well, this is my number I'll be more than happy to replace … whatever." She looked toward Daria then handed him the coaster.

"Wait, what's your name Ms. 202?"

"Melanie," she smiled and kept walking.

Once outside again, she pulled out the glass she'd hidden beneath her jacket. And without missing a step tapped it against the painted cinderblock wall, letting the shards fall into the groundcover. Melanie shook her head. She hadn't consciously taken the glass – it was instinct. Leaving fingerprints was always a bad idea.

Irrational, Melanie knew.

She said nothing of the incident to her friends.

Early the next morning with her radio strapped to her arm, her phone hooked to her shorts and her hair in a ponytail, Melanie followed the coast south.

It was June and summer was in full swing. Bright umbrellas speckled the beach at 7:30 on a weekday morning. Melanie walked barefoot along the shore. The cool water washed over her feet, erasing her footsteps. She had nowhere to be and all day to get there, and was not about to spend another day scrapbooking with her mom and Cheryl.

The jealously of her sister-in-law's relationship with her mother came unsuspected. Rita and Cheryl spent hours together, picking out papers and choosing scissor designs to create a "life" album for Olivia. Cheryl was calling Rita "Mom" and they palled around like teenagers. Melanie had joined in for two days, on the third they had moved over to Cheryl's house. Melanie was hurt. Too much spare time had always been a problem. She'd attributed her intense, hard-driven focus to her inability to cope with emotion. Whenever feelings went awry Melanie found herself at work, putting 110 percent of her attention into things she could control.

You have way too much time to think and now ... now you're starting to feel?

Feel. The word left a bad taste in her mouth. Heated blame was aimed at Ty for her sudden surge of hormones.

Seven years of celibacy, then some hot kid lays a wet one on you and you get weak in the knees. But the truth was she had been "feeling" since Hawaii.

Effortlessly her daydream flowed to the man with the green eyes and she wondered how the rest of his evening had played out. Her thoughts swirled like the tide, sweeping in and flooding her senses, only to be washed away by the arrival of the next.

Her phone rang. In an exceptionally bored moment last week she'd changed her ring to the William Tell Overture.

"Hello?'

"I'm calling for Melanie."

"Yup, speaking," she said, nearly trampled by three boys that only had eyes for the water.

"Hi, this is Adam. You probably know me better as the guy wearing the red wine."

"The man in merlot," her smile reaching through her voice.

His laugh was deep and Melanie's self-pity vanished.

"Yeah, I guess that's me."

"I was just thinking about you," she blushed. "I wondered about the rest of your evening."

Melanie walked to dry sand and sat while she listened to Adam talk about driving Daria home.

"Your home?"

Her home.

Melanie was feeling sick, and she realized his voice had awakened a confused rabble of fluttering butterflies.

"I thought if you didn't have plans for tomorrow we could do something."

Her heart skipped.

"I'm free during the day but I've got…" She hesitated then tossed him the information. "I have a blind date in the evening."

"A blind date, huh? So, you're not married with half a dozen kids. That's good to know."

His voice was low and soft.

"What about you and the vocal blonde?"

Melanie closed her eyes letting his deep husky voice soak into her skin.

"Nope, there's no one," he said slowly. "What else do you want to know?"

Melanie bit her lip, giddy.

"What else do I want to know?" Melanie repeated thinking of how to answer. *I want to know why your eyes are so green and why my heart goes into overdrive just thinking about you.* "How about a confession? Anything you wouldn't normally tell someone on the first phone call." *Sure,* she thought, *it was easy to be brave over the phone.*

"Hmm ... all right. You have the most beautiful smile I've ever seen, and when I saw you last night I had to stop myself from kissing you."

Melanie froze, barely managing to get the words out of her throat. "Well, that's pretty good."

Unconsciously, she bit her lip.

The noisy beach was forgotten while they spoke and she concentrated on being charming, getting lost in conversation. That is, until a woman in a one-piece bathing suit bellowed at her two toddler sons and stormed to the water to catch the mischievous duo, who were streaking naked to avoid being lathered with sunscreen.

"Where are you?" Adam asked.

"At the beach among thousands of my closest friends."

"We've been talking for 20 minutes. How 'bout I meet you there and we'll have lunch?"

"Where do you work that you can take off to lunch with someone you don't know?"

"I work in a restaurant. How about lunch?"

"You'd never find me."

"I'll find you. What beach?"

Thirty minutes later Melanie waited for Adam outside a Denny's. She begged a woman in the bathroom to borrow some lipstick and ran her fingers through her hair.

"You should keep the hat on," suggested the woman with the lipstick.

"Ya think?"

She nodded and Melanie pulled her hair back and slipped her ponytail through the back of her baseball cap. The parking lot was a stream of moving vehicles, a constant trading of spots – one car out and another in line to take its place accompanied by horn blowing and hand gestures. Nervously she traveled across the curbs, balancing on and hurdling over the short barriers.

She recognized him cutting through the lot from a distance. If she'd been savvy she'd have waited to let him approach but instead they met awkwardly between two towering SUVs.

Adam looked like he'd stepped right off a fashion shoot, in a pair of loose shorts and a white T-shirt that fit snugly across his shoulders. It was a different look but suited him well.

"Hi," he greeted, as he took off the silver framed sunglasses, exposing his beautiful eyes. She exhaled and froze as he bent to give her a quick hug.

"I'd have worn a nicer tank top had I known we were going to meet," Melanie said, looking down at her outfit starting with the old running shoes that looked even grungier than they had this morning.

"You look nice. Sporty."

"Thank you," she said, thinking, *for saying the right thing*.

He was taller than she'd recalled. She barely reached the top of his shoulders.

"Are you hungry? There's a great hot dog stand a couple of blocks away."

"Is it the restaurant where you work?"

Adam laughed. "No."

The hot dog lean-to was set up on the sand's edge, along a row of shabby businesses that included equipment rentals and a swimsuit/ T-shirt shop. The entire structure looked unstable, and Melanie wondered how it stood up against the strong Pacific winds.

The beach was packed, uncomfortably crowded. In another hour every square foot would be occupied for miles, too many people with too much bare skin smeared in coconut oil. The hot dog shack had about a dozen tables, each with four chairs and a red and white umbrella. Melanie and Adam stood in line with two-dozen others.

"So, Adam, at the restaurant, what do you do? Waiter? Bus boy?"

"Chef."

"Chef?" Melanie repeated as they arrived at the order window where two men in white paper hats served specialty dogs. "Aren't hot dogs against some culinary Hippocratic oath? 'I will never injure or give poison in the form of various animal scraps to my diners'?"

He laughed. "What's wrong with an occasional deviation?"

"Hey Adam, how ya been?" said one of the men from behind the counter, his little white cap clinging to a sparse clump of thinning hair.

"Hi Joe. I'd like you to meet my friend Melanie," he said, his hand flat on the small of her back.

"Nice to meet ya. So ya going for the colossal with the works? What about you?" Joe asked, gesturing to Melanie.

"She's going to have the same," Adam said.

"Hey, Ervin, get Adam his drinks at no charge."

"Thanks, Joe."

By the time Ervin got their two cups of Coke and Adam paid the bill, Joe had slid over their dogs and was onto the next customer. Two seats opened up at a table for four and they enjoyed the comforts of aluminum chairs.

"Are you ready?" Adam asked, slipping a waxed paper boat off the tray.

Somewhere beneath a mound of chili sprinkled with cheddar cheese was an entire hot dog and bun. As she looked around at the other people to learn how to tackle this beast, a chunk of the chili slid off the dog and onto the wax paper wrapper.

Adam picked up his dog and took a huge bite.

He nodded. "The best."

Melanie smiled. How could she eat this and retain a sense of mystery about her? She couldn't. Adam watched, grinning, as she picked up her hot dog and took a bite. She nodded her approval while using the side of her hand to wipe a glob of chili from her lip. Adam handed her a napkin. He'd taken his sunglasses off and their eyes locked. For that moment she felt she could read his mind and him hers. He was thinking about kissing her and her lips tingled in anticipation.

"Maybe I should have told you a different confession."

"No, I liked that one. How about another?"

"Another? All right, but then it's my turn to do the asking."

"Fair enough."

"Something about me, right? Okay, well, I've been looking at some property in L.A. to open my own restaurant. It's a great building, old brick with lots of windows, a decent parking lot..."

His statement dropped off as he thought about the potential. If it was possible for him to become more attractive Melanie thought it had happened right at that instant.

He appologize for zoning out momentarily, then explained. "I'm meeting with the agent next week and I've been working out the offer for the past three days."

"Wow, you don't need to apologize. I think it's great."

"It's a risk, but I'm really excited about it. So, now it's your turn, tell me something about you."

And that's why this was a dangerous game. Her mind flipped through the possibilities. She wanted something with substance but was trying to avoid looking like an idiot. Melanie struggled with her minimal options.

"Okay, then, I've lived in the same apartment for eight years but I still don't call it home. I'm never there," she said, with a tinge of fear. It was not a habit to share information about her life with anyone, even more difficult was that she was telling the truth. But she continued, trying to make it light. "I don't cook. My fridge is littered with old Chinese food boxes and maybe a moldy cube of cheese or a bottle of water. I clean it out only when I remember I have a refrigerator and that's usually when I'm placing another half empty box of Kung Pao inside."

"Well, it was nice meeting you," he stood and shook her hand.

Melanie laughed.

"You leaving?" asked a boy carrying a tray with three giant dogs.

"Sorry, buddy, but you can take that empty seat," Adam said.

"Thanks." He was a skinny, shirtless teenager with wet swim trunks that hung indecently off his slim hips.

"What kind of work do you do, Melanie?" Adam asked, after the kid settled in and consumed one of his hot dogs in two bites.

"I set up communications systems."

"What does that mean?"

"It means I travel to third-world countries and set up phone, internet and satellite systems for companies so they can capitalize on the cheap labor."

"Noble."

"Don't judge," Melanie said, raising her eyebrow.

"Okay, and for fun?" His smile captivating, even as his eyes laughed at her.

"I set up communication systems," Melanie smiled, idiotically. "I don't go out too much unless it's work-related. Believe it or not I love my job."

Melanie sat across from Adam, the first man she'd been interested in in years, and now she was thrilled to be talking about work.

You're sick, seriously demented – have you forgotten you quit?

"Would you want to walk to the water?" she asked, wanting nothing more than a distraction.

"Yeah, are you finished?" he asked, tossing their trash into the garbage.

The kid was downing his third dog when they walked toward the mayhem on the beach.

"How about we go somewhere less popular. My car is just around the corner."

Around the corner and through a narrow alley Adam stopped at a black BMW X5.

"Nice car. I had no idea chefs were so highly compensated."

"Only the good ones." He opened her door and waited as she settled in on the soft leather seat.

The radio was off, though it was one of her tests; Dennis had played a classical CD, Phil had no car, Lee's "Rose" had echoed Gloria Estefan and Ty, well, he had his own band, she was dying to find out what Adam's radio was tuned to.

"Do you mind?" She asked pointing to the CD case in the center console.

"Go ahead."

She felt him watching her as she flipped the pages. Bob Dylan, Bob Dylan and more Dylan. Who knew the guy had put out so many CDs?

"Approve?"

"Late '70s classic rock and mostly from an artist I can't even understand," she laughed. "I guess it's better than Britney or a collection of Broadway Musicals."

"Okay, what's on your iPod?"

"Christmas songs, only Christmas songs. It's my favorite time of year," she teased, to avoid a lie. There was no music on her iPod, just languages, biographies, and non-fiction psychological insight books. Who would want to date that?

The traffic from the beach spilled over onto the streets, the short drive to the bay longer than expected. Adam pulled off the congested street at the park.

"Can I ask about the woman you were with last night?"

"Daria is our hostess. I like to check out the new restaurants but I don't like to go alone." They settled down on the grass beneath the shade of a tall elm. "And what about your blind date?"

Oops.

"My mom's idea." She skimmed over her current situation, leaving out blocks of information.

"I can't wait to meet your mom."

The thought caused her heart to beat double time. Adam in the same room as Rita? The thought was horrorfying and yet possible. She was liking this man more and more. He was intriguing, handsome and funny, and if she were looking then this would be exactly the right guy for her.

CHAPTER 11

Memories swept in like a hurricane the moment he walked into the apartment building. An odor from his past that he hadn't noticed at the time, a mixture of burnt bread and cigar, caught in his lungs. Taking two steps at a time, he climbed to the empty apartment on the third floor. The scent faded as he climbed, but it had already provoked thoughts that he'd just as soon forget.

Distracted, he assembled his gun.

He remembered the boy, 19, in pain and full of regret, in the days leading up to the end of innocence. The boy amid "friends" in the living room of a brothel, pressured and wanting to try the drugs that were set out before him. Women giggled in the background, standing in doorways, ugly women and beautiful girls in scant lingerie. Leading men into the various bedrooms.

He had become a regular client but the drugs were new.

The killer of today closed his eyes and watched the boy, wanting to stop him before evil engulfed his mind and body. The killer wanted to shout at the boy to run, but in a well of depression, the boy could only see darkness and no longer cared if he lived or died.

The killer opened his eyes, leaving the boy to make all the wrong decisions.

The scope was set and adjusted. He sat on the metal folding chair next to the window and waited for the judge, a man in his mid-sixties with a full head of silver hair, a thick neck and an unwavering belief in justice.

Routinely, the killer didn't know his marks, but this was different – a high-profile case involving brothers from Colombia. Drug lords with money and power. Closing his left eye, he waited for the judge, who stuck religiously to his rigid schedule and who would leave his New York City brownstone for the last time.

In a bight blue jogging suit, the judge stretched at the top of the steps, looked in both directions before grabbing his chest and gasping his final breath.

CHAPTER 12

"Melanie, are you all right?"

"Yeah, I was just thinking," she said, breaking from her trance.

"Well, your date is at the door. Didn't you hear the bell?"

Melanie looked at her list to remind her of who the date was tonight. Nick Brody, a pilot, Carla's selection.

"Hi, Nick Brody," he said with a strong handshake.

"Nice to meet you." Melanie quickly ushered him out the door, not wanting anyone to linger too long with her mother so near.

Nick wore dark jeans and a leather jacket and his short white hair curled at the ends and looked bright against his tan skin.

"I'm taking you to the hottest place in town," he said as he drove faster than the speed limit. "My co-pilot had these reservations but wasn't able to use them so he gave them to me." Nick looked over at Melanie, then dropped his gaze down to her leg.

She did a quick check. *Yup, too much thigh exposed.* She shrugged, feeling generous.

The restaurant was quaint, with queen palms and a homey porch welcoming them inside. The outdoor tables were lit with tiny white lights twinkling in the trees overhead. An antique rust color warmed the dinning area, with painted grape vines climbing up to the bamboo ceiling fans. Tea lights flickered in votives on each table.

Nick spoke with the hostess and within minutes they were seated at a candlelit table for two.

Nick ordered drinks – a gin and tonic for him and a red wine for her – calling the waitress, "Honey," as he'd done with the hostess who seated them.

"The food is supposed to be outstanding," Nick said, his eyes following a woman's rear as she passed their table. He looked back to Melanie without a hint of apology. "Did Carla tell you I'm retired military?" She shook her head.

"She said you were divorced at least once."

"Twice. I flew for the Air Force for more than 20 years. Have you ever been up where the captain sits?"

She shook her head, lying.

"There's nothing like the power of the cockpit," Nick said, lifting his glass.

Melanie ignored his play on words, wink and the smirk on his smug face.

Nick spoke only of Nick and his adventures at 35,000 feet. He guzzled down three lowballs before their meal arrived – an array of pasta, grilled salmon and fresh vegetables.

Because of his monologue, Nick took twice as long as Melanie to finish his meal. She sipped her wine and was relieved when he declined dessert. Was there anything left to know about Nick Brody?She wondered and hoped to God he'd finish. But he continued on about how women love the thrill of sex during a flight. It was enough, Melanie stood. Nick dropped a couple of bills on the table and eagerly followed her into the cool night air.

"You'll have to thank your co-pilot for me. The food was outstanding."

"You have to thank me first," Nick said, licking his bottom lip as he opened her car door. "Would you like to get a drink?"

It was still early and her momentary hesitation was a moment too long.

"My place," Nick said, his fleshy cheeks rising with the upturn of his mouth. "I thought we could sit by the pool and get to know each other better. You could thank me there."

Melanie groaned, "You are incredible." She didn't mean it as a compliment.

He shrugged his shoulders. "We're two single, unattached adults. What's the harm? Besides, I'm on an early flight to Heathrow in the morning."

"You're right," Melanie smiled and shut the car door. "I'm over 30 with no prospects of a husband … and I'm ovulating. Sounds perfect. I'm ready, what about you, *Nick*?"

"That's okay with me, Honey, I've been fixed," he smiled.

She laughed. "You're an ass."

It was afternoon and the sun was still hidden behind an overcast summer sky. A breeze chilled the air and the whitecaps looked dramatic above the gray water. Melanie's daily run had taken the same course it had yesterday. She ran quickly to the spots she'd spent with Adam and then slowed, picturing herself with him once again. Jason Johnson, her sixth date, had called to postpone until Sunday, giving her the opportunity to catch up with her friends.

Melanie called Carla as she strolled the last quarter mile of her run and gave her the update on Nick and his highly testosteroned view of women.

"I thought he'd be good for you, you both travel and are never home," Carla said.

"Yeah, well, Nick is definitely out," Melanie said, "but I think these dates are weakening my resolve. I honestly don't know what would make me happy."

"We all struggle with that question," Carla sighed. "Was there anything redeemable about last night?"

"The food was out of this world. Have you been to Oscar's Bistro? I had broiled swordfish with stuffed mushrooms."

"It's all the rage."

"Did you read that in a headline?"

"Actually, I think I did. How about we go there tonight? I'll have Ted's rep call for a reservation and pick you up at 8."

"Sounds great."

"Bye, Hon."

Melanie took her place in line at her now-favorite Starbucks. Lately she'd become a regular and was even greeted as such, her order being called out even before she spoke.

"Have a nice day."

"You, too," Melanie said as she answered her ringing phone. "Hello."

Melanie giggled, shaking her head in disgust at her idiocy, "Hi, Adam."

"How are you?"

His deep voice was as smooth as melted chocolate. Her heart pounded as she managed her way through the slippery slopes of the English language, but she refused to behave like a 12-year-old girl gushing over a boy. Only her mother could reduce her to such childish theatrics.

"I'm terrific," she said as she paced the sidewalk beside a towering tree whose roots had cracked the cement, making for dangerous terrain. "How are you?"

"I'm good. So, how was your date last night?"

"Let's just say I'm glad there are only two left." She didn't particularly like discussing her dates with Adam. "I got home early and spent most of the night on my dad's porch swing. You know what I miss?"

"What's that?"

"Stars. When did they all fade?"

⁂

Though Carla flexed her political muscle, she couldn't get a reservation that night. The woman on the phone suggested they show up in case of a cancellation – which, at a quarter to nine, they did.

Shocked, Melanie recognized Daria instantly. She was standing behind a mahogany pedestal wearing a slinky burgundy dress with spaghetti straps, her long blonde hair flowing down her bronzed shoulders. She presided over table assignments with her worn grease pencil like a warden under the Stalin regime. Melanie used an eight-foot potted tree as a screen, keeping an eye on Daria as she pretended to admire an oil painting with Jenny. Carla and Trish did their best to compel the hostess to find them a table for four.

"I'm sorry, but there are no tables available. I don't know who would have told you to arrive without a reservation. We're booked solid for weeks," Daria said snootily.

"But we're starving. Don't you have seats at a bar or something?"

Daria rolled her cold brown eyes. "The best I can offer you is Monday, July second, if you can wait."

"Now what?" Jenny asked, as they huddled in the parking lot.

"I say Burger King. I'm dying," Trish suggested.

Melanie teetered on the curb, letting the three of them come up with a solution. She could still see Daria through the glass doors, guiding guests to their tables. Melanie knew that beneath that beautiful exterior resided a lunatic.

"Melanie?"

She felt a warm touch on her shoulder.

"Adam."

"Hey, what are you doing here?" he asked, enfolding her lightly in his arms.

Disappointed, she held on for seconds longer. He didn't pull away, but whispered, "Too many eyes here."

His cheek rubbed against hers slowly, a private acknowledgment. Melanie closed her eyes. He smelled nice – delicious actually, garlic and lemongrass. His ability to evoke such emotion startled her and she ignored the red flags flying like confetti at a New York parade.

"This is where you work?"

"Yeah, didn't I tell you?"

"No, but I just saw Daria."

She pointed back through the glass but her eyes couldn't turn away from him. His bright blue dress shirt, with the first two buttons undone and the cuffs rolled up, made her heart skip and her palms sweat.

Hell, Melanie, you're becoming a desperate woman, losing IQ points just looking at him. But, God, he might be worth it.

He smiled. "You look incredible. Are you here with a date?"

"No, friends."

Carla, Jen and Trish were still arguing over where to eat. She felt the need to justify.

"We don't have a reservation and Trish wants to go to the Burger King on the corner but Carla is refusing to drive her there.

Jen is on a diet and can't eat carbs so I'm waiting for a compromise. You smell nice, by the way." She added quickly not looking at him but at her friends who hadn't yet noticed Melanie's absence.

"Thanks," he said, amused. "I think I can help with this. Come on."

He held onto the tips of her fingers as they walked. Melanie tugged on Carla's sleeve, motioning for them to follow.

"Daria, what can you do about getting these women a table?"

"Umm … let me see," she said, clearly troubled. "Sure Mr. Chase I can do that for you."

"You're a sweetheart."

Her big brown, "anything for you, Mr. Chase," doe eyes narrowed like a Banshee as she recognized Melanie. Melanie felt the burn.

"Right this way, please," Daria said, an artificial smile plastered on her unblemished face.

"Thanks, Daria," he smiled and turned back to Melanie. "I've got to get back to the kitchen but Daria will take care of you. We're still on for tomorrow, right?"

Anything you say, Mr. Chase.

"Tomorrow?" Carla mouthed, her eyes big.

"So, Daria, who is Mr. Chase?" Trish was asking as Melanie caught up.

"He's our head chef," she said, directing them to an empty table in the back and handing each of them a menu.

"He cooks?" Trish looked over to Jen.

"No, he designed our entire menu and created each dish personally. He is our *head* chef."

"Then why doesn't he wear the funny outfit?" Trish giggled and Daria sighed. Melanie could feel Daria's eyes roll to the back of her head.

"How do you know this guy, Mel?" Carla asked.

"Clumsily, she drenched us with a bottle of wine and completely ruined my favorite dress," Daria said before falling back into her prepared spiel. "Your waiter will be here shortly. Welcome to Oscar's."

The girls eyeballed each other, containing their giggles until Daria had turned the corner.

"You really spilled wine on them?"

Melanie nodded and told the story.

"No wonder she didn't seem to like us very much," Carla giggled.

"I think Daria has the hot-and-heavies for Mr. Head Chef," Jen said.

"Can you blame her? I think I've got them, too," Trish smiled devilishly. "Maybe our celibate friend has also been infected."

Melanie wanted to say something but the waiter arrived to rattle off the specials and take their drink orders, allowing her to change the direction of the conversation. The subject of Adam did not re-surface and Melanie was grateful.

"Dee-lish," Trish said, dropping her napkin onto the table next to a half-eaten bowl of Zesty Shrimp Salad. "Why have I never heard of this place?"

"Because there aren't any strippers," Jenny offered.

Melanie lifted her glass of wine. "To Testosterone Nick."

"Testosterone Nick."

"How many dates have you got left?" Trish asked.

"Two. Tomorrow is Don Avery and then Sunday is Jason." Melanie looked over at Trish.

"I am really sorry about Jason," Trish said to Melanie.

"No big deal. He was really nice on the phone. A true gentleman." *Please make sure that Trish knows I called and that I'm not a schmuck,* Jason had said over the phone earlier that morning.

Melanie had promised.

"Still, I'm disappointed in him." Trish continued, lowering her voice. "I'm not going to let Daria sink her claws into Mr. Chase," she said, reaching into her bra and enhancing her cleavage. With a little jiggle she rested her breast on the edge of her low-cut blouse and then continued to even herself out.

"Jeez, Trish, are those the same ones from college?" Melanie asked, staring.

"No, I replaced those about three years ago. These are safer and bigger." Trish's brows raised. "What about Mr. Chase, Mel? If you don't, I'm gonna."

Melanie bit her lip, feeling her brow furrow.

Trish is going after Adam! You can't compete with her. How much do you want him? Her mind raced. *A boyfriend? You can't do this, remember? You still have your job, it's only a matter of a day or two.*

"Melanie," Carla said firmly, "you like this guy, I see it all over you. It doesn't have to end like Dan."

Melanie shot a glance at Carla. "Why would you bring him up?"

Nobody ever spoke of Danny; he'd been a closed subject for years.

"Because that's where you're stuck," Jenny added, loudly. "Get over him already."

"While you guys argue over this I'm going to have some fun," Trish scooted out of the booth seat and adjusted her skirt, exposing more of her long legs. Smiling, she waved.

"Don't you wish you could do that?" Jenny said. "Just be so confident."

Carla snorted, clearly disappointed.

Melanie knew what Jenny meant but at the moment she almost hated Trish. Her head throbbed as she kept an eye on the direction Trish had gone. The light conversation continued, each woman disregarding the elephant at the table.

Five minutes passed. The waiter cleared the dishes and brought dessert.

"We didn't order these," Carla told him.

"Shut up, Car," Jen scolded. "Look at this chocolate cake."

"Mr. Chase sent them over and he's taken care of your bill. Is there anything else I can get for you?"

"We're good, thanks," Melanie said, wondering what Trish was doing to get the free meal. "Jen, I thought you were on a diet."

Melanie was agitated and her fuse short.

"Who cares about carbs?" Jenny said, putting a forkful of cake into her mouth. When her eyes rolled back into her head from pleasure Melanie reached over with her own fork.

"Get your own," Jenny guarded her plate with a thrust of her fork.

Four dishes had been scraped clean when the waiter returned.

"I am too full," Jen said, leaning back in her chair, having consumed two of the delicacies. "That was awesome, as RJ says. Can you believe he's going to be 10 next month? Ryan thinks that RJ will be an amazing…"

"There they are," Carla said, interrupting.

Melanie had already noticed. They were walking side by side until Adam stopped to speak with four elderly ladies drinking chardonnay.

He leaned in to say something to Trish before giving the women his full attention. Trish strutted her way back to the table.

"Well?" Jenny asked Trish anxiously.

Melanie couldn't look at her.

"He's into Melanie, no big deal."

Melanie breathed, her head dizzy from a sudden rush of oxygen. It *was* a big deal. Trish wasn't used to rejection and it had to sting.

"Seriously?" "Really?" Both Carla and Jen asked.

"He refused my best offer," her confusion was in her words. "He must really like you. Hey, did you guys eat cake?" She slumped back in to the seat, her arms crossed across her chest.

Melanie watched Adam interact with his guests. He looked up, catching her stare, and she read his lips as he said, "Thank you for coming back. I'll see you next week." He walked directly to Melanie's table without breaking eye contact.

"How was everything?"

"Amazing. It really wasn't necessary." She said, feeling guilty under his gaze.

"I wanted to."

"I think I gained five pounds," Jenny said, in her unusual way of mixing a compliment with a snide remark.

Adam walked them out to the dim parking lot as the brisk night air blew through the small canyons of large SUVs.

"You know, your friend just hit on me," he said, pulling her to the side when they reached Carla's Navigator and the others piled in.

"I know, I'm sorry about that but I'm glad that..." How was she going to finish this?

Adam gave her a confused look. "Did you know she was going to … see me?"

Melanie nodded.

His eyes narrowed, "Did you think I'd like her?"

Melanie shrugged.

"I'm not looking for that." His glance shot to Trish, sitting in the back seat, then bending to Melanie's eye level. "I don't sleep around and I don't do casual."

Now it was Melanie who was looking curious. "That's good to know."

"I'm picking you up early, 8 or 8:30."

"I'll be ready."

He was close she could feel his breath as he said, "I can't kiss you here."

"I wasn't going to let you," she whispered back.

"Tomorrow," he smiled.

"Maybe," she replied.

He smiled. "Good night."

He opened her door and helped her into the vehicle.

"What happened?" Carla asked, revving up the engine.

"I guess I'm going out with him tomorrow morning," Melanie said, waving goodbye and pulling the seat belt across her chest. "Where are we off to?" she asked, in a happy mood.

"How about drinks at my apartment?" Trish offered.

Trish's apartment was a fully feminine experience, decorated in pinks and floral prints. The couch was covered with pillows – lots of pillows. But like Melanie's apartment in D.C., her refrigerator contained a variety of take-out boxes.

"I may not have food but I've got margarita fixins." Trish danced around her small kitchen pulling out glasses and a blender.

"I'll just have water," Carla said. "A DUI for the wife of a congressman in an election year would make headlines for a week."

Jenny found a radio station that played "oldies" and the girls were taken back to their college days. Dancing, drinking and laughing, they reminisced about old times. Later, Melanie sat on the carpet and leaned against Carla's chair while Jenny and Trish sat on opposite ends of the florid couch.

"It's great being here with you, guys," Melanie said, "I'd forgotten how much fun we have."

"Just like old times," Carla agreed.

"When are you going to get out of this apartment and buy a house?" Jenny asked Trish.

"Probably never. Have you seen the prices of houses? Besides, I like living in an apartment, everything is taken care of with one phone call. It really is the life of luxury." Trish leaned back on the many pillows and placed her forearm over her eyes.

"It's a nice apartment," Melanie said, laying flat on the floor and reminding herself never to invite Jenny to her own barren apartment.

"Of course you think so, you live in an apartment, too." Then turning to Trish, she continued. "Getting life advice from Melanie is like asking a..."

"Easy now, Jen," Melanie cautioned, sitting up, as Jenny paused to think of her simile.

"All I'm saying is that you don't hold the same values that we do."

Melanie put up her hand, stopping Carla, who was about to say something.

"Okay Jen, values?" Melanie sat up, placing her glass on the coffee table. Her patience was worn thin and her nerves still raw from the Trish incident.

"Jenny, stop," Carla urged.

"No, why should I? I'm tired of having to walk on eggshells around Melanie. No one can ever say anything. She finally gets a date so stop the presses. It's always all about Melanie even though she never calls, writes or even e-mails. Her secretary sends cards and gifts on all the appropriate dates but I doubt Melanie even knows what she sent any of us for Christmas or our birthdays. Do you?"

She didn't.

"You swoop in on your company's plane, flaunt your big life and as quickly as you come you jet off again, and we're supposed to stop our lives for you?"

"You don't know me, Jen. You know nothing about my life." She was preparing for a girl battle not yet seen by this configuration of friends.

"Melanie, these are just my observations, they aren't meant to make you angry. I'm sorry if you can't accept criticism or if the name Dan sends you into a tailspin."

"That's it, Jen. I'll admit I'm not perfect, but the reason why I 'swoop' in is because I'm embarrassed about how long I stay away. And I don't stay long because it hurts to know how much I miss being here, and Danny, well, that hurts, too."

"You know I did feel bad when he crushed you in college, but then you closed up and were so completely pathetic. Do you remember?"

Melanie nodded, not breathing. Her dry mouth reached down to her parched throat.

"Please, that was a decade ago. Seriously, Melanie, you need some perspective."

"Perspective, is that what *you* had when Ryan had his affair? I didn't judge you for staying with a cheater, I let you live your life your way. Even when you entrenched yourself in religion and started preaching morality. You can wrap yourself in the gospel, Jen, but it doesn't give you control of any moral compass."

"Ryan had an affair?" Carla asked, too shocked to remain hidden in her chair. "When?"

"How do you know all this? Trish?"

"I never said a word." Trish raised her hands but leaned forward.

"I pay attention. And my radar is picking up on something now. So, is he cheating again?"

Jenny didn't say a word – she didn't have to, her gaping mouth and bulging eyes were enough.

It's not like she didn't deserve it, Melanie thought, justifying her words.

"Jen?"

Carla and Trish moved closer, putting their arms around Jenny as she wept into her hands. Melanie stayed seated uncomfortably on the floor, soaking in a pool of her own guilt.

"It's not Ryan," Jen muttered, "it's me."

"It's okay, Honey," Carla comforted her and glared at Melanie.

Hypocrite, she thought, swallowing a shot of tequila and then another.

"Are you leaving Ryan?"

"No," she sounded terrified. "He doesn't know and Tom, well, Tom's married, too."

Melanie walked out onto the balcony. Trish's apartment was on the second floor of a two-story historic building in Point Loma. The view wasn't much – a two-lane artery connecting Ocean Beach to the city bypassing Interstate 8. At 11 p.m. the traffic had all but ceased, allowing the rustling palm fronds to play out their symphonies.

Melanie tried to absorb the serenity of the summer night, the smell of the freshly mown lawn, the rapidly moving clouds that hung low as they passed over the slumbering city.

"Mel, I'm going to drive Jenny home," Carla said, poking her head outside.

"I guess I should go with you, then."

Carla would pass La Jolla to take Jenny home in Oceanside, easily an hour's drive.

"Why don't you stay and I'll come back for you," Carla stepped outside, rubbing her arms against the chill. "Jenny is pretty upset and I want a chance to talk with her alone."

"She's mad at me." Melanie shook her head. "You know this has nothing to do with me, I'm just a convenient rack to hang her shame."

"I don't blame you, but you were harsh."

"Have a safe drive." Melanie didn't want to hear it.

Inside, the tiny apartment was warm and Trish had blended another pitcher of margaritas, stronger than the others had been.

"Well, that was something," she said, filling two glasses to the brim.

"Did you know?"

"Hell, no. After she's been giving me the third degree about my lifestyle, Jesus."

Melanie exhaled, "I won't apologize, she provoked me and ... I guess I do regret it ... but I'll need another drink to think it over."

"I'm glad we have some time together," Trish said, folding her legs underneath her body as she sunk into the couch. "I owe you a huge apology. I'm not used to being with women I care about and I guess I've just gotten a little out of control."

Melanie looked up at Trish, her droopy lids covering most of her eyes.

"Forgive me?" Trish asked.

Melanie rubbed her eyes and sat on the edge of a chair facing Trish.

"Only if you forgive me."

"That's easy, you haven't done anything wrong."

Melanie let out a laugh, "I am really sorry about absolutely everything, but she just pissed me off. I should have kept my mouth shut – I didn't know she was having an affair."

"She and I haven't been very close since she joined her church group, probably to repent her lurid deeds with Tom," Trish stated.

"Well, she was right, I can be a jerk. It breaks my heart that I've been separated from all you guys. I am so sorry."

"Don't get so bent out of shape, we're really not all that great," Trish winked and lifted her glass. "I think that of the four of us you and I could be close," Trish smiled. "I work with 98 percent males and the women I know are just as bad as I am. I miss having friendships."

"I'll drink to that."

"So, we're okay, I mean with the chef and all?" She made a childlike sad face.

"We're okay."

"Then can I ask what's up with you two?"

Melanie took a deep breath, "I've got this enormous crush." *And when he looks at me with those intense green eyes he literally takes my breath away. It's overwhelming, debilitating even, to feel this much.*

"What are you going to do?"

"I don't know," Melanie shook her head.

Trish's eyes softened and Melanie wondered if it was from pity or the tequila.

"Well, he really likes you. I found him in his office and at first he was fine but when he realized what I was there for, I think he got mad." She brushed her blonde curls out of her eyes. "He changed the subject back to you each time I advanced. Finally he just said that he respected you and there was no way it was ever going to happen between us."

"I'm sorry you got your feelings hurt."

"Yeah, well, can I tell you a secret?"

Melanie nodded.

"I have an enormous crush on Jason."

"Why did you hook me up with someone that you're interested in?"

"I don't date the players, never have, if you can believe that. I figured if I can't have him then you should." With a devilish smile Trish continued, "Besides, there is a world of men to meet and I'm not a lonely girl."

"Do you mean that, or are you trying to convince yourself?"

Trish smiled, sleepily. "I have to admit that I am smitten with Jason. He's funny, sweet and loaded with cash, but I can't."

Melanie understood completely.

"Trish, before you pass out there is another thing." Melanie felt her nerves beginning to tingle and took a long drink. "It's been a long time since I've … had a boyfriend."

"So?"

"So, what if I've forgotten how or what if I'm clumsy?" Melanie bit her lip, waiting for Trish to respond. "It's been a long time."

"Are you talking about sex?"

Melanie nodded.

Trish looked shocked before she started to laugh.

"It's not funny," Melanie said.

"What do you want to know? You've done it before, there was that guy a couple of months ago. Just do what you did to him."

"I can't, I made him up. I've made them all up." Melanie pulled her mouth down in a frown.

"What?"

She shook her head, "I've made up every boyfriend I've talked about." Melanie's nervousness came out in a half-hearted chuckle, "You look so funny right now."

"Shut up and explain," Trish looked less drunk and more angry.

"You've met my mom. It was easier to make believe than to actually date. I'm not all that capable of being available."

Trish's shrunken eyes were a bit more sober, but whether they were wide with concern or horror it was hard to tell.

"So who, when was the last time you had sex?"

"I don't want to tell you, and get that wretched expression off your face."

"Just spit it out or I won't give you any advice, and trust me, I give excellent advice."

"Hmmm." *How desperate am I?* "Bobby, about seven or eight years ago and it only lasted a few weeks."

Melanie watched Trish's reaction.

"Are you sure you're not a lesbian? Because, you're going to have to explain this one." Trish blinked a few times, pushing away the alcohol and the drowsiness.

The margarita had been effective with Melanie as well, liberating her defenses and loosening her tongue.

"I'm not gay, I'm just celibate."

Trish's mouth gaped and Melanie was reminded of a blowfish she'd seen while scuba diving. But as Trish stared Melanie thought of Bobby.

They had been on a job in Chile in early spring when a warm front hit, causing an avalanche. The plunging ice cascaded down the mountainside, encapsulating them in their tiny cabin. All of the equipment, along with a navigational beacon, had been packed, ready to vacate, in the truck that was swept five miles to the bottom of a rocky ravine. Storms and high winds further delayed their rescue and sometime after they'd tunneled to the surface Melanie succumbed to one of Bobby's advances. Bobby was a few years older, with light red hair and clear blue eyes – not unattractive physically, it was just that his personality repelled her. He'd caught her at a vulnerable time.

"Are you ever going to say anything?" Melanie asked.

"Wow, you are seriously fucked up." Trish slurred, laughing as she gulped down the last of her drink.

"I know."

"Why don't you tell me anything? I would be so mad at you if I were sober." Trish pointed her finger at the wall behind Melanie.

"But I still need your help."

"Okay, okay, well if you're talking about Adam you don't have to worry because he knows exactly what he's doing. You just have to lay back and enjoy," she laughed.

Melanie fell back onto the chair and held her forehead in her hands. "Come on, I don't want to seem incompetent."

"Would you be more comfortable with a graph or a chart of some sort?"

"Ugh, please. Do you know you're an obnoxious drunk?"

"All right, do you know how to strip?"

"Like in a strip tease?"

"Yeah," Trish said, pulling herself up. "You move your hips and your shoulders while slowly peeling off clothing. Granted, for the first six months you'll be naked in less than five seconds," she laughed and walked a crooked line as she demonstrated. "Use your sensuality."

"I don't have any. Am I supposed to fall over, too?"

Trish locked eyes and with a mysterious grin dropped her blouse to the floor. She moved closer and began to unzip her skirt, pulling it lower until Melanie could see the pink lace of her thong.

"Now it's your turn," Trish said, stumbling as she bowed and tried to reach for her blouse.

"I *cannot* do that."

"Yes, you can, anyone can. I saw it on Oprah."

Melanie stepped to the corner of the room and let out a deep breath. *You can do this. Spy Melanie can do this.*

Sauntering like Trish had done, she untied the string to her blouse without breaking eye contact. She walked, pushing out her hips and arching her back. It wasn't until her skirt hit the carpeting that Melanie returned.

"Well, I am one hell of a good teacher. Jesus, Melanie, I'd do you."

"Yeah?"

Trish nodded, "But what the hell are you wearing, Grandma's underwear?"

Melanie dressed and sat with Trish. "I feel better, but I'm still worried."

"I need more margaritha, margarisha, whatever," Trish kept talking while she emptied the pitcher into their glasses.

"I can't understand you. Maybe you've had enough margarisha." Melanie couldn't stop laughing.

"I've got an idea." Trish leaned over the side table and rolled off the couch.

"Are you all right?" Melanie pulled her back up and threw the pillows to the ground.

The TV flickered on as Trish fumbled to find the right numbers on the remote.

"You have porn?"

"Keep stripping like that and you, too, could have illegal cable from a very robust cable guy." Trish leaned her head back, her eyelids struggling to stay open.

Melanie intruded on a couple in a hotel room whose lurid acts both mildly disturbed and aroused her. You can do this, she told herself as she studied the woman's moves.

"Well, I am not doing that," Melanie said to a sleeping Trish. "And I'm definitely not doing *that!*"

"Hey, I'm back," Carla called from the door.

Melanie jumped out of her skin as she fumbled for the remote to turn off the set.

"What are you doing?" Carla scrutinized Melanie then looked at the dark screen of the TV.

"Nothing." Melanie shrugged and struggled to clear her mind of the erotic images. "How's Jen?"

"Upset."

Melanie nodded, cooling down from her naughty research.

"The affair has been going on for months." Carla sat on the chair across from Melanie shaking her head. "I probably shouldn't be telling you this but I can't get the image out of my head. They've been having sex in the back of their minivans."

"Oh, thanks," Melanie said, grimacing.

"I convinced her to tell Ryan."

"Really? Are you sure that's the best idea?" Melanie strained to sober up.

"Yes, of course. Besides, he cheated first."

Melanie wasn't sure it worked that way but hey what did she know?

"I can't believe you knew about Ryan and didn't tell me. She said you hired a cleaning service for her after RJ was born. Why?"

"I thought she was going through a hard time and shouldn't have to worry about the laundry. Anyway, I didn't tell because I really didn't know for sure."

"Is she all right?" Carla asked, nodding to Trish who'd started snoring loudly.

"Passed out."

"Why is her shirt on backward?"

Melanie grinned. "Don't know."

CHAPTER 13

"Melanie?" Her mother's strident voice cut into her dreamless stupor, giving way to near-consciousness.

When did my mother's voice get so shrill? she wondered, the ache behind her eye cutting like a blade into her brain.

"Melanie," Rita repeated. She knew *that* tone, stern and under control yet at the cusp of intolerance.

A rough shoulder shake caused the residual alcohol soaking her brain, to fire up an angry hangover. She swallowed back the foul stench rising up in her esophagus, groaning an incoherent "What?" to her mother.

Wincing, she opened one eye. She was on the couch with Rita bending over her, and behind her mother's shoulder the room was caught in a nauseating spin.

Rita sighed. "I do wish you'd sleep in your own bed once in a while," she said, giving another shake, then adding, "Sometimes I find her on the porch swing."

Melanie knew, the instant Rita had spoken the words.

"Oh crap, what time is it?" she asked, grabbing her splitting head that felt as though it must have an ice pick protruding from her frontal lobe.

"Eight-thirty," Adam said.

She heard his amusement and to add to her discomfort a stampede of rushing blood pounded its way up to color her face.

"Melanie, are you drunk?" Her mother's sharp tone of disapproval stabbed into her head.

"No," she huffed and squinted at Adam. "I am so sorry. Give me 10 minutes?" Melanie asked, avoiding breath contact.

"No problem. I'll just hang out here with your mom."

"I'll be down in six."

Melanie threatened her mom to behave with one forceful, evil look.

"Take your time, dear," Rita grinned.

Melanie willed the room to stabilize and gingerly took the first few steps. Easy.

She swallowed three aspirin, washing them down with the water from her two-minute shower. Every moment that passed meant another embarrassing moment of her life exposed to Adam. Her body was still damp when she slipped into a pair of Capri pants and pulled a white cami over her tropical print bikini.

"Hey, what's going on?" she asked, feeling human again, her hangover settling into a kindlier purr.

Adam's face was bright. He and her mother were hunched over the kitchen island. Rita was giggling and chatting rapidly.

"We're looking at your family photo albums," Adam said, his green eyes glimmering with new knowledge.

"Oh, dear God, what year?"

"Your trip to Mexico. You're in high school."

"Blonde highlights?"

Adam laughed. "Yeah, I saw that."

"Okay! We're done here." She glowered at her mom, "You know that's just wrong."

"Honey, you're too self-conscious – you are a beautiful girl."

Melanie walked to the opposite side of the island and closed the album. Right after the year of blonde highlights was an especially ugly year of acne that she'd rather keep a secret.

"He's handsome," Rita whispered.

"I know and he can hear you." Melanie whispered back, grabbing a baseball cap off the table on her way out the door. "Great idea with the pictures, Mom."

"Mrs. Ward, it was a pleasure meeting you."

"Please, call me Rita."

Outside the heat of the day was rising, the air had lost its moist, earthy fragrance and the soft sounds of nature were drowned by those of human development. She waved to her mom as Adam opened the car door. Rita ducked behind the sheer kitchen curtains.

"Should I wait to kiss you until your mom isn't watching?"

Melanie laughed, "How long has it been since you had to ask that question?"

"I have to admit it's been a while." He quickly and lightly placed a peck on her cheek. "It's sweet, you're sweet – even with a hangover. How about we stop for some coffee?"

Sweet? Is that what I'm going for? I stayed out late drinking and watching porn with my girlfriend. Who's sweet now?

"Coffee." She could already smell the aroma and the power of the stuff working its magic on her headache.

"Did you have a good time last night?" His voice was peaceful, unassuming. "I was surprised to see you."

"Not as surprised as Daria."

"Yeah, well, nothing I can do about that."

"My friends were all really impressed with you," she said. "Especially Trish." *Shut up, you stupid, stupid, drunk girl!*

"Yeah, about that," he said, parking at a metered space in front of *her* Starbucks and waited in the customary seven-person line before continuing. "Melanie, I don't understand how you could agree to let your friend..." He shook his head, and she wondered what exactly

Trish had said or done.

Speechless for a moment, she considered how to answer. "I thought you might..." she struggled, squinting back the pulsing throb behind her eye, "...like her. She's beautiful and I..." she sighed, "have no claim."

The muscle in his jaw twitched and his smooth, curvy lips tightened into a hard line. The girl behind the counter saw Melanie and rattled off her drink, a Venti caramel macchiato with a shot of soy, and Adam ordered a small black coffee.

"You drink coffee?" Adam asked one eyebrow arched to a concerned height.

"Occasionally. I might have been here once or twice."

"Bye, Melanie. Bye, Melanie's friend."

The awkwardness of Trish lingered.

Ready to break the tension she said, "I bought one of these for my dad the other day," pointing to her cup as Adam drove, one-handed and looking smoking hot. "And he said, 'I hear that people are paying three bucks for a cup of coffee.'" Melanie laughed. "I didn't have the nerve to tell him I'd paid almost five for his."

Adam maintained his stoic stance but added his appreciation for her mother. "I enjoyed talking with Rita."

Hmm, she thought, wondering if he had any idea how fuming mad she was with *Rita*. "Yeah, I could tell," Melanie cringed from the awfulness.

Mentally she flipped through the pages, most were of her in sporting events, track and field in high school. Those she was okay with, it was the rest that she hated. Bad hair, bad outfits, braces and just all around embarrassing.

"It wasn't too bad." A bit of his smile returned.

"Then why do you keep laughing?"

"I'm sorry, it's just not often I get to see a beautiful woman wake with a hangover."

"Not at the beginning of a date, anyway. We seem to be doing things backward, you and I."

She paused, daring to move her gaze from the harmless streets to his risky eyes, "Are you still mad at me?"

"I wasn't mad, it's just..." He cleared his throat. "I like you, Melanie, and I thought, well, I thought you liked me. But if you're willing to, to hand me off to your nearest available friend ... then I'm not so sure."

Ouch.

His eyes narrowed and he pulled his brows in so they nearly touched. "Unless, that's what you wanted." His voice was soft, "Did you want me to choose Trish?"

"No," she said, her stuttering heart felt unpleasant. It was comparable to being stranded in the middle of the desert with no water and surrounded by aggressive rattlesnakes. "I leave for D.C. in a few days and she stays. I don't know, maybe at some level I thought she was better for you." Melanie bit her lip and stared down at her hands that were wrangling each other in her lap.

"Melanie, I get to decide who's better for me," he said, covering her hands with one of his.

Melanie smiled. The weight of his hand felt nice, soothing. It was the touch she'd ached for in Hawaii.

Strange, she thought, *to get something you wanted, then not know what to do with it.*

"So, Adam, who's going to be on this boat trip?"

"Just us."

Melanie glanced back at the three grocery bags on the back seat.

She bumped the back of her head against the headrest. "I knew I should never have eaten that hot dog, now you think I'm a glutton." She refused, even in her darkest hour, to call herself a pig – she had her limits.

He smiled, this time not taking his eyes off the road. "I wasn't sure what you liked so I brought a selection. And I like you as much as I do partly because of that hot dog."

"I'm not exactly sure what that means but I'll take it as a compliment." She relaxed a little.

At the marina rows of white boats rocked gently in their berths. Melanie carried one of the grocery bags along the wooden plank dock to the 35-foot sailboat at the end.

"Adam, she's gorgeous."

The boat glistened merrily in the placid waters.

"Yeah, she's my escape."

Unlocking the door to the cabin, Adam, opened his world to Melanie. She stepped down into the living quarters, the galley, the control panel and a seating area. To the back, through a partially opened pocket door, was a bedroom with a door to the head.

"Can I get you something to drink?" he offered, while stacking the multitude of containers in the cabinets and the small refrigerator.

"I'm good, but can I help?" She picked up a clear plastic box and, tilted it, tried to figure out what was inside.

"I'm good." His fingers caressed hers as he removed the box from her hands, setting it on the table before settling his hands on her waist. "Do you realize you have perfectly shaped lips?"

She bit down on her perfectly shaped lower lip and hoped she wouldn't have to wait too long for a kiss.

His hands moved up to her neck, his thumbs slipping beneath her chin to tip her face upward. She stopped breathing.

He bent low, his shallow breath, warm and pleasant, on her cheek. She liberated her restrained lip just in time to meet his mouth. Melanie was overtaken by three careful, sensual, contact-and-break kisses.

Her arms twined around his neck as she rose on her tiptoes and curved her body into his. His closeness swirled in her head, his scent and the intimacy of his tongue skimming along her lips and pulling at the strings of her consciousness.

In his arms she weakened, succumbing to his kiss, moving her mouth with his.

Breathing his air, her chest molded into his and her fingers tangled in his hair. She pulled him down to her.

It was as close to losing control as she'd ever been, but still she felt the hoisting of her protective shield.

Melanie peeled herself away, her lips the last to part. Adam smiled down at her, his joy flowing from his eyes, brightening his wide grin.

When she kissed Ty she'd known his motivation, but with Adam – the bed glaring at her from behind a thin partition – she was less certain. More certain, though, was her resolve to keep a safe distance from his bed sheets.

"I think I'm going to get some air," she smiled back at him, his face too close.

"I'll be up in a minute."

Outside, the summer sun beamed lovingly on the Southern California coast. A steady lapping of the water against the cutter's hull calmed her.

The cobalt blue cushions along the bench seat were comfortable.

She waited for Adam to emerge, hoping his hold over her had somehow broken during the last two minutes. She closed her eyes, her head spinning, whether from delight or alcohol she couldn't tell.

"How are you doing?"

"Clearing my head," she answered, her heart racing.

Adam motored out of the harbor as she sat starboard and enjoyed the warm sun and gentle breeze. She shook out her damp hair to dry in the wind. Once out in open water Adam raised the sails and they zigzagged across the dark blue sea, the whitecaps splashing over the deck and spraying mist high into the air. Up and over the rolling waves, the water was darker and colder than it had been in Hawaii. Melanie looked back at Adam, his green tropical shirt pressed firmly against his chest while the back whipped in the wind. He smiled and motioned for her to hold on. She braced herself as best she could on the slippery fabric. Changing course the boat picked up speed, leaping, bounding and flying through the water.

He navigated expertly, making it look easy, shifting directions and letting the sails drop. She made her way to where he stood.

"That was amazing!" Melanie laughed.

"I thought I was going to lose you a couple of times."

He worked, lowering and tying down the slackened sails as she watched and admired.

"Watch this," he said.

A bright blue canopy opened automatically, shading the U-shaped seating area in the aft of the boat.

"Nifty," Melanie said, now sitting in the shade.

"That's it? Nifty?" he smiled brightly without a hint of offense.

"What do you want me to say? The whole thing is a babe magnet," she said, reminded of the old movies her father used to watch, with the playboy's apartment decked out in the latest gadgets.

"A babe magnet?" he repeated with distaste. "Is that who you think I am?" he asked, with a look of concern. "That's not me, Melanie, I'm not a player."

"You don't use this boat to lure women?"

"Today is my first time. How am I doing?"

Melanie laughed. "Failing miserably."

"I guess I'll have to try harder," he said, scooting in next to her. "But honestly, Melanie, you're the first person I've invited on my boat."

"Is it brand new?" she teased.

"Hmm," he rubbed his chin and studied her. "You're dangerous, aren't you?"

"It's funny because I was thinking the same thing about you." Her stomach rumbled, a loud, embarrassing complaint. "I wonder if I'm more or less dangerous when I'm hungry."

"Well, either way I can't have you hungry." Reaching beneath the seats he pulled out a rectangular tabletop and a pole. "I'll get lunch, and you can set the table, if you don't mind." He handed her the tools and grinned.

She surveyed the latches and clips along with the base, fitted with slide-out attachments that connected to the Formica tabletop. Her hands moved quickly as she assembled the structure and secured it to the footing in the floor.

Done, with time to spare, she leaned back and enjoyed the peace.

Her belligerent stomach moaned for attention as the smell of food wafted from the open cabin door.

"I'm coming," he called, anticipating her impatience. "Hey, nice job." Adam situated plates and containers across the table.

"I'm getting drinks, why don't you get started? These are the appetizers." He opened two dishes, one labeled "crab cakes" and the other "spring rolls."

It was all she could do to wait.

Adam came out with two tall glasses, iced with a deep pink liquid.

"What is that?"

"Strawberry agua fresca and you're my guinea pig. Do you mind?" He handed her the cold glass.

"I don't mind," she said, though she sniffed the sweet-smelling drink before taking her first sip. "It's good." She nodded and took a deeper swallow. Her stomach wasn't distracted by the fluid, it wanted food.

She picked up a crab cake, and although he wasn't watching, she knew he was tuned in to her reaction.

The toasted buttery crust melted on her tongue. "Oh my God," she looked into his green eyes, "you have to have one."

Adam looked, pleased yet not surprised. "Good?"

"Very, but of course you know that."

He shrugged, "It's nice to hear."

Melanie picked up a bite-sized piece and held it up to his mouth. She hadn't intended the gesture to be arousing but her toes curled the instant her fingers made contact with his lips. She looked up to see him gazing at her with the same reaction.

She held her breath and this time she leaned into him, encircling her arms around his neck and with a somewhat shy movement she kissed him.

"I'll have to remember crab cakes for you."

It wasn't just the appetizers that worked her up, his entire menu was outstanding – tortellini salad, sea bass with lemon and herbs, chicken Florentine and chocolate cherry cake.

His food was an aphrodisiac.

Melanie kissed him like he was the oxygen she needed to breathe. Lost in the power of his touch she wasn't sure when she'd moved, straddling his lap and holding his face in her hands.

He brushed back a loose strand of hair that had fallen into her face, and that simple gesture was the trigger. It was so Danny that Melanie couldn't shake the feeling.

Adam's jaw suddenly felt wrong, too strong and too clean shaven, his neck too thick, his shoulders too broad and too muscular – he felt *wrong*.

She pulled off his lips and lap in one quick movement, like yanking off a Band-aid. Melanie was panting and Adam looked confused. She needed a moment alone to understand what the hell was going on. Off went her Capri pants and white camisole top. Adam's expression was wide with distress. She felt guilty and embarrassed.

"I'm going for a swim."

The water was cold and dark, both freezing and burning her lungs. Melanie swam downward, kicking vigorously until she figured she'd used up half of her air. Hanging suspended in a black abyss, her tears blended with the ocean.

Who are you? The person I know wouldn't have had her legs wrapped around a guy she'd just met. No, she'd be fighting like hell to get her damn job back. Melanie, where are you?

She knew what she had to do.

Focusing on the spot of light that barely penetrated the darkness she kicked upward, following the bubbles that escaped her mouth. The surface was farther than she'd thought. She'd miscalculated her depth and felt her body closing in on her. Her focus remained on the slow-growing circle of light above her head. In a Superman position, arms extended upward her kicking was less energetic, she was tiring but she didn't know failure.

The water invaded her body, as she screamed in the cold blackness. She felt something wrap around her waist. She fought it, striking at it and trying to swim away, but it pulled her up, fast.

It was Adam. They exploded out of the surface of the water. Coughing and wheezing, she struggled to fill her searing lungs. Adam kept her from bobbing back under and dragged her toward the wooden boat steps.

Effortlessly he lifted her, setting her on the step. The air helped reduce her coughing. Adam was still in the water, resting his forehead against her knees.

His hair was curly wet. She touched the base of his neck, behind his ear, and the spirals coiled gently around her fingers.

"Are you all right?" he asked, looking up from her knees.

"Yes."

In one fluid movement Adam was standing beside her on the step, reaching down with his open hand to pull her up to her feet.

She shivered and he draped a towel over her shoulders then wrapped his arms protectively around her.

"You scared me," he said, tightening his embrace. "What the hell was that about?"

She felt the change, from concern to anger.

"I…" she shivered, his bare chest was warm, "I was on my way up."

"I know." His lips pressed down on the top of her head. "I had no idea you could hold your breath that long."

"I'm sorry."

"What happened?"

I got scared, was too much truth, so she settled for, "I'm not ready for *this*."

"You're going to have to be more explicit." His arms slackened and the anger had morphed into something else.

Her radar was activated and monitoring every fluctuation in his tone.

"I go back to work this week. And I just can't start something when the inevitable result is disappointment."

The quiet was maddening. The boat creaked gently.

"Come to L.A. with me. I leave Monday to close on the building for the restaurant. I can get you back in just over an hour. We can figure something out."

"I can't," she said, instinctively opposed, the hairs standing on the back of her neck. "You've obviously have never been in a long-distance relationship." She didn't like to use the word "romance" if she could help it.

"No, but..." He looked down at her, "have you?"

"Once."

Adam sighed and he released his hold.

"Are you still cold?"

She shook her head.

"Adam, can I ask you something?" Their eyes locked. "Just before I dove in, you had a peculiar expression. I was just wondering what you were thinking."

His slightly embarrassed, regretful smile was attractive. "I thought you were ... undressing."

"Then why the unhappy look?"

"I wasn't unhappy, I was surprised." He hung the towel across her shoulders. "I told you, I don't take sex casually."

"Oh," she nodded, comprehending. "You would have turned me down?" The image of her standing in the buff while being rejected made her cringe.

But Adam shook his head. "I wouldn't have said no."

Melanie squinted up at him, the sun in her eyes making it impossible to read his face. Her heart sped up and beat hard against her ribs.

"Now I wish that was what you wanted," he admitted.

"Adam." Her voice was flat.

He was the first to break away, clearing the dishes and taking them from the table to the cabin.

On the edge of the bench, Adam had folded her clothing. She dressed, the wet bathing suit saturating the dry fabric. Sitting cross-legged she searched the horizon for – nothing, anything, a distraction.

Her empty feeling intensified when Adam sat next to her and stared.

"What happened with the long-distance relationship?"

She felt the downward turn of her lips but couldn't reverse the bend.

"You were in love with him?"

Melanie hesitated. "Um, yeah, I thought I was. Is that the same thing?"

"I don't know."

Melanie sat up straighter, repositioning her legs, nervously tucking them beneath her, agitated from the mention of Danny. She understood that Adam was expecting some sort of explanation and her throat tightened in response.

"I was in college and he was my fantasy guy."

"Really?" Adam's eyes widened and his eyebrows raised with interest.

"Really," she smiled, blushing, a little ashamed of her girliness. But suddenly she wanted to tell him. The gentle, cradle-like movement of the boat plunged her into a sense of nostalgia. She spoke slowly, remembering each detail.

"His name is Danny." She cleared her throat.

How long has it been since I've said his name out loud?

She exhaled softly to settle the jitters. He waited patiently, not moving. His gaze was soothing and finally she found her voice.

"Right before graduation, he broke up with me. He was moving up and I was in the way. But when he got to New York he found himself alone, and Danny was never alone. I was already in D.C., and it seemed like such a short distance to the city. We did the three-hour almost-no-distance thing successfully for about eight months before we both got too busy. We planned train schedules, work schedules but it just fell apart, slowly, so slowly that neither of us noticed. It's not like we ever officially ended it – it just faded. One day we had our last phone call, our last kiss, our last goodbye. We didn't even know it was our last, or at least I didn't."

Adam wore the appropriate solemn expression, "When was the last time you saw him?"

"Seven or eight years ago. He's a rugby player and out of the blue I happened to check out his team's Website. There was a big picture of him with a woman. He looked happy. The team was congratulating them on their upcoming nuptials. There was a bio. She was the daughter of one of the owners, rich and beautiful, and Danny was handsome and talented." Melanie sighed. *What else was there to say?*

"Wow, what'd you do?"

"What could I?" she shrugged. "I went to work. Forty minutes later I was boarding a flight for a job in Chile."

"Do you still love him?"

Melanie thought for a moment. "No, that was a long time ago, but I'm still cautious because of him." This was something she'd only recently learned, as recent as the words that had just rolled off her tongue.

Adam nestled closer, his arms tenderly drawing her toward him. His intense emerald eyes were steady as his lips brushed her across her cheek. She untangled herself from his hold, pressing her hands against his broad shoulders. Adam loosened his hold, brushing back a strand of fallen hair and caressing her face.

"I want to take away all of your pain."

"I'm not in pain."

She took his hand in hers, it was calloused and scarred, by years of culinary mishaps. But on her skin they'd felt soft and smooth.

"Are you kidding?" He pulled back to get a better look at her expression. "He's the real reason you're pushing me away."

"No," she shook her head, uncomfortable with the direction of conversation.

"Okay," he said, shuffling and readjusting his seat further from her. "I guess we should we start heading back," he said, moving away testily.

"Do we have to?" she asked. "I mean, can't we talk?"

He looked unsure.

"You must really like L.A." she tried.

"Why do you want to know, Melanie? You've made it clear that *this* isn't going any further."

"Because we still have today."

"Okay, but if I end up kissing you again, we're out of here." His laugh wasn't the same.

She didn't care what he talked about so long as they were together, even if it was only for a few more hours.

"I chose L.A. because I can't open a place in San Diego. I signed a contract with Oscar. Los Angeles seems reasonable."

"Did you always want to be a chef?" she asked, cautiously.

"No, it had never occured to me. I was all set to play football at Florida State."

"A jock," she chuckled. "I bet your mom has an amazing family album." She knew he had to be as gorgeous in high school as he was now.

Adam's eyes steeled and it took him a moment to answer. "My parents were killed in a car accident a few years back."

"Oh, I'm so sorry." Melanie held her breath and watched his lips relax to their normal fullness and coloring.

"It's okay." He nodded. "My mom did have a set of three-ring binder photo albums. But I doubt they were any better than your mom's."

"Did you bleach your hair blonde?"

"Never."

"Then it's no contest," she said, giving her teenage-self an eye roll. "What happened with Florida State?"

Adam's green eyes looked right through her as he hesitated. She knew the pause, she *used* the pause – the how much to tell? Pause.

"You don't have to say anything, I'm sorry," she said, feeling the innocent question had hit another target.

"Where'd you learn your interrogation techniques?"

Melanie held her breath, but he was being playful. "My mother. You did meet her, right? Do you want to start heading back?"

Adam dragged his front teeth across his bottom lip. Melanie's heart flooded, that was *her* nervous gesture.

"Do you want to go?"

"No, but I thought I was being too nosey." She said, shifting to find a more comfortable spot on the hard wood planks.

He stretched out his legs and adjusted to sit beside her. "Any way to make this work?"

"I'm in D.C. and you're in L.A."

"Right."

"Are you going to tell me how you got from football to crab cakes?"

He exhaled. "Florida State. Football ended on prom night, senior year, with a 1966 Ford Mustang and a giant oak tree."

"Were you hurt badly?" She asked, though this was obviously a delicate topic.

"I wasn't in the car: Three friends, their girlfriends and my girlfriend. So, physically I wasn't touched, but I *should* have been in that car. Instead, I was putting the moves on Mary Ann Reynolds." He squinted at Melanie, "You want to hear my ancient history?"

"I do." She really did.

Adam took a long look at her. "Kristen and I fought a lot; that's why I wasn't in the car. But when I heard the sirens I just knew, I ran the two miles. Nicole was in the street, the Mustang was a mass of metal and the police were trying to extract the bodies."

"Oh, Adam."

"Gruesome. Not one made it to the hospital."

"You felt guilty?"

"I still feel guilty."

"Even if it wasn't your fault?"

"Logically, I know what you're saying but I can't convince myself that's how it works. Believe me I've spent years replaying that night."

"Do you let yourself appreciate how lucky you were?"

"It's taken a long time."

"Well, I'm grateful to have met you."

Adam leaned into her shoulder and kissed the side of her head.

"Anyway, to answer your question. That summer I spent inside my room and had no intention of ever leaving my house. Until, I overheard my parents talking with the school shrink about a grief boot camp. I raced back up to my room and, serendipitiously, on TV was an infomercial about a culinary school in Mexico City. I dialed and four days later I packed."

Melanie wished she could be that woman who knew how to balance it all. She wasn't. And even if she could learn – eventually – right now wasn't the time.

"Are you okay?" He squeezed her shoulder.

"Shouldn't I be asking you? The thing is..." She quickly added, "I don't want to say goodbye."

"You're just not ready, I get that."

"I thought I could..." she said, opening her eyes then wishing she hadn't. He was so handsome, so close and it would be so easy, at first. She swallowed. "I wanted to try a friendship, relationship ... I don't know, *something* with you. But my job, my life..." she was beginning to ramble. She'd already allowed him too far inside.

"You don't have to explain," his expression was kind.

She felt both relieved and disappointed.

They both knew there was nothing more to say and the silence crept up on them.

The sun angling under the canopy signaled that the close of day was near. Adam, already late for work, quickly and ably raised the sails.

"Come here," he motioned for her to stand at the helm. "You said you wanted to sail."

"You don't have time," Melanie protested as he easily moved her in front of him, putting her hands on the wheel.

"The restaurant is all set and isn't this our day together? Time to step up, Melanie."

Melanie didn't pretend to know less than she did, but she did take the long way back.

The marina was quiet and they held hands as they walked to his car.

"Thank you for an amazing day," Melanie said, standing toe to toe with Adam, inches from her front door.

His fingers entwined with hers, Adam was looking directly into her eyes.

"I think we did all right for our one-day romance." His smile brightened up the dimming evening. "If you're ever in L.A., hell, if you're ever in California, give me a call."

"I will."

It was their last moment and she clung tightly to his hands.

"I don't really care for goodbyes," he said, not moving.

There was a peacefulness in his last kiss.

She wouldn't have changed one second. It had been a perfect day that, even in years to come, she wouldn't be able to beat. He was halfway to the curb when the calm morphed into a panic that rose to her throat. Skipping down the steps she flew into his arms.

Ask me to go with you again, ask me to dinner, ask me anything!

"You take care of yourself."

"You, too."

Say something, her mind screamed.

She waved at the back window of his BMW as he pulled away from her curb.

CHAPTER 14

Melanie would rather have crawled under the covers and avoided all humans, but she couldn't. Tonight was her date with Don Avery, an entrepreneur in the local dry cleaning industry. 15 minutes late, he arrived in a delivery van. His *So Clean So. California* slogan, with giant clothes hangers looped the Os, was painted on both sides, on the back door and again on the hood of the vehicle.

"Sorry I'm late," he wheezed. "Got caught up at work."

I'm more disappointed that you showed up at all.

"What's the plan?" Melanie asked, slowing her step.

Don was 300 pounds plus, 5'10" with short legs. She was at the mailbox waiting for him to make his way gingerly down the three steps off the porch. She noticed that the gardenia bushes were blooming and that it'd been at least a week since her dad mowed the lawn.

"If it's all the same to you, I've been craving Chinese food," he coughed after situating, adjusting and buckling.

"Sounds fine."

Melanie imagined Adam sitting in his office with a glass of wine. Maybe he was thinking of her, too.

"There's a place in Kerney Mesa, an all-you-can-eat, that puts out shrimp on weekend nights. They do raise the price to $13.95 but I think it's well worth the bump."

Don continued talking, enlightening her on the dry cleaning process, and Melanie did what she could to stay focused. He talked the entire drive, he talked picking out a table and continued while they slid their trays along the buffet line. Melanie would add an occasional "uh-huh" or "oh yeah?"

Placing his tray with two loaded plates, a giant Diet Coke and a wedge of pecan pie onto the table he said, "I think I've been talking too much."

Melanie's grin was weak, but she was grateful for his chatter. "It's all right."

"I'm just nervous and I tend to yammer on. You can just slap me if I get started again."

She agreed on the punishment.

Don let out a deep breath before attacking his plates. She didn't hear a peep out of him for five minutes. Melanie ate slowly. She wasn't hungry.

"Would you excuse me for a few minutes?" he asked, shuffling out of his seat.

Melanie played with her food as she sat uncomfortably, daydreaming of Adam, his body wet with sea water dripping on the deck. His skin had been warm, even with the cold water, and his heartbeat erratic as she'd rested her cheek against his chest.

He thought he was rescuing me. She smiled to herself, thinking it was very sweet and romantic of him.

"Sorry about that," Don said, interrupting and arriving with a vanilla cone. He smelled of cigarette smoke. "I noticed you've got a wine stain there on your jacket. I could get that out for you at no charge," he offered, swirling his tongue around the ice cream.

Melanie's heart filled, looking at the corner of her leather jacket. "Thanks, but it's sort of a memory I'd rather save."

Don's face wrinkled in confusion. "But that's a gorgeous jacket and I could make it like new again."

Melanie smiled. "I appreciate that but I don't think of it as a blemish." She knew he didn't get it. In Don's eyes all stains were meant to be eradicated. "Would you want to catch a movie or something?"

Melanie asked on their way back to his van, still full of deliveries in the back.

"Well, I don't really know how to put this," he paused, opened the door for her and walked around to the driver's side. The van groaned as he sat down, and he shuffled trying to get comfortable. He unwrapped a mint he had taken from the restaurant and popped it into his mouth. She declined one when he offered but he said nothing as he started the ignition and drove out of the parking lot.

"Cheryl said this was only dinner. If we went to a movie with popcorn and a drink it's another 40 bucks." He was taking her home. "The offer on the jacket still stands." He grimaced at the red wine that had stained the leather.

Sunday, Melanie went to Mass with her parents. She daydreamed through the entire sermon and decided she just met Adam at the wrong time, pushing away the question of when would have been better.

She spent the rest of the day helping her mom with Sunday dinner, fetching, measuring and pouring over a new Paula Deen cookbook. It was a day meant for her 'improve relations' project. Jealousy over her relationship with Cheryl was only bound to get worse once the baby was born.

That Sunday Bruce arrived early. Jason Johnson was a San Diego Padre and Bruce was thrilled wearing his Johnson baseball jersey. He approved of Melanie's outfit an hour before Jason arrived. Then leaned against the kitchen sink, keeping a watchful eye on every car that passed.

Bruce hollered and Melanie looked out her bedroom window

and saw that parked out front was a gorgeous burgundy convertible Porsche. From the top of the stairs she could hear Bruce's nervous voice.

"Yeah, she'll be right down. I'm her brother, Bruce. I am a huge fan and let me tell you how great you are doing, fantastic! Worth every cent."

"Thanks, man." Jason slapped Bruce on the back and whistled when Melanie walked down the stairs.

She smiled.

"Okay, well, you two have a great time tonight," Bruce said, nodding in approval. He was as giddy as a school girl as Melanie and Jason walked out the door. "Stay out as long as you like. It was really great meeting you."

Melanie shook her head at her silly little brother and turned to say something but Bruce quickly shut the door.

"Nice car."

"This baby isn't even a month old." He caressed the hood as he trotted to his side of the car. "Do you want me to put the top up so you won't get your hair messed up?"

"No way." Melanie wanted the wind in her face.

Jason sped through the streets. "I thought we'd take a little drive before dinner."

"Love to."

She leaned back into the new leather interior and closed her eyes, imagining she was with Adam driving to L.A. It had been difficult to stop the daydreaming. He was even trying to creep into her reality. Everywhere she went she noticed his car or someone who looked like him.

Jason cranked up the stereo – rap music. He drove way too fast, tires squealing around corners, then pulled into a secured driveway and unlocked the gate. Carefully he avoided the huge potholes that dotted the pavement. Rounding the bend the land opened up, and Melanie realized they were driving along the marsh that swung in about a quarter mile from the sea. The road coiled around the outskirts of a bog. Towering eucalyptus trees lined one side of the road as it cut through a hill that held the 5 freeway.

"I like to take her out here for a spin."

Jason put the car in gear and like a bullet they sped along the unmaintained path. The force molded her into the seat, and her adrenaline kicked in.

Desperate to preserve the familiar feeling, she asked, "Do you think I could give it a try?" Melanie was exhilarated, longing to hold onto an old friend.

Jason hesitated. "Can you handle this car?" he asked, looking down at her small frame.

Melanie smiled, "Yeah, and I'll tell you what, I'll even put in a good word for you with Trish."

He put the car in neutral and gave her pointers as they traded seats. Melanie rolled her seat closer to the pedals and floored the accelerator. She shifted gears and hugged the curves, holding onto the power and control.

Melanie, she thought with a pang of heartache, recognizing herself and missing this person.

The scenery blurred as she pushed the vehicle up over 100 mph. Whipping around, the car came to a dead stop at the end of the path.

"Whew! Where did you learn to drive like that?" Jason asked, leaning back in his seat. "Incredible."

Swapping seats, Melanie pulled the seat belt across her chest.

"I really need to get me one of these."

"I do recommened it." Jason raced back the way they had come.

Melanie's head was forced back on the headrest as he pushed past 110 mph. Hitting a rut in the road Jason lost control and the Porsche fishtailed. Frantically he tried to regain control, but the vehicle seemed to be gaining speed, spinning them across the road. Dust rose around them, clouding any possible view. Melanie waited for the right instant before she unfastened her seatbelt and partially leapt and was partially thrown into Jason's lap, grabbing hold of the wheel and stepping on his large feet to shift gears. She turned the key to the accessories mode to kill the engine while allowing her the ability to steer and pulled the emergency brake. Unsure if it would work, she held her breath as the car screamed to a stop with a hard, rocking jerk.

She leaned her head back on Jason's shoulder. His heart beat wildly and his body trembled beneath her.

Her blood coursed with excitement. As the dust settled, one of the ancient trees appeared eight inches from the passenger side door.

"Wow, that was close," Melanie exclaimed, her knees momentarily weakened.

The irregular pavement had been marked up behind them and Melanie examined the circular patterns burned into the road. There were gaps in places where it seemed the car had lifted off the ground. Jason was still in the car with his eyes shut.

He was devoid of color. Melanie knelt down beside him and cupped his face in her hands. She tilted his head to face her. Had this been one of her agents she would have slapped him, but he was a civilian.

"Jason, look at me." She got into his face as his blue eyes focused on her. "We're okay, everything is fine."

"I'm sorry," he whispered over and over.

"It's okay, we're fine." She assured him of this by extending her arms and standing. "Look, I didn't even break a heel," she joked, bending back down to his eye level.

Jason's color was returning but his body was still shaking. "I almost *killed* you."

She brushed his hair off his forehead, touched by his vulnerability.

"Come on, let's take a walk." She held his hand as he got out and leaned against the car.

He didn't want to see the marks the spin-out had caused and he especially didn't want to see how close they had come to wrapping around the tree.

"Melanie, I am so sorry." He pulled her into a tight embrace.

She enclosed him in her arms and was taken by the incredible sunset. The clouds hanging in the sky had taken on a pink glow, and the orange sun was hanging just above the horizon.

"Thank you for saving my life," Jason stuttered and squeezed her hand, too hard.

A bond had been forged and Melanie recognized his wholesome quality and a little-boy charm. He wasn't blatantly handsome, but she found herself understanding Trish's interest.

"We'd better think about getting back," he said.

"Do you want me to drive?"

"I'm okay," Jason smiled, sheepishly. "You know, you're like an angel."

"Hardly."

"You're not going to tell anyone about my ... my cowardliness."

"You are *not* a coward – it was scary."

"You weren't scared."

"Yes, I was."

Jason drove cautiously, his hands at ten and two, around the bends and even more so on the freeway.

"So Jason, what are your feelings toward Trish?" She decided not to beat around the bush.

"Should we be talking about this?" He moved only his eyes to look over at her.

"I'm just curious because if you were interested and had good motives I think I could get you two together."

"Yeah?! Well, if you could do that then you really are an angel. I'm crazy about Trish. I've asked her out dozens of times and she keeps telling me to look her up when I retire."

Melanie laughed. "She's determined, but I think this is a good thing."

"I even considered getting injured just to be near her."

"I think I've got a better plan," Melanie said, looking up as Jason parked. "What are we doing here?"

"It's my favorite restaurant. The chef is a good friend of mine."

"Adam?"

"Yeah, you know him?"

"We went out a couple of times." She felt as sick as Jason had looked after she'd pulled the brake. Her stomach flopped and churned. "Can we go someplace else?"

"Sure, but he doesn't work Sundays so you're safe." Melanie looked around the parking lot – no signs of his vehicle. "The date went bad enough to avoid him? Doesn't sound like Adam." Jason looked at Melanie in curiosity.

She shook her head. "It wasn't bad." Conceding she added, "Let's get dinner."

Jason was a star at Oscar's. Daria went gaga over him and practically tripped over her own jaw when she spied Melanie.

Sitting at a small romantic table, Melanie used her excess energy to plot out a campaign to put Trish in Jason's arms. She didn't mind being mostly on her own as their conversation was interrupted, constantly, by fans. But when he did speak of Trish a light shone in his eyes and Melanie's resolve was confirmed.

Shit, I hope this works. If not I could damage another friendship.

"Jace, hey man, I heard you were here."

Jason stood to shake Adam's hand and they exchanged a quick, manly, embrace. "I didn't think you worked on Sunday."

Melanie noticed a slight note of guilt in Jason's voice.

Adam opened his hands, "What kind of greeting is that?" He asked, his laugh light, before even noticing Jason's companion. "Melanie?"

"Hi," she said, absently pulling on her bottom lip, extremely aware of his handsome face.

"What's going on?" He bent and placed a soft kiss on her cheek.

"My blind date, buddy, so lay off the lip action." Jason smiled, pulling an empty chair from a nearby table. "Take a seat." He motioned to Adam.

"Thanks, Melanie is your blind date?" He pulled the chair closer to Melanie, their knees almost touching.

She hoped the stirring in her abdomen didn't show on her face.

"Yeah, she's Trish's friend. You remember."

Then looking bewildered, he looked to Melanie for clarification. "Your friend Trish is the physical therapist for the Padres?"

Melanie nodded.

"Get this, man, Angel here is hooking me up with her." Jason was giddy delivering the news.

Melanie cringed at the memory of Adam's brief experience with her.

"Angel?"

"Yeah, she's an angel, isn't she?" Jason watched her with admiration.

Adam nodded reluctantly.

"He's just grateful," Melanie explained.

"Hell, yeah." Jason's eyes lit up. "Wait 'til you see her."

Adam fessed up, admitting to briefly meeting her the night the girls ate at Oscar's.

"That's great, Jace, but how'd you land Melanie as a blind date?" She tilted her head and refrained from rolling her eyes.

"It's a miracle."

"That's enough," Melanie stood abruptly. "We'd better go if you want to meet up with Trish."

Adam walked them out to the parking lot.

"Give us a minute," Adam said to Jason, holding onto Melanie's wrist as Jason took his seat behind the wheel. "Hi," he smiled, and her heart thumped. "You look beautiful. I'm glad you came by tonight. I've been debating whether or not to call." His eyes traveled her face down to her hair that covered her shoulder. "If only things could have worked out differently for us."

"I know," she whispered.

His kiss left her breathless and she quickly took her seat next to Jason, her knees wobbly.

"Bye, Adam."

"Jason, you drive safe, no funny stuff. Understand?"

"You got it, Pops."

Adam scrutinized the Porsche. "What's with the dust?"

"Yeah, about that, I gotta get it washed." His voice was tight – he was obviously a terrible liar.

Adam's eyes narrowed on Jason before moving onto Melanie.

"Maybe I should drive you home."

"Come on!" Jason laughed.

"I'm fine." Melanie said, though she would have preferred the extra time alone with Adam.

He stood, hovering, before relenting. "Okay," he nodded. "Bye, Melanie."

She swallowed hard and nodded.

Jason pulled out of the parking lot gingerly. "What'd you do to my friend? I've never seen him like that."

"Like what?"

"He's not much for PDA. Even his girlfriends only made it to hand holding or a small, quick kiss. Public, open-mouth kissing was definitely out."

Melanie tasted her lips. She could still feel him there, warm and soft.

"And look at you, all quiet and mannerly." Jason's laugh was more of a boom.

"What?" Her brow furrowed with mock annoyance.

"You like him, too."

"Just drive, Jason."

"Yeah, all right," he said, still laughing. "But Adam is a great guy."

"Really, there is no need to sell him."

"Then what's the problem?"

Jason was taking care to obey all the traffic laws.

"Logistics," Melanie sighed, tired of talking about it and definitely sick of thinking about it. "He's opening a restaurant in L.A. I live in D.C. And if the 3,000 miles weren't enough, a new business takes time – all of his time – and effort. It's just bad timing." She was happy to be pinning the blame on Adam, though in her heart she knew it was all her doing.

"I guess," Jason said, rubbing his smooth, freckled chin.

Melanie stayed quiet, immersed in her own thoughts the rest of the way home.

"So, you're clear with our plan?"

"Not science. I show up and she falls lovingly in my arms."

Melanie shook her head. "It's a bit more complicated" – though, admittedly, not much.

"Are you sure you know what you're doing?" Jason asked, standing on her porch.

The light was on and Melanie knew Bruce was still inside waiting for details.

"I'm sure. Trish is going to be happy to see you."

"I was talking about you and Adam."

"Oh, that. Well, that I'm not sure about at all, but right now it's how things have got to be."

"You're the boss." He lifted her off her feet in a big bear hug.

She laid the groundwork with a single phone call. Trish's voice was a rigid mix of jealousy and anger as Melanie asked permission to use Jason to get over Adam. And now Jason was on his way to her apartment with pints of her favorite ice cream, Ben & Jerry's Chunky Monkey.

Melanie prayed she had made the right decision as Jason's red tail lights faded out of sight.

❧

Melanie never slept that night. Thoughts of Adam were becoming more intrusive, and with her dating obligations behind her she wanted nothing more than to get back to work. It was time to call Mike.

"Melanie, my love, how are you?"

His voice was like home, "I'm good. God, it's great to hear your voice."

"I wish I had better news for you," he said, finally in an unfamiliar tone.

"What's up?" she asked, sounding calmer than she felt.

"Nothing, that's the problem. Things seem to be running smoothly. I mean, it was a little rough the week after Ben left, but Parker seems to have found his footing. Hey, I know that's not what you wanted to hear, and I'm as surprised as anyone, but what can I say?"

Melanie was steady.

"That can't be right." Parker was incompetent and that wasn't a negotiable.

"I'm not in the know like when you and Ben were running the operation, but he struts around like he owns the place. I keep my head down but the agents are really starting to respect Parker. Cases have been light so I guess he's farming more out to the FBI, he's juggling the load," Mike continued speaking but Melanie couldn't hear another word.

She was miles ahead of Mike.

"Tell me, Mike, how could the case load be light? We're rounding up on the Fourth of July."

Holidays always caused a spike in terrorist activity, always.

Mike stammered.

"Where's Ben?" Her voice held authority as if she'd never been gone.

"He's a nut job but I'm telling you, the Agency is backing Parker. I seriously doubt Jackson is even coming back."

"Get me Judith, now."

A quick discussion with Ben's secretary, now assigned to the front desk of Spy Manor with the security guard, yielded Ben's new number.

"Ward."

His deep voice was her warm blanket. She trusted him more than any person on the planet. He'd saved her life on many occasions and she treasured the moments spent strategizing in his office. He was her mentor, her confidant, and at one time her advocate. But apparently, now she was "Ward."

"How are you, Ben?"

"I've had better days but Lilly's a trouper. She would've made an excellent agent."

There was a pause while Melanie debated the right words.

"Well, to what do I owe the pleasure of this call?" Ben asked.

She clenched her teeth, angry that he felt the need to continue with the game-playing.

"I spoke with Mike, and I'm confused about what the hell is going on."

The heavy sigh, from a man with too much on his shoulders, filled the receiver. Guilt quickly replaced her selfishness.

"From what I know the Board is pleased and the country is as secure as it's ever been."

"Ben, I'm sorry, but you don't buy that for a minute. Get me back inside, I can get to the truth." Desperation smothered her.

"Melanie," Ben started in his parental voice, "when I pushed for your resignation I had every intention of returning as director and bringing you back. I was keeping you apart from Parker for your own good. Now, however..."

"No, Ben."

"Hear me out." He was again her superior. "These past weeks with Lilly made me realize, I'm an old man who has missed out on a key aspect of life. I've put so much energy into the job that I'd forgotten the beauty of pure existence."

"No..." Melanie could feel her rising panic but forced herself to listen.

"Honey, you need a life outside of the job. You've done so much good for humanity, now it's time you focus on being happy."

Bullshit.

"Ben, that's crap. What is happy? I'm happy!" Her fingers pressed into her temples.

"My point exactly. Find your laugh, Melanie. I love you like a daughter, and I wouldn't allow my own flesh to continue the way you've been ... I can't let you. This is your chance at freedom."

"I'm going back, Ben, with or without your help." She felt like a defiant child. "You *know* I can."

She had dirt on Hugh Parker. She could do whatever she wanted.

"Let it go, Agent."

"Are you kidding me?" she asked angrily, "you think I can be *happy* sipping piña coladas while everything I've worked so hard for falls apart? Jesus, Ben, are you wishing for a catastrophe? I could own the Agency with the stuff I've got on Hugh."

"You can't use that." His voice was suddenly stern, defensive.

"Hugh has been very gracious with Lilly throughout this whole ordeal and I am not about to disrupt that. Do you understand?"

"You, Ben? You sold out."

"Damn it, Ward! This is my wife's life we're talking about."

Melanie shut up. He was outraged, with cause, and his voice shot fear into her bones.

"Hugh Parker is an influential man with a long reach. Even you couldn't beat him, so don't try."

Melanie was shaking.

"Melanie, I'm sorry. I've been under considerable stress and it was Hugh who got Lilly to the top of the transplant list. I'm worried about her and would do almost anything to keep her with me for a few more years. I've been a terrible husband, Melanie, and I need to do this to make it up to Lilly. Do what you have to, just please keep me in your heart when you act."

"I promise. Give Lilly my best," she said, not recognizing her own timid voice.

Things were changing and Melanie was terrified.

"What's the matter?" her mother asked from the doorway. "You're as white as a ghost."

Melanie clutched her phone in a daze.

"Roger! Roger!"

"I'm all right," she said, not sure if it was true.

"Sit down, Honey." Rita pulled her to the nearest chair. "Roger, get some water for Melanie."

"What's going on?" her father asked, rushing inside, his voice filled with concern. "Annie?"

"I quit my job," Melanie muttered.

It felt strange saying the words. It'd been true for weeks but it was the first time she'd felt the certainty.

"When?"

"Is it because you're taking a long vacation?" Rita asked.

"I quit before I got here but it was supposed to be temporary." She looked up at her parents. "What am I going to do?"

Her mind was racing, trying to come up with a solution.

"I've got to go." Melanie said before rushing up the stairs to her room.

In the bottom of her duffle bag shoved in the back of her closet was her gun. She wanted to hold onto the old Melanie, Spy Melanie. And she had an overwhelming urge to shoot something. In her father's Chevy Nova she drove to the Agency's local office.

"I'm sorry, Ms. Ward, but you aren't in our database. I can't let you in."

Melanie stood, bewildered, at the security desk about to be escorted out of the building.

"Can't you call Mike Hanson in the D.C. office? I've got his number right here."

The unrelenting uniformed guard shook his head.

"Agent Ward?"

Melanie turned toward the voice. "Agent Clark," she said, with a grin that stretched from ear to ear.

"It's okay, I'll sign her in."

Lenny Clark was a Vietnamese American whose soldier father had fallen in love during his tour of duty and came home with a very pregnant wife. Lenny was born in L.A. but now spent most of his time as an undercover operative. Years spent with society's underbelly had changed Lenny into a shady, unapologetic character. Outspoken and as deviant as the people he monitored, Lenny made no excuses about his sinister outlook on life. Melanie respected his integrity and loyalty.

"Thanks," she said, once the door's lock had been disengaged with the familiar buzz. The pent-up tension releasing, she was grateful she wasn't going to have to take hostages. "I just came to practice at the shooting range," she faked a serene smile.

In the soothing, cold white hallways pretending would be easier, now that she was back in her element.

"I heard about your termination," Lenny said under his breath.

"It was a mutual thing," she growled, contradicting her tone by shaking her head with a laugh. "Sort of, anyway."

"What's going on in Washington? I've been back a couple of days, fucking pulled from deep cover and nobody knows what the hell is going on."

Melanie shook her head. "I don't know, Len."

"Fucking Parker. Things need to change, so whatever it is you need to do, Agent, do it." His brown-eyed gaze was piercing. "I'm on my way back to the Orient and hope my fucking cover hasn't been compromised or I'd help bring down the house, but you know *my door is always open to you*."

He stopped as they approached the shooting gallery. His eyes narrowed as he evaluated her. An agent began target practice firing off five quick rounds.

"Good luck, Agent Ward," Lenny said, saluting her.

"Thank you," she grinned and Lenny walked away. "Lenny," she called, when he turned she nodded and he responded in the same manner.

Melanie found her way through the corridors to Lenny's office. The door was unlocked. She smiled, switching on the light and easing into his ergonomic chair. The small space was cluttered with boxes, papers and binders. One wall was covered with personal photos tacked into the plaster. Lenny was divorced but there were pictures of him with his wife and daughter. Melanie shook her head at the little girl who'd never know what a hero her father was to the world, though he'd never be her hero.

"Okay," Melanie said to the blue computer screen.

Knowing she no longer had her clearance, she stumbled around searching for the phone database. She still had some access – after all, her phone was operational. Mike would have set up a new identity for her. Melanie closed her eyes and imagined Mike, a technical wizard who lacked social skills, idolized the agents and spoke using exaggerated hand gestures.

He's not an agent, he's technical.

She typed LISA ABERNATHY, her last alias.

Confirmed.

Melanie smiled. *Now for the passcode.*

Yakimoto, No.

Hawaii, No.

Melanie breathed out, clearing her lungs.

She tried again, three more times, nothing.

She searched her memory. *What had he been impressed with?*

Swingers.

Bingo! The gates opened and Melanie had full access to the agency's files. She poured over the endless stream of data, not knowing exactly what she was looking for.

"Hey, Trish," she said, answering her phone while still typing on

Lenny's computer.

"Hey? That's all you have to say?"

Oh shit, she'd forgotten.

"How was your evening?"

"I cannot believe you did that to me."

Melanie waited for as long as she could, trying to decipher if Trish sounded angry. "So, are you mad or not?"

"I should be furious."

"But you're not! Oh, thank God," she said, relieved that something had gone right. Melanie refocused on the computer. "I'm so relieved, you have no idea, but I can't talk right now. I'll call you back, okay?"

"Seriously, you're ditching me? What are you doing?"

"Trying to get my job back."

"What does that mean?"

Melanie huffed and briefly recapped. "I'll explain more later. But I am so happy for you. I like him."

"He's super sweet, right?"

"Super. Love you, bye."

Melanie skimmed over the vast information. She followed the path from Parker's first day, the cases, his e-mails and the assignments, perusing for a pattern. There wasn't much time before Mike would figure out she was on and boot her from the system.

"Melanie?" Mike sighed her name into the receiver.

"Speak of the devil," she said, casually. "What gave me away?"

"I was leaving for the day so I did a quick sweep and guess who I see is online." Mike lowered his voice to a whisper. "You can't be doing this, Mel. Did you break into Agent Clarke's office?"

"He's always on assignment anyway. I don't even know why he

needs an office. In theory it's not my fault."

"I'm glad this is fun for you, because you're breaking the law and now you're involving me."

Melanie smiled victoriously.

"So, you'll let me finish?"

Mike blew a loud breath, letting her know it was a big decision for him, but she already knew he was a major pushover where she was concerned.

"I need four more hours."

"Four! Are you kidding me? You can have 20 minutes."

"Three hours, but that's my final offer," Melanie smirked.

"One, and if something comes up I'm pulling the plug."

"Deal."

Melanie checked her watch. Rummaging through Lenny's desk she found three jump drives that she loaded with every file she could find that had anything to do with Parker. Hastily she scanned the information, looking for an obvious change of tide in Parker's behavior. Her phone rang.

"Time's up, Princess."

"Wow, it's been an hour?" Melanie looked, blurry eyed, at her watch.

"Two and a half, I fell asleep." She could hear him yawning. "Hold on, someone's at the door."

"Hey, Ed?"

It was Finn Parker's voice.

"I'm Mike."

"I need to know if it's possible to delete information from a person's file."

"Delete? We usually re-classify the file to a higher level of authority."

Melanie stayed quiet.

"Just tell me if it's possible."

"Yeah, it's possible." Mike said. "Do you want me to take care of it for you?"

Parker's grating chuckle sent a shudder down her spine. "Right, like I trust you."

"He's gone," Mike said, "but, Mel, you've got to end this fishing expedition. I shouldn't have let you stay on at all. Parker would literally kill me if he knew I was helping you. His ego's the size of a large planet. It's like he thinks nothing can touch him. I hate to do this, but I'm going to have to shut down your phone access. God, that was scary. I swear I cannot stop sweating."

"You did great, Mike, please let me keep the phone."

The length of Mike's pause was disquieting for Melanie. She'd trusted him with confidential information more times than she cared to admit and his jumping ship caused distress. She stayed quiet, waiting him out and not letting him off the proverbial hook.

"Mel," she could visualize his down turned gaze as he slowly shook his head, "I don't like this. I'll give you another week but no longer, and I'm not interested in any of your ploys." His voice was weak. "I'm sorry but I've got to consider myself. I told you he's like all-powerful now."

"That only happens in comic books, but I got it." *Loud and clear*, she thought.

CHAPTER 15

Melanie divorced herself from everything but hunting Parker. Locked away in her room she scoured documents as the summer days gave way to increasingly longer nights.

"Hey, stranger."

Melanie smiled and rubbed her strained eyes, grateful to give her brain a rest. She put the call on speaker phone and stretched across on her untouched bed.

"Hello, Trish. Are you married yet?"

"Ha-ha, very funny. But I do have to say that things are wonderful," she said in her giggly, "it's great to be me" voice. "I'm going to start calling you Angel, too. Did you hear about Jenny?"

"No, what happened?"

Melanie hated to hear, knowing it would be bad.

"Ryan left her after she confessed about her romp with Tom the good parishioner. I guess she's pretty distressed, curled up in a fetal position and refusing to get out of bed. Her mom's stationed herself over there and is taking care of the kids. That Ryan has got some nerve. I swear I never liked him."

"What are we doing for her?"

"*I* was going over this afternoon but you should stay away. She's still mad at you."

"Unbelievable."

"I know, but it's easier to blame you than herself or Ryan. But that's not why I called. You'll never guess who we had dinner with last night."

Melanie hated guessing games. She played along less than whole-heartedly.

"Gandhi?"

"Come on, Mel, play."

"Okay, um, I don't know. George Foreman."

"I'll give you a hint: his first name starts with an A and you like to kiss him."

"Adam? Really? Did you go to the restaurant? Because I called last Thursday and they said he'd be out until tomorrow."

She let out a small grunt. "Nope, you can't even imagine my horror when Jason introduced us. I was afraid Adam would say something about the night I, well, you know."

"He wouldn't do that. But how did he look?"

She pictured his dark hair curling at his ears and the shallow creases leading to his sparkling green eyes. Just the memory caused her blood pressure to rise.

"Not as good as I remembered. Plain, actually, with really big ears."

Melanie smirked.

"He asked about you."

"Yeah? What did you say?" She cowered, waiting for the answer. She never knew what Trish was going to say.

"That you lost your stupid job and that you were literally morphing into a big, ugly, pasty hermit crab. Never leaving your room."

"Trish!"

"Seriously," her voice changed, losing its playful tone. "He works tonight, I think you should call him."

"Maybe I will."

"Promise?"

Melanie laughed. "Promise."

"Good, good, okay." Her delight returned when the topic changed to Jason, who was currently en route to Pittsburg.

The night fell quickly as Melanie prepared to visit Adam at work. She'd thought of nothing else since Trish's phone call, even shutting down her computer. She wore a chocolate-colored wrap dress that could have come right out of a disco circa 1975. Her hair curled, and her makeup applied, she clutched the steering wheel of her father's metallic green Chevy.

A group of weary seniors gathered at the entrance to Oscar's as Melanie snuck a glance toward the hostess pedestal. Daria, looking unbearably shrewish in yet another elegant gown, was in command. Not wanting to be noticed, Melanie waited a few minutes and slipped in with a large party. She veered off toward Adam's office as the others made their way to the dining room.

She'd always considered desire a weakness, and right now she felt very weak. Her rapid breaths betrayed her nervousness as she clipped down the tiled corridor. What was she going to say? That she'd made a mistake?

His door was like the ones at her elementary school with a big square window. Instead of artwork he had mini blinds and his name painted on the glass. The door hung slightly ajar.

It was the hushed giggle that stopped her knuckle from rapping against the door. With the tips of her fingers Melanie pushed the door open just enough to peek inside. Adam was sitting on the floor gazing into the eyes of a woman, a candlelit dinner beautifully laid out on the coffee table.

"Maybe she's his sister," she hoped. Then Adam cradled the woman's face and kissed her.

A small squeak escaped her throat, the scene was romantic and intimate. Melanie closed her eyes, rolled back against the wall and wished she could disappear into the wallpaper.

∾

The night stretched out unbearably. Images of Adam with the other woman gave way to Finn laughing as he kicked his heels up on Ben's mahogany desk. The collision of her two worlds felt cataclysmic, with nowhere for her to seek solace.

Forcing the fresh pain of Adam into the darkest reaches of her over-active imagination, she chose to focus on what she could control. Finn.

Her hours of research had opened the doors to Parker's decision or lack of decision process. At first it was fun and games, assigning friends to "cases" in the south of France and Bali. Until the stream of increasingly negative e-mail brought an especially heated letter from his father. It was a reminder to honor the Parker family name and suggested Finn accomplish matters through "alternative means." Melanie understood Hugh's translation of "alternative" and figured Finn had taken the advice because a week later the nasty e-mails were tilting to an affirming tone.

Rita began rustling in the kitchen, Melanie rubbed her eyes and was surprised to see the soft sunlight beaming through the lace curtains. She went down looking for company, her mom was fooling with a pot of coffee.

"You look terrible," Rita said, taking her glasses off the tip of her nose and letting them hang to her chest. "Have you been crying?"

Melanie filled the largest cup in the cupboard without answering. Rita said nothing, but hovered over Melanie as she swirled vanilla creamer into her dark java.

"Everything's fine, Mom, I just had a long night."

"You have noticed that I've been giving you your space."

"Yes, I have. Thank you."

The coffee was hot and bitter. Melanie added more flavored cream and stirred in two teaspoons of sugar.

Rita moved her weight to a stool next to Melanie's.

"So, if you want to talk about whatever is on your mind, I won't pressure you."

The bloodhound had caught a scent and Melanie, having less strength than her mother, gave in.

"I went to meet someone last night and it turns out that I was too late."

"What does that mean, you were late?"

"He's got a girlfriend."

"Nonsense," she said without hesitation.

"Mom, he does, I saw them kissing."

"Is he married?"

Melanie shook her head.

"Then it's not too late. How do you think I landed your father?" Rita asked, raising her eyebrows.

"No," Melanie gasped, forgetting her own misery. "Dad always says he pursued you. You were at the punch bowl in the yellow dress when he first saw you and fell in love instantly." She recited the story she'd heard dozens of times over the years. "Love at first sight."

As a child she'd gaze at the photo of her parents and imagine them at the party, where her father worked as a waiter and her mother was a debutante. It was all very vivid in Melanie's mind, as if she'd been there herself.

Rita wore a Mona Lisa expression. "Phhh," she waved off the

notion. "I'd seen your father around town for a month. He was dating Penny Pimpleton at the time."

"Her name was Pimpleton?"

Then this unfamiliar woman leaned forward, her hand on Melanie's, wicked delight humming out of her words. "No, but that's what I called her."

"Mom!" Melanie wheezed, wide-eyed.

"What?" she asked, innocently. "I planned the whole thing." She shrugged. "I simply did what was necessary, and if you like this man, you should, too."

With that, Rita put her glasses back on the tip of her nose and continued reading an article from the morning paper, looking very different from the woman Melanie had always known.

"Does Dad know?" Melanie was aghast that such a key part of the Ward history was a sham.

"Heavens, no," she said, not looking up. "Besides, his version is so much more romantic."

Melanie, harboring a renewed sense of hope, put down the awful coffee. "I think I'm going for a run." She smiled. "Thanks, Mom."

"Have a good time, Honey."

Melanie could have sworn that her mother, from behind her bifocals, gave her a wink.

It was a beautiful morning, and Melanie ran along the streets of La Jolla down to Pacific Beach. Adam had mentioned on their date that he'd missed a beach volleyball game to spend the morning with her on his boat. That had been a Saturday morning. It was Saturday morning now.

Summer tan lines were visible, kids had been released from school and Melanie – her radio strapped to her arm, hair pulled up into a ponytail and cell phone clipped to her shorts – navigated through the crowded sidewalk.

Tourists mixed it up with the locals and she could blend. The sun seeping into her skin warmed her and she could almost imagine feeling like her old self again. The heavy salt air filled her lungs and she was absorbed in the moment.

The beach bustled with joggers, bikini-clad women rollerblading on the sidewalk and families dragging ice chests and inflatable rafts toward the water. She didn't even mind that her pace was slowed. She felt completely normal behind her sunglasses. Her spirits were curiously lifted by her mother's 35-year charade.

A volleyball tournament caught her attention. Three games were taking place simultaneously, Miller Lite was sponsoring with banners announcing the fifth annual championship. Quickly she glanced at the spectators on the sidelines and players before falling on just one man in a blue jersey.

Melanie stopped jogging and hopped the three-foot retaining wall that separated the sidewalk from the sand.

Her heart pounded as if keeping time with a marching band. He spotted her almost immediately. The game he was playing in had been suspended and he jogged over to greet her.

"Melanie?"

"Hi," she said, wishing she'd taken a few minutes to create a plan.

With three long steps in her direction he was within arm's reach.

"Hi," he said, looking at her curiously. "What are you doing here?"

"Just out for a jog."

"How have you been?" He asked, his curiosity seeming to intensify,

"I mean, I was sorry to hear about your job."

"Yeah, sucks. I, um, tried calling you but you weren't due back until tonight," she admitted.

"I was surprised to hear that you were still in town," he said, clearing his throat. "Did you know we had dinner with Trish and Jason the other night?"

Melanie nodded, then corrected. "Well sort of, I didn't know about the girl. I found out about her last night when I went to the restaurant to see you and you were engaged in a picnic on the floor." Melanie tried to soften her tone. "I don't think Trish wanted to be the one to tell me."

"Oh, I'm sorry you had to find out like that."

They stood looking at each other, he was standing close, she leaned back on her heels.

Shifting her weight in the sand she wondered how she was going to remind him that … what? Her chest felt heavy just thinking of what she wanted to say.

"Well, she can't play!" a stocky man shouted, treading heavily toward Adam. "Damn fool, her finger isn't broken, that medic is a fucking kid with maybe a year training. Jesus, and now we're going to have to forfeit because we have to have at least one woman on the team." The man was a sweaty beet red, from the top of his balding head down beneath his blue jersey. "Who's the chick?"

"Stan, this is my friend Melanie."

Friend.

"Does your 'friend' play volleyball? We need a woman."

"I don't know, do you, Mel?" Adam set his glasses on top of his head. "I get it if you'd rather not."

He's manipulating you with his gorgeous green eyes.

"I can play."

"All right!" Stan said, racing away. "Hey, ref we've got our player."

"Thanks, uh, Mel..." he was about to say something when Stan hollered.

"Hey, love, what's your name?"

"Ward, Melanie Ward," she told the man who was writing her name on a clipboard.

Melanie was introduced to the team, and tossed a blue jersey.

"Okay, then, time is up, folks." The judge blew his whistle and clapped his hands together.

"Tiny thing, aren't you? I hope you can play. If not, just stay out of the way," Stan said, patting Melanie on the back.

From the first serve Adam tried to protect her. "You can't cover both our areas," she said. "Really, trust me."

"These guys play rough." He wasn't trying to be condescending.

"I'm fine. You can't win if you're worried about me. I've got this."

She did. And once he realized, they fell into sync. The sun burned and sweat dripped from her body. With the back of her hand she pushed back a strand of hair, sand scraping her forehead, then she called the score and served. The ball volleyed a few times before Melanie saw it head straight for an open corner. She lunged for the spot. Lifting her face, as she crashed, skidding across the coarse sand. The ball bounced off her wrists as a sharp pain seared from her hip. She heard the cheers as she pushed to her feet.

"We did it!" Adam shouted as he scooped her up in his arms and spun her around.

For an instant their eyes locked and without thinking Melanie bent down and pressed her lips to his. Her breath caught and they both hesitated. He tasted salty and she could feel his heartbeat quicken beneath his sweaty jersey. This was where she wanted to be, she reengaged in their kiss. Still in his elevated embrace, his fingers gripping her back, he lowered her. But their gaze didn't break until his teammates pulled him away to celebrate.

Her heart was racing and she was feeling light-headed, mostly from the salty kiss but a bit from the pain. She hobbled gingerly off the court, pulling open her shorts to admire her crimson hip.

"Anything I can help you with?"

Melanie looked up at the man from the opposing team. His shoulder-length jet-black hair was slicked back into a ponytail and his accent was a Portuguese dialect. His gaze started at her hip and rose slowly up her body to her eyes.

"Are you a doctor?"

"Almost," he smiled. "Well, it has always been my mother's dream."

Melanie chuckled.

His bright, white smile was enormous and he stretched out a hand.

"Javier Santos."

"Melanie Ward," she said taking his hand. "Brazilian?"

"Yes! Brava Melanie."

He placed a soft kiss on the back of her hand, never taking his brown bedroom eyes off hers. Javier was tall and fit, each muscle well defined under bronzed skin. His brown eyes were almond shaped, and on first impression Melanie was reminded of a sleek, untamed panther.

"Melanie," her name rolled off his tongue like a gentle breeze through a field of wheat. "Maybe I can teach you to speak my native tongue over dinner?"

"Sorry, I'm going to have to pass."

"Another man? Which one?" His brow furrowed.

Five yards away he stood with Stan, her radio in his left hand. "Adam."

Javier reviewed Adam before turning his attention back to Melanie. "Yes, he has a certain charm but no passion. A woman like you will become bored."

Melanie shrugged.

"Here is my card. Melanie, call me."

Sexuality oozed from his body. He kissed her hand and smiled powerfully enough to strip her of every piece of clothing.

"'Bye, Javier."

She read his card: car salesman, Luhan Motors.

Should've known.

Melanie walked toward Adam as people trudged across the burning sand, seeking out valuable beach real estate. The sun was almost directly overhead and the wind had momentarily stopped, allowing her to feel the scorching rays penetrating into her skin. She did her best not to limp.

"You all right?" Adam asked, putting his hand gently on her bruising hip.

"I landed hard on that last dig. I may have bruised my hip. It's not a big deal."

"I think the medic is still here. Maybe he has an ice pack or something." Adam put his arm around her waist, supporting her as she walked.

Melanie tried to protest as she wrapped her arm around his back, acutely aware that her deodorant was no longer giving off its spring mountain scent.

The medic looked to be in his early 20s and was disappointed to learn there was no gaping wound to treat.

Melanie wondered how much training this kid had received and was reminded of how pissed Stan had been. She sat on the bumper of the emergency vehicle, swallowing the two tablets she'd been given with an icy bottle of water.

"This ice pack is the best I've got. I brought some tape so you can stick it to your skin."

He handed her the thin, rectangular frozen pouch and a roll of emergency tape.

"An ice pack and some Tylenol, the duct tape for the medical profession."

Adam smiled, lifting her heart to a new height. The wind and humid air had put a curl at the ends of his dark hair, which the sun had lightened to a chestnut brown.

"Mel," he said, rubbing his sweaty forehead. "I feel like I need to explain. I met Gigi in L.A. after you and I had ended things."

"You don't need to explain. I'm not going to say that I'm not disappointed but..."

"Just for the record, I've thought about you a lot, probably too much."

"I saw that last night." She couldn't help herself.

He shook his head. "Believe me when I tell you that I've missed you."

Melanie wanted to believe him, but what difference did it make?

"I just thought there was something between us, and to see how quickly I was replaced is surprising."

"I thought you'd left."

"That's not the point, Adam. You know what, forget it." She clenched her teeth.

"Jesus, Mel."

"Jesus, Mel? Really?" She matched his volume level. "All of your sermonizing about not taking sex lightly and looking for the right woman and then within days you've suddenly found her?"

"You ditched me, remember?"

Melanie was about to counterattack when a woman's voice cut through the din of the beach.

"Adam?"

Melanie looked up toward the parked cars. A woman, *the* woman, was waving at Adam.

"She's here?" Melanie was furious.

"She was meeting me after she got off work."

"So you two are really coupled," she said under her breath. It wasn't a question.

Melanie couldn't take her eyes off the woman, Gigi, walking across the blazing sand, wearing a business suit and waving her silver heels over her head. A sadistic pang of enjoyment comforted her when Gigi gave a rapid assortment of yelps, her brain finally realizing that her bare feet were smoldering.

"Bright girl."

"Mel, she's a real estate attorney in L.A."

Melanie rolled her eyes.

The volleyball players and their families cleared the sidelines gathering their chairs and ice chests.

"Hey, Adam, we're meeting in 30," called out, one of the teammates.

"I'll catch you there," Adam shouted back with a wave.

"You're coming too, right Melanie?" Stan asked.

"Wouldn't miss it," she lied.

"Great, great game, both of you. Nice kiss, too." Stan chortled, a pair of orange beach chairs swaying from each arm

"It was a nice kiss, you know," Melanie whispered, regretfully.

"They always are with you."

"Why her, then?"

"Mel, you'll like Gigi once you get to know her."

"Are you kidding?"

He stared down at her and Melanie looked at the woman he'd chosen. Gigi was still tussling with her shoe, trying to wedge her toes between the straps while standing on one foot.

Melanie only partially listened as Adam pointed out the similarities between her and Gigi.

*Blah, blah, blah, w*as all she heard until the final sentence that she couldn't ignore.

"Friends? We're not friends." Melanie spat.

"You serious?"

They stood toe-to-toe and for the moment Gigi, with one shoe on, was forgotten.

"What'd you think, I wanted to be drinking buddies?" Melanie looked at the boy medic who'd been hanging on every word. "Am I done here?"

"God damn it, Melanie, why do you want to make this so difficult?" Adam asked, yanking off his sunglasses. "I hate this. You don't get to control everything."

"But I do get to control who my friends are and who are not."

He glared, "We're not friends. So, what? We're nothing?"

That hurt.

"I guess so."

"You are so frustrating. I don't understand what you want from me. Mel, we had one date and I feel..." He growled. "I have a girlfriend now and you are too complicated, too confused."

Now she was angry and embarrassed. "Yeah, you're right."

Melanie clenched her teeth to stop the tears. Adam pushed back the top of his hair and shoved on a cap.

"I asked you if I was done here!" she blasted the kid.

"Uh, yeah," he said, looking scared as he backed out of her way.

"You suck, Adam."

"*You* suck, Melanie."

Melanie took another glance at Gigi, who was attaining Amazon status with each enormous foot forward. She was as tall as Adam and now she was kicking sand out of her shoe after each step like a cat with something stuck to its paw. She gave the impression of a giant buffoon until Adam stepped up and lifted her in his arms and over his shoulder.

Hurt and humiliated, Melanie pushed through the throng of annoying tourists with their arms full of beach crap.

"Excuse me," she said with heated sarcasm.

"Pardon me."

Melanie recognized the voice. She bit her lip and looked up into the panther's eyes.

"In a hurry, Melanie?"

"I'm sorry, I didn't see you," she said, hidden behind her sunglasses. "I was trying to escape an awkward situation."

Javier looked over Melanie's shoulder and she could tell by his expression that Adam and Gigi were still within sight.

"Apparently he already has a girlfriend." Melanie smiled, tried making light of her embarrassment.

"I guess that means you're free tonight."

Melanie laughed at the simplification. "I guess so."

"I've got a special event and I'm in need of a date. Do me the honor?"

"Javier, I don't know."

"Please."

Reluctantly, she agreed.

Javier arrived at her door right on time wearing a loose, off-white linen shirt and dark chinos. His shiny black hair was slicked back, like it had been earlier but without the ponytail and tucked behind his ears.

"Hi," Melanie said, holding open the screen door for him.

"You're breathtaking." He stood directly facing her, placing a kiss on each cheek. "Beautiful."

"Hello," Rita sang, peeking around Melanie.

"Hello," he said in his thick accent, a smile lurking at the corner of his lips.

Melanie made the introductions. Rita had been overjoyed with the news that Melanie was going on a date.

"I now know where your daughter gets her radiance."

Rita giggled like a schoolgirl. It was uncomfortable seeing such an intensely sexual person flirting with her mom. Melanie had to escape before her mom did something scary like flirt back.

"It was a pleasure to meet you." He kissed the back of Rita's hand.

"You, too."

"I did not know you lived with your parents," Javier said, as they walked to the silver sedan with dealer plates.

"Yeah," she snorted, embarrassed.

"It's sexy," he said, making Melanie laugh.

She did a quick narration of her current circumstances in the car as jazz flowed softly from the sound system.

"I promise by tonight you'll have forgotten all your problems."

She was sure he'd like to try, but she wasn't going to let him. Javier was smooth and was not only at the right place at the right time but he also had the uncanny ability to say the right things. Definitely not "falling in love" material but he was doing wonders for her self-confidence.

"My cousin's wedding," Javier said, in the packed lot of St. John's cathedral.

The stone basilica was ornate and grand, rivaling any 17th century European cathedral. Melanie navigated her spiked heels over the cobblestones and up to the huge wooden entry doors. They had reached the top when a long white limo pulled up and out stepped a beautiful bride in a flowing white gown. Her entourage in periwinkle desperately tried to keep the train from sweeping the ground.

"She's beautiful," Melanie gasped.

"She's a princess."

Melanie agreed. As they entered the vestibule a young man in a tuxedo greeted Javier warmly. He received a hug and a kiss on both cheeks and once introduced, Melanie received an equal welcome.

The church was imposing, with arched ceilings flanked by stained-glass windows depicting each of the Stations of the Cross and a series of holy men including the 12 Apostles. The setting sun was perfectly positioned to glow heavenly through the colored glass.

Melanie and Javier were escorted to their seats. Sharing the hard wooden pew with men in tailored suits and designer clad women, Melanie heard the murmurs as she passed.

"My family," Javier grumbled in her ear. "They're all against my bachelorhood, every last one of them."

Melanie was unsure, but she thought she caught the faint scent of gardenia.

"It's Carmella's favorite flower," Javier whispered.

The groom, in a black tux with tails, rubbed his hands together, looking increasingly anxious. His blond hair, not dark enough to frame his pale face, faded into the background. He seemed to be miscast as Prince Charming in this fairy tale wedding.

The organist began playing "The Wedding March" as the doors squeaked open and everyone stood to witness the bride's arrival. The procession began with the ring bearer and flower girl, eight bridesmaids and finally the bride. She walked slowly with a distinguished gentleman, her bright smile sparkling behind her laced veil. Carmella was one of those people with such seemingly flawless beauty that caused you to feel self-conscious. Taking her place next to her future husband, her glow overshadowed the gaunt man.

Melanie listened, critically, as the priest gave his interpretation of the institution of marriage. She was a skeptic. The odds of such an illusion actually succeeding were close to nil, her parents being the wonderful exception. To pledge your undying love and devotion to someone you know in your 20s or 30s seemed utterly foolish. For Melanie, the astonishment wasn't how many marriages fail, but that any could survive 50 years of change and annoying habits.

The couple repeated their oaths to love, honor and obey looking at the other so utterly convinced that a fantastic rush of hope welled up in her eyes.

Carmella and Charming held limitless possibilities, and this was an innocent start of their new life. The fundamentals of marriage suddenly seemed overwhelmingly beautiful, and holding her breath, Melanie awaited the kiss with tingling sensations in her tear ducts.

Blinking back the moisture, she stood mesmerized when the priest proclaimed, "I am proud to present Mr. and Mrs. Carmichael."

The fresh air outside brought Melanie back to reality and Carmella's wedding felt like a fantasy she'd seen in a movie ages ago. The colorful glow streaming from the stained-glass windows, the scent of gardenia, the beautiful princess in her spectacular white gown and the words of a charismatic priest had played with Melanie's head, teasing and pulling at the speck of hope she kept hidden.

"It's been years since I've been to a wedding," she said as they descended the stone steps of the church.

"Me, too. I try to avoid any situation that gets my mother to think about her future grandchildren. 'Javier, when?' she asks. 'I am not a young woman,' she says."

Melanie laughed. He used a kinder voice to mimic his mom than she used for hers.

Carmella's wedding was a momentous occasion in the Santos family. Relatives from across the States, South America and Europe flew in for the event.

The reception was as extravagant as the ceremony, the entire second floor of the Veranda Hotel was devoted to the party. Sequined white linens covered the round tables, with candles illuminating the gardenia-and-lily centerpieces. Low-hanging chandeliers glowed softly from above, and a string quartet played on the dance floor as guests queued up at the receiving line.

"Javier, thank you for coming," the bride said, giving her cousin a hug and kisses and reminding her new husband that he'd met Javier months ago.

"This is my friend, Melanie."

"Javier?" Her eyes opened like saucers to stare at Melanie. "Is this serious?" She laughed, exposing her unnaturally white teeth.

"Carmella, let's get through your wedding before you start marrying me off."

Javier sounded jovial as he and Carmella exchanged pokes from what appeared to be a long-standing family joke.

"We're delighted that you were able to be part of our celebration," squeeked the timid voice of Carmella's husband.

"Thank you, it was a lovely ceremony," Melanie said, looking uncomfortably into the man's barely blue eyes.

"We'll speak later, Cousin." Carmella's promise sounded like a challenge.

"I look forward to it," Javier raised her gloved hand to his lips then shook the pale, thin hand of the newest member of the Santos family.

"Champagne?" asked a tuxedoed waiter holding a tray of fluted glasses.

"To a meeting of two souls and an evening filled with laughter and love," Javier toasted.

"Cheers."

The room was beginning to fill as they made their way to a wonderfully loud table. Three older women, two of whom sported the same color and hairstyle as her mom's, were laughing heartily.

"Olá, Mãe," Javier said, happily leaning down to kiss his mother on the cheek.

"Javier! Come here." She cupped his face roughly but with love and kissed him.

"Olá, Tia Luisa, Tia Natalia." He went to each of the other woman and greeted them with kisses as well. "Mãe, tias, este é o meu amiga, Melanie."

They each tried but stumbled over her name. She followed Javier's example and introduced herself with a kiss for each woman. Javier held out a chair for Melanie right next to his mother.

"These are our seats," he said, lifting the place cards that said Juanita and George. "My sister and her husband. She's eight months pregnant with twins and has been confined to bed, so we're taking their spots."

"Yes, my first grandchildren and I've been blessed with two," said Mrs. Santos. "When I'll have more, God only knows."

"Congratulations," Melanie said.

"So, how long have you known my son?"

Mrs. Santos was a woman of business and the two other eased in to hear every syllable.

"Not very long."

"And yet he brings you to a family event." Her eyebrows raised above her round, plastic-rimmed glasses.

The women agreed, flying off into their own rapid-fire conversation.

"Melanie is fluent in Portuguese," Javier said, putting his arm across the back of Melanie's chair and leaning forward.

He was close enough for her to notice his left earlobe held evidence of a long-ago piercing, his shave was close and the scent of aftershave clung on his smooth skin. Two parallel laugh lines framed each side of his full lips. A tingle of excitement arose in her abdomen.

"Melanie?" Mrs. Santos said, breaking the moment.

The questions began, the women wanted to know how she'd learned Portuguese, where, why and everything about her background.

"This is Carmella's wedding, not an inquisition," Javier protested.

"It's all right," Melanie said, answering the questions at truthfully as possible.

"Oh, Javier, look there's Marcos," Mrs. Santos said, waving to a young man. "You really should say hello."

Melanie had to marvel at the woman's tenacity. There was no way she'd get the scoop with Javier lingering, blocking each of her questions.

"Marcos!" Javier jumped out of his seat to embrace the man.

As they spoke Melanie understood. Javier and Marcos had been childhood playmates and Marcos had just arrived from Brazil.

"Melanie, do you mind if I go visit with some old friends?" he asked. "I won't be too long, I promise."

"I'm okay, you go and have fun."

Javier absently kissed her cheek and escaped with Marcos into the crowd. It was the least sexual gesture he'd made all evening, and the most potent. Melanie looked at her glass, full again … when had that happened? She hadn't noticed the waiters refilling the bubbly.

"My son is very independent. We're all waiting for him to settle down and find a woman to marry."

"Javier doesn't seem ready for marriage."

"Maybe you could change that?"

Melanie's laugh was sarcastic.

"He obviously likes you," piped in one of the aunts.

It took Melanie some effort to convince the women that she wasn't interested in marrying the most eligible bachelor in the family, and still they held onto hope.

Melanie did learn a great deal about Javier. He'd never been married, never even close, and behind his sleek exterior was a humanitarian.

Okay, this is all from the perspective of a completely devoted mother, Melanie reminded herself, but she liked what she heard. Javier had a degree in psychology and volunteered with troubled youth. The man was nearing sainthood when he returned in time for dinner.

It was Melanie who made the first move during the lobster bisque, placing her hand on his thigh. Javier smiled and set his large, heavy hand on top of hers.

Melanie never had an accurate account of how much champagne she drank but she did know was that her spirits were high and she felt only bliss.

After dinner Mrs. Santos insisted Melanie join the 50 single women on the dance floor for the bouquet toss. Melanie stood to the side, having no intentions of vying for the coveted spray. The drums rolled and Carmella pranced about before flinging the arrangement high into the air. It bounced off a low-hanging chandelier and smacked right into Melanie's chest.

I caught the bouquet, was all she had time to think before it was snatched out of her hands by a more exuberant bachelorette, leaving Melanie only a sprig of gardenia.

"Thank God you were not left with that bouquet," Javier whispered, winking one of his cat eyes as they traded spaces and he took his spot among the single men.

His soft breath on her neck had sent shivers down her spine. Melanie enjoyed the tickle that dashed up her spine.

"You should have held tighter," scolded Tia Luisa.

"But did you see, it flew right into her arms. Did you see that?" Tia Natalia asked around the table, nodding. "That's a good sign, and at Carmella's wedding!"

The groom appeared very uncomfortable holding the white garter. His pale complexion flushed bright pink as he pulled back on the garment and flung it only inches from his black wing-tip shoe. The men roared while one good samaritan lunged three feet onto the parquet floor to win the prize and save the new Mr. Santos from embarrassment. That good fellow wasn't Javier.

"Dance with me," he said, holding out his large hand with a twinkle of mischief in his eyes.

Her interest in Javier had been building all night and Melanie was unclear if it stemmed from the alcohol flooding her bloodstream or the chorus of praise sung by his mother. As she moved slowly within the confines of his arms she felt peacefully content. It was the tremendous curiosity she felt about his sensuous lips that held her in a gravitational pull as Javier spun her around the dance floor. She wondered if he'd dare kiss her out in the open or if they'd have to find a secret spot. She didn't have to wonder for long. Their first kiss was both electric and soothing. She was swept off her feet.

The band was playing the Tony Bennett classic, "The Way You Look Tonight," when she gave into his words, his hands and pushed away hope.

CHAPTER 16

Melanie squinted her cloudy eyes at the bright blue blurry numbers that shone from his bedside clock. 3:10. Javier slept peacefully on his back, the white sateen sheet covering the bottom half of his naked body. His chest, stripped clean of hair, rose and fell in a gentle rhythmic motion as Melanie slid out of his low platform bed. Her clothes had been discarded somewhere in the living room. She padded across the plush carpeting to the master bathroom, silently closing the door. Finding a switch she abruptly dismissed the darkness and caught a glimpse of herself in the mirror. Her hair, a matted mess, was only part of the problem. She couldn't look at who she'd become. Melanie quickly flicked the light back off.

What are you doing? she asked, wrapping herself in a bath towel. She wanted to sob.

Scolding, piercing thoughts bellowed into her brain and she leaned against the marble basin. The tangy residue of the sparkling wine loitered in the back of her throat and Melanie rinsed her mouth, spitting the bad taste into the sink. She turned away from her reflected silhouette with a heavy sigh, her head in the palms of her hands, regret and disappointment commingling beneath her skin.

What were you thinking? she wondered, shaking her head and scolding herself, again.

She dragged her fingers through her tangled hair and wiped the goop out of the corners of her eyes. Melanie steadied her breathing, censoring vivid images – she'd rather forget.

Startled by a knock on the door, Melanie flipped on the light and tried to behave normally.

"Hey," he said with a smile.

A pair of unbuttoned Levi's hung loosely to his hips, which led up to his finely toned chest and arms. He was incredibly, irresistibly sexy and suddenly she felt better about her decision. At least she could understand how it'd happened.

"Everything all right in here?"

She nodded. "I was just thinking."

"That can't be good." Javier, still smiling, leaned against the basin next to her. "Do you want to talk about it?"

"Not really."

"He is with another woman."

"What?" Melanie was startled. "No, I wasn't thinking about, I mean this has nothing to do with him. Of course, I was upset this afternoon but…"

Giving her a sideways look, Javier apologized for his assumption.

"It could be considered a sin if such a beautiful woman wallowed over an undeserving man."

A nervous laugh escaped her lips. "It's just that I think I was falling for him."

"Melanie, there will be many other Adams if you want there to be. He is fine for an average woman but you are not average – you are exquisite."

Her spirits were lifting and again she understood what had brought her to this point, expressing her deepest emotions in the wee hours of the morning to a very well-known stranger.

He caressed her bare shoulders and moved closer. "To me you seem a woman who is always in control. You need to relax and enjoy life's pleasures. How about this time we focus on you?" A devilish smile appeared on his face and there was mischief in his cat eyes as he said, "Let me show you what I mean."

"I don't know, Javier," she said, feeling very exposed and intrigued.

"I promise you won't want me to stop."

He lowered himself to her height and began kissing her neck at the spot right below her ear. Melanie wrapped her arms around his bare shoulders as his tongue massaged circles down to her shoulder. Javier scooped her up and carried her out of the bathroom. Her towel fell to the tile.

"You won't need that," he said, his words spoken into her mouth. He carried her into the darkness of his lair.

<hr>

California's sunrise was not as spectacular as its sunset, but the morning's soft sorbet yellows streamed magically off the billowy clouds. The dew was still hugging the greenery as Melanie and Javier said their goodbyes on her front porch.

"Thanks for coming with me last night." His hands caressed her knowingly, and she blushed. "I'll call you later," he said with a kiss.

In dramatic contrast to the purity of Carmella's wedding, Melanie's night had been full of pure lust and she'd enjoyed every wicked moment, every wicked touch.

Still she knew waiting for a call from Javier was about the last thing she needed.

"Javier, I had an amazing time with you but we both know what this was." Again she blushed, remembering. "Let's not pretend it was something more."

His narrowed eyes reminded Melanie of her initial impression,

Javier the panther.

"You are an incredible woman, Melanie." His lips covered hers with a whisper. "If you want any more of what it was, make sure you call me."

"You'll be the first." She smiled a satisfied smile.

Melanie filled her lungs with the morning air. He had made good on all his promises, leaving her with no complaints.

If this turns out to be a bad decision, she thought, *at least I'm not regretting it now.*

A moment later she was tiptoeing up the stairs to her bedroom wanting to scream and dance. She leapt onto her bed and sprawled out. She felt tired but invigorated. The thought of spending this particular day investigating Parker seemed inappropriate.

Instead she rolled on her stomach, daydreamed about the evening and waited for a decent hour to call Trish.

"Melanie, you're just the girl I wanted to talk with," Trish said in a hushed whisper.

An hour later, after a shower and a change of clothes, Melanie bounced out her front door at the sound of Trish honking the horn.

"Oh my God, it's true!" Trish said, even before Melanie had shut the car door.

"What are you talking about?"

"You had sex!" Trish was gaping at Melanie with round eyes. "What the hell, they were right. I can't believe it. I told them no way, there was no way you slept with someone."

Trish chattered on, not really even speaking to Melanie.

"Who told you?'

Trish gawked as she spoke. "Adam came over really early this morning and he was all in a sweat."

"Adam went to your apartment?"

"No," Trish paused. "I've been staying at Jason's. I guess I've sort of unofficially moved in with him. I think I'm going to keep my place just in case, you know," she said, veering off course.

"What does 'unofficially' mean?"

"Well, he asked and I'm leaving some of my stuff, but I'm going to sleep at my apartment at least twice a week."

Melanie wondered if those good intentions would last a single week.

"And Jason's place is so big and masculine, well, you know, I'm just not as comfortable."

Melanie had no idea, she'd never been to Jason's house, but wanting the conversation to focus back to Adam she said, "So, Adam showed up at Jason's this morning?"

"Yeah, they went into the game room. When I went in to say goodbye they pulled me into the conversation. He said you tripped during some game and hurt your hip."

Melanie huffed. "I didn't trip, I … never mind."

"Anyway, Adam said he met you at the beach and when he and Gigi were leaving you were with some Mexican guy." Trish was speed talking. "And boy did you piss him off when you said that you wouldn't be his friend. He went on for 15 minutes before asking if you'd always been an extremist."

"Whatever," Melanie said, her aggravation returning.

Trish's car hummed, curbside of Melanie's house.

"I'm really sorry I didn't tell you about Gigi. I had no idea you'd find out the way you did." A blush rose to Trish's creamy cheeks.

"What do you know about her?"

Trish looked guilty. "We've gone to dinner with them a couple of times." She shrugged, "What do you want me to say?"

"I'm just curious."

"She seems nice, and he likes her. She's an attorney. I think she said she did some modeling in college."

Melanie nodded. "Great, sounds perfect."

"Don't be so jealous."

Sighing, "Me jealous? Why would I be jealous? I mean, look at my life. I have no job, no prospects and I'm 32, still living with my parents."

Trish scrunched her nose and scrutinized Melanie with her big blue eyes. "You're 33, and although I never knew this, you are seriously fucked up," Trish laughed.

"You said that before."

"Did I?"

"You were drunk."

"Well," she thought for a second, "that doesn't make it less true." Melanie agreed.

"Then tell me who's this Mexican guy that you couldn't do without." Trish laughed. "What on Earth possessed you to do the nasty with him?"

"His name is Javier, he's Brazilian, and don't call it that."

"Wow, Mel, look at your smile. You must really like him."

Melanie shrugged.

"When do I get to meet this Latin lover of yours?"

"Never," Melanie said, curtly. "Javier was a one-time deal."

"Really? Was he no good?"

"No, quite the opposite." Melanie shivered.

"Then I say you screw him until you get bored or he gets serious. Jesus, Mel, this is so unlike you."

Melanie described Javier.

She tried to explain his panther-like qualities – muscular with zero body fat, black silky hair, deep, almond-shaped eyes.

"But I do think that I set my standards too high with Javier."

"Tell me all the details," Trish urged.

"No way! You're a weirdo," Melanie laughed one instant but was somber the next. "He seems to really like her. Doesn't he?"

Trish nodded slowly. "At least I thought so, but Mel, he was totally upset about you and Javier. Angry, mad, like furious with you."

"Did he tell you I kissed him?"

Trish's eyes grew big. "Adam? No! When, on the beach?"

Melanie nodded. "He kissed back, too."

"I don't know, Mel."

"It doesn't even matter. He's with King Kong, anyway."

"She's really not that bad."

"Shut up and take me to lunch."

"There's more I need to tell you," Trish said, seriously. "Don't be mad, okay?"

Melanie froze. Nothing good ever starts with 'don't be mad'.

"Just tell me."

"I'm really sorry, Mel." Trish's eyes darkened. "When I walked into the room, the guys were talking about how you had sex with … well, with Javier. You have to understand that I totally didn't believe them. But Adam was positive and I couldn't convince him that you weren't that way, or so I thought," Trish grinned slightly and shrugged her shoulders. "So I may have mentioned that you'd been abstinent."

Melanie knew she was getting the sugar-coated, best-case scenario. She decided that it was okay.

"And I might have accidentally let it slip that it'd been 10 years."

Trish winced.

"You didn't!" Melanie said, her heart pounding.

She wanted to correct her – it had only been seven years. But at this point a freak was a freak, and three years didn't change that.

"I'm so sorry. At the moment it seemed rational but when…" she paused, "they both stopped and stared at me I knew I'd said too much. But it was out there and I couldn't take it back. I tried to fix it by telling them about how after Dan you got married to your work and now you're grieving from losing your job. It's like going through a divorce and I might have said that you're afraid of commitment."

"Trish," Melanie sounded almost pleading. "You psychoanalyzed me in 30 words or less?"

"It all came out so wrong. I didn't mean to sabotage you. It just snowballed. Everything I said to fix the thing I'd said before just made everything worse."

Melanie looked out the window, there were no buildings crashing down. She was glad Trish remained silent, not attempting to further explain herself. After a few minutes of watching the breeze rustle through the trees, she had come to terms with her humiliation.

"It doesn't matter, Trish, really," she said to ease Trish's mind. "It doesn't matter," she said again to see if she could be convinced. "It's okay, everything you said was, almost, accurate. I didn't know how much I liked him."

"Do you want me to hit Jason up for the full scoop?"

"Naw, I'd just as well let things alone. I didn't think it could get worse with Adam. The whole damn thing was just wrong from the start. We broke up before we even started dating. And now we're cheating on each other." It would have been funny had it been someone else's life. But it left her with a crack in her heart, right along side the scar

Danny had left.

"You could fight for him, maybe."

Melanie shook her head.

"Are you sure about cutting the panther loose?"

"The panther was a one-night thing. But it looks like you and Jason are in full swing," Melanie said, changing the subject. Her heart ached and she couldn't think any more about Adam, but she was curious to know how Adam had found out about Javier.

Trish hesitated about discussing her relationship in the midst of Melanie's current situation. Melanie welcomed the distraction.

"Hey, Jason's going to Chicago tomorrow. How about we get together, just the two of us?"

Melanie smiled. She was being asked out on a pity date.

CHAPTER 17

Pre-dawn Tuesday Melanie finally uncovered a potentially important e-mail from Parker to one of the deciphering technicians. In the short request Parker mentioned a disc he had retrieved while in Paris. A cloud drifted between her bedroom window and the moon, darkening her small world like an omen. She felt the customary prickle that came with a meaningful discovery – the piece she'd been searching for.

It was her last resort, but after hours of spinning her wheels she concluded that she couldn't get her job back without Mike's help. The strain in their relationship had been palpable during their last conversation. Melanie hoped the friendship was as strong as she'd always considered it to be and picked up the phone.

"Hi, Mike," she said, trying to sound casual.

"Melanie? Hold on a sec." His voice muffled as though he'd placed his hand to cover the receiver.

Melanie strained to decipher the mumbles.

"Melanie, hey, I'm glad you called," he said. "How've ya been?"

"Good, good. How are things on the front?" Her heart fumbled to find a rhythm.

"Getting stranger each day. I swear, you'd never recognize this place."

Melanie waited for him to elaborate, but he didn't, so she seized the best opportunity she'd was going to get. "We've been friends a long time and you know I wouldn't ask something of you if I didn't absolutely have to, but…"

"Stop with the butter, Melanie. What is it you want?'

"I need you to recover a disc from Parker's office."

He released a huff of air so big Melanie could feel it hit her cheek.

"The disc and the hard copy were sent via inter-office on Friday. It'll be on his desk no later than tomorrow. I need that report."

"Have you had a heat stroke or are you just insane?" Mike whispered frantically. "I can't break into his office and lift evidence from his desk. *You're* the agent. I sit at my computer, away from direct danger."

Melanie knew he'd balk but she pressed on. "I can't do it. There's no way I could get into the building without being noticed. I was going to intercept it in the mail but there's no telling its exact route. Believe me when I tell you I've considered every other alternative. You're my last hope."

Another hefty blow into the receiver. "How important is this information? I mean, is there *any* other way?"

Melanie's resolve cemented. "I wouldn't be asking if there were. I'll send you everything I've got and if you don't think it's pertinent then forget I ever asked. Deal?" She held her breath.

"I'm not promising anything."

"Understood."

Melanie didn't waste any time working on plans C and D. Plan A had her doing all the legwork, but to get into the agency without being arrested was highly unlikely. Mike was B. Plan C included eliciting help from Judith while D was more of a fantasy – snatching Parker in his sleep and torturing him until he confessed his treason.

She wasn't resting. Her blood coursed as if replaced with caffeine and she decided this was more stressful than any assignment. It was personal, and although everything to this point felt like a strange dream – as if she were peering into someone else's life – she knew it'd be permanent unless she acted.

Melanie paced for twelve hours, checking her phone every five seconds, eager not to miss Mike's call. She was expecting his response any minute.

She was startled when her phone vibrated in her hand. The caller ID read Carla Bradley.

"I think I knew a Carla once," she said, absently chewing on her bottom lip, calculating the probability of Mike actually agreeing to help, and wishing to hell he'd call.

"I know, I know. But I've called to find out what your plans were for tonight."

"Tonight? Nothing." *Even if Mike calls, I still have to wait,* she thought as Carla spoke.

"Good, because Ted can't make it to Lena's annual Fourth of July party until after 10 and I'm in need of an escort."

"Escort, huh? Are you sure you dialed the right number?" Melanie said, looking at her calendar, having forgotten that today was the Fourth.

"A slow case load," Mike had said, the burn still blistering. It stung knowing that this year she was completely out of the loop.

Carla continued, "Don't be silly. It's an absolutely fabulous party. All of the who's who will be there, dressed to the nines and eating the finest cuisine from the trendiest caterers. After sundown she sets off a spectacular fireworks display. Believe me, you don't want to miss this."

"Sounds great, and it'll give us time to catch up. It seems like forever since we've had a chance to talk."

"I know, it's an election year and I've been swamped doing my part for Ted. But definitely tonight it'll just be the two of us. And by the way, Lena's parties are high-fashion events so you'll want to wear your very latest summer outfit."

The day passed and she began to wonder if she should start working on Judith.

Melanie took her time putting together an outfit for Lena's fabulously fashionable party. She was more than ready, excited even, when the limo pulled up to her door.

Tonight is about the party and spending time with Carla, she thought. *You can worry about the rest tomorrow.*

Melanie grabbed her bag and headed out wearing a short white strapless shift dress and a pair of wedge gladiator sandals.

"Nice ride," she said, slipping into the back and giving Carla a squeeze.

"Thanks for coming."

"My parents are tired of me hanging around. My mom practically threw me out of the house." Melanie laughed at how relieved Rita had been at the mere mention of a party. "Bruce says I'm a cat away from becoming a spinster."

"Well, there will be loads of single men, you can have your pick." Without pause she jumped topics, "I spoke with Ted and he thinks he can get you a job with the city and there may even be trips to D.C." Carla was all about being responsible, and being unemployed definitely didn't mesh with being a useful member of society.

"I really appreciate that, but I'm still feeling my way around this new life I've been given."

You are such a liar, she thought of the hours tucked away in her childhood bedroom with the lavender wallpaper, tackling her obsession with Parker.

The black limo took the windy, narrow streets slowly before

stopping in front of a modern two-story building that looked more like a complex of offices than a home.

"This is hands-down the best party of the year. It's by invitation only and you do *not* want to be dropped from Lena's list," Carla said eagerly as they walked up the narrow walkway lined with large leafed foliage.

The front doors were open wide, beckoning guests to continue on into the marble-tiled foyer.

"Mrs. Bradley!" Exclaimed a petite woman with shoulder-length, frosted blonde hair.

"Lena, hello," Carla said as the two exchanged a hug and dramatically kissed the air above each other's ears.

"Stunning as usual," Lena said, holding onto both of Carla's hands. "This must be your escort." The appraisal took less than a heartbeat and Lena's brown eyes were firmly back to Carla. "Ted is planning to grace us with his presence later, right?"

"Of course, he wouldn't miss your party for the world. He'll be here before the fireworks. I would like to introduce my very oldest and dearest friend, Melanie Ward."

"I'm pleased that you were able to join the festivities," Lena said halfheartedly. "There's food, music and lots of spirits, so help yourself." Her eyes already moving to the next wave of arriving guests. "Oh, Melanie, I just adore your entire ensemble. You'll have to tell me where you made such a find. Later, okay?" Lena asked, releasing them with a small waggle of her fingers and a flight attendant-style, "buh-bye."

"Wow, a compliment from Lena. Nicely done."

Melanie shrugged, a few steps from the entrance the room opened to a platform high above the living area. The house was built on the side of a cliff and the view of the Pacific was breathtaking. The west wall was made up of sliding glass doors that had been opened, letting in the salty breeze. Under the arched patio people clustered around long tables covered edge to edge with delicacies. Two bars with tenders in flag shirts were at each end of the patio and from her angle, Melanie could see the edge of a lower patio with another bar and a bubbling Jacuzzi.

Carla was already gone, her low, proper heels clicking down the tiled stairway. Melanie took another look at how the other half lived and then followed her friend. The living room had gold carpeting, two monochromatic couches and four matching chairs. Above the fireplace, water cascaded down a mosaic of sea-glass into a grate on the mantel. She caught sight of Carla in her green sundress with a flower pinned to her dark hair, already engaging in conversations.

Coming in on the middle of campaign talk Melanie stayed silent and tried to appear interested. Carla flittered about the room, pollinating supporters of the Bradley for Congress crusade. Melanie tagged along, getting trapped every so often by contributors interested in "the oldest and dearest" of all of Mrs. Bradley's friends.

"What do you do, Ms. Ward?" they'd ask.

Melanie felt that an out-of-work 33-year-old living with her parents wouldn't help boost Ted's popularity so she did what she did best – she lied.

When Carla wasn't around Melanie became a professional snowboarder, a NASCAR announcer and only got in trouble as an archeologist specializing in ancient Greece.

It was the only thing making this fabulous party bearable. An hour into the party Melanie gave up on any quality time with Carla. Carla had switched to promotion mode months ago and she'd be almost useless until after the November election. Melanie searched for an available bartender.

"Did you see who just arrived?" Carla asked, sounding thrilled and squeezing Melanie's arm.

Melanie glanced up to the bridge above the living room, thinking maybe Brad Pitt. Instead, a Hispanic gentleman, looking very Cary Grant in a dark blue cashmere jacket, strode down the stairs. He was holding the hand of a woman who may not have had a face; all Melanie could focus on was her plunging neckline exposing a pair of full double-D's.

"That's Salvador Luhan."

Melanie ran the name through her brain's database, "As in Luhan Motors?"

Carla's face twisted with apparent exasperation. "Yes, but he's the man who thwarted the bomb."

Seclusion had its drawbacks. The only bomb she'd seen, when she'd sneaked a peak at the television, had been stamped ACME and Wile E. Coyote was strapping it to his wiry back.

Carla whispered the account of Luhan's escapade as Melanie watched him prance around, shaking hands like a celebrity.

Three days earlier, Sal Luhan had rear-ended a red Ford Taurus a mile from Nimitz Naval Base. He got out of his truck to check on the other driver, when the guy sprung out of the car, knocking Sal to the pavement, and ran. One knee injured, Sal chased the 22-year-old two blocks before tackling the kid to the ground and holding him until the police arrived. In the trunk of the Taurus they found enough explosives to take out a two-mile radius.

Melanie was intrigued, as was everyone in the room. But while most centered their attention on the charismatic leader, Melanie was hypnotized by the tall man standing to Sal's right. His dark, sleek hair was pulled back into a short ponytail and his panther eyes locked onto Melanie's. Immediately, his broad white smile contrasted with his bronzed skin, sending her chills of delight. Javier's black shirt was untucked, hanging loosely from his broad shoulders.

"Yes. He owns a dozen dealerships across Southern California." Carla kept talking as Javier swaggered toward them.

His eyes ran up and down her body. She resisted the temptation to check herself and allowed his x-ray vision to explore.

"Hello, Melanie." He lifted her hand to his lips without taking his eyes off his prey.

"Hello Javier," she said, joyfully, "I'd like you to meet my oldest and dearest friend, Carla Bradley."

"Enchanted. So it is true that beautiful women come in pairs," he said, kissing Carla's limp hand before turning his attention back to Melanie.

Javier's typical M.O. – the corny lines, the smooth touch, the eternal eye contact – was more than any woman could endure without caving.

Even stone-cold Carla must be feeling his Brazilian heat.

Suddenly this fabulously boring party had become interesting.

"You look incredible," Javier said, widening his cat eyes and grinning from ear to ear. He took a step closer. "I've been thinking about you."

"How many different women have heard that this week?" Melanie put her hand on Javier's chest to stop his momentum.

"Melanie, may I speak with you for a moment?" Carla said with a sour tone, raising her index finger to Javier.

"Give me a minute?" Melanie said, looking apologetically at her predator.

"You may have all the time you want. I'll get us some drinks." Javier winked and stood in line for the bartender.

There was no question, she knew exactly what Carla wanted – or more accurately didn't want.

"Javier and I went out on Saturday night." Melanie confessed before Carla could start. "We had a good time. I didn't want to tell you about him because I knew you wouldn't approve but Oh My God, Car…" Melanie shook her head.

"What about the chef, what was his name?"

"Adam. And I told you he has a girlfriend now."

"That's right, but I thought you were going to try and…"

"He's got a girlfriend."

"So, you're dating this guy?"

"We're not exactly dating," Melanie said, devilishly manipulating Carla's prudish strings.

Her little pixie face hardened with a look of reproach that might as well have been spoken.

"I'm a big girl, Car."

"I don't want to know any more." Carla shook her head.

"Carla, you need to lighten up. You're becoming judgmental and anal. I understand image is important but you're taking it to the extreme."

"I cannot talk to you right now." Carla turned and left for more suitable company.

Melanie did the same.

"What would you like?" Javier asked.

"Two dirty martinis."

There were so many different emotions surging through her body.

For weeks she'd been experiencing drastic highs and plummeting lows. She wondered if this was how normal people felt – if they struggled with radical emotions on an hourly basis, or if maybe she was suffering from bipolar disorder. She tossed down the first martini, slid her olives off the little yellow sword and left the empty glass on the bar. Both Javier and the bartender gaped at her but she felt better.

"I believe that people in the psychology sector call this self-medicating." Melanie lifted her second glass.

His eyes scanned her face, a smile curving his full lips as his gaze moved down her cleavage.

"Don't think you're getting me drunk so that I'll sleep with you."

He leaned in close. "It worked last time." The pressure from his kiss lingered on her cheek.

"That was different," she replied, feeling flushed.

Everything about Javier was sexual, and she guessed that more than one deal was closed when he sold a car. Even a talk about the weather held the promise of a bedroom interlude.

"You are beautiful and very sexy in this white dress," his smile broadened. "You have a fantastic body. I know, remember?"

His flattery was more effective than she cared to admit. Conversational flirting with Javier was turning out to be the highlight of the evening.

"Maybe we should find a cozier spot and get reacquainted."

Melanie laughed nervously at his relentlessness.

"Have things been crazy at work with Salvador being the big hero and all?"

"More hectic, yes, but very good for business." He hooked his arm around her shoulder, guiding them to a sheltered corner of the balcony. "Have you thought about me?" He asked, his fingers leaving an icy chill along the smooth skin of her jaw. "I've thought about you."

"I'm sure."

Javier stopped mid-caress, leaned back on his heels and looked into her eyes.

"What?" She asked, feeling his gaze penetrate beneath her skin.

"Are you not over him?"

He was looking too deeply, she couldn't pretend – but she could lie – instead she joked. "He was so last week, I can't even remember his name."

"Melanie," he said sadly as if feeling her innermost pain. "If you need, I have a shoulder to cry on, ears to listen with, arms to hold you and…"

"You had better stop there." She warned when a mysterious sparkle returned to his almond eyes. "Seriously, Javier, as much as I appreciate your offer I'm really fine."

"Really fine," he repeated.

Melanie tried to change her expression. She was not going to talk about Adam anymore.

"That woman with Salvador, is that his wife?"

"We're talking about Sal?" He sighed, and glanced over her head. "Okay then, he's divorced. That's his latest girlfriend."

On cue, the couple strode out the glass doors and over to them.

"Javier, my best employee." Sal greeted him with a handshake.

"Hello, Sal, Becky, this is Melanie. She's very interested in your adventure."

Salvador Luhan began to retell his tale of heroism with zest, giving Melanie the impression he'd told this same story many times in the past few days.

"There I was, turning onto Sports Arena Boulevard, when out

of nowhere this car cuts me off. I slammed on the brakes hoping to avoid a collision but my truck hits the Taurus. It was completely unavoidable."

This is the legal notation at the bottom of a contract, very small and very CYA.

"My head banged on the steering wheel, see, right there." Salvador pointed to a quarter-inch scratch above his left eyebrow. "Anyway, when I went to check on the other driver, a kid, at first I think he's knocked out but he pushes open his car door and knocks me down. Then he starts running, tripping over me, stepping on my leg. He takes off. Well, I know trouble when I see it, I've been around the block. So, without thinking, I pursue." Sal smiled and gripped his bicep. "I work out and am in pretty good shape for my age, aren't I, Mama?" he asked his buxom companion.

"How far did you chase him?"

"Three blocks, easy. When the cops arrived they found the explosives in the trunk. I really don't see myself as a hero, just an honest guy in the right place at the right time. Anyone would have reacted the same."

It was the exact story Carla had told and Melanie knew if she asked any more questions someone was going to ask for her press badge.

"You two have a nice evening. Come on, Mama." The couple pranced off in search of another set of fresh ears.

"Is your curiosity satiated?" Javier asked, staring down at her with an amused expression. "Because I'd like to get back to more pressing matters."

"Can you get through a whole day without sex?" She laughed when his hands went to her waist.

"Of course. But I like you. Would you rather we talk?"

"No." *God no!* He was too insightful.

Melanie ignored the expanding party and paid little attention to the enormous orange sun setting the horizon ablaze.

"Why do you taste like vanilla?"

"Sunscreen," Javier said. "I enjoy sharing it with you."

"You are a very generous man, Javier Santos."

"You, more than anyone, ought to know." Javier's mischievous smile returned.

Melanie felt the heat rise from the bottoms of her feet, igniting her cheeks.

"I'm fond of that color pink, it goes well with your skin tone," he said, scrutinizing her. "It's endearing and innocent yet we both know you're not so innocent." His soft whisper tickled her ear.

"Stop, now you're embarrassing me on purpose," she pushed at his shoulder.

"There is something intoxicating about you," he said, taking her face gently in the palms of his hands. "You could be hazardous to my bachelorhood."

"Not me. Believe me I'm no threat. It is what it is, remember."

His grin broadened, "Thank God one of us is thinking straight."

He kissed her cheeks and pulled her into his chest. Holding her close she accepted his kindness and fit her body against his.

"Hmmm, hmmm."

Melanie looked out over Javier's arms.

"Trish!? What are you doing here?" Melanie squealed, hugging her friend as if she were long lost.

"I'm here with Jason. The better question is, who are you doing here?"

Trish eyeballed Javier as Jason approached.

"I'd like you to meet Javier."

"So you're the infamous Javier."

Trish stepped back to take a better look.

"Infamous? I like that," Javier said, eyebrows lifted high on his crumpled forehead as he winked at Melanie.

"This is Trish and her boyfriend Jason Johnson."

Javier extended his hand and for a moment Melanie feared Jason wouldn't reciprocate.

"You play a wonderful game."

Jason shook the man's hand and the two began a common-ground conversation.

"He's hot," Trish said, leaning in close with a hushed voice, "but I think you're right to end things quickly." Her eyes were traveling up Javier. "He could be dangerous." Her smile flashed wickedly.

"I know." Melanie was watching Javier, too. "He's attentive, seems genuinely interested and is caring." She shook her head. "And look at him."

Trish laughed, "A man–whore with sensitivity."

"Don't call him that," Melanie said defensively.

"You know he's got another girl around here somewhere."

"At least one."

"FYI, Adam's here." Trish tried to sound casual.

"What? Is *she* here, too?" Melanie's eyes shot up at the crowd.

Along with the nerves came a feeling of betrayal. Trish was cavorting with the enemy. Even if it was irrational, Melanie was hurt. "We went to Jason's game." Trish said defensively, feeling the condemnation. "What, am I supposed to ignore her? Adam and Jason are friends and she's his girlfriend."

"Right, whatever. I really don't want to hear it."

"You *cannot* be mad at me," Trish sounded surprised.

"Can't I? Because I think I am."

"You totally dumped him and I am not choosing sides by going out to dinner with them."

Melanie clamped her jaw shut until her teeth hurt. She had nothing nice to say.

"Hey, Trish," two voices sounded from opposite directions.

Carla and Gigi merged simultaneously, like the midget and the giant converging at the center ring of a three-ring circus. Melanie swallowed the lump in her throat and gawked up at Gigi, the Amazon, with flowing coarse black hair that draped down to the middle of her enormous back. Everything about her was long – from her seemingly extra-knuckled toes to her extra-high forehead. Though she couldn't deny a certain attractiveness – dark brown eyes with sweeping eyelashes – Melanie took solace in her evil thoughts. Perhaps Gigi hadn't yet stopped growing because she seemed much larger than she had the day she had hopped one-footed on the hot beach.

"Hello, I'm Carla Bradley," said the pixie, when Trish faltered in the introductions.

"Oh, sorry Gigi, these are my friends Carla and Melanie."

"Gigi Sullivan." She acknowledged them with a curt nod and scanned, above their heads, at the crowd. "Can you believe the people that are here?" she cooed.

Gigi was as impressed with the guest list as Carla, who at the moment, was still ignoring Melanie.

"Oh my God, I see a couple of judges. I need to go introduce myself," she enthused to nobody in particular. "A definite boon to get on their good side, if I'm going to be moving here."

Melanie looked at Trish's blank expression.

"Moving here?" Melanie asked, her arms folded across her chest.

"Yeah, I'm moving in with my boyfriend." Her bulging brown eyes flickering down at Melanie then back at the notable crowd. "Adam Chase. Do you know him?"

Melanie nodded. Yes, she knew Adam.

"I thought he was moving to L.A."

"So did I," she chuckled. "But after he bought his building he turned around and leased it to a gay couple. Can you believe that? Now I've got to relocate to San Diego and I don't know if it's the best career decision. But love can make even the most sensible do crazy things."

Love? Melanie's heart crumpled. She'd forgotten about Javier until his arm snaked around her waist. It was comforting.

"Javier Santos," he said, reaching for Gigi's enormous paw with his free hand.

"Hello, I'm Gigi." Her smile widened and she actually looked at him.

Javier let Melanie loose and focused his concentration on Gigi. His voice dropped to a purr and he inched closer.

Melanie smiled. A warmth crept beneath her skin as Javier's magic made giant Gigi flush a deep crimson.

Carla looked alarmed while Trish looked away as if she hadn't noticed. It was a triangle of silence. Presently, Melanie was angry with everyone except Javier, and he at the moment was doing her a favor.

Melanie scanned the sea of faces and found a sliver of Adam behind a group across the patio. The view of him flowed through the movement of the mass of bodies, like a current drawing him closer.

As people parted and swayed, she caught glimpses; his jaw, his eyes, his ear, until he made his way out. Mesmerized by a dark curl on his tanned neck, Melanie stared, not breathing.

"Melanie," he spoke quietly, his expression shy. He ran his fingers lightly along her bare shoulder, breaking her out of the trance.

"Hi." She sounded raspy and breathy.

Javier sidled alongside Melanie, while Gigi quickly distanced herself from Javier.

"Javier, good to see you." Adam offered.

"There you are." Gigi was still blushing as she turned from Melanie's panther.

Adam didn't have to bend down to meet her lips and his hand automatically rested below her waist.

"Have you met Margaret?" he asked.

"I'd really rather be called Gigi." Her smile faded and there was an edge to her voice. "And yes, we've made all the appropriate acquaintances."

The circle hushed.

"I think I'm going to do a little networking," Gigi said, pressing her two yards of body against Adam and hanging her long tentacle across his shoulders, pushing back the stray curl. "Okay, Baby?"

When she left, the little group rearranged with Melanie and Adam standing apart from the rest.

"How's the job search?"

"It'd help if I were looking," she said, looking past him to the gathering crowd at the bar. She'd lost track of her unfinished martini and was suddenly very thirsty.

"You look beautiful."

"Don't do that." She met his emerald gaze.

"You're still set on this not-friends business?"

"I need a drink," Melanie twisted, hoping to catch the nearest bartender or waiter with a drink tray.

"I'll get it for you. What would you like?" he asked.

"Two dry martinis."

"Two?"

"Hey, are you getting drinks?" Trish asked, "I want two martinis, too, please."

"I'll have a wine spritzer," Carla added.

Javier was next to put in his request for a beer, anything imported. Melanie smiled as Adam and Jason left to fill the order.

"He's trying to be my friend. And did you see her 'Okay, Baby?' Ugh!" Melanie said with distaste to no one in particular.

"Why can't you just be his friend?" Carla asked, exasperated.

Melanie exhaled, and looked at both Carla and Trish. They didn't understand. "Because when I look at him I can't breathe, my toes curl and my brain stops. And whenever we were together I'd be looking for any opportunity to…"

"Good reason." Trish patted Melanie's shoulder. "Don't be mad at me. I feel stuck and if it bothers you this much I won't socialize with them anymore. Just don't be mad." Trish had the perfect pout, jutting lips and weepy eyes.

"I'm not mad at you, either of you."

"You hanging in there?" Javier asked. "I'm going to check on Sal and Becky, okay, *Baby*?" He said and nudge her with his elbow.

"Thanks for everything, *Baby*."

"My pleasure," he licked his vanilla lips. "We could irritate him one last time."

She took a quick glance. Adam looked away when their eyes met.

"No, but I do appreciate the offer."

"You underestimate yourself. You could get him back, if that is what you truly wanted."

"I don't think so."

"That is why I said you underestimate. They're not in love, Melanie."

Melanie paused. "You are very sweet."

He shrugged, lifting his palms and smiled gently. "My mother likes you. What else can I do?"

She stretched and he bent, meeting her halfway.

His warm lips brushed across hers, softly at first, but this was Javier and he didn't know how to hold back. His kiss was so intense that Melanie could feel the flush rise from Carla's pale skin as they parted.

"Bye," he whispered, "Call me."

Melanie exhaled as he turned and sauntered off.

"Wow," Trish giggled. "Are you sure you should cut him loose?"

"I'm not sure about too much these days."

"You always get the best kisses. Ted has never kissed me like that."

"Adam is going to go ape shit."

"Why should he? He's moving on with Godzilla." Melanie looked down at the lower balcony where Adam's Amazon was impossible to miss. Standing taller than most of the population she comically towered over the two older men she was trying to impress.

"Look at her."

"She's not that bad."

Melanie rolled her eyes. "Shut up."

"What about those clothes?" Carla asked, "Did she grow since she got dressed?"

Melanie couldn't stop the vision of Lou Ferrigno busting out of a pair of light blue capris and three-quarter-sleeve blouse with a pair of paisley blue kitten-heel flip flops. Melanie was wiping the tears away when Jason arrived with a tray.

"Here are your drinks, ladies."

"Where's Adam?" Trish asked, lessening Jason's load by one martini.

"He went to find Gigi," Jason answered quickly, handing Carla her spritzer.

"Did he see Javier leave?" Trish took a second glass and handed it to Melanie.

"He saw."

Trish flicked her chin up at Melanie and they raced to empty their glasses.

"Jace, did you know that Gigi was moving in with Adam?"

"I heard."

Trish loaded the drained stemware back on the tray and replaced their empty hands with two fresh glasses.

"I hate her," Melanie observed casually.

"Okay, I think I'm going to return this to the bar. You guys have fun."

"I can't believe I'm so jealous," she said, twirling the glass between her fingers.

"Oh, there he is," Carla said, pointing out Adam stealing Gigi away from the honorable arbitrators.

Melanie's eyes were stuck on them, though it was like watching your own home go up in flames. "Can we please talk about something other than them?"

The sunset had turned dark, the pastels, pinks and yellows swallowed up by indigo blues and violets. Carla took the opportunity to provide the lowdown on the guests. Melanie was beginning to feel the comforts of 80-proof vodka.

She wasn't even mildly interested in who had escaped a DUI or whose home was going to be featured in *San Diego Living*. Briefly, her eyes scanned the room from the reformed porn star who was currently a best-selling novelist to Congressman Ted Bradley.

"Ted's here, Car. He looks really good."

Ted was wearing his signature khakis, which looked like Dockers but were 10 times more expensive, and a long-sleeve dark blue button-down shirt. His brown hair was cut short and his smile showed off a set of dazzling white teeth.

"He's getting ready for campaigning," Carla said, as her eyes drifted lovingly over her husband.

"Wow, Car, Ted *is* looking hot!" Trish said, ogling Ted purely to annoy Carla.

"Hi, Honey," Ted said placing a small peck on Carla's lips. "Hello, Melanie, Trish." He placed an equally passionless kiss on each of their cheeks. "I'm a lucky man to be standing with the three most lovely ladies at the party."

Ted was forever the politician.

"Did you see Randall Nelson and his wife are here?"

"No! Where?"

"And there's a photographer here from *San Diego Magazine*," Carla said, and then they left to work the party, leaving Trish and Melanie to talk about them for the few moments before the lights flickered.

"Everyone to the terrace," Lena announced, waving her pencil-thin arms. "My annual fireworks spectacular is about to commence!"

Jason cozied up beside Trish just as the herd began its stampede to the patio.

"I've got to pee," Melanie told Trish, escaping the barrage.

The gathering crowd was tightening in as Melanie pushed and struggled, weaving her way against the flow.

"Melanie."

She stopped at the sound of her name, lost in a sea of torsos.

"Mel." His hand reached through the horde and clutched her arm. "Come on," he said, keeping her tightly behind him as he shouldered his way out of the masses.

Her cheek rubbed against his shoulder, he smelled of vine tomatoes and green olives. She'd missed him, missed his cooking, his strength.

The darkened living room was empty, and as he slid the glass doors closed, the whistle of the first rocket being launched from a vessel floating somewhere offshore.

Ripples of "oohs" and "aahs" filtered through the crowd of admirers. A flash of gold reflected in Adam's green eyes. The rockets erupting in the night sky were the only source of illumination.

The force of the explosions rocked her, sending her heartbeat into an uneven palpitation. It was difficult to read his expression through the strobe of colored lights, though Adam stood close, his face hidden in darkness. He was holding both her hands and she could feel his rapid heartbeat through his palms.

"I've been wanting to get you alone all night," Adam said.

She felt a calm excitement, her emotions obstructed by the alcohol pulsating through her bloodstream, pleasantly numbing the tips of her fingers and toes.

"Mel, I need to apologize for my behavior at the beach." He stepped closer, pressing his fingers into her arms. "I am so sorry about the things I said. I never meant to hurt you." His soft eyes pleaded for forgiveness. "I feel as though I have to explain Gigi."

Okay, Melanie thought, not exactly how this is supposed to start. She waited for the, "You're beautiful, I made a horrible mistake, I want only you" dialogue to begin.

"She and I met in L.A., *after* you and I had parted. I thought you were gone and when I met her she was so uncomplicated. You had been very clear about your intentions," his voice was low and deep.

Melanie stared, concentrating to link the words to their meanings. Trying to make them fit, but she knew this was not right. She couldn't think – damn vodka!

"Melanie, maybe we could go out with you and Javier. The four of us could…"

He kept speaking but she heard nothing else.

"Stop," Melanie said, realizing his intention. "A double date?" she asked incredulously, garnished with a sarcastic laugh.

"I just want to be able to see you, somehow, as friends," he whispered.

"No. I can't do this." She shook her head and walked across the room, grinding her teeth. Not wanting to lose control she blinked back the moisture forming on her eyelids. She looked up at the glistening waterfall above the fireplace.

"Melanie?" He followed, standing too close.

"You just don't get it." Of course she'd known she'd fallen too quickly, too irrationally but there had been small signs that he too … Melanie closed her eyes to shut out the world and came upon an understanding.

"Please."

"You were right – I'm the one that didn't realize," she'd mistaken his kindness for intimacy. She'd been lonely and vulnerable and had completely lost her freaking mind.

"So, we can be friends?" he asked cautiously.

"No. Nothing changes for me." Melanie had to let go, she felt woozy, lightheaded. "I can't socialize with you and Gigi, I can't be around you." She felt sick. The reverberation, the vodka and the smell of sulfur from the rockets were having an unpleasant effect.

"But, I care about you, Mel, and if we could just get over this…"

"I can't 'get over this.'" Her breathing shook as she turned to stare into his tender green eyes. Her voice softened, but she wanted to make herself clear.

"Please, Melanie."

"You don't understand. I'm not *choosing* this, it's…us…this, right now I've got nothing. I keep making mistakes that I don't know how to fix. I'm floundering for some footing in my life."

"I can help, really, maybe. We could talk, somehow stay connected. I don't want you out of my life."

What he was asking was impossible. "Listen, I understand why you chose her, really, I get it, but consider my side." He tried to interrupt but she quickly continued. Melanie's face tightened, realizing she was going to have to spell it out. He was unaware of how entangled her feelings had become.

It was difficult to explain, she paused and he stared.

"I … I," she stumbled, then opened up in a rush, "Adam, from that first look I've been falling in love with you. I know we've only been on one date but…" The words spilled out, flooding her usual boundaries. "I've tried to get over you … but I can't, I'm overwhelmed. It's worse when I see you, when you're so close. I want to kiss you and I want you to hold me and make love to me. I want you to want those things, too. I can't be your friend. I can't sit and have dinner or stand at your wedding. I'm sorry, but I'm just not that strong. *This* is breaking my heart." Instinctively her hand covered her chest. Her chin began to quiver, she was done.

Adam's face was frozen in shock. He looked as sick as she felt – pale and ready to puke. Behind a wall of plate glass and a million miles away from the tiny world they occupied stood 100 people with their eyes raised to the sparkling heavens.

"What the hell is going on here?"

It was Melanie who broke the gaze to see all 6'2" plus heels of Gigi, her arms akimbo and the glare of the red rockets reflecting in her angry eyes.

"You again. Why don't you go back to your car salesman and…" her lasers seared into Melanie, "get the fuck away from my boyfriend. Don't look at me like you haven't got a clue. You've been ogling him all night and I'm tired of it."

Melanie was startled out of her heartbreak, her irritation bubbling, but Gigi wasn't wrong.

"Look, whatever problem you've got it's with Adam, not me," Melanie said, as if she hadn't just been on the verge of tears.

"Just shut up," Gigi's entire body shook as her voice thundered with the rockets outside. "Adam, tell this skank to take a hike."

"Gigi," Adam started but Godzilla advanced, her eyes scrutinizing, cutting him off.

"What's going on here? You're off hiding in the dark with this circus midget."

"It's not what it looks like."

"Is there something going on with you and this ..." she eyed Melanie, "bitch?"

That was it. Without a thought to consider the consequences, Melanie's gladiator sandals went right on top of the glass-and-wrought-iron coffee table. Reaching eye-to-eye with her opponent. A controlled storm behind her eyes, she said, "Call me one more nasty name and I *will* take you down."

Gigi's expression was not unfamiliar. Ten years of life experience had coated her in a tough armored shell, which proved useful in situations where she needed to wield a power of intimidation way out of balance with her exterior appearance.

Melanie stood stoic and unflinching, her jaw taut and her gaze fixed. She was going to enjoy this, she thought as she analyzed her prey. Gigi stood frozen in astonishment; her mouth gaped and her huge eyes bulged.

"Hey Angel, why don't you get down from the furniture?"

Jason, with his hands out ready to help her down, was out of place.

"Can you take me home?" she asked, embarrassed. She was at a Fourth of July party, not a political insurgence.

"Sure, come on," he said, holding her arm as she stepped off the table.

"Mel?" Adam reached for her as she passed with pure pity in his eyes.

She shook her head. Caught in a whirlwind all she wanted was to get out and go home, hide, die, whatever. The staircase seemed much further than before and she caught sight of her friends' faces pressed up against the window.

"Jace, no stunts, drive safely, understand?" Adam asked in a thick baritone voice.

It's just what he says, she thought, saddened. Adam glanced her way, his complexion pallid. Behind him, Gigi was fuming.

"Yeah, man, I hear you." Jason clapped Adam on the back.

From the top of the stairs she took a last, fatal, look. The picture was clear: Adam was pleading with Gigi, arms crossed, as the lawyer in her weighed her negotiational pull. Melanie imagined Adam explaining how 'she' was nothing, just a girl he dated once, and it was the giant ogre that he loved.

Melanie sighed and hurried across the marble tile out the foyer and onto the narrow path to the valet kiosk. There was no humor left in her.

"Man, Angel, you've got a set of balls!" Jason jogged to catch up with her. "Gigi is like a foot taller and a good 70 pounds heavier." He gave his ticket to the man in a red vest.

She ignored him. More than just her body ached, her mental state was in anguish as well.

"You okay, Angel?"

"You don't have to call me that, I know I'm a huge disappointment," she said, before a pair of uncontrollable tears slid down her cheeks. Jason folded her into his arms, "Are you kidding? You're entertainment and besides you'll always be my Angel. Guardians come in all sorts of packages – even tiny, little crazy ones."

She felt his chest lift with his laugh.

"You know what sucks the most about this fight between *them*?" She finally managed to say, wiping her eyes and pulling out of his embrace.

"What's that?" Jason asked, exchanging a bill for his set of keys.

"Make-up sex."

The valet opened the door for her, unaffected by her comment.

Jason put the vehicle in first and sped away from Lena's annual Independence Day Bash.

"I don't understand either of you," Jason said, carefully managing the curves. "I swear Adam is crazy about you."

"I screwed things up," Melanie said, lowering Eminem to a soft blare on the stereo.

"That's funny, Adam said that he was the one to screw it up."

"He said that?"

"Yeah, tonight when we were watching you with Javier."

Melanie considered it for a moment. "He's just being polite. Crazy little package, remember?" She pointed to herself with a laugh.

"What's with you and that Javier?"

"Javier." She let out a breath. "He was what he was."

Jason studied her from the corner of his eye and said nothing for a few minutes.

"You looked happy with him."

"Did I? He's really not what you would expect, an enigma, he's kind and caring and he makes me feel, what … valued, alive, worthwhile, maybe." She couldn't pinpoint exactly what Javier quality.

"From a guy's point of view, he's an asshole."

"Yeah, well, I'm not going to disagree with that either. But, there is something very appealing about him. He can make a woman feel as if she's the only one in the world."

Jason stopped at her curb and sighed. "During the fireworks I saw him with someone else. Trish wanted me to tell you."

Melanie shrugged. "He and I aren't together, we're just … friends."

"Now that I don't get." He watched her. "If you could just be that with Adam ... he'd be less nuts."

"I can't be his friend. It's different. Trust me, Adam is better off. My life is a mess."

Melanie leaned over and kissed Jason on the cheek, trying to lighten the mood, wanting to forget the last half hour. "Thanks for the ride and the concern. I'm completely embarrassed about everything tonight."

"Listen, Angel, I'm pulling for you."

"Jason, it's one thing to root for the underdog and completely another to hope for a lost cause."

A crooked grin crossed his face. "Well, I do know you were cool tonight. You stepped up, literally...like, *on the table* stepped up." He laughed.

"I take back my 'thank you,'" she groaned, her head aching. "Goodnight, Jason." She opened the car door. "He thinks I'm insane, huh?"

Jason shook his head, "Oddly enough, he doesn't." Jason's eyes sparkled as he shrugged his square shoulders.

"I bet he does now."

"He doesn't."

Melanie walked cautiously up the front steps. She held the doorknob and listened for Jason to speed down the narrow, tree-lined street before stepping back into the night.

"Jack Scott," Melanie said, smiling broadly at the approaching figure.

Martinis, Adam, his Amazon and her grief were instantly dissolved.

She'd spied Jack sitting behind the wheel of a car parked in front of the Jeffersons driveway as soon as Jason's Porsche had rolled to a stop.

Jack was laughing, the chuckle she'd grown accustomed to while in Hawaii.

"Good to see you haven lost your edge," he stepped onto the sidewalk. "Hey, was that Jason Johnson?"

"You already know that. What are you doing here?"

"The Board sent me to bring you back," he said, his tone turning formal.

"They should call Ben."

"Agent Jackson lost his wife last week. My orders are to facilitate your immediate return. That's a direct quote."

"Where's Parker?"

Jack squinted at her, and lowered his voice to below a whisper. "Gone, disappeared. No one knows if he left or was taken, but I've been instructed to brief you on the flight to D.C. The Board is willing to accept any of your conditions," he lifted his eyebrows.

"Good, I've got three."

She listed them: full control without intervention, her salary doubled and Ben to regain control when he was ready. Jack pressed redial on his phone and spoke for less than 30 seconds before flipping his phone shut.

"Done."

Melanie looked at Jack and he at her. They both smiled.

"It's good to have you back, Agent Ward."

"It's good to be back." Behind her calm exterior, Melanie soared. "I'll be out in 10," she nodded, her stature three inches taller.

The TV flickered in her parents' bedroom as she reached the top of the stairs. Melanie flinched at the thought of that conversation.

Agent Ward was returning as a new woman. She changed into a pair of dark jeans, a long-sleeve blouse and heels. She filled her duffle bag with new style and dropped it on the carpet outside her parents' room.

Melanie knocked twice before entering.

Rita was reading a book while Roger watched television.

"Hi," Melanie smiled.

"You're home early," Rita said, looking above her glasses.

"Yeah, I've got some news."

Melanie sat at the end of their 40-year-old bed and explained the change of events. She started off delicately, not wanting to lose any of the ground she'd worked so hard to gain over the past weeks.

"It won't be the same as before, I promise."

"We always knew you couldn't stay here forever," her father said, tying his robe closed, "We're not upset. When do you leave?"

"Soon," Melanie said, motioning her head to the bag by the door.

Rita let her bifocals hang to her chest and put her arms around Melanie. "I miss you already," she said.

"I miss you guys, too," Melanie laughed to hold back the tears.

"Keep in touch with your mother," Roger said, his voice revealing more sentiment than his words.

"Every day," Melanie said, knowing it would be true. "I love you," she said through tears.

"You just stay safe, okay?"

Melanie nodded, taking one last look at her folks while a wave of sadness filled her heart.

CHAPTER 18

Jack carried her bag up the steps of the Agency's fastest jet. With a three-inch stack of files and a computer for company they went straight to work.

"Before we get into all this," Melanie motioned to the paperwork, "why don't you tell me what's going on?"

Melanie didn't need to know about the cases – she'd caught up through her research on Parker. What she needed to know was the delicate intangibles that couldn't be detected from a computer screen. It was the mood of the agents – where their heads were, their loyalties and any allegiances to Parker.

"The transition was ... rocky, to be kind. He's a class A dick."

Melanie knew this but she listened intently.

"The Board backed every lame-brain decision," he shook his head. "There was no misinterpreting their agenda. Finn was in charge. It silenced the murmurs and the agents had no choice but to succumb to the Parker dynasty." Jack spoke for 40 minutes ending with, "Mel, agents are bumping into each other out there. It's a mess, assignments are blurred, agents are working on more than one case while undercover. It's just a matter of time before someone is compromised."

"Tell me, Jack, why are you here?"

"Before he left, Agent Jackson assigned me to monitor Parker, confidentially," he tilted his head and there was a slight boast to his words. "When the Board contacted Jackson regarding current events he instructed them to speak with me and reinstate you."

She was almost afraid to ask. "The catalyst?"

"Parker vanished on yesterday. At first we thought he'd been kidnapped but we received no ransom demand, and then we found this."

Jack pressed a few keys on the laptop and Melanie watched a convenience store video surveillance recording, of poor quality. Scratches on the film from years of taping and re-taping over the same videocassette reduced the quality but Parker at the ice cream freezer was clear. He was speaking with two Hispanic males and his demeanor showed no signs of resistance or tension. He was there of his own volition. Melanie looked at the date stamped on the bottom of the snowy black-and-white image on the screen, 1:17 p.m. July 4. Today.

"Mike's working on cleaning up the resolution."

"Do we know these men?"

"No."

⊂⊗⌿⊃

"Good morning, Ms. Ward."

Melanie looked up the staircase. "Good morning, Sir." The old man was wearing a pair of knee-length plaid shorts and a Polo shirt with a cigar clamped tightly between his front teeth.

"Let's go in here," he said, leading the way into a study off the entrance hall. "I must say I was pleased to hear you'd come back willingly." He snorted a laugh as he flicked on the lights.

"There are conditions," she reminded him, the most senior of the Board members.

He waved her off and pulled the corner of a portrait to reveal a wall safe. "You don't know what you're walking into over there," he said, shuffling through the contents.

"I guess I'll find out."

"You are tenacious. That's what you are – like a bad penny always showing up." He found what he was looking for and grinned. "You've got top clearance, a new badge and some other computer crap that I don't know what the hell is for ... but it's yours." He handed her an envelope with one hand and pulled the cigar from his mouth with the other. "Good luck, Ward. And do me a favor – find that Parker boy."

His politics were unclear but she agreed heartily.

Jack was dozing in the sedan when she returned. Melanie sat quiet for a moment enjoying the revelation.

"How'd it go?" Jack asked.

"Strange." She contemplated for a moment wondering if Jack would understand. "He's just an old man." She laughed lightly, amused and curious about how her perception had changed. "Not iconic or heroic. He was wearing plaid shorts. I'd never pictured any of them out of their black robes." She looked back at him, and rolled her eyes. "You know what I mean." Suddenly she recognized her feelings, she was happy. "Jack, what do you think about assisting me? I'm going to need your support."

"I'd be honored, thank you." He stuck out his hand.

Melanie was back in a world of men and their dependence on custom. Relieved and grateful she shook his hand.

The large conference room was buzzing. A dozen large coffee cups were scattered across the table and 12 familiar faces, each with a different expression, stopped speaking as Melanie entered the room.

"Good morning," she began, placing a stack of files at the head of the rectangular table, Ben's spot. The chatter dropped to a few rumbles and the ordinary sounds of sipping, chewing, scooting and throat clearing.

Agent Masters stood. "It's great to have you back, Melanie."

A burst of clapping erupted from more than a few others.

"Thank you," Melanie said, after a minute. Surprised to receive such a welcome from a group that had never shown her much solidarity. "As you all know Finn Parker has not been seen since Tuesday afternoon. At this time we do not believe that he's been abducted, but we are not ready to rule out the possibility. There is a team working around the clock to determine Parker's whereabouts. In the meantime we need to get the Agency back up to standard." Melanie looked into each face. "We've got a lot of work to do and it's going to take everyone's full effort. So, with that said, I need to know now if anyone *isn't* on board."

Some of the agents shifted in their seats and glanced at their neighbor, but no one protested.

"Okay, then, let's get started."

She had outlined her strategy on the flight from San Diego, and now handed each agent a copy. For two hours they hashed out the details, and by the end she felt she had the support of most agents. She wasn't offended by the few who were aligned with Parker and had benefited from his reign.

When the last of the agents exited the conference room, impatient to implement the plan, Melanie asked Jack to locate both Jane and Judith while she grabbed her first opportunity to speak with Mike.

He was exactly where she expected, sitting intently in front of three computer screens, typing ferociously away at his keyboard with a pair of headphones over his ears.

"Mike?" she said, touching his shoulder.

"Aaagggh," he shouted, half jumping, half falling out of his chair.

Melanie couldn't help but chuckle. "What the hell is wrong with you?"

"Jesus, Melanie," he breathed as he tussled with the wheeled chair and tried to get back on his feet.

Melanie held the chair steady.

"I swear, you shouldn't sneak up on people." He was almost panting as he slowly sat back down, pressing his palms to his chest.

Melanie rolled a second chair close to her pale friend and sat.

His eyes shifted around the room. Melanie turned to see two other technicians immersed in their work, much as Mike had been.

"We need to talk, but not here," he whispered. "Follow me."

He led her into a small storage room that housed extra cable, monitors and boxes of spare electronic parts.

"What's going on?" She'd never seen Mike so out of sorts and her concern was building.

"I did what you asked," he said, looking up at ceiling tiles and the air vent.

"Aren't we secure?"

"Yeah, yeah, but give me a break, I'm a technical expert, not a spy."

"Okay, sorry," Melanie smiled.

"Anyway," he said, his tone lowering still. "I got this disc from Parker's office after you called." He reached inside the front his pants and pulled out a mini disc. "I wanted to keep it safe."

Melanie eyed the item without touching it. "That's a copy right?"

Mike's forehead had started sweating, dripping down his temples as he wiped the side of his face with his arm. "I didn't have time to copy it." He looked guilty. "I was planning on returning the original but he ... he showed up. And, Mel, he went berserk. He came running into the 'war room.'" Mike put up imaginary quotes and rolled his eyes. "He was frantic, and asked me to pull up surveillance on his office. He stood behind me for 20 minutes as I skimmed through hours of footage. He didn't even realize we were looking at the wrong day. I wanted to call you but it got crazy here and then I heard the Board had sent Jack for you."

Melanie was no longer laughing.

"He was swearing and pulling at his hair, and all the while his disc was under papers on my desk. He left after that and no one's seen him since."

"What is on the disc?"

"I don't know yet. The encryption is pretty advanced, and with all of this hullabaloo I haven't had time to work on it."

"Have you had any luck with the facial recognition of the men at the convenience store?"

"Are you kidding? I've been freaking out about this." He waved the disc.

"Okay, I want you to work on the surveillance video. Locating Parker is your priority. I'll take care of the disc..." she thought of where it'd been and continued, "you can hold onto it. Thanks."

Melanie left the communications center and headed to what was now to be her office. Stepping into the cozy, wood-paneled room she was hit with the loss of Ben. In the two months since Parker had taken over he'd taken Ben out of Ben's office. The decanters usually filled with clear to amber liquids sat empty on their silver tray. The sense of order Ben brought to everything he touched had vanished. Jane and Judith sat on the couch, leaning into their conversation.

Jack had rounded them up from the menial jobs Parker had assigned them to and brought them back to assist in the redevelopment of the agency. When Melanie entered the room both stood with willing faces and broad smiles.

"Hello, Agent Ward. It's good to have you back."

"How are you, Ma'am?" Jane asked.

"I'm well, thank you. Judith, any word from Agent Jackson?"

"Not since Lilly passed away."

"Well, I've got a big task in front of me and I am going to need your help." She sat on the leather chair across from the couch.

Like she had with the agents, Melanie laid out a strategic plan with daily reports and a step-by-step guide to manage their goals.

"Knock, knock," Jack said from the door. "Am I interrupting?"

"No, come in. We're just about finished here. One last thing," Melanie added as they were standing in the doorway. "About my personal calls – I'm going to need you to put them through no matter what the situation."

Melanie turned to survey her new office. It was dark, stuffy and she pushed aside the heavy drapes, flooding the room with natural light. Outside the window an old elm tree, dense with waxy green leaves rustled silently in the summer breeze.

"Ha, there really are windows behind those old curtains."

"Look at that, they even open. I thought they'd be painted shut for sure," Melanie said as soggy air crept in, making her rethink the idea. She pushed the window closed and decided Mother Nature had the lighting right but couldn't beat central air.

"How loud is the grumbling out there?" Melanie asked, sitting on the corner of Ben's desk.

"Not too bad. Some, but mostly I think people are glad to have you back." Jack took a seat. "How are you holding up?"

"I'm great," Melanie said, actually feeling great.

"You look it, too," he said, awkwardly. "Anyway, the last senior agent is en route and we're on schedule. Your design to alleviate agent congestion in Europe was brilliant, by the way."

"I'd rather you not do that."

"I'm not kissing ass, I'm seriously impressed," Jack said, with an embarrassed expression.

"All right then, thank you. But I'm going to rely on you for honest input and that can't happen if you tiptoe around, understood?"

"Yes Ma'am," Jack smiled.

CHAPTER 19

The South of France, with its acres of vineyards still barren and dormant, looked dry and dead, but with spring approaching, life was exploding just below the surface. At the tip of the stem undeveloped buds waited to meet the sun for the first time. The beauty of the patchwork countryside went unnoticed by the man behind the dark sunglasses.

On a desolate stretch of road he stopped at the house of his target: a converted stone barn tucked 30 yards inside a field of grapevines.

He observed.

A family: man, woman, red-haired girl with ringlets like her mother's riding her tricycle, a baby balancing on wobbly legs. Laughing, the woman scooped up the toddler and the man lovingly leaned in to kiss her porcelain cheek. The older girl remained determined, struggling to pedal on the gravel driveway.

Before long, the father lifted his nose into the air, catching the scent of death. Coolly, he ushered his family to the safety of their home.

The killer had been detected.

The target, tall and thin with blonde hair and a beard, took long strides to the waiting car. Squatting down to eye level he asked, "Could you give me a day? I don't want my family to be here or to see…" he cleared his throat. "My boy is just a baby but this would haunt my wife and daughter."

He didn't beg – accepting his fate – he negotiated on behalf of his family. His past had caught up with him. But the killer did the unexpected: he looked deep into the eyes of his target, full of vitality and sadness. He did not want to be the one to extinguish the life from this man. He wanted to *be* this man.

"You don't have much time," he said in a deep grumble.

The man did not thank him but stepped back as the car sped away.

The killer did not return the following day, instead, he flew to London, unplugged his computer and formulated a new plan for his life.

CHAPTER 20

"You look like crap," Jack said, lifting her feet off the couch so he could sit. "Why don't you sleep in the apartment upstairs?"

"I was just taking a nap," she rubbed her burning eyes. "I should be used to no sleep by now." The pressure had been relentless, scrutinizing eyes were upon her and she knew more than a few hoped she failed. "Is it day or night?"

"Both," Jack answered.

"What is that I smell?" Now her eyes were open and sat up. "Pepperoni? Yum. Jane has been feeding me salads all week."

"I brought beer, too."

He handed her a steaming slice, cheese dripping off the sides. Melanie ignored the inferno melting her taste buds, draining half a beer to cool off her singed her tongue. She closed her eyes to enjoy.

"I thought we should celebrate," Jack said, clinking his beer to hers. "In two weeks we've cleared up the festering problems, the system is mostly mended and the assignments are finally smoothing out."

"You're right," she said.

Melanie had arranged cases like a master puzzler and Jack had been invaluable. They were finally noticing a reduction in the strain. The need for intervention lessened each day. Reaching the point where the emphasis was no longer on cleaning up, instead she was taking on new cases and actively moving forward in securing the nation.

She'd even maintained a personal life, even if it was only a few moments each day.

Melanie leaned back and listened to the scraping of tree branches against her window.

"I like what you've done with the place." He nodded toward the flat-screen TVs that took the wall space where the file cabinets had once stood.

Melanie glanced at the headline news and dug into a second slice.

"Thanks," she said, raising her second bottle.

"I had no idea you were starving."

Shoptalk was the only thing they had in common, and with the planet under control their conversation waned. She closed her eyes. The beer, combined with a full stomach, added to her fatigue.

"You look stressed," Jack said, walking around the couch.

"I do?" she asked drowsily.

Jack's mumbled words were just beyond comprehension as she nearly drifted off to sleep.

"What are you doing?!" she asked, suddenly frightfully awake.

"Giving you a massage."

It was true – his hands were on her shoulders, moving up to her *now* highly tense neck.

"Thank you, but…"

She searched for a gentle way of telling him to get the hell off her.

"Your muscles are tight."

Melanie turned her body, placing her back out of reach.

"Think about it, Mel, why don't we give it a shot, you and me?"

His voice was an octave higher, his eyes wide, and Melanie knew he wasn't kidding.

"Jack."

"Who knows the demands of an agent better than another agent? We wouldn't have to lie to anyone about where we are and what we do. It's the perfect solution."

Jack hopped over the back of the large black leather couch and sat facing Melanie, who was stunned.

"What … when did all this happen?" she asked, thinking back for signs she may have missed about his intentions.

"We have a chemistry, your words."

"When did I say that?"

He inched nearer.

"Jack, you know I like you and you've been a great friend these past weeks, but truly, this isn't going to happen." His blue eyes were hazed and unconvinced. "Don't look at me like that, I'm serious."

Before the period had been placed on her sentence Jack's lips were pressed against hers and he was pulling her into the confines of his arms.

"Jack," Melanie said, wiggling out of the odd embrace. "Jack, really."

"Just agree to think it over."

Melanie shook her head. "No, there's nothing to…"

She was stopped in mid-sentence by a knock at the door.

"Can I help you?" she asked, shooting Jack an angry glance.

"Excuse me," a young man said. He was obviously embarrassed at witnessing her and Jack's exchange. "I'm Dom DiRito."

Bad news, she thought looking at her watch. *Good news doesn't arrive after 2 a.m.*

"I know who you are, Agent DiRito. Why don't you come in and have a seat?"

"I'm sorry to be interrupting," he gave Jack a sideways glance. "But I was told by my supervisor that the matter couldn't wait for him and since I was at the Manor, I mean since I was here I was to speak to you directly."

"It's fine, Dom, just tell us what's on your mind."

"Two months ago when I was part of a team in Turkey bidding for a set of stolen nuclear devices. Agent Levine and I were tying to ascertain if the offer was legit. But before the transaction was authenticated Agent Parker pulled the operation." Dom DiRito's round face was filled with anticipation. "Ten minutes ago I received a phone call from the line we used for that assignment. It was from a man who said he was in possession of one of the devices. I agreed to meet him at a motel just outside of Tampa tomorrow … well, today, at noon."

"What's the name and address of that motel?" Melanie asked, already grabbing hold of her phone to make the first of several calls.

They were going to need blueprints, satellite feed, an explosives expert and a sharpshooter.

Jack waited until Dom was outside of earshot.

"Do you think this has something to do with Parker?"

Melanie shrugged, "He'd better hope not."

❦

Her first breath of Florida air was oppressive. It was steamy and thick, even in the early morning hours, leaving nothing to look forward to as the sun would soon be beating down from directly overhead. Melanie didn't mind the perspiration that came from physical labor, but sweat running down her back as she walked to the SUV just wasn't right.

Waiting for her, Dom and Mike's assistant Ed, were fellow agents Colleen Bricks and John Roberts.

"Colleen, how've you been?" Melanie asked once the A/C was cranked to full blast.

Colleen was the utmost expert in armaments, a major feat considering how difficult it was for a woman to succeed in a man's field.

"Busy. I've been meaning to call and congratulate you on your promotion," Colleen smiled.

"Hello, John."

John nodded.

Inside the SUV, Ed, almost as non-verbal as John, immediately went to work linking his computer to the flat-screen.

"This is the motel," Ed said, pointing to a green building in the center of the screen. Showing off, he zoomed quickly in on the structure, leaving only a narrow image of the surroundings. "We're in real time."

Melanie took over. "Larry Schuster checked into room 214 last night, making two phone calls. The first was at midnight to his ex-wife, and the second to DiRito. Schuster was released last week after serving two years of a three-year sentence for battery."

"Where'd he get the suitcase? Any possible scenarios?" Colleen asked, studying the picture.

"We lost him from the time he was released until he arrived at this motel. The local PD has been staking out the motel since 4 a.m. and was able to hold off the news crews until about an hour ago," Dom explained.

In the satellite pictures Ed had brought up on the computer Melanie could identify police cars, media vans and the popular freeway that butted up against the old building, which would be bumper-to-bumper in a few hours. In the hours before the city dressed for another business day, Melanie assigned each of her agents a task. The motel was a two-story 60s-style relic. Cars parked right up against the first-floor rooms while two stairways led to the second-floor breezeway. The doors to the balcony and parking lot were the only ways in or out of each room.

It was remodeled 11 years ago, enabling Ed to pull up the blueprints.

"I have the decoy you asked for right here." Colleen gently patted a silver suitcase resting against her leg.

Melanie looked to John. Going over possible outcomes, the one that caused the least pandemonium was his "suicide." It could have gone easier had the ex-wife not called the police. But now there was no way to bring Schuster out of this alive.

"I'm ready," John said.

Melanie wondered if he was as bored as he sounded, or if taking lives had taken his soul. They revisited the plan one last time.

From a thicket on the northern end of the motel, Colleen and John would crawl through the ventilation system to Schuster's room with a low-grade, homemade bomb in a suitcase. Colleen would inspect Schuster's device, disarm it and bring it back safely, leaving the decoy. John would interrogate Schuster before injecting him with a lethal dose of heroine.

The entire case was resolved three hours after touchdown.

Colleen transported the bomb to her lab and Melanie spent the day with the Agency's Tampa personnel.

The heat of the day was behind them as the aircraft lifted off the sweltering tarmac heading toward dusk.

She returned phone calls and cleared up loose ends before dialing Carla.

Voice mail, again. Trish didn't answer either.

Dom and Ed's voices carried in the small comfortable cabin as they laughed and spoke cheerfully. The two men had had a very good day.

The lights and the level of noise in the fuselage were both dimmed, as if on one switch, for the descent into D.C. From her oval window, Melanie, like a novice astronomer, made out the familiar constellations of her city: the brightest lights from the Capital Building, Lincoln Memorial and the long dark stretch across the mall to the Washington Monument were the planets in this solar system. She closed her stinging eyes, shutting out the city. The most powerful city in the world, filled with corruption, lies and empty promises. It was no place for the weak or complacent. Melanie was tired. She missed the Southern California sun.

Gravity forced her back against the seat and for a moment she wondered where the hell Ben was and when would he return.

Melanie's heels tapped along the asphalt runway toward her waiting car as Agent DiRito called out to her.

"Agent Ward?"

His suitcase teetered on one wheel as he ran to catch her.

"What's up?" Melanie asked, attempting to keep exhaustion out of her tone.

"I was wondering if you wanted to grab a drink?"

"Agent, I'm going to pass on that, but you did a fine job asking," Melanie laughed, stepping into the company car.

He stuck his head inside before she could get the door closed. "But, Ma'am, I was hoping to discuss my career options. How do you think I did today?"

She was too tired for this.

"If there's a position you're interested in have your supervisor submit your name. Goodnight." She shifted her gaze to the car door.

"Right, sorry," he said, jumping back. "Thank you. Goodnight."

"Home please, Marcos," Melanie said as she slid into the back seat of the cool car.

The evening was still young but she wanted nothing more than to sleep in a real bed with sheets and a soft pillow.

After making arrangements for a 5:30 a.m. pick-up, Melanie stood outside the little iron fence, admiring her old place. It hadn't changed in 50 years, much less in the two months since she'd packed her bags and left for San Diego. The neighbors were still arguing and she wondered if they'd even noticed she'd been away.

Melanie skimmed her fingers above the door for the key, exactly where she'd left it. The lights still worked and she held hopes that the air conditioning unit would soon be humming along. She lugged her bag up to the loft, where her bed was still unmade, the sheets half off the mattress in a crumpled heap on the floor. Absently, she switched on the TV she headed toward the bathroom for a cool, refreshing shower.

Afterwards, she pulled on an old T-shirt and a pair of shorts that were balled up at the back of the closet, and called one of her old haunts, The House of Wang.

"An order of the house lo mein."

She gave her address to an unfamiliar voice and popped open a bottle of beer from the fridge. Melanie sat on the orange Formica countertop, leaned against the dark wood cabinets and stretched her legs over the sink. It was a comfortable position, one that developed gradually over many years of wearing out the same spots in the yellow linoleum.

Fifteen minutes later her stomach growled at the slamming of a car door. It was her Pavlovian response, hunger at the sounds of take-out delivery.

"Hello," the driver's face was well known as Melanie handed him a bill. "I'm glad to see you, you just won me 20 bucks. We thought you might have died."

Melanie nodded. "Nice. Congratulations."

Steam drifted out as she opened the little white box filled with soft noodles, vegetables, mixed animals (pig, cow and chicken) and a crustacean. Ripping open the corner of a soy sauce packet she drained its contents into the container, then broke her chopsticks apart and rubbed them together, smoothing out the rough edges. Grabbing another beer, she climbed the steps to bed, where she'd eat and fall asleep to the nightly news.

Melanie wasn't surprised the Tampa story hadn't made it on every cable news network. Thanks to her team it had been a non-event. Sure, there had been wide-spread evacuations and a multitude of traffic jams but Melanie had seen much worse escape mention.

Instead, she watched a newswoman reporting from the White House. Earlier in the day the President had met with a handful of Senators. Economic strategy was the topic and from behind the correspondent Melanie watched Hugh Parker. A big, toothy grin stretched from one side of his devil face to the other as he shook hands with the Commander-in-Chief.

"... it is a unique idea," the woman was saying. "Senator Parker has been the biggest proponent to alternative fuel. Some see it is and end to his presidential aspirations, before this 'flip-flop' he topped the list for presidential candiates. Now, well, we will have to wait, Senator Parker is known for his inovation. Maybe this is a part of his grand scheme. This is Natalie Hart, with the latest from Washington."

Fifteen minutes later the story repeated. Melanie watched Hugh closely. He didn't seem like a man concerned about his missing son.

She picked the shrimp and beef out leaving half a box of noodles, and set the TV's sleep timer for 30 minutes. Sinking down into her pillow she watched inattentively. The next moment, or so it seemed, she was snapped awake by the ring of her cell phone. The television was off and her room was dark.

More bad news, she thought as she answered with a raspy voice.

A voice on the other end said only her name, "Melanie," but that was all it took for her heartbeat to quicken.

"Adam?"

Now she was fully alert.

"It's too late to be calling, I know, I'm sorry."

"Is everything all right? Trish?" Her heart pounded, bracing for the bad news. There had been no answer when she'd called earlier. Her blood drained to her toes.

"No, Mel, she's fine, it's nothing like that, I didn't mean to scare you."

"Are you sure?"

"I promise. I had dinner with Trish and Jason."

Melanie breathed, letting out a sigh of relief. She ran her shaky hand through her hair. "Okay." It was going to take a minute for her muscles to relax. "So, how've you been?"

"Good, well, sort of. I've been thinking about you and wondering how things were going?"

"Busy," she said. Her deep, calming breaths weren't working.

"So..." he started and Melanie's mind flashed to their last meeting.

"Before you say anything – if it's about the Fourth then please don't. I would really rather forget the entire evening." She listened to the silence and wondered about the conversation she'd just stopped. If it was about that night, she decided she was better off not knowing. But her pulse was the rapid beacon that told a different story. She wanted to hear what he was going to say.

"Melanie, I would really like to see you," he said, interrupting her thoughts, his voice calm and even. "I'm going to be in D.C. tomorrow and I *was hoping* to take you to dinner."

Her brain was still calculating the risks when she surprised herself by saying, "I'd like that."

Adam sighed, like he'd been holding his breath. "Great. Daniel's Dragonfly, tomorrow night?"

"That place is impossibly packed," she said, reeling from her impromptu response.

"I know a few people. I'll pick you up at 7:30."

"How about we meet there?" Her heart compressed. She was going to see Adam.

"Whatever you want. Mel, are we okay?" He cleared his throat and sounded insecure.

She hadn't thought of Adam since she'd returned to the Agency. And now her feelings were re-surfacing. He was trouble.

"I want to see you, but don't have expectations."

"I won't."

"Tomorrow, then."

"I can't wait."

She swallowed back

"Sweet dreams, Mel."

She stayed motionless in her pitch-black room.

Throughout her morning of meetings Melanie carried on business as usual, wrestling with her emotions behind a large disposable cup of vanilla coffee.

A tingle of life initiated in the pit of her stomach. Adam's butterflies had been revived.

She called Trish.

Flying through the obligatory pleasantries she told Trish about Adam's call and their plans to meet.

"Aren't you happy?"

"I don't know. Since I got my life back I haven't even thought of Adam or Javier. I've pushed my pathetic summer behavior out of my mind and I like it that way."

"You want to go back to being the celibate workaholic you've always been?"

Melanie sighed. "No, but I don't want to be the irrational, love-sick teenager, either. I care about Adam, but I don't need him. I needed him when I was in San Diego, without a job, without a purpose, and he was frolicking with the mammoth."

"He split up with Gigi for you," she said, matter-of-factly.

"They're separated? When did that happen?"

"During the Fourth of July party, right after Jason took you home. I don't think you were even to Jason's car before he told her." Trish lowered her voice. "She would have made a scene if not for the guest list."

"Why didn't you tell me!?"

"He asked me not to. Then he disappeared for a week, but he's asked about you every day since he got back. He checked in twice yesterday. I guess he got tired of waiting."

Melanie sat speechless lost for the moment in her thoughts. "Well, he shouldn't have done that. It's too late – I'm in D.C. now. It's not for forever, but I'm content."

"Jesus, you are so pig-headed! The guy's in love with you and you're acting like a bitch."

"Ouch." Melanie grimaced. "That's harsh."

"How about spoiled brat, then? Either way you won't listen. Mel, I love you – you're my best friend, but you're so stubborn, just like your mother, and if you snub him I swear I'll beat you senseless."

The feelings of that horrible night came tumbling back – too many martinis, too much said by everyone involved. She felt the hangover pushing its way back.

"Wow, just like my mother? I think I'd rather be called a bitch."

Melanie looked up to a knock on her office door and waved Jane inside as she finished her conversation with Trish.

"I've got to go, but I'll think about what you said, except for the mean parts. And I'm not like my mother." Was she? "Hey, have you heard from Carla? I've been trying to reach her all week."

Jane lingered after placing a DVD on top of a pile of folders on Melanie's desk.

"Last I heard someone new threw their name in for Ted's seat. Carla's been scrambling with their campaign manager, complaining about airtime. She's fine. Call me tomorrow," Trish commanded, "and Mel, I'm sorry. I go too far, sometimes."

"Yeah, well, sometimes I need that. Bye."

"Love you," Trish said.

"Love you, too."

Jane loitered inside the door, uncharacteristically paying close attention to every word. "Was there something more?"

"Um, the DVD is from Mike. He just dropped it off and said it was extremely urgent, and I guaranteed him I would hand it to you personally." Her voice trembled slightly at the end of each word. "Um," she said again, "I'm sorry to interrupt."

Melanie's eyebrows lifted.

"I was wondering about Agent Scott?" Jane's pale brows pulled in tight as her face flushed pink then feverishly added, "I'm sorry, I was out of line by asking. I usually don't pay any attention to the rumors about you. It's just that he invited me out to dinner, I just automatically thought…"

"Jane," Melanie said, calmly.

Jane, her face glowing red behind her fashionable rectangular eyeglasses, asked, "yes?"

"Jack and I are not romantically involved."

"Really?" she asked, forgetting her embarrassment and stepping closer to Melanie. "Are you sure?"

"Pretty sure," Melanie nodded with a laugh.

"Of course you'd know, what a stupid question. I'm sorry," she giggled and exhaled.

Melanie watched Jane walk dreamily out the door, then backtracked a pace.

"Agent Ward?"

"Yes?"

"So, you wouldn't mind if," her face twisting, "I accepted Agent Scott's invitation?"

"I wouldn't mind one bit," Melanie relaxed.

Melanie chuckled as she settled back into her chair and slid the

DVD into her computer. Mike had finished deciphering the encryption, a formula for an achievable alternative to petroleum gasoline, more efficient than the corn product used in Brazil. Melanie spent the next hours trying to connect the dots. Her mind traveled back to the clip on the news. What was he up to? She wondered, was it money? Finn didn't care about monetary gains – the Parker boys were all about power – or were they?

Well, I have a piece of their puzzle now, she thought slyly.

Melanie brought in a team to further explain the formula and what impact it would have on the economy.

It was just after 5 p.m. the next time Melanie looked at the clock. She left the room filled with experts who could speculate without her. The day had run like a roller coaster, slowly dragging on for hours, then suddenly the hour hand behaved like second hand and time flew.

Hurriedly, she walked the bustling halls, ignoring the whispers as she passed the kitchen and living areas of the old building. They were probably gossiping about her and Jack.

Let them, she thought and smiled hello to the storage room filled with costumes and disguises of every nature, including cocktail dresses. She knew the layout well and went directly to the rack with her size, grabbing the first dress that caught her eye and folding it into her shoulder bag. Next was a pair of matching shoes and a silver clasp purse. Like the spook she was, Melanie snuck out the door, down the corridor and disappeared into the waiting car.

CHAPTER 21

The heavy wooden doors, forged with black iron hardware, were like portals into the past. Stepping across the threshold of Daniel's Dragonfly was like taking a trip into medieval times. Cold, uneven slabs of yellow stone covered the floors and climbing plants clung to the rough slate walls. In the central atrium Melanie gazed up to the glass ceiling that stretched two stories high, where perfumed flowering vines reached for sunlight.

"May I help you?"

Melanie looked at the source of the voice, a gentleman in a tailored dark green waistcoat and green plaid tie. "I'm admiring your cubicle," she said. When he didn't crack a smile she added, "I'm waiting for Adam Chase."

"Yes, Mr. Chase is in the bar." The man pointed his stubby finger at a pair of swinging doors with stained-glass windows.

"Thank you," she said, and pushed open the door.

A highly polished bar stretched across the length of the narrow room. She looked at the tables with iron chairs and mosaic tabletops. Most seats were filled with politicians and lobbyists, their ties loosened and top buttons undone. Tightly pinned men and women during the day, unwinding and speaking in low voices over brandy snifters and highballs.

Her breath caught.

His broad shoulders were covered in a dark suit that blended seamlessly with the rest of the Washington men. Except he was irresistibly handsome, so much so that her heart ached at the sight of his strong jaw, his dark hair cropped close behind the curve of his ear. Mindlessly she bit her lip and held her breath.

He spoke with the waiter, his tan deeper than only two weeks earlier. He glanced at his watch.

I'm here, she called out silently. She had forgotten how powerful her physical reaction was to him.

He turned, as if having heard her. She waited for the recognition to sink in, watching the corners of his mouth lift into a brilliant smile. Melanie stood frozen, her silver heels adhered to the floor, not breathing she waited for him to cross the room.

"Hi," he said. "It's great to see you."

"You too," she whispered.

"I got us a table and a bottle of wine," he said, leading her to a small table with an image of a golden dragonfly in flight over cobalt blue glass.

He gave a nod to the sommelier, whose livery matched that of the maitre d', and held the chair for her.

"How've you been?" she asked, enjoying the feel of his leg against her knee.

"Pretty good," he chuckled. "That's what I'm supposed to say, right?" his eyebrow arched playfully.

"Oh, right." Melanie said, not understanding unless it meant he was missing Gigi. The wine steward arrived with an aired bottle of Sauvignon.

"I left Oscar's," Adam said matter-of-factly as he raised his glass to check the color of the wine.

"Really? Are you opening your restaurant?"

"Not yet, but it was time for change," he smiled and without pretension sipped and accepted the bottle of wine.

Two glasses were generously filled.

"I heard you broke up with Margaret," Melanie said, playing

nervously with the stem of her own glass and unable to call a grown
– *very grown* – woman "Gigi."

"I should've done it sooner."

She looked up into his incredibly intense, breathtakingly handsome
face.

"Are you surprised?"

"I thought you two were very…" what was the right word? "…
connected." Gigi had called it "love", but Melanie couldn't.

"Hmm? No, I wouldn't say that. I'd say we were convenient."

Melanie wondered at convenient. *How could that be?*
He'd humiliated her for convenient?

"It didn't seem convenient when you left me standing alone on the
beach." Her passion leaning toward anger.

She felt his eyes scrutinizing her every expression, analyzing her
reaction to him.

"I know," he said, dropping his eyes. "I know I have no right to
ask anything from you but I was hoping," his voice cracked and he
still looking down, "that you could forgive me." He slid his gaze to
meet hers. "I screwed this up, Melanie, and if I could take it all back
I would. Sorry doesn't even begin to cover how I feel."

Everything about him cried genuine remorse and that sincerity
pulled at her heartstrings. Thumping painfully in her chest her
imprudent heart melted in forgiveness and compassion. She reached
to touch his hand, and his fingertips were cool, a signal of nerves.
His hand tightened around hers and they both took in a breath.

"Well, it wasn't just you. I have regrets of my own."

"Do you?" His eyes pleaded.

Javier came to mind, clearly it was what Adam was thinking,
though she hadn't necessarily meant him. Melanie considered which

part of Javier she regretted. She didn't. But she could be sorry for the pain it was causing Adam. Later she might add the sex part but at the time *that* was what kept her sane.

She swallowed the expensive wine too fast, she knew, but there was an entire bottle and she could use the fermented grapes.

Adam smiled. "Would you rather have a shot of tequila?"

"You're going to think I'm an alcoholic," she said, but didn't refuse.

He motioned for the bartender. The rims of the heavy glasses clinked as they each licked a sprinkle of salt from their hands and swigged the shots before biting down on wedges of lime.

Melanie's heart fluttered. His smile was bright and the liquor burned down her esophagus to her empty stomach.

"Were you nervous about tonight?" she asked.

"I'm still nervous. You?"

She nodded.

His smile dropped and the vein in his neck throbbed.

"You know, there really isn't anything to forgive."

"Mel," he said, with a look that proved he was unconvinced, shaking his head.

"I was wrong, too," she said. "Consider yourself forgiven."

The fragileness in his eyes was fleeting. Clearing his throat, he asked, "Just like that?"

Melanie didn't look away. She wanted to see him vulnerable, doubting there would be many opportunities to peer into his soul.

"Yeah."

"Do you think we can start over?" he asked, quickly composing himself.

She wanted to say yes, she wanted to hold onto this feeling.

"I don't know how that would be possible."

"Then say maybe. I'll take a maybe."

"Maybe." The knots in her stomach multiplied.

The moments of silent staring continued as they were led from the bar to the restaurant. A surreal quality embodied the restaurant, extending further than the visual illusion of a castle: a maiden with blonde braids sat upon a wooden stool plucking a six foot harp, and the roasted duck in a rosemary/cranberry sauce smelled of ages past.

When Chef Daniel, stout with ruddy cheeks and strawberry/orange hair, emerged from the kitchen to say hello, even he seemed illusory.

Scooting into the booth, pushing Melanie toward Adam, he smiled and wound his ample arm along the top of the booth.

"So, this is the girlfriend that you're so eager to impress?" his accent fluctuated between Scottish and Irish as he appraised her. "Too skinny" had been his verdict.

Melanie looked at Adam, who took the question in stride and made the introductions. Daniel, as it turned out, was robust and jovial, laughing loud enough to be noticed by all.

"Finally a woman who is able to tie this one down," he said, leaning in close enough for Melanie to catch a whiff of garlic and body odor. "He was quite popular," he added a wink of his bloodshot eye. "Did you hear what happened to Gibson?"

Daniel threw out a few more names as he leaned across Melanie's lap to grouse, completely forgetting to carry on with the ruse of the accent.

"How did you two meet?" Melanie asked, pulling as far away from the man as possible without being rude.

"We were competing for the position at Oscar's."

"Really?" she asked, catching a clumsy moment between Daniel and Adam.

"Yeah, but Adam was more popular," Daniel snorted and dragged his weight to the edge and heaved himself out of the booth. "It was lovely meeting you, Melanie, and Adam, stop by anytime you're in town. We can chew the fat."

"I'd like that, and thanks for the table."

Daniel snapped his fingers at a passing waiter and returned to the kitchen.

"He's enthusiastic. I can see where this place gets its personality."

"He is unique. We met just after I arrived in San Diego. He was a big-shot chef even back then."

"But *you* got the job at Oscar's."

"Yeah," he nodded, concentrating on the past.

"You told him I was your girlfriend?" she asked, amused. "That's a bit of a stretch."

He shrugged. "It was easier than explaining the truth," he chuckled, his expression turned boyish. "I'm happy with a maybe." He brushed his fingers along her cheek then rested his warm hand on the back of her neck.

"Do you miss her?" she couldn't help herself. Consumed with curiosity and jealousy, she was unable to let it go.

"Who?"

"Gigi."

"Why would I miss her?" He leaned in, his brows knitted in tightly. "God, Mel, the only time I've thought of her was when I agonized about how I hurt you." His hands rubbed down her arms. "The night of the party you said some things."

"I was pretty drunk." She felt drunk now, her toiling brain

cloudy.

He nodded. "I hope not too drunk."

She couldn't breathe.

"You said exactly what I was feeling." His intense eyes drilled into her.

Melanie was speechless.

"I fell for you the second I saw you. It was an arrow straight through my heart, taking me by surprise and leaving me defenseless. I know I screwed up and I can't take back the things I said and did, but..."

"I forgave you, Adam."

"Mel, I don't forgive myself."

"I am as much to blame as you. I pushed you away, remember?" she smiled, "Jumped overboard."

"I remember." The tense muscles in his face relaxed, a bit. "At the beach, the volleyball game, did you know I was going to be there or was it a coincidence?"

"I knew."

"How? I don't recall ever mentioning I played volleyball."

"You did. On the boat you said you were missing the game to be with me."

He nodded, thinking.

"You could have been mine?" He jaw tightened and emotion rose to his eyes. "You kissed me," he rubbed his temples, "but Gigi showed up and she was so easy. I tried to believe that ... I don't know ... but when I saw you with Javier ... I imagined..." He clenched his jaw, his emerald eyes steely. "I was angry."

She felt his pain although even though he called it "anger."

"I gave up on us. I'm sorry." He squeezed her hands and Melanie knew he'd been berating himself for weeks. "I knew that we were meant to be together but I got scared. I can't believe how quickly and desperately I fell for you." When he looked back at her his eyes were clear, remorseful. "Mel, I need to know … about the 'maybe' – is it because you don't feel the same anymore, or is it Javier, or something completely different?"

"Can't you see how I feel about you?"

She released his hands and he cupped her face to look into her face.

"I can't read you," he gritted his teeth, struggling, confused. "I don't know how you feel and I'm terrified that you're just sitting here to be polite and that I've lost you."

His touch lingered long after his hands were gone.

"My feelings haven't changed," she lost her voice to a whisper.

His tendons in his jaw flickered and his lips disappeared into a narrow line. "Really?"

Melanie could only nod.

His desire was in his voice as he said her name and on his lips as he gently kissed her. "God, you are so beautiful," he said, holding on tightly. "Whenever I think about you, I think, she couldn't possibly be as beautiful as I remember but then I see you, like tonight, and you are, even more than I remembered."

That was it, her heart was let loose.

After dinner, the fresh air did nothing to clear her mind. Even the distinctive scent of a well-used cab couldn't undo her euphoria.

"Two stops." Adam told the driver once they were settled in the back. "We'll drop you off first."

Melanie rattled her address. Adam's smile was simple and open and it gave her courage.

"Adam," she said, pulling her bottom lip between her teeth. "I thought we could spend tonight together."

"I'm not going to rush you. I'm determined to wait for as long as you need."

Melanie wanted to laugh.

"There'll be only one stop," she said.

She was taking Adam into her unimpressive habitat. Either that or she would do the Saturday morning "walk of shame," exiting his hotel in her previous night's dress.

"Are you sure?" he asked suspiciously. "Because the last time I moved too fast, you bolted."

"That was completely different." She couldn't contain the laugh. "I was lost in San Diego – I can't even explain my mental state."

"And things are better now?" His posture and the raised eyebrow signaled his doubt.

"Yeah, I have my job back, purpose and equilibrium has been righted within the universe." She was happy and chuckled merrily as Adam rubbed his chin. "I want you to stay with me tonight. At least come in, and we can decide what we should do next."

"I don't want to make a mistake," Adam said as the cab rolled to a stop in front of the wrought iron fence that surrounded her tiny yard. Her dreary-looking brick duplex seemed romantic in the glow of the moonlight. In the front seat she noticed the cabbie angling his head to catch Adam's answer. Adam's green eyes looked gray as he gazed back at her. "But I think the mistake would be in missing another moment with you."

Though she couldn't make out the exact words of congratulations, she did see Adam smile as he paid the driver his fare.

His hand was still cool as he caressed the back of her neck as she fumbled with the lock.

The air conditioning was on and the lights were off. *Perfect,* she thought.

"Would you like something to drink?' Melanie offered, knowing she had only one Samuel Adams in the fridge and doubting there was any ice for the tap water.

Adam shook his head as a slow grin spread across his shadowy face. He stepped toward her, closing the door behind him. Their eyes locked, and Melanie felt uncomfortable, awkward and suddenly nervous.

Adam bent down and placed his lips on hers, pulling back to read her reaction – she didn't blink and he smiled. He kissed her again, closing his eyes and pressing firmly against her. His fingers were hooked in her hair and he glided the side of his nose along her neck, kissing her skin along the way. "Melanie," he said, his breath tickling her skin. He stopped at the edge of her shoulder and stepped back.

She'd never seen him look so dangerous, handsome and hungry – her body reacted. He stared at her as his index fingers laced beneath the thin spaghetti straps of her dress. Then dragging the straps over her shoulders he let them drop. The dress fluttered to the ground.

A weak moan escaped from the back of his throat as Melanie stood in heels and lacy black underwear. He lifted her and climbed the stairs.

❧

Melanie desperately wanted to know what time it was, but Adam was on that side of the bed, blocking the view of her clock. Her arm was wedged between him and the mattress, the best she could do was keep still and try not to think.

She'd done something stupid. Even she, who knew none of *Cosmo's* rules on dating, knew she'd made a colossal mistake.

What did she really know about Adam? Wasn't he too good to be true? Were there red flags scattered around her feet that she'd chosen to ignore, scarlet fluttering by her blind eyes even now? Why had she been so willing to trust him? Because when she looked into his brilliant green eyes she felt as if she'd known him since time began? Melanie could even convince herself that their hearts were somehow connected, a bond that when she breathed, he breathed.

Utterly ridiculous, she thought, becoming more and more appalled. *Face it, Mel, it was old-fashioned primitive lust.*

In the darkness she could hear the regularity of his breathing, as rhythmic as the tick of his watch. Sliding to the floor, she put on a pair of shorts and an old T-shirt that said something about a charity run she'd participated in back in college. Cautiously, she descended the stairs, hugging the wall and avoiding the creak of the third step. She was as silent as a breeze. Scooping up the beaded purse that carried her cell phone, she padded her way across the barren living room to climb out the window.

Melanie took no interest in the starry Washington night sky, which was currently blocked by feathery clouds, and instead sat stiffly on the front stoop she shared with her neighbors.

She hit the third number on her speed dial, knowing – but not caring – that it was too early, or late, to call.

"Hello?"

"Trish, it's Mel."

"Are you all right? Because if you're not I'm going to hurt you."

Melanie chewed on her lower lip. "Adam's here and..."

"Jesus, Mel. You *scared* me," after a few beats she added a side note to Jason, "No, it's Melanie, she's just freaking out 'cause she and Adam did the nasty."

"Stop calling it that," Melanie said, already feeling a bit better, "and stop talking to Jason."

"Okay, so, how was it? And feel free to go into details," Trish laughed. "Jace and I will reenact it later."

Melanie rubbed her forehead with her free hand. "Trish?"

"Okay, I'm moving into another room. Go ahead, spill."

Melanie leaned against the iron handrail. "It was … it was amazing." She felt the warmth of her blush.

"Really? Better than the panther?"

Javier? Melanie considered for a moment. "No comparison."

"Really?" Trish's voice raised to a higher pitch. "So, what are you doing talking to me?"

Melanie gulped, her eyes rolled and her mouth went dry. "I did something stupid." Trish quietly waited. "I told him I loved him." Melanie dropped her head to her knees.

"During?"

"Yeah, and he didn't say it back." Melanie could feel the horror of her words on her contorting face. "He'd been talking, saying things, you know and then after … I said what I said he was quiet for the remainder of the … time."

"Adam was talking, during?"

"You're missing the point."

"Adam's a talker? I'd never have pinned him as a talker."

"He's not a talker. He was just talking."

"What'd he say?"

"Just, Trish, I don't know, nice things, sweet actually." Melanie smiled at the memory. "Focus, Trish, I said it and he didn't say it back."

Her friend sighed into the receiver. "Well, there's nothing you can do about it now, so just forget it."

"I can't. Why am I such a loser when it comes to Adam?"

"You're being too hard on yourself. Besides it's Adam, and he's totally into you. I bet he's just waiting for a more appropriate activity to tell you."

"You think?" She wanted to hope that was true.

"Definitely."

"But what if he was just into the chase?" she groaned.

"No reception inside?" His voice was husky from sleep.

Oops! Melanie twisted looking up at Adam standing in the doorway. Her heart skipped.

"I gotta go," she said to Trish. "He's right here." She didn't bother to continue in a clandestine manner. There were no secrets here.

"Call me later. Love you."

"Thank you!"

"What are you doing out here?"

Melanie scooted over to share the step with Adam.

"Trish." She held open her hand to exhibit her phone.

He hesitated before speaking. Then he slid his index finger along the bottom of her jaw and pulled her face until she was looking him directly in the eye.

"Melanie, I know you have your friends, but I also want you to feel like you can share things with me, too."

She looked at him guiltily. "Talk to you *about* you?" she chuckled, "what a concept."

"How else will I know when I do something wrong?"

"You haven't done anything wrong."

"Then what are we doing out here?"

Okay, she thought, *tell him, tell him what's eating you. Here's your chance to change, to become an adult in an adult relationship.*

"I don't have the best judgment when it comes to you. I think I might already be in too deep."

And you might break my heart.

"Too deep?" he smiled, sweetly, "you mean your feelings for me?"

She nodded and now he chuckled.

"It's not possible for you to be in this deeper than I am." His hands were soft as he squeezed hers. "Can we go inside?" He asked, his dress shirt partially buttoned.

"Yeah, but there's nowhere to sit."

"Strangely, I think I saw a bean bag in your front room," he said, the corners of his lips curling upward.

"Are you making fun of my apartment?"

"A bean bag?"

She laughed. *Okay it was difficult to defend a 1970s throwback,* she thought, deciding instead to go for distance, dis-ownership. "It was here when I moved in, all right?"

The light from the streetlamps filtered in from her still open escape hatch. She scrutinized her apartment from Adam's eyes; the barren living room, with orange shag carpet that simply looked grubby in the shadows, a blue bean bag and two yellow hooks she'd screwed into the ceiling to hang her bicycle above a scrap of carpeting to catch oil drips. Embarrassing.

"Why'd you climb out the window?" he asked, taking her hand and leading her to her seat.

"The door *usually* squeaks and I didn't want to wake you." She gave an angry gaze to her traitorous door.

Melanie squished into the blue nylon bag as the synthetic "beans" squirmed and settled beneath her weight.

Adam knelt down on the shag carpet in front of her. There was only one bag, but even if she'd had two she still couldn't picture Adam snuggling down among the beans.

"Melanie," Adam, delicately ran his fingers across her lips and their discussion from outside picked up without interruption.

"I feel foolish, I think I may have misinterpreted your intent."

"You didn't."

"Why is this so difficult?" *Danny wasn't difficult, he was simple. Granted it didn't last but...* "Maybe we're forcing this, Adam."

"I'm assuming that we're talking about," his turn to hesitate, "what you said ... when..."

She sighed, relieved that it was awkward for him as well. "Yes."

"Mel, I've only told three people that I loved them; my parents and my high school girlfriend, Kristen. I told you what happened to her, right?" Even in the darkness, Melanie felt the heaviness of the question.

"I remember," she said, softly. She and other friends had been killed on prom night.

"A year after that car accident ... my parents were hit by a semi in a head-on collision."

"I'm so sorry," she sucked in a full breath.

"I'm not in any rush to lose you, too." He brushed back a strand of her hair and tucked it behind her ear.

"You think you're cursed?"

Adam shrugged. "I'm not willing to gamble."

"Maybe," Melanie thought, "the curse is on the people who love you."

He looked amused, "Others have said it and they're all still walking, unless they didn't mean it."

No, they meant it.

Outside, the crickets continued their incessant high-pitched chirping.

"Mel, you *know* how I feel." He moved closer. "I've never really been in love before, so I don't know how it works but I promise this will get easier. I just can't say those three words until I'm sure that you're safe. I'm not going to lose you. Can you live with that for the moment? Is it enough?"

"I can live with that."

Adam smiled. "How do you feel about Venice?"

"Venice?"

"Yeah, no cars." He stroked his lips along her cheek. "We'll buy a villa overlooking the canal with its own boat garage."

Melanie awoke in her room, Adam still holding her, with her cell phone ringing downstairs. It was difficult to maintain a sense of dignity while trekking down a flight of stairs in the buff.

Her voice mail had picked up the call – it was Jane. Melanie redialed.

"Oh, Agent Ward, I'm so glad you called. It's almost six and no one has heard from you and I was worried you'd been abducted like Agent Parker." Jane's voice wavered as she spoke.

"Parker deserted, he wasn't abducted, but I appreciate your

concern. Jane, could you send Marcos for me in about an hour and a half?"

Melanie heard Adam shuffling about upstairs as she closed her cell phone.

How strange to have someone else in this makeshift house, she thought as she stretched out flat next to Adam, smiling and wondering if this was going to be a regular thing.

I'll have to get some furniture, she considered, *maybe a set of dishes.*

"Good morning," he said, winding his arm around her waist.

"Hi," she said, snuggling in close to his warm body. He was comfortable and for the first time she regretted having to go to work. "I wish we could stay here all day."

"We can't?"

Melanie shook her head. "No, I've got to go in for a couple of hours. But after that, if you're free, we can meet up."

"Since you are the only reason I'm in D.C., I think I can make time for you." He looked handsome with his hair in disarray and eyelids heavy from lack of sleep.

Thirty-five minutes later she and Adam had showered and dressed. He rummaged through her kitchen cupboards, refrigerator and freezer as she sat in her usual spot atop the heinously colored counter.

"What is this?" he asked, the refrigerator light shining on a couple of bottles of water, three beers left from a six-pack and an old package of individually wrapped slices of American cheese. He held up a square Styrofoam box.

Melanie laughed and shook her head. She couldn't ever remember seeing that container, none of her usual deliveries used those kinds of boxes.

Adam returned it to the top rack.

"And, Mel, you have only one pan." He couldn't hide his dismay.

"I have a pan? If I'd known that, maybe I'd have cooked something."

"Come on, do you even live here?" His brows were knit in tight and when he shook her shoulders she could tell it seriously bothered him.

"I pay rent, yes, but I spend most of my time at the work. It's easy, convenient and they've got showers, so mostly I stay there," she stroked his forehead to smooth out the lines. "Don't worry so much."

"Have they got beds?"

"Yeah, and really comfy couches." Melanie hopped off her makeshift orange bench and cozied up against his freshly cleaned body.

"I hate that you live like this."

He rubbed her back, closing the refrigerator door and setting her one pan on the old Formica counter. "Where do you eat?"

"Here on the counter or up in bed."

He sighed in resignation, his shoulders dropped and he kissed the top of her head. "Okay, so, where can we grab some breakfast?" he asked, shaking his head.

"There's a little bakery down on the corner. We could walk there and be back in time for my driver to take me to work and you back to your hotel."

"You don't have some aversion to furniture, do you?" Adam chuckled and unlocked the front door. "I mean if I were to happen to run into a chair or let's say cookware and brought it back to this apartment, you wouldn't break out in hives, right?"

"I'm not sure!" she giggled, actually giggled, as she stepped out onto the portico.

A hint of autumn was in the warm morning air as she locked the door and slipped the key into her jeans pocket. She had no plans to rid herself of her ear-to-ear smile anytime soon.

"Hey, did you just…" inside her front yard Adam stood with two men and all three were staring at her.

Standing shoulder to shoulder just off the steps she recognized the men instantly. Fear oozed from her body and out the bottom of her feet. Adam. Her empty stomach twisted into painful contortions – she had to keep Adam safe. But the men from the surveillance video were not concerned with Adam. Actually…

Shocked into silence, Melanie worked to unscramble the puzzle that lay before her. The older man's arm rested on Adam's shoulder, clasping him on the back, engaging in what looked like a reunion of sorts. Adam was smiling, laughing and speaking perfect Spanish.

Holy shit!

Her glance flipped to the young man anxiously waiting off to the side, his brown eyes holding fast to her. Unwavering, he didn't even blink but gripped a pistol tightly in his right hand. Melanie sensed he was scared enough to use it.

"You'll have to excuse my rudeness, Agent Ward. You see, my very good friend Adam and I have not seen each other for years. But I have not forgotten about you." His mouth warped, in a leer, both his thin upper and lower lips disappeared into his dark, cavernous mouth. Dark raisin eyes glowered from beneath heavy brows and the pleasure in his voice was chilling, raising the hairs on the back of her neck.

She was in danger, trapped and completely vulnerable. She took a risk and gazed at Adam, six inches taller than his compatriot. His expression was foreboding. His posture had changed, stiffened. His chiseled jaw was clamped shut, the furrow above his eyes was hard, his shoulders were squared. But it wasn't the physical change that was the most alarming. It was his once-dazzling emerald green eyes. They were lifeless and stone cold. A shiver rose along each vertebra.

"Let me introduce myself. I am Hector Ortiz. This is Raul, and of course you know Adam." He stepped uncomfortably closer.

"No, I don't know him," she answered with more confidence than she felt.

Hector laughed. "Very well, this is Adam." Giving a nod to Raul he turned back to Melanie. "Okay, Ms. Ward, disrobe."

"What?" Melanie glared back, doing her best to maintain her composure and waste time.

"You heard me, do it," Hector commanded and Raul lifted his right hand.

"You're fucking with the wrong person."

"I ask nicely only once," Hector snarled and Raul followed the example.

"No." Her eyes settled back on Hector, boldly.

"Do it." Adam's voice was a growl.

Raul's sneer morphed into a grin.

Melanie tightened her lips and looked up and down her street. Not a soul. Holding back the frustrated, angry stream of emotion, she bit down hard on the inside of her cheek.

The first two buttons were the hardest.

Stripped to her underwear, she stood defiant.

"Everything."

Raul exposed a set of gray teeth as his grin widened, unabashed, and he lifted his eyebrows.

She did as instructed, not wanting to give them an extra minute to anticipate the show. She looked directly into Adam's dark, dead eyes as she unhooked her bra.

"Ha, very nice, my friend," Hector chortled and ogled simultaneously.

The three men enjoyed themselves before Hector tossed her a blue jumper. Without instructions Melanie dressed, shoving one bare foot in after the other and then quickly pulling up the long zipper.

Unceremoniously Raul corralled her to the back of a Ford Taurus.

"Get in," Hector demanded, opening the trunk.

"Go to hell."

She glanced out the corner of her eye in hopes that someone would come.

She didn't see the backhanded slap coming, but she felt the tiny asphalt pebbles wedge into her palms and the side of her cheek when she hit the street.

She tasted the blood on the corner of her mouth where his knuckle slammed into her tooth.

"Fuck you." She spat the blood on a leather loafer.

"Get in," Adam's voice was ice, and Melanie had to look to make sure it was he who'd spoke.

She strained for one last glimpse down the empty street as a pair of hands grasped the back of her blue jumpsuit and heaved her into the trunk. It slammed shut before she even had the chance to pick her road-rashed face up from the floor. Her intuition pressed her to quickly investigate the tail lights, the spare tire and the keyhole, but the entire cavity had been cleared. She did, however, discover that if she leaned her ear against the back she could hear the conversation in the front.

She closed her eyes and listened to what she did not want to hear – Adam and Hector chatting.

"I've wondered about you through the years. It's good to see you again, my friend."

"You're looking great, you haven't aged a day."

"I'm a medical mystery," Hector laughed, "I owe it all to plastic surgery and having no conscience."

Melanie winced as the car erupted in laughter.

"So, Adam, tell me, who hired you?"

"Ah, but I don't take names, remember? My concern is the target and my bank account."

More laughter.

"How are Terese and the girls?" Adam asked.

"Terese has gotten into another one of her phases. She's selling jewelry on that television show. And the girls, well, they're teenagers now."

Melanie could listen no more. She sunk down into a ball and did what she could to keep herself from panicking. Exhaust was seeping into her cave faster than fresh air and she was unnaturally sleepy.

CHAPTER 22

Melanie roused from her unconsciousness with a burning pain in her ribs. Groggily, she blinked her unfocused eyes, trying to ascertain where the hell she'd been taken. The stale air was heavy with chemicals, and the summer heat was sweltering.

Her head weighed a ton and her stiff neck ached. Her arms were stretched above her head with her wrists shackled to a wooden rafter. A scent of decay and mold hung in the dust of what appeared to be one of the many abandoned barns that speckled the countryside of D.C.'s neighboring states. Aged gasoline and oil stains still marked the dirt floor that reached across to the oversized sliding barn doors. A work bench, long ago forgotten, was cluttered with jars and paint cans connected by cobwebs and covered in dust.

Melanie surveyed her environment and her situation, locked in heavy chains and bound to a sturdy beam that structurally supported the dilapidated building.

Sunlight was gently streaming through the cracks in the wallboards and ceiling.

Assessing that it was sometime around one or two o'clock meant that she'd been missing for hours. The protocol, as she knew so well, was that if they'd known where she was, she'd have been rescued.

Painfully she swallowed, her dry tongue sticking to the back of her throat. She could hear her captors behind her left shoulder, but they were out of visual range. The three men were playing a loud game of poker as Melanie was being pulled like taffy. Her arms were stretched taut, causing her sides and lungs to ache and the manacles to dig further into her already broken skin.

She'd been deceived – tricked in the grandest way. Along with the rest of her body, Melanie's heart moaned with grief. Her cherry-red toenails peeked out from under her blue jumpsuit. She'd painted them only yesterday for Adam and now ... now she felt ridiculous. But even in her sorrow she discovered a cement foundation had been poured around the beam. It was three inches high and two inches deep – just what she needed to gain extra height and release the pressure from her wrists. A foot on each side of the post and up she stood, enjoying the relief for a mere moment before the stiff barn door was dragged open. She looked toward the afternoon light and the dark figure of a man slid the old door shut.

Her eyes adjusted and he spoke.

"Have I missed anything?"

It was Finn Parker.

In a rush of emotion Melanie was surprised and sickened but stood expressionless as Parker walked closer, his face drowned in absolute happiness.

"No, she'll be out for awhile."

Melanie glared into Finn Parker's sea-blue eyes and he looked into hers.

"I think we can begin the torture."

His lips curled with an odd combination of hatred and pleasure, a gruesome grin that beamed directly at Melanie.

I'm going to die right here, chained to this beam.

She had wondered about her death back when Diane March's body had been found, and here it was. Her heart hammered, but there was a certain satisfaction in knowing.

The scraping of chairs along the dirt floor was immediate.

She stood, stoic and rebellious, staring out above their heads.

"Well, good afternoon, Agent Ward. I hope you had a comfortable nap," Hector said with arrogance.

Melanie said nothing.

"Business, then. Parker tells us you've stolen a disc that belongs to us."

"I don't know what you're talking about," Melanie lied.

"You know exactly what he's talking about," Parker piped in, "you stupid bitch."

"Well, either I'm a stupid bitch or I know exactly what you're talking about, which is it?" Melanie asked in a tone filled with loathing and impudence, considering her current circumstance.

"You had someone break into my office and steal that disc. I know you were behind the theft."

"Jesus, you're a whiny little prick."

Parker looked at Hector and back at Melanie, his face pink.

It wasn't until the laughter began and his face turned to scarlet that Melanie knew she'd gone too far.

In two strides Parker was peering up at her and, although she didn't think he could reach, he balled up his fist and landed a direct hit to her face. He cocked back his arm and Melanie prepared for another punch.

"You need to learn to control your temper," Adam said, grasping onto Parker's arm.

"What? Who the hell do you think you are?" Parker asked, ripping his wrist from Adam's clutch.

The left side of Melanie's face pounded. He'd struck her in her cheekbone and eye, and the blow had knocked her off her cement perch. The manacles sliced deeper into her wrists. It was all she could do to keep from passing out.

"Who's in charge here? Hector?"

"Look, man, do whatever you want to do. But if he knocks her out, we're looking at another hour."

Hector scrutinized Adam.

"Hector?" Parker asked, wanting a decision.

Hector narrowed his already squinty eyes but his shoulders relaxed a bit as he nodded. "Well, now perhaps you'll be more willing to cooperate with us, Agent Ward."

"Sorry, but I don't have it on me. Maybe you've figured that out already." Her face was throbbing and she felt it beginning to swell.

"I'm losing patience with you."

"All this for alternative fuel? *Who* are you working for?" The muscles in her arms burned and she was getting lightheaded. *Maybe another slap would be helpful*, Melanie mused. "It doesn't work, you know, the formula. There's some problem at the final stage. My people checked it out, something about a boiling problem."

Hector gave Parker a sideways glance.

"She's lying!"

Melanie shrugged. "My tech guy can explain." She rattled off the number to Mike's direct line using her code. Hector put the call on the speaker.

"Melanie! Oh my Lord, where are you?"

Mike's typical frenzy at any other time would have made Melanie smile, but today she had to choke down a wave of emotion that such a welcome voice brought to her chest.

"With whom am I speaking?" Hectors rigid voice would have Mike scurrying to trace.

"Um ... Mike," he said, his keyboard rattling away.

And with that the speaker was turned off and Hector roamed to the far side of the old barn so Melanie could not hear the rest of the conversation. She felt pity for Mike, he frightened so easily, but he could find her, more so than Jack. She had no choice but to involve him.

Parker looked lost in thought. Melanie smiled. Parker had confused Mike with Ed.

"He wants to talk with you," Hector stated with an air of superiority.

He thinks he's already won, Melanie thought as Mike's voice once again filled the old place. She sighed.

"Melanie, Melanie are you there?"

"I'm here," she smiled, but the left side of her mouth didn't move. "Mike, it's all right. Do you know which disc he wants?" she asked, assuring herself that Hector had been straight with both of them.

"Yeah, the one from inside my pants."

"Yeah, that's the one. Hey, look, Mike, I just want..."

A dial tone echoed from the speakers.

Just as well, she thought. *It's bad luck to say goodbye.*

"Now we wait." Hector kicked back in one of the wooden chairs and examined Melanie.

"Melanie Ward," Parker's voice, sticky with a mixture of glee and abhorrence. "I've dreamed about this moment for years." He glided toward her, his right hand weighted by a gun.

Her blood rushed to her ears, her breath felt heavy and the sharp pains in her body eased as, gratefully, she went numb.

"This isn't happening now," Melanie said.

Parker laughed. "It'll happen when I pull the trigger."

Hector shook his head. "What do they teach you? Raul, take his gun."

Beneath her blue jumpsuit a slow drizzle of blood trickled down her arm to her elbow.

"Could I get some water?"

Hector snapped his fingers twice and Raul responded with a squirt from an open water bottle that had been left on a nearby workbench.

The warm water mostly washed her face but the small amount that she did taste held the distinct flavor of O positive.

"Thanks."

Melanie gently dabbed her swelling face on the shoulder of the stiff cotton jumpsuit.

"I'm curious." Hector turned his chair, its back to her, and straddled the seat to face her. Looking intently at Melanie, he asked, "Did you have any suspicion?"

Adam.

Painfully her heart filled with dishonor and shame. She ignored the question.

"No hints? I'm surprised. No offense to my friend," he said, nodding toward Adam. "But I've heard such stories about her intuition. Agent Ward, you had no inkling as to his true motive?"

Melanie didn't respond, again.

Leaning forward in his rotting chair, showing piqued interest in the subject, he asked, "Did you fall in love?"

Melanie didn't answer but she reacted, her body tensed. Hector's squinty brown eyes penetrated into hers.

"Did he tell you that he loved you?" he pressed.

"Hec..." Adam began, only to be silenced by the palm of the man's hand.

"Agent Ward, did he tell you he loved you?"

Melanie stared out, across the old barn, dust particles glimmered in the shafts of sunlight.

A booming laugh erased the tension eased on Hector's wrinkled face.

"Women always believe they'll be the one to capture the King of Heartache." His cheerfulness continued. "Would you like to know who you fell in love with?'

"No."

"What else do we have to talk about? And I'm curious."

"And all this time I thought you were a lesbian," Parker sneered.

Melanie rolled her unswollen eye. "Yeah, well, you're an idiot. I give you three months before it's you they've strung up."

Melanie could see the hate steaming off his skin.

"Adam was the best assassin in the world a few years back." Hector ignored them. "No assignment was off limits *if* you could afford his fee."

"How'd you do it, become the best?" Raul asked. It was the first time Melanie had heard him speak.

"He rid himself of any conscience and simply pulled the trigger. He's a heathen – it's not something you can learn," Hector continued. "Attractive and charismatic is a deadly combination. Adam is the only man I know who walks into a whorehouse and walks out hours, or even days, later without charge. Do you remember?"

Adam sat tilting his chair, balancing on the back two legs, laughing heartily and looking very pleased with himself. Hector looked on like a proud father. Raul dreamed of the day he'd be the best and Parker fumed alone in the background.

"Adam has always been blessed. I don't know how many times I found him passed out with an empty bottle of whiskey on one side and a line of coke on the other. Tempting death is one of the things Adam does best, even in prison. We were in a Mexican prison, mind you, and Adam, well, he can make the best of friends and the worst of enemies, no?"

"It seems that way," Adam answered, his laughter gone.

"I hate to break up the party but the file has finished downloading," Parker said, looking at the laptop on the table.

Melanie's mind raced. She yanked on her chains, ignoring the pain in her wrists.

The beam was solid, the chains were thick. There was no way out.

Grasping at life, her mind whirled and her heart pounded when her eyes deadlocked with Parker.

"You know, you can still come out of this," Melanie persuaded. "We can say you were doing undercover work."

"Good idea. Maybe I'll try that after you're dead."

"Hugh is going to destroy you if these guys don't kill you first."

"Do you think I'm doing this on my own? Isn't it time to kill this bitch?"

"Raul, she's all yours," Hector gave the go-ahead, looking up from the computer.

Raul, looking as terrified as she felt, raised his firearm.

"Adam," she choked out.

She looked directly into the dark eyes that had seemed so loving. "What?"

"Could you let my family and friends know that I love them?" Melanie's mouth was dry and the words cracked. "That I was thinking about them. Could you do that, please?"

He cleared his throat. "I can do that."

She exhaled, relieved that she had some control over her death. She relaxed her shoulders, leaned her head back and breathed slowly.

She was dizzy, lightheaded, but she got the last word to her loved ones.

"Thank you," she said when she had her emotions under control. "Okay." She nodded to Raul, breathing.

"How very moving, but this is bullshit! Hector, it has been understood from the beginning that I get to pull the trigger."

"Step back, Agent Parker, or *you* will be Raul's first hit."

Not to cause a distraction, Melanie held her breath. Raul's raised gun was now aimed at Parker. As much as Parker wanted to be the one to kill Melanie, apparently it wasn't worth his life. He stepped back.

"Wise decision. Well, Agent Ward, it has been a pleasure."

Hector winked at her then gave a slight nod to Raul. Feeling nothing, Melanie stood and watched the last seconds of her life play out in slow motion: Hector striding away, Adam to her left was watching, Parker seething behind Raul and Raul standing purposefully before her. Melanie drew in a deep breath, smelling and tasting the dusty mold, then she gave her own nod of readiness and closed her eyes.

The explosion echoed in her ears.

She gasped as the first shot rung out, but it was the second that sent bolts of pain through her body. Her face. Like she'd been hit with a brick instead of a bullet. *Shot in the face*, she thought, wheezing in short puffs of air. Coughing out mouthfuls of dust, the pain was excrutiating.

Her eyes were clamped shut and her ears rung as she instinctively reached for her face. The shackles were still attached to her wrists, but the chain had been shot clean through, and she was face-down on the ground.

Quickly, she ran her hands along her body. She hadn't been shot. The pain was from colliding with the floor. Her instincts jumped to survival mode as movement caught her attention. It was Parker crouching low, crawling out the barn door. Raising up on her elbows Melanie turned to see Raul inches away, already dead, his brown eyes frozen in wide shock. Blood had begun to pool in his open mouth.

A sense of hope eased some of the pain as she heard the argument between Hector and Adam. The words were inaudible but Hector was on the wrong end of the barrel and he was enraged. Melanie ignored the two men and focused on building upon the meager amount of strength she had left. Struggling to her feet she fought the ache as another shot rang out.

Fear weakened her knees and her legs buckled under her, bringing her back to the dusty ground.

"Melanie!"

He's coming, Melanie's heart raced in a panic. The adrenaline rushing, coursing, giving energy where a second before there was none, prompted her to stand. Anger gave her strength, and she waited until he was close enough before she pulled back her arm and swung, throwing the force of her entire body at him. Adam was quick – he leaned back, missing her fist, but he hadn't allowed for the extra expanse of chain that hung from her manacle. A streak of blood cut across his left cheekbone as he caught her in mid stumble.

"Melanie, the place is going to blow!" he shouted, disregarding the slice. "You can kick my ass once we get out of here."

Easily he captured her in his grasp and lifted her securely against his chest. Kicking at the rickety door through which Parker had escaped minutes earlier, Adam broke off a section large enough for them to squeeze through. The dry, stale air outside was perfumed by the concentrated odor of gasoline. A quarter-mile down the narrow dirt road, Parker's SUV was kicking up a cloud of dust.

Only the chrome bumper glimmering in the evening sun was still visible. The old barn, with its peeling red paint and leaning walls, was smoldering. A fire had already consumed the bottom half of the structure and, in the time it took Adam to run 30 yards through waist-high brown weeds, the loft collapsed with a great plume of smoke.

He was running toward the tree line, pressing her head into her chest.

"Keep your head down, it's not over!" he shouted over the roar of the crumbling building.

She ducked her face into Adam's shirt as the force of the blast hurled him off his feet. He landed on top of her in a clear spot among the pines. His arms wrapped around her head as they bounced on a thick layer of pine needles.

"Baby, baby, are you okay?"

Melanie did her best to squirm out from under his weight. Using her legs, she struggled against the soft earth. Even with extreme effort she moved only inches. She'd tasted freedom and she was determined not to die today.

"Get away from me," her voice sounded strange to her – strangled with panic. Infuriated he'd heard her fear she struggled harder, scrambling until she smacked into a tree.

"Melanie, No!"

Using the trunk she pushed herself to stand.

"Okay, look, I'm not going to hurt you." He stepped backward with his palms out in the "don't shoot" position, Hector's laptop tucked beneath his arm. "I'm going to reach in my pocket, see."

When his hand came out it was holding a small, dark key.

"It's for the cuffs. I'm going to unlock them." His voice shook and his movements were deliberately slow as he knelt down and gently freed her from her chains.

"Oh, Jesus, Melanie." His eyes darted from her wounded hands up to her wounded face. "I'm going to use my shirt as a bandage to stop the bleeding."

Melanie nodded, leaning against the tree. He pulled off the white dress shirt she'd watched him put on that morning and tore it into strips. His hands worked quickly, efficiently nursing her wounds.

"Who are you?" she croaked.

His eyes were green and warm, filled with concern.

It was *him*.

A small sound of alarm squeaked out of her throat.

"I'm the man you're in love with, the same man," he said, still kneeling before her, gazing up.

"I don't know you."

"I'm so sorry, Melanie," he said, dropping his head and leaning into her abdomen.

Melanie pressed her fingertips into his shoulders, pushing him off her.

"And you work for...?"

He shook his head. "Nobody."

"Right," she said, realizing she wasn't going to get answers but persisted. "When did you know who I was?"

"Today when Hector told me. I had no idea, Mel. If I'd known you were Secret Service I'd have run in the other direction. Honestly, I left this life five years ago when I moved to San Diego. Hector saw me with you and he assumed you were a target. I let him. There was no other way to keep you alive. I thought he'd see right through me. I couldn't look at you, Melanie, but I had to become *that guy* again." He was still kneeling, pleading with his eyes for her to believe.

"But that's not me anymore. You *know* me." Gently he took her hand and opened it against his chest where his heart was pounding against his rib cage.

"I'm too exhausted for this. Just tell me, where are you taking me?"

"I don't know, to the hospital?" He tilted her face to the side to take a look at the damage. "You're bleeding pretty badly."

"Head wounds do that," she said, confused. *Is he saving me?*

"I know, but I don't want to take any chances. Isn't there someone you want to call? I lifted Hector's phone," he swallowed, like it was a difficult memory. "He really was like a brother to me – at one time, anyway."

She felt no remorse for the loss of either Hector or his protégé. But here she was, outside of the burning tomb while Adam's associate lay charred.

"You're s-s-saving me?"

"Yes." He slumped against her body, his arms hugging her tightly around the waist.

Her hands went to his head, her fingers in his hair. Blood was already beginning to seep through her neatly bandaged wrists. Could this be right? Was she comforting the assassin?

Police and fire sirens sounded from somewhere beyond the trees.

"I can't be found here, I need to get away." She said, looking into his eyes and wondering how there could be such evil underneath.

Adam hit the redial button and held the phone for her.

Her throat cracked when she heard Mike's voice.

"Melanie, jeez, I've been trying to locate you. Keep the line open for two more seconds." He was breathing heavily before yelling, "I've got you! Okay, the chopper is already in the air. 15 minutes. There's a strip of highway due east of your current position."

"I'll be listening for it, I'm making my way to the road," she said, but all she wanted was to rest.

Adam flipped the phone closed and lifted her in his arms. "We've got to get you closer to the highway,"

"I can walk."

"I know you can, but let me carry you."

It was awkward being in his arms, pressed against his bare chest. Conflicting emotions of love and fear.

She wanted to hate him, she wanted to feel only contempt, but Melanie closed her eyes and opened her ears, listening to his heartbeat.

Stop! You can't still be in love with him! He's a killer with cold dead eyes and has the devil as an acquaintance. But ... she breathed in his scent, felt his skin and he held her so tenderly. *You're an idiot.*

"How can I ever trust you?"

Adam knelt with Melanie still confined to the safety of his arms and said, "Melanie, you're my family. I've spent my entire adult life alone, making the wrong decisions. I won't make excuses for what I've done. Most of what Hector said is true. What I'd like to say is that when I did *those* things I wanted to die. I taunted death, challenged him, I *wanted* him to win. I never expected to be allowed to be happy. You've changed everything."

"I don't know. I have so many questions."

"I'll answer anything."

There were too much – too many questions. She didn't know where to start.

Adam continued. "Hector was my translator at the culinary school. When we first met we both had aspirations. He wanted to be a chef and I wanted to forget. In that first year at school he kept me going when I wanted to hide beneath a table. Then the oil refinery was closed and his family lost their jobs. Hector joined his father in protesting – Mr. Ortiz was a radical. I knew what I was doing when went along on the raids. I was caught. That's how I ended up in jail.

"For months my parents got nowhere fighting the legal system. They flew to Mexico City to speak with officials, pleading with both governments to facilitate my release. On their way to the airport their taxi collided with a semi. The coroner said they died on impact.

"Prison was brutal and I thought I'd die there. Hector aligned with the new company who had purchased the refinery and they worked their magic to free me. I was in their debt and the price was that I join them. I swapped one prison for another. I sold my soul. I don't really remember much about the following years. I numbed myself with whatever was available. I was 26 when Hector and I had a falling out over money so I went out on my own. I gave up the addictions and honed my craft and by the time I walked away I was considered the best."

"You're proud of that?"

"I was."

"What made you quit?"

"I was hired to kill a man, an ex-assassin who decided not to play the game. He had a wife, baby son and a little girl with curly red hair and I couldn't do it. I watched them all day outside their farmhouse. He had everything I wanted; I just didn't know I wanted it until that day. I left, gave back the fee, unplugged my computer and vanished."

Adam stared past her at the thick trees blocking out the sun's evening rays.

"When my friends died I lost my mind. When my parents died I lost my heart. I didn't care about anything or anybody. But, Melanie, you've given me my heart back. I was so scared today that I would screw up and I'd lose you, too."

He closed his arms around her and she felt him shudder. A surge of emotion, kindness, love and affection washed over her as he held her protectively against his bare chest. Melanie leaned her cheek into the crook of his neck.

"You're hurt," he said, stroking her hair. It was the only spot that didn't ache.

"I'm okay."

"I've never loved like this, I don't know how to act." Melanie's heart fluttered. "I love you, Melanie. I've been in love with you since the beginning of time. And I almost lost you without saying those words. God, I was foolish. I love you and I *will* protect you from the danger that causes."

"Adam, I don't know, I can't think. I mean, aren't you a fugitive?"

"There isn't anybody actively seeking me. Hector was the only person who knew me and now," he shrugged, "there's Agent Parker."

He was a problem.

"Could you still love me?" he asked, dragging his teeth over his bottom lip. "I'm not a monster anymore."

How could she answer? She did love him – but would she after they were apart and she had time to think?

His weary eyes were pained and turning distant. Melanie recognized a crucial moment. Her heart hammered and she was suddenly scared, not of him but of losing him.

"I do love you." She reached out with her bandaged hands and drew him to her. Her mouth was sore but she gently pressed her lips to his.

His eyes were tearful when she shifted away.

In the distance Melanie heard the helicopter. There wasn't much time left.

"What do we do?"

He shook his head, unknowing.

"What will you do? Where will you go?"

"Please, don't worry about me."

"How will I see you?" Melanie asked, her breath coming rapidly.

"I'll come to you."

"There isn't anything else you're going to spring on me later, right? This is it?"

He lips curved upward. "Isn't this enough?" He tenderly cradled her face. "There's nothing more. You know more about me than anyone ever has." He looked above the trees. Melanie knew he was judging the ETA. "I have no more secrets from you." He let out a deep sigh. "Except…" He squinted and his green eyes sparkled, even beneath the shadowy pines. Her heart beat irregular. His confession could be anything and she braced for the worse. "I slept with Oscar's wife to get the job."

She paused. This was unexpected.

"I was just starting my new life – it was a relapse but I haven't slipped since ... unless you count today." He was serious, concerned.

"I don't."

"I'm sorry. I know I'm not who you expected." His shoulders dropped as he lifted her to her feet. There was no pain in their goodbye kiss. "I love you, Melanie."

His gaze was misty as she turned to make her way through the last few rows of trees. The shadows had consumed all the light on the forest floor, causing Melanie to stumble into a shallow roadside ravine. She scrambled to her knees and waved her arms at the low-flying helicopter, folding to the asphalt as the rescue team landed on the vacant two-lane highway.

"So, this is where you've been hiding out? We've been looking for you," Jack said, bending down to help her to her feet.

"I think I've got broken ribs, Jack," Melanie winced at the pain.

Straining to maintain control over her pain, she held her breath, closed her eyes and tried to focus on something else.

Parker. Retribution.

And Adam.

The sparks of a plan were ignited as she staggered to the helicopter. The blades of the chopper whirled overhead and she was about to succumb to her exhaustion but she was overcome with joy. From the hatch, looking worried, was her mentor, the cavalry…

Agent Ben Jackson.

Living Lies

EPILOGUE

He stood cloaked in darkness, at the edge of her hospital bed. It'd been over 24 hours since he left her at the forests edge and now half her face had swollen, unrecognizable. How could he have allowed himself to believe that the Universe or who ever controlled fate would grant him happiness?

He loved her. And that love nearly killed her. Adam tried to swallow down the grief – he felt as though he'd already lost her. What if Melanie had died? He knew for certain that she would if...

He stared longingly. His heart ached at the sight of her bruised and broken body lying there with an IV attached to her arm. How was he going to stop loving her?

Adam could feel the darkness enveloping him, the old familiar feeling of despair creeping inside his bones. He stood watching over his beloved as he fought to keep his demons at bay. He had sworn never to return to his old life but there was no choice. He saw the look in Parker's eyes – he would not stop until Melanie was six feet under.

The cold was beginning, turning his heart to stone when a remarkable thing happened.

Melanie stirred, opening her eyes – though the left was only a slit. She moved her arms, reaching with the one not attached to a tube, and yanking the needle from the inside bend of her elbow. A soft guttural groan escaped her throat. She bent her arm, fingers to her shoulder, minimizing the pain. Then, before he could stop her, she kicked her legs off the bed and crumpled to the floor.

"Where do you think you're going?" He asked, rushing to her side.

"I'm getting out. What are *you* doing here?" She asked, gripping his shirt to help pull herself up.

"I was checking in on you and now I'm putting you back to bed." He tried to lighten his dour mood. "You need to rest, Mel." She leaned into his chest. Adam's heart swelled. "Sweetheart, let me get you back into bed."

Melanie nodded. "Unless you can sneak me out of this place."

"Are you being mistreated?"

"I don't like needles. The morphine makes me feel ... yucky."

"Back to bed," he grinned, lifting her as carefully as humanly possible.

"Will you hold me?"

The moisture filled his eyes, "Of course." How could he leave her? He set her down and crawled in beside her. She leaned back into his arms and slept. "Melanie?"

"Hmm."

"I'm going to have to leave soon. I need to fix some complications and I don't know for how long I'll be gone." He swallowed the lump in his throat.

"We can work together," she said drowsily. "A team."

"No. It's better for both of us if I leave."

She opened her eye, it was clear, alert.

"What are you saying, exactly?" Her words slurred slightly from her inflated lips, and he heard the tremor in her voice.

He said nothing, knowing his voice would crack if he tried.

After a long silence she muttered, "Your curse has ended, I'm alive."

He shook his head.

"I didn't die, Adam. If you hadn't noticed I'm right here."

"You're in a hospital bed, Mel."

"This? This is nothing I've been in worse shape plenty of times. Besides if not for you I'd never have made it out of that barn."

"Shhh. No more talking." He said stroking her hair and kissing the side of her head. "Everything is going to be all right."

To be continued ... Summer 2010

ACKNOWLEDGMENTS

Thanks to my pint-size support system,
Samantha and Sydney for forgiving my imperfections.
Thank you Mom and Dad, Frank, Ralph, Kris,
Steve and Linda for all the great family discussions.
Thank you Jill Spitz for making this a better story.
Anne Kellogg for your enthusiasm
and grammatical expertise.
Scott Barker for making me try harder.
Angie Chiara for lifting my spirits, staying
up late to read and for great book selections.
Thanks Amy for being the first to read *Living Lies*.
A special thanks to PowWow Publishing for your
tireless efforts and belief in me. And thanks to
Brent for foregoing homemade cooking.